Alfred Flett was born in Sunderland but
emigrated to New Zealand with his parents
when he was eleven. He has been a
journalist for some time and now works in
Fleet Street. He lives in Balham. *Never
Shake a Skeleton* is Mr Flett's first novel.

Never Shake a Skeleton

ALFRED FLETT

SPHERE BOOKS LIMITED
30/32 Gray's Inn Road, London WC1X 8JL

First published in Great Britain by Michael Joseph Ltd 1973
Copyright © Alfred Flett 1973
Published by Sphere Books 1975

TRADE
MARK

Set in Intertype Lectura

Printed in Great Britain by
Hazell Watson & Viney Ltd
Aylesbury, Bucks

To Puddin', a second and
much happier choice, without
whose gentle persuasion this story
would never have been told

ONE

NEVER SHAKE A SKELETON

Hodges. There was no one else. I finally made up my mind at ten o'clock. So it was a wild night, with rain pelting down. Too bad. As I shrugged into a mac I wondered about the photograph. I might as well have it with me, just in case: I didn't have to produce it unless I wanted to.

My hand on the doorknob, I paused. Hodges: the grittiest bastard of them all. But at least he'd remember. He'd been part of it all, when it happened. And because he'd remember I'd probably get my face pushed in by an expert at pushing in faces. It took a long, deep breath to force myself out through the door into the passage, and another to let myself out of the house.

Halfway down the long slope of Leigham Court Road I stopped, turning my hunched back to the wind and the rain. I was wasting my time. The chances were he wouldn't live there any more. But maybe he did; I hadn't heard anything to suggest he didn't. And once you've served in the Shop the ordinary bits of chat you hear can mean more than they do to anybody else.

I turned again into the storm and trudged on down to the station. I took a ticket to Victoria, and sat in my own steam bath in the heat of the train. I battled through bad-tempered crowds down to the tube. Maybe he wouldn't push my face in: maybe he'd just dial 999 and call an ambulance, and tell them to bring a strait-jacket as well.

Old habits die hard. I took my time up the stairs at Earls Court station, loitered a bit in the foyer, patting my pockets and looking sort of anxious. The coloured porter had that cold look on his face. He'd seen and heard it all before. But the crowd off the train was thinning by then and no one was taking any notice of me, other than the porter.

Then I found the ticket, grinned at the lad in uniform. He flashed white teeth back at me. I hunched my head down into the wet collar of my mac and splashed my way out into the noise and the brightness and the clutter of Kangaroo Valley. Turn left and left again. I made myself trip, giving myself a chance to stop, rub my ankle and look back the way I had come. Nobody. Why the hell should there be? I felt ridiculous, trudged on. I didn't have to look at the numbers; I'd recognise the house. Then I began to wonder if I would. There'd been a lot of changes in the years since I'd last trod this street. Bed-sits and cheap hotels cluttered the once stately houses. Maybe Hodges would've moved, but I stubbornly hung on to the belief he'd still be there. You don't build up a cover to chuck it away just because times and people change.

The rain was easing off when I went up the steps into the shelter of the high portico. My eye ran down the lighted panel of buttons at the side of the big double doors. There it was: Hodges. G for George; V for Victor: Hodges. I stared at it, and damn near turned round and walked away. It took an effort of will not to. Instead, a finger found the bell. After only the slightest hesitation, I pressed. Then I leaned down, my ear hard against the tiny speaker grille. Nothing. Perhaps he wasn't at home. The thought made me happier. I bent against the button again and held it just a little longer. I looked out behind me. The rain had stopped. Perhaps I'd be able to go home, dry out and forget all about this.

The speaker crackled. I'd moved away, and thought about keeping on going. But I went back and bent down to the grille.

'Who is it?'

The voice hadn't changed. It was still like wet gravel in a tin pail. Who was it, he wanted to know, but it was useless to tell him.

'Who is that?' Hodges sounded scratchy. Or maybe it was just a poor connection in the speaker.

It had to be now. I put my mouth close to the grille. 'Eppler,' I said. 'It's about Eppler.'

I had my ear back to the grille quick. The silence sounded very loud. The next time I heard Hodges his voice was tight.

'Who're you?'

'I need your help.' I took a long, sucking breath. 'I'd like to give the place a new coat of paint.' God, that dated back a long, long time. But Hodges was old enough to remember, if he wanted to.

That was when an ancient and very noisy MG battered its way to a stop right below me. A girl with long, silver hair fell out of it. She was laughing fit to kill. So was the hippy lout with her.

I was mouthing words savagely, urgently. Come on, Hodges,

open the bloody door . . . push my face in if you have to, but open the bloody door . . .

The couple down on the street were having a ball. He had a hand down her blouse or whatever it was, and she was trying to bite his ear. They were telling all of Earls Court just what they had in mind once they could climb the steps. A window opened and an Australian voice bellowed some advice in rich strine. The lout and his bird thought this was very funny. They really got into the laughter act. The girl pulled up her top piece and waggled a sizeable pair of mammary glands in the general direction of the anger.

My ear was hurting. I had it pressed against the grille so hard. 'It's open,' I heard Hodges say. The voice was soft, gentle. I swallowed. This was bad, very bad. I pushed against the door, slipped inside, shut it behind me. Then I leaned against it. This was going to be rough. There was scuffling and wild laughter muted only by the thickness of the wood. I ignored the lift, chose the stairs. It was only two floors: I could cope with that.

I didn't have to search for number 27. I'd been there before. Along the corridor, turn right, and the door was at the end of a little cul-de-sac: a sensible site for a man in the business Hodges was in.

Take it easy, I told myself. No sense in buying trouble.

'Go right in,' said Hodges. His voice was behind me. The hair stood out straight from the goose pimples on the back of my neck.

You get rusty after a while. You tend to forget obvious things like flat number 29, which I'd walked past before turning into the cul-de-sac — the one that had a connecting door from 27. But maybe it was just as well I hadn't been clever and opened the door of 29: Hodges, waiting behind it listening for me, mightn't have appreciated it. I walked ahead of him through the door. At least I hadn't turned round. It's best to do what you're told when there aren't any alternatives.

The place hadn't changed much. There were different drapes, bits of bric-a-brac I didn't remember, some new titles on the bookshelves, and the television set took up a corner where once there'd been one of those impressive console radios; but the lumpy lounge chairs were the same in spite of the camouflage of patterned covers.

The door clicked shut. I stood there in the middle of the room trying not to feel like the clot I must've looked.

'Sit down,' said Hodges. It was an order, not the hospitable gesture of host to guest. I sat down where I knew he'd want me to sit: in a narrow armchair that didn't permit too much manoeuvre.

He stood in front of me. It made me feel a bit better to see he hadn't changed much. He was older, of course, and so was I. But, unlike me, there was no fat on him. He was lean, hard, with a suspicion of sun-tan lingering on firm skin. His hair was as dark as it had ever been, his eyes were as alert, as pale blue, as horribly cold as I'd always remembered. He was not very big, but put together in just the right proportions. He'd pass for forty, even to a woman – which was pretty impressive, one way and another. He was still a natty dresser, with the same old thing about dressing-gowns. Over what looked like an expensive shirt and well-creased pants he was wearing a sort of silk kimono. A kimono on Hodges? No. More likely karate-style. I used to rib him about his dressing-gowns. That's how long ago it was.

'I'm waiting.'

And not too patiently. He still balanced light on his feet. I wished I'd worn as well. I sucked in a long breath.

'Well, it wasn't easy. Coming here, I mean . . .'

'I'll bet.'

'But I had to talk to somebody. It could be important.'

'It'd better be.'

'That Eppler bit . . .'

'You had nothing to do with Eppler. Anyway, he's dead.'

He wasn't making it easy. But then I hadn't expected this to be just a bus ride. So Eppler was dead. I wondered how and where and when . . .

Hodges moved sideways, watching me. He flicked open a cupboard, took out a bottle and a glass. For just a second I was grateful. My throat was like sandpaper. Then I saw the label on the bottle: lemonade. He splashed some into the glass, stood there sipping it. There were other, more exciting, labels in the cupboard. So Hodges still didn't touch hard stuff. He kept it, though, for friends: and enemies. He offered me nothing. I licked dry lips.

He held up the glass. It held perhaps two inches of lemon-ade. 'That's how long you've got.'

He sipped again. The level fell maybe a quarter of an inch.

This was when I'd get my face pushed in. On the tube I'd

had all sorts of ideas about how to approach this without actually mentioning her name. But it wasn't on. I had to do it the hard way.

'It . . . it's about . . . about . . .'

My mouth just wouldn't shape itself right. And the bastard just stood there, supping that stinking lemonade.

I got my tongue right for the sibilant. It came out like a hiss. 'Sophia.'

I pressed against the back of the chair. Hodges stared at me, his face unchanging. He quietly drained the glass, put it down on a shelf without once taking his eyes off me. I didn't see him move but I felt the sting of his slapping palm across my eyes before I heard the contact of flesh on flesh. He stepped back. No hint of anger in him at all. But now he'd listen. And he'd listen good.

Something warm was trickling into my left eye. The pain was just a throb now. And I wasn't going to give that man the satisfaction of watching me lift a hand to check the blood. Because I could see he still wore the plain gold ring on the third finger of his right hand: the ring with the microscopic spike just long enough to break skin and draw blood. And blood in the eyes didn't help if you were slugging it out with a man like Hodges.

'You just never learn, do you?' he said.

I wanted a drink. Even lemonade. How can you talk when your tongue's just a hard bit of rubber choking a dry throat? And the vision in my left eye was on the wonk. That'd be the blood. But I still wasn't going to give him the satisfaction of watching me dab at it.

Hodges just stood there. Waiting. Those long delicate fingers, fine as a woman's and as tough as tempered steel, played gently with the gold ring. It was more than a hint. He was telling me to get on with the talk. I tried. I swallowed, tried to get some spittle into my mouth. At last I managed a sort of croaking mumble. 'This . . . this afternoon. It was this afternoon . . .'

It wasn't any use. Now I was trying to tell it, all of it sounded crazy. And it was best never to talk crazy to Hodges. I started to sweat a bit, and began to hunt for the words which would make it as sane and as sinister as it had looked to me.

This time I felt the biting scratch of the spike dragging across where the first wound still throbbed. I couldn't help it. It was reflex and pain and the shock of not having seen him

11

move: my hands went up, one to cover the sticky wetness over my left eye, the other, far too late, to ward away the sweeping arm.

His voice was just a murmur. 'Sophia, you said. This afternoon, you said.'

I had to throw my head back. The blood was dripping on to my pants where they stretched tight across my thigh. The still figure of Hodges was just a smudge through the haze of blood and the tears mingling with it.

'The Sophia file was closed. Thirty years ago.' The voice was still, flat, quiet. 'You know that. You closed it.' A hand flashed forward. The vice-grip of those steel fingers grabbed a handful of shirt and collar and tie, jerking me forward. 'You closed that file!' he said. The wet gravel was swishing about in the tin pail of his larynx now. 'You mucked it up. Didn't you? Didn't you bloody well do it?'

The air supply was cutting off. I wrenched at his hand. I nodded once, twice, three times, ignoring the throb of pain over my eye. He jerked the gripping hand forward. My head hit the back of the chair. I gulped oxygen. He waited, quite still and quiet. He just stood there, watching me. I wanted to wipe away the mess around my eyes, but I wasn't going to reach into a pocket for a handkerchief, not with Hodges four feet away. I used my fingers to smooth away the veil of blood and water.

He was right. The file had been closed thirty years ago, and I'd closed it. Hodges had never forgiven me for that. I remembered the last time I'd been in this room. Hodges, standing pretty much where he was now, and the controlled but gritty calm of his voice as he'd said: 'Keep away. You hear me? Keep away from me. Get under my feet just once and I'll tear your head off . . .'

Like he'd said, I never learn. Because here I was, near enough to under his feet. And he'd started the head-tearing bit. But there wasn't any other way, not after this afternoon.

This afternoon? How the hell was I going to make any sense of the telling of that? Of what had happened while I'd stood in the Press Club bar, Benson boring the ears off me, not even remembering Sophia?

'You said "this afternoon",' said Hodges.

I nodded again. The breathing was easier now. If I could find the right words, words that made some sort of sense, he'd listen all right. He'd have no choice, not after what happened all those years ago. I'd read somewhere that you should never shake a skeleton. Some of the dead bones might fly off and hurt somebody. But this was a skeleton that had to be shaken. So maybe a new world history had been written since those hard, grim days when a lot of us had fought our own war in the bars and cafés and lush flats and dark alleys of a Cairo seething with troops.

Hodges had been there. So had I. And so had a woman named Sophia.

TWO

SOPHIA

Grayling said, 'We don't deserve to win the bloody war.'

There wasn't much point in my telling him that the way things were going it didn't look as though we would. So I didn't. He was squinting out into the bright winter sunshine and picking his nose. That was always a sure sign Grayling was troubled. He wriggled restlessly inside the khaki serge battledress uniform with the green war-correspondent flashes on the epaulettes. Grayling really resented having to wear it.

'Christ,' he'd say, 'they'll be giving me a gun next. And then where'll we all be?' A man given much to blasphemy and profanity, he knew his limitations.

The gharries and taxis were doing a brisk trade outside what had been the Italian Dopolavoro Club opposite. It now housed the New Zealand Forces Club and the distinctive lemon-squeezer hats with the colourful regimental puggarees dominated the busy Sharika Malika Farida.

Grayling morosely finished his zibib and yelled for two more. Little Ahmed came running, the black tassel on his fez bouncing impertinently. He liked Meester Grayleen immensely.

'I tell you, they're bloody idiots. Bloody morons.'

I reminded him gently that I didn't know what the hell he was talking about. How the hell could I, he wanted to know. He was always a bit bellicose about my neutral background and the fact that I could wear comfortable civvies. The Republic of Ireland had low priority on his list of things worth recognising.

I let him simmer on. Grayling was too good a newspaperman not to want to tell a good story. Over the fourth zibib it came tumbling out. Suitably censored, this is what he told me.

Before the British Press colony had beaten an undignified retreat in the face of the Nazi occupation of Hungary, Grayling had known of an Englishwoman who kept odd company in Budapest. She'd been several kinds of a bitch, and worse, if Grayling was to be believed. She'd consorted with dubious Hungarians and with known members of the German fifth column.

14

'And yesterday, only bloody yesterday,' the voice was choked, 'who do I see walking along bloody Soliman Pasha large as bloody life, eh? That same bloody tart, large as bloody life.'

Careful probing got me nowhere. Grayling didn't know her name. Oh yes, he'd heard it. Thought it began with a C. 'But damn it, you don't invite a bitch like that to have a drink,' he ranted. 'How the hell should I know her?' He hinted darkly that he could have understood it if the bloody woman had been Irish . . . but a bloody Englishwoman, going on like that!

That night, in the club on Malika Farida, a New Zealand soldier punched a Greek civilian. Next day one of my chores was to run a check on the two complainants, who'd issued statements to the military police. One was signed 'Yanni Phillipides', and was just a recital of his version of what had happened. How, with a companion, he'd gone to visit friends in an apartment at the Dopolavoro Club. He'd mistaken the floor and had found himself in a room full of 'drunken soldiers'. One of these had objected violently to a 'wop' coming in, had hit him, had broken two of his teeth.

It was the second statement that damn near stopped the clock. Yes, she'd been with Mr Phillipides. Yes, they were going to visit friends. Yes, she confirmed what the soldier had done. She described herself as English, a refugee from Budapest. She signed herself 'Ida Clapham' . . .

I could hear Grayling. 'Oh yes, I've heard the bloody woman's name. Think it began with a . . . a C. Yes, a C . . .'

Grayling would have been pleased if he'd known what was going to develop, because a soldier did some time in the military nick for belting a civilian. The lad should have had a medal . . . or so we thought at the time.

The flood of humanity from beleaguered Europe was stretching the security services in Cairo to their limits, trying to sort deserving wheat from political chaff. The situation was tailor-made for Hitler and his bully boys. Even the suffering Jews had to work their way as best they could through the tight security-screen on the Middle East frontiers. A lot could be done with a Jew whose wife and family were still in Nazi hands in Germany. But Ida Clapham was lucky: she was English, holder of a British passport. Nobody, it seemed, worried too much about the Budapest part of it. She was on the run from the enemy. That was good enough. 'Just hand in the passport to refugee control, sign these forms, collect a subsistence allowance and here's a chit for the pension where you'll live.'

The Lebanese in charge of the refugee control-office was helpful. Yes, a Mrs Ida Clapham was registered. Yes, he was holding the passport. Yes, yes, yes (he was becoming a bit impatient), she was at the hostel as far as he knew, drawing her money, behaving herself.

The photograph in the passport was like all similar pictures. Not flattering. It made Ida look like a very plain horse. She looked older than the thirty-seven years debited to her. She'd moved around Europe quite a lot. That tallied. Her occupation was given as 'saleswoman'. The thought occurred to me that she would have to be pretty good at her job if she hoped to interest any man in her personal wares.

'You want the other passport?' the Lebanese wanted to know.

'What other passport?'

'Daughter of Mrs Clapham,' he said.

It was a French passport. And not even the smudgy picture could destroy this woman's beauty.

Name: Sophia Kukralovic. Birthplace: Cracow, Poland. Age at date of issue two years before: twenty-nine. That bothered me a bit. If she was Ida Clapham's daughter I'd stumbled on a biological miracle that was going to knock the Immaculate Conception into a cocked hat.

'Mrs Clapham's step-daughter,' said the Lebanese. Fortune and fame winged their way out of an open window . . .

It took time and no little skulduggery to set up the meeting. The Lebanese was persuaded to write a letter. He grudgingly accepted that we'd been friends for years. Yes, he said, he'd naturally be delighted if I dropped in at his office after a trip to the Sudan. My boss took a bit of persuading, too. When you're just a sergeant in a security section you don't pull much weight with captains.

'Look,' he said. 'Get this check finished fast, skiving about spending taxpayers' money isn't our job.' I reminded myself to ask sometime about how he could afford the blonde from the cipher section. 'You get a report on those women and I'll pass it on.' But he did let me have the section's battered green Chevvy when we got a signal from the Lebanese. Ida and Sophia would be at his office at eleven o'clock on the Tuesday morning, to sign some forms replacing those his staff had lost. This must have stuck in his craw. He was a character, I suspect, who never lost anything. The women would be there, he

16

thought, about fifteen minutes.

I walked through the outer office, pushed open the door of the little cubicle and suffered the garlic-laden embraces of my old and very dear friend. Over his shoulder I saw Ida Clapham. I'll bet she hated her passport being impounded: the picture in it flattered her. Beyond her, staring out of the window, was a blonde-haloed vision in a white silk blouse and brown jodhpurs, idly tapping a riding-crop against her leg. She turned lazily and smiled. And for the first time I saw what I later learned was a mannerism: when she smiled she raised two long tapering fingers of her left hand and caressed a dimple in her cheek.

Plain Ida Clapham may have been, but she knew a thing or two about winning friends and influencing people.

The two of them had seemed grateful when I said I had a car outside. And when I jerked open a back door, Ida got in. She told Sophia to ride up front with me. And then Ida asked if it would be any trouble to drop her off in the Midan Opera? After that, perhaps I'd take Sophia on? The trouble was that this trick was old hat. Split up, and the tail has only one chance in two of staying with the target that matters. Maybe, after all, Ida Clapham was the brain and Sophia just the bait. But when you're young, a little nibble at the hook's hard to resist, so we dropped Ida Clapham in the Midan Opera, and I went to work on what I had left. For a while, work was what it seemed like. Sophia thanked me prettily enough for the offer of lunch, but she already had an appointment. I pitched the tale of a journalist with a rare day off. No uniform to attract the girls – just a lonely neutral a long way from home: all horrible corn but, if I do say it myself, well delivered.

What swung it I can't be sure. 'But,' she said, 'I'll have to make a telephone call. And change.' I offered to drive her home and wait.

'No,' she said, the fingers caressing the dimple. 'Tell me where and I'll meet you. At half-past one.'

She wouldn't be shifted from that, and I was prepared to push only so hard. So we agreed on Groppi's after I let her out in Kasr al Ainie. I pushed off, but not too far – just out of her line of vision. I hopped out and watched from inside a café. She'd walked perhaps a couple of hundred yards, not too obviously interested in what was going on around her, but interested just the same. Then she hailed a taxi. Now why should she do that, when she had the Chevvy for free? That was when I reckoned I'd be lunching alone: which just goes to show how wrong you can be, because I was only halfway through my first zibib in Groppi's bar at twenty-eight minutes to two when in she came, all cool and pale blue and damn near edible. Honestly, the blokes in that bar just stopped nattering and boozing like snapping your fingers.

'Sorry I'm late,' she smiled, the fingers on the dimple. And thank you, she'd have a Campari. Yes, with ice and soda. Oh, and lemon, please.

For a consideration, Mahmud had said he'd keep us a table. We sat down to eat at ten past three. She'd drunk a lot but was possibly rather more sober than I felt. She talked freely enough about inconsequentials, like the weather and how pleasant it was, and how prices were rising, and wasn't *Gone With The Wind* a splendid film? She asked questions about my job. But there wasn't any depth in them. There was no probing. We talked a bit about Ireland, a country she said she'd like to visit one day. I tucked that away for future use.

Her English was as good as mine. Only the accent betrayed foreign birth. When I complimented her she was surprised.

'But I lived in England for many years,' she said. Then, shrewdly, 'As you have, I think.'

She was extremely clever. When I tried the obvious gambit of guessing her nationality she encouraged me, as a sort of social game, to place her. I kept well away from the Cracow of her passport, and from France, where the document had been issued. I didn't want her tying too many things together too quickly. Anyway, she wasn't French. She could just have been Polish, but even in those days I was developing little nervous tics about what people told me. I studied her features. She posed, smiling, the fingers on the dimple. The thumping I felt had nothing to do with nervous tics. This was plain physical. Her blouse was unbuttoned, just far enough for the deep cleavage of full breasts to be glimpsed. I was content to look and allow erotic imagination to run riot.

'Well?' she asked.

I tried to concentrate. Kukralovic: Slav, of course, and a name she should never have had. It was too hard, too harsh for a woman as ... as ...

'You are not a very good journalist, I think,' she said.

So I had to say something. 'Russian,' was what I said.

The blue eyes widened, the full red lips formed a delicate O, to show just how impressed she was. 'You are so nearly right,' she said, a hand reaching out, covering one of mine, squeezing it gently. 'But we people from Georgia do not say we are Russians.' There was a little toss of the proud head. 'We are Georgians.' There was a hint of anger when she added, 'We are a Soviet Socialist Republic on the maps. But we are Georgian, not Russian. We existed as a people before there was a Russia.'

I buried my nose quickly in a drink. Born in Cracow said the French passport; born in Georgia, said Sophia Kukralovic.

She glanced at her watch, an expensive-looking piece of jewellery. She stood up. 'Now I must go,' she said. No messing about: this was a definitive decision. She was going to go. She declined my offer of the Chevvy, insisted on Mahmud calling her a taxi. And she was equally determined that I stay to finish my drink. I cursed for not having kept pace, but there was also the bill. I asked if I could see her later. She pouted in thought for a moment. 'Tomorrow,' she offered. 'Lunch? But out of town, please. Where the air is fresh.'

I suggested Sans Souci. She said half-past one. And then she was gone.

My boss wasn't pleased at all when I said I needed the Chevvy again next day. It didn't impress the cipher blonde, riding around in a pool car. And he nearly had a fit when I showed him the Groppi's lunch bill.

'This is a routine check job. What makes you think you're in the spy business? How the hell am I going to get expenses like that through?'

I gave him a fast briefing on what I'd picked up. That stopped him. He rubbed his chin. 'Look,' he said. 'This is getting out of the section's depth. Give me a report on what you know and I'll shove it along.'

'That doesn't make sense,' I argued. I saw the look on his face and quickly added 'sir'. And it didn't, did it? Here I was, making ground of a sort with the woman. How easy was it going to be to feed in a stranger?

'Because they're experts,' the captain told me. But I could tell he was weakening. He was figuring how he could swing rank and buy into the act and get himself some kudos as well. There are a lot of politics in the military.

'Look,' he said. He scratched the side of his nose. 'You'd better keep that lunch date tomorrow. I'll see how much money I can drag out of them for you. Oh, and you'd better have the Chevvy. But use it, man. Find out where she's living. But then you'll write a full report for the other people. They won't thank us for muscling in on their territory.' He thought for a bit. 'Come to think of it, I'd better come with you.'

This was going to be tricky. He was all right at the job he was doing, I suppose. Running a security section probably wasn't much different from what he'd been doing eight months ago. Except that he'd gone down with gyppo tummy when the regimental band he looked after was posted away, he'd done pretty well, or so the grapevine had it. And the military mind being what it was, he'd got this job when he came out of hospital at Helwan. But he was right. This wasn't our province at all, once it got past running a quick check on who was what.

The trouble was he wore civvies as if there were still three pips on each shoulder. And his target with any woman was laying them on their backs just as fast as he could find any reasonably flat surface. He mightn't wait that long once he got an eyeful of Sophia.

So I said, 'Thought you were running the Suez road check tomorrow.' I tossed in the 'sir' more smartly this time.

'Damn!' said the captain.

I was late getting to the Sans Souci. Getting money had been the hold-up. There'd been some argument in the military secretary's office, but the boss, bless him, had got me the funds. Then I'd got stuck behind an army convoy that was tangled with a camel train. So I was in a bit of a panic when I'd parked the car and hurried into the gardens. She wasn't at an outside table: not many people were. Inside, it was more crowded, especially up at the bar. There were several blonde heads but no Sophia Kukralovic. And it was nearly twenty to two. Maybe she'd been held up. I half-turned towards the bar, then on impulse decided to wait outside. I might spot at least the direction she came from. I found a table behind an ornamental shrub. I could see the garden entrance through the leaves. To anyone coming in I'd be a shapeless something. It would do. A waiter bustled up. I ordered a zibib: no sense dying of thirst.

At ten to two I was ready to pack it in. That was when I heard the squeal of brakes. I looked behind me, over the hedge. Maybe thirty yards away a taxi had stopped. Sophia stepped out, then turned and spoke to someone inside. Then she was listening. She laughed, fingers on cheek. I put my face in my glass, heard the taxi door slam, the gears grate. I peeped through my defensive shrub. The cab was going past the gate.

There was a man in the back. I couldn't see much of his face in the shadow, but he was wearing a fez. Then Sophia was walking into the gardens, gorgeous in an outfit I hadn't seen before. She moved gracefully, without hesitation, her eyes searching without any urgency. I reckon she knew I'd be waiting.

I stepped out behind her.

'Hello,' I said. She turned, smiling, hand stroking dimple.

'I am very sorry I am late,' she said. 'But the soldiers take all the taxis. It is very difficult.'

We picked up where we'd left off the day before, surprisingly easily, but I felt her mind wasn't wholly on conversation or the drinks or the food, which she decided she wanted pretty well straight away.

'What's the trouble?' I finally asked her.

How observant I was, she told me, eyes wide, those lips forming the little O of wonder. Yes, I thought, observant like I can see a brick wall at two feet.

'It is Ida,' she said.

Wondering why she was suddenly laying on the accent so thick, I played it dumb.

'Who's Ida?'

'Oh, you know. My friend. Mrs Clapham. You met her. Yesterday.'

'Sorry. Yes, I remember Mrs Clapham, of course. She's a friend of yours, then?'

'A friend? She is my greatest friend.' She turned her head away and I swear she dabbed at her eyes. It was quite a performance.

'She had an accident or something?' I asked.

'Oh, no. But I am terribly afraid for her.' Suddenly she was leaning across the table, both her hands grasping one of mine. It was a pleasant sensation. 'Will you help us?'

She certainly didn't waste any time. She'd become a little girl all lost and bewildered in a great big world.

'If I can.' My hand answered the pressure of hers. Not too obviously, I hoped.

'She is such a good woman. She saved my life. And now she is in such terrible danger.'

This I wanted to know about. From the little I'd seen of Ida Clapham she didn't seem the sort to get involved with what could be remotely described as danger.

'It's the secret police,' Sophia said. 'They are watching her. All day and all night they follow her everywhere.'

21

'You're telling me the Egyptian secret police are . . .'

'No, no. You do not understand. It is the English secret police. She is very frightened. You must help us.'

This was getting more screwball by the minute.

'Will you come with me? Now?' Sophia asked. I nodded. 'You will see. I told Ida you would help us.'

'But if what you say is true, what can I do?' Lying valiantly, I added: 'I'm not even British.'

'It is better that you are not.'

'But Ida . . . she's British, isn't she? Name sounds like it.'

'Oh yes, she is English. That is why we are afraid. Please come now. Quickly.'

I paid the bill. By the time I'd rejoined her, Sophia had called a taxi, had the door open. I shut it firmly, gave the puzzled driver a few piastres. 'I've got a car. Come on.'

We clambered in. 'Where to?' I asked her. She gave me an address in Bab al-Sharia. It wasn't the address my Lebanese friend had.

I drove in silence. I had a lot to think about. I'd have had more to worry me if I'd known that this meeting was to lead me to confrontation in London thirty years later with a man I didn't know called George Victor Hodges.

THREE

LONDON: THE WOMAN IN THE CLUB

'I'm waiting,' said Hodges. He'd poured himself some more lemonade. He just stood there, swilling the stuff gently around the glass. God, I'd have given an arm for just a drip on my leather-dry tongue. I tried to activate the saliva buds. How the hell could I tell him anything without spit to lubricate the words? A bloke with his experience should know that.

'You'd better have this,' he said. The tumbler, steady as a rock, was under my nose. I grabbed at it, spilling driblets as my clumsy hands closed round the glass. I gulped at the drink. Sure enough, some of it got down the wrong pipe and there I was coughing and choking, tears smarting my eyes. He took away the glass and just stood there, watching me. I groped towards my pocket. Steel-hard fingers were on my wrist, jerking the hand away from the pocket where my handkerchief was. As my body twitched in a paroxysm I was hardly conscious of the slow numbing of my hand as the blood supply was checked by the vice of Hodges' grip. A hand was patting the pocket. The pressure on my wrist relaxed. One last violent convulsion cleared my windpipe of the lemonade and I fell back in the chair, tears in my eyes, snot trickling out of my nose, the throb of pain pulsing like a hammer against my forehead. At last I was able to hide my shame behind the curtain of the handkerchief. The bastard! I shouldn't have come. I knew it had to be like this. But there wasn't anybody else. Only him: only Hodges.

Then I took my hands from my aching face. Hodges was dropping the glass I'd used into a cheap, hideously-coloured litter basket. That was like him. All that man's taste was in his mouth. But that didn't . . .

'This afternoon,' he said. What patience he'd shown had gone. Hodges never used words when a change in voice-tone would do. And those two words sounded just like fingernails dragging over sandpaper.

I nodded, swallowed. 'Yes, I was at the Press Club. With Benson.'

'Who's Benson?'

23

Hell, he really meant to start at the top. Trouble is, I talk too much. 'I was at the Press Club' would have been enough. But me, I've got to tag on 'with Benson'. I had to be careful. 'Benson,' I said, 'is a reporter. On one of the Sundays. Bright lad. A bit brash, but going places.'

'I didn't ask what he is. I asked who he is.'

'Oh.' I'd have preferred to have notice of a question like that. 'Young chap. Middle twenties. Could be edging thirty maybe. Been on Fleet Street about four months. From the provinces – Sheffield, I think. Made a bit of a name for himself as a feature-writer up there. Journalist of the year. Something like that.'

Pray God he doesn't press this. I didn't want to have it beaten out of me that Howard Benson was starting to get in the hair of a few people at the Ministry. Not seriously, not yet. He had the defence beat and was playing it according to the book – just dropping in at the Horse Guards Avenue entrance, saying hello, taking away whatever handouts we had. Sometimes he'd phone in for what we could give him on running stories. His pieces were models of good reporting, intelligently and brightly written. But he had a knack of phrasing, of emphasis, that made what appeared under his by-line just a little – what? We didn't know what. It was as though he was scrawling in foot-high capitals the message: 'Now, this is what they say. But don't you believe a word of it.'

The trouble was that we could analyse his stuff for hours at a stretch and be right back where we'd started. Either what he was doing was his natural journalistic style or he was hearing things he shouldn't and playing it safe till he latched on to something worth spelling out in words of two syllables. And so those of us who had anything to do with him grabbed every chance we could of enjoying his quite lavish expense account. Now how the heck do you parcel that up in a couple of sentences to a man like Hodges?

'He spends well,' I said. 'And Her Majesty's servants in the PR business don't get paid so much.'

Would that hive Hodges away from Benson? It did.

'Christ,' he said. 'You don't change, do you? Never learn, do you?'

I sat there and let him say it. 'Go on,' he said.

'Well, we were at the bar. He was bashing his gums at me. Boring me stiff.' I had to do what I could with Hodges, get him away from Benson. 'Still, he was paying for the booze and the grub. Then he stopped talking. Just like that. He was staring past me. I had my back to the lobby.'

I wasn't exaggerating. Benson's mouth was hanging open on a word he never finished uttering. And when I turned round my mouth must have dropped open, too. There she was, posed in the doorway. Eric Lawson was standing back to let her through, and Alistair Pemberton had a gentle, guiding hand on her elbow. It was just as though the Government had announced legislation to outlaw newspapers. The bar was pretty crowded at one o'clock, but the gabbing and the guzzling stopped dead.

The woman glided into the room, Pemberton grotesquely out of character behind her, Lawson nodding in a condescending sort of way to the rest of us. Then she laughed, a tinkling sound that echoed like a bell in my memory. Suddenly, the pile of rich blonde hair, the milky complexion, the startlingly blue eyes, the ruby-red mouth didn't belong to her at all. Here was a ghost of thirty years fleshed and breathing. I literally had to shake my head, place my feet firmly in the carpet to avoid the impulse to go to her. I told myself it couldn't be. It wasn't possible. Sophia was a long time ago: thirty years ago.

Then, as the conversation stuttered again into life, she laughed at something Lawson had whispered. That was when I knew. Beyond any shadow of possible doubt, I knew. As the pearl-white teeth parted, two long fingers stole softly to her cheek and stroked the dimple at the side of her mouth.

Not a muscle moved in the expressionless face staring back at me. 'What did you do?' Hodges wanted to know, his voice flat.

'Do? Why, nothing. I . . . I just turned back to my drink.'

That was true. I had to concentrate on something else other than the guest of Pemberton and Lawson. I wanted to sort out what had to be done.

'Excuse me,' said Benson. 'Chap over there. Haven't seen him for months. Just say hello . . .'

I watched him go as I quickly drained my Scotch. He pushed through the lane that had opened to allow the blonde and her escorts up to the bar. It didn't surprise me at all that Benson pushed in behind them to grab at Lawson's hand and pump it up and down. He was being a bit enthusiastic about a chap he hadn't seen for months . . . like last Thursday, to my knowledge. I wanted another drink, but Tommy and Brian were competing to serve the newcomers. The woman was being helped on to a bar stool, short skirt riding high on a tights-clad slim thigh.

'So I walked out,' I told Hodges. 'I rang the office, said I didn't feel well. I went home.' I hadn't felt too good. You don't have a chunk of that kind of your past dumped in your lap without feeling a bit sick. I had to have time to think.

All of us had known Sophia had a child – a daughter – somewhere in her background. It was something she never kept secret. Which made the visitor to the Press Club probably older than she looked. But she had to be Sophia's daughter. The face, the figure, the whole physical set-up of her. But the clincher had to be that mannerism. And if heredity meant anything, then this woman had to be thought about, seriously. Add to all that a man named Lawson. He edited the left-wing weekly *Podium* that somehow managed to survive in the jungle of Fleet Street. Forty-ish, running to seed and not apparently too well heeled, he was an unlikely suitor for the hand of Sophia's daughter. But Pemberton was the bigger puzzle of the two escorts. Too far to the Right even for *The Times*, he was making a good living out of one of the more sensational tabloids sniping at the Establishment, to which he genuflected when he wasn't actually sitting at his typewriter. He was an odd fish, but not a woman's man: a man's woman, said his colleagues on the Street; that is, if you weren't too fussy, and were inclined that way.

Lawson, politically so-so at best: a security blot at worst. Pemberton, an amoral leopard changing its spots. It didn't make sense. But it was Sophia's ghost who troubled me most. So it had to be Hodges.

I didn't much like the look on his face. It had got very tight. And darker.

'I don't believe your memory's that good,' he said.

'Good enough not to be wrong.'

The bad part had to be over. Now that he knew, he just had to be reasonable. There wouldn't be any more of the pushing-in-faces technique. So my confidence was building up. Not too much, because you could never know with a man like Hodges, but enough for me to commit myself to telling him what I believed to be true.

'Thirty years?' he sneered. 'You remember a face after thirty years?'

'Yes,' I said. I hesitated, but before I reached inside my jacket, I let him know what I was doing. 'I've still got her picture.'

That didn't please him. I watched him rise on the balls of his feet. I braced for the shock attack, but then he settled back again on his heels.

'Why?' he wanted to know, his voice in a whisper.

Why does anyone hang on to a yellowing photograph for thirty years? I couldn't think of any good reason why I had. I just dug into my pocket and held it out. He didn't take it, just stepped forward a pace and stared down at the postcard print. My hand started to tremble, holding it at arm's length. His fingers locked around my wrist.

'Why?' he asked again.

I just shook my head. There wasn't any reason I could tell him about.

Slowly and deliberately, he twisted my wrist until he could read the inscription on the back of the picture. The pain was excruciating, but I had to put up with it. His mouth framed the words: my name; hers, in the spidery Russian script; Cairo; the date: that's all there was. But he spent a life-time reading it. Then he turned my wrist back again. That was almost as painful as the first awful twisting. He stared at the likeness of Sophia for a long time. She looked like an angel. The smooth face, calm and serene, framed in the fur hood of her jacket: a silk handkerchief peeping out of the pocket over the full left breast. She'd been beautiful all right. That was something I'd never forget.

He dropped my wrist suddenly. The shock of release made me drop the photograph. Clenching and unclenching my numb right hand I bent forward, my left arm reaching down. His foot was on the card lying on the floor.

'Tell me why you kept it,' he said.

I sat back in the chair. 'I don't know,' I told him, and I swear to God that was the truth. The conviction must have reached him, because he stepped back and I bent forward again and picked up the picture with my left hand. I was about to slip it back into my pocket, but I didn't. You could never tell with Hodges. So I just held it, feeling foolish.

'There are hundreds of women in London right now as beautiful as she is,' he said. 'How can you be sure the bird in the Press Club's any relation?'

'She's the spitting image,' I said. 'And how many women in London rub a dimple when they laugh?'

Hodges turned away, got himself a fresh glass from the cupboard and splashed some lemonade in it. He didn't offer me another drink. I could have used it. My throat was dry again, and my eye was throbbing, though the bleeding seemed to have stopped.

'It's not only the likeness,' I said. 'It's that, of course, and rubbing the dimple. But there's Lawson. And Pemberton.' I waited, but he just sipped from the glass, his eyes boring into me. 'They must be in the files,' I ventured.

'That's none of your business,' he said. But there wasn't any venom in his voice. He was simply stating a fact as he knew it.

'It has to be worth a check.'

He sipped some more lemonade. 'Know your trouble?' he asked. I didn't even bother to shake my head. 'You're not one of us. You never were. You don't think like we do. You get half-cock ideas.'

'Look,' I said. 'She exists. Right here in London. The daughter of her mother. And she's matey with Pemberton and Lawson. So it's half-cocked, maybe. But I'm not doing anything about it, except telling you. So you say I buggered it up thirty years ago. All right. Now *you* have a go. Somebody's got to do something. But I'm staying out of it. That's why I'm here now. Just so none of us has another Cairo round our necks.'

FOUR

CAIRO: IDA

It wasn't easy driving to Bab al-Sharia. To the normal hazards of camel-trains plodding their slow and unpredictable way through the crowded narrow streets and the honking, snorting arrogance of impatient taxis there was added the maze of military vehicles trying to dominate the Egyptians even if, at that time, the British weren't able to dominate the enemy.

In spite of the concern she'd shown earlier, Sophia was calm enough as I hauled the wheel this way and that, trying to get through the busy Cairo streets. Out of the corner of my eye I could see her, her head turned away slightly from me as she watched the traffic. I wondered what she was up to. If Ida Clapham was in trouble with the British secret police – whoever they were – what made her think I could help? Then I started to wonder just what the connection was between these two oddly diverse women: one, plain as a calico pillow, the other, all peaches and cream and blonde bedworthiness. There seemed to be no dispute about the fact that they'd arrived in Cairo together, as refugees, duly accounted for, apparently cleared by the security control at Haifa – if the Lebanese official's records were correct. Haifa. That presupposed they'd travelled across Turkey from Hungary . . .

Beside me, Sophia gave a sharp cry. I jerked the wheel over, grazed a camel's rump, revved the engine to drown the splutter of Arabic curses and to slip between an army seven-tonner and a loudly blaring taxi.

'Sorry,' I grunted.

She gave a little laugh. Up went the fingers to caress the side of her mouth. 'But it is exciting,' she said.

The street was less crowded. I stole a sideways glance. Her lips were slightly parted. The full breasts were rising and falling quickly. She was enjoying herself all right. Maybe I should crash the bloody car so she could really have herself a good time! I had to ask her the way. Bab al-Sharia, tucked in behind the Mousky, was a maze of alleys and lanes and cramped little streets. Sophia was guiding me into a warren I didn't know at all, into places where no car should have been driven.

'It will be better if we leave the car, I think,' she said.

That's when I started wondering if Sophia was as bright as I'd suspected. The characters in these streets wouldn't have left even an oil-drip to show where a car had been parked.

'You just tell me where,' I suggested. I had my eyes on the road again, but I sensed that she shrugged.

It finally became impossible, of course, so I either had to ditch Sophia or risk the boss's car. Keeping my fingers crossed, I locked the car. Then I stood quite still and looked for an honest face. In Bab al-Sharia! Sophia seemed suddenly to remember Ida Clapham and the secret police. She plucked at my sleeve.

'Do hurry,' she urged me. But I kept right on searching the alley with my eyes. And there was a giant Nubian, his galabiah sparkling white, red fez at a jaunty angle. At least he looked clean, and that was something in Bab al-Shira. He was sitting outside a doorway, his chair propped back against the white wall. I hoped he spoke English or French. Piastres changed hands. His fractured English was good enough. Yes, the car would be quite safe. I believed him, unless he was going to strip it himself. I hurried after Sophia who was heading for an alley that looked like a pathway to hell. Squalid buildings seemed to lean across the passageway in a sort of arch. Refuse littered the paving. Fly-blown coffee-coloured children played listlessly, and a lemonade-seller wasn't doing any business in spite of the insistent tinkling of his bell. I caught up with Sophia. 'What the hell, she doesn't live here, does she?'

She nodded. 'It is to escape the secret police.'

It had to be something, because maybe the hostels provided by the refugee people weren't five-star, but compared to these hovels they were palaces. The place became more stinking the further we pushed into it. Was this why Sophia hadn't allowed me to go with her after our previous meetings? Looking at the back of her neck – there wasn't room for us to walk side by side – I couldn't believe that. She couldn't live here. She belonged to Shepheard's, Groppi's, the Gezira and Maadi Sporting Clubs. This wasn't her world: refugee or not, she didn't belong here. I didn't like the way some of the locals were staring at us: they looked as if they were calculating how much our clothes would fetch in the Mousky. What I had in my wallet – peanuts probably, by Sophia's standards – could maybe keep any one of these families for a couple of months.

'Christ,' I said. 'Does she have to live here?'

Her head bobbed impatiently. 'I told you,' she said. 'It is because of the police.'

We ploughed on through the stench and the garbage. I was lost, but Sophia walked on confidently. Then we were in a cul-de-sac of broken masonry, discoloured walls, with nothing but sand under our feet. I'd seen similar places in the Dead City: there should have been a few tombs resting on the ground. Right at the end, Sophia pushed open a small door. It creaked on rusting hinges. She plunged on into the darkness of a smelly passage. I followed her up some broken stairs to a landing on which there was only one door. It was in startling contrast to those we'd passed. It was clean. Sophia went on through it. No knock; no warning; just straight in. For a woman supposed to be scared stiff of secret police, the security was pretty lax, I thought.

I paused on the landing. The voices inside sounded mighty relaxed. A feminine voice said, 'Hello, darling.' And a man said, 'Is he with you?'

'Yes,' said Sophia, and poked her beautiful face through the door. 'Do come in,' she invited me.

I wondered if the man was the Yanni Phillipides who'd signed the complaint against the soldier in the Dopolavoro Club. His voice had an accent thick enough to chew.

No matter how broad-minded you are it's always a bit of a shock to walk into a room for the first time and see in bed a woman you're meeting for only the second time. It was obvious she didn't have any clothes on. Ida Clapham was just throwing back the single not-over-clean sheets as I came through the door. She swung her legs off the lumpy-looking mattress and said, 'Hand me my dressing-gown, love.'

The man finished tying the tape of his pyjama pants before he picked up the dressing-gown and threw it on the bed. He wasn't wearing a jacket. He was painfully thin, his rib-cage looking rather like a concertina, and he hadn't shaved for several days. His beard and body-hair were jet black, contrasting sharply with the pale sallowness of his skin.

Chuckles rippled waves of laughter when Sophia said: 'You really mustn't mind Ida and Yanni. They enjoy making love in the afternoon.'

I re-set my features into a sort of smile. Shrugging into her dressing-gown, Ida said, 'You're a nice chap. Looking after Sophia, I mean.'

Yanni stepped over to me, held out a bony hand. 'Hello,' he said. His grip took me by surprise. He smiled when I winced at the strength of it crushing my fingers.

Ida was taking her time about fastening the gown. It fluttered behind her as she moved. I wondered why I'd remembered her as a plain woman. Only one word could describe her body: voluptuous: not fat, but firm, and splendidly distributed.

'Drink?' Ida asked, smiling. That gave me a second chance to put my face right. Her teeth were awful. Funny – I hadn't remembered that.

Sophia burst out laughing as Yanni kissed her cheek. 'Perhaps he hasn't seen a woman before,' she suggested, pointing a shaking finger at me. Ida smiled again. She held the robe open. 'But a body's very ordinary, isn't it?' she said. She bloody well knew hers wasn't. I hoped my face wasn't reddening.

'Yes,' I said. 'I'll have a drink.' I turned to face Yanni, hoping that by dismissing it I would get used to having Ida's body flaunted at me.

'It is good of you to come to us,' Yanni said. 'Here. Sit down.'

I slid into the chair by the rickety table. It was a frightful little room, cramped, scruffy, untidy. Off it was a minuscule kitchen. The ice-box was in an alcove housing a shower with a ragged curtain and a hole-in-the-floor loo. It was a primitive place. Sophia looked like a rose growing on a dung heap.

Ida tied the sash of her gown while Yanni, yawning, went to the icebox and came back with a bottle of zibib. Ida got four glasses from a curtain-fronted cupboard and brought them to the table, her fingers holding them together inside the rims. I began to ask myself if I wanted a drink, after all.

Sophia was standing by the window which overlooked the fetid lane we'd walked along. The cries of the children and the street hawkers was a constant background of noise.

'Here,' said Yanni. He pushed a glass, almost half-filled with neat zibib, across the table. To gain time I asked him for some water.

'It is cold,' he said.

'But I can't drink this stuff neat,' I said.

He looked puzzled, splashed himself a good-sized tot, sniffed it, drank it. 'Very good,' he said. Not a trace of a shudder or a stutter.

'Good,' he said again. He filled the other two glasses. Ida took hers. 'Cheers,' she said and swallowed the lot. Sophia, sensible girl, stayed by the window, not looking at any of us.

I put my lips to the tumbler and sipped very, very gently. The raw spirit seemed to take strips off the membrane of my throat. I fought against it, but I had to splutter. Yanni grinned. Ida patted me solicitously on the back. 'Go down the wrong way, love?' she wanted to know. I nodded. Behind the protection of a handkerchief I tried to sort out these screwball people. For a woman supposedly terrified of some threat from secret policemen, Ida was amazingly relaxed. Her relationship with Yanni didn't seem at all odd. She was a common woman, probably from London's East End if I was any judge of accents. What didn't fit was Sophia Kukralovic. What was it Sophia had said of Ida? 'She is my greatest friend.' And where did Yanni the Greek fit into the triangle? There had to be a reason other than sex that he was with the two women.

The coughing fit ended. 'Are you all right?' Sophia asked. She had crossed to the table, was fingering one of the glasses. To Yanni, she said: 'What are you trying to do? Poison him?'

'I drink it like that.'

'Perhaps. But ordinary people do not have a tin tank for a stomach. Get him some water.'

Yanni shrugged, but he didn't argue. He went to the kitchen. I stared up at Sophia, jerked my head a fraction of an inch in the direction of Ida who was disappearing into the bathroom, my eyes two question marks. She laid a delicate finger on her lips.

Yanni was back at the table. He sloshed water into my glass. 'For babies,' he said. Then he sat down, poured himself another large tot and drank it neat. Ida came out, paused in the doorway, then went to Yanni and sat on his lap, indifferent to a gaping dressing-gown. I waited. There didn't seem anything else to do. Sophia still stood beside me. All the concern she'd betrayed at the Sans Souci had gone. She was placid, still.

It was Ida who started. 'You told him?' she asked Sophia. I sensed Sophia's little nod. Then Ida leaned forward, an arm still around Yanni's neck.

'You will, won't you?'

The ball was in my court. Believe me, it was easy to play it dumb. 'Won't I what?' I asked right back.

Almost sharply, Ida said, 'Sophia says she told you.'

It was time Sophia got into the act. I looked up at her, but she was still staring out of the window. Yanni was pouring himself still another zibib. So it was my turn again. It looked as if I was going to have to play this alone. 'She told me some crazy story about you and the secret police. The *English* secret police.'

'It's because of Yanni,' said Ida. I stared at the man as he poured the drink down his throat. Yanni was a new dimension in something I didn't understand anyway. So I sipped my zibib and waited.

'They don't like people who make trouble for soldiers,' Ida said.

I damn near did it, damn near opened my big mouth about the punch-up at the Forces Club. I actually had my mouth shaped to start saying, 'You mean Yanni and the . . .' With my mouth open I had to do something. I made it into a sneeze. I hoped it looked like a real one. The dumber I played this the better. 'I don't know what you're talking about,' I said.

Ida swung off Yanni's lap and faced Sophia. 'I told you to tell him,' she said, an edge to her voice.

'I told him enough,' Sophia snapped. 'It's your problem.'

Yanni leaned forward and plucked my sleeve. 'Look,' he ordered. He opened his mouth wide. It was a revolting sight: coated tongue, stained broken teeth, and his breath didn't remind me of violets. He pulled his cheek back. Two of the yellow molars were missing. The sockets hadn't healed.

'The swelling's gone down, though,' Ida volunteered. 'You should've seen his face after it happened.'

I swear to God it just popped out. 'The secret police did this?'

Sophia giggled. Up went the two fingers to the side of her mouth. Ida turned on her furiously. 'I want to talk to you,' she said. She grasped Sophia's arm more than firmly and pushed her towards the door none too gently. To my amazement Sophia went without protest. The door slammed behind the two of them.

'What's all that about?' I asked Yanni. He yawned, poured himself a drink, shook his head, shrugged. 'That Ida, she is a very strong woman.'

'Tell me, Yanni, what's all this about secret police?'

For some reason he thought this was funny. He laughed, throwing his head back, revealing again the awful mouth.

'It is that Ida,' he chuckled. 'She believes this.'

'And you don't?'

He shrugged. 'Why should the police be interested in Yanni Phillipides?' he wanted to know. 'I am a simple Greek. I make no trouble.'

'Then what the hell's all the fuss about?'

'Ida, she will tell you.' He just wasn't interested in the conversation. 'You do not drink?' He pushed the bottle across the table. I pushed it back. 'Enough here, thanks.'

The door opened and Ida came in. She was smiling, her long, thin face looking a bit like a comic mask. 'Sophia is waiting for you,' she said.

I got up, said, 'Nice to meet you,' to Yanni and headed for the door. Ida stood in front of me. I had no choice but to stop. Deliberately she untied the sash of her dressing-gown, let it fall open, then put her arms around me and drew me close. I looked sharply over my shoulder. That handshake of Yanni's had been pretty powerful. But he was pouring still another drink.

'Don't worry,' she whispered, then kissed me on the mouth, rubbing her body against me. I shut my eyes. Her face, but only her face, was off-putting.

'You have a telephone?' she wanted to know, her mouth against my ear. Oh God, I thought.

Over her shoulder I saw Sophia, standing in the doorway. It gave me an excuse to break away. I muttered a thank-you, went out and shut the door behind me. Sophia's smile stretched from ear to ear. She guided me back to the car. The major-domo was standing beside it, his smile expectant. I dug into the money I'd have to account for later, opened the door for Sophia, slammed it, then went round and got in behind the wheel.

Before I started up I asked, 'Now where?'

'Would you like to come home with me?'

You bet I would, I thought. But this could cost money. I did some rough mental calculations. I had about eight hundred piastres in my pocket.

'Yes,' I said, keeping my fingers crossed.

She told me the address, and I damn near wet my slacks. The Dopolavoro Club, she said.

I had sense enough to keep my mouth shut while I twisted and weaved through the late afternoon traffic. I parked a block away from the Malika Farida: no sense in tempting wallop-happy soldiers on leave to go joy-riding. We walked up to the entrance of the Dopolavoro building. The street and the lobby were swarming with noisy roistering troops, and guiding Sophia through the crush wasn't any fun at all. The whistles and

35

invitations and the touching just had to be tolerated. Sophia did it well, the smile on her face friendly enough but by no means inviting. The insults she ignored. So did I. To one persistent, red-faced, very drunk corporal's demand to know her price she smiled softly and said, 'Marriage.' The laughter this sparked off followed us into one of the lifts.

Sophia pressed the seventh-floor button. I already knew the military had commandeered only up to and including the sixth floor. Had Yanni been pushed in the mouth because he and Ida had been visiting Sophia and had mistaken the floor? Or pressed the wrong button in the lift? I also knew that the Dopolavoro apartments had cost luxury rents before the war. The prices must have risen sharply after the pressures which accompanied the arrival of the Allied forces.

Sophia unlocked a door. I followed her into a small but magnificently furnished hall. Three doors opened off it. All were ajar. One was a well-appointed bathroom. Another was a bedroom, I supposed. I stood in the lounge, a splendid room of taste and comfort. Off this was a modern kitchen.

Sophia's flat matched her clothes, in style and in cost. She should have been employed by a bank. To live as she was living on a refugee pocket-money allowance of the equivalent of half-a-crown a week showed a remarkable talent for financial manipulation.

'I feel dirty,' she said. 'Come and talk to me while I have a bath.'

FIVE

LONDON: SARA

Hodges said: 'Yes. You buggered up Cairo all right.'

He finished his drink. Slowly. I looked down again at the picture in my left hand. So I was all those years older: I still felt an itch where it mattered when I remembered her taking that bath in her flat.

'You still living at Streatham Hill?'

I nodded. Who was he fooling? I'll bet he knew damn well where I was living. I'd even bet he knew to a penny just how much rent I was paying for that crummy bed-sitter.

He poured himself more lemonade. Then he paused, looked over his shoulder at me and put his glass down. He reached into that hideous rubbish container and picked out the glass I'd used. He didn't wipe it. Just splashed lemonade into it, handed it to me.

'You look like you could use a drink.'

I gulped it down, feeling grateful to the bastard.

'You sure nobody saw you come here?'

Holding the picture in my left hand, the empty glass in my right, I said, 'I'm sure.' He still looked doubtful. 'I checked and double-checked all the way. Right up to the front door.'

'You're a liar,' he said, without any emotion at all.

Oh, Christ, was it going to start all over again? 'I tell you . . .' I started to tell him.

'I heard them. The others. When I picked up the door phone.'

It took maybe a second for the penny to drop.

'Oh,' I said. 'The hippies. You can forget that lot. Just a bird and a bloke fooling. Drunk. And some Aussie opposite yelling at 'em to shut up.'

'So three people saw you, then? Two of 'em close enough to see which button you'd pressed.'

'Come off it,' I told him. 'Nobody could've seen anything. Doubt if the hippies even knew I was there. All mad keen to get to the cot, from what I heard.' Hodges wasn't really listening. He was just staring. 'Anyway, if half the bloody street saw me come in here, does it matter? It's your business to see people, isn't it? I mean, an insurance bloke'd starve to death if he wasn't talking to people, wouldn't he?'

I was grateful to him again because he didn't use the hand with the ring. He used the other: open, flat, but I felt it. Oh, yes, I felt it all right, dragging across my cheek, my nose, my mouth. I dropped the glass and the photograph. He was a blur. My eyes were watering and my nose was dripping something. I hoped it wasn't blood. Couldn't be. It hadn't been that sort of a blow.

'You talk like you know a lot of things about me,' he said. His voice was very flat.

I was past the point of no return so what the hell? I just pulled out my hanky and dabbed at my eyes. I watched him sit down, his fingers tracing patterns on the glass of lemonade.

'You'd better tell me,' he said. His voice sounded almost kind. I didn't like the sound of it at all.

'Listen,' I said. I was getting a bit desperate. I tried to sort out words that would make sense to him.

'I am listening.'

'When I saw her I knew I had to talk to somebody. There was only you. You were part of it all. But I knew how you felt. That's why I took time off to think about it. But you were the only contact left. It had to be you. So . . . well, I came.'

That was lame, the last bit. But truth often is, isn't it? It doesn't sound convincing, like a good round lie. It might have been better if I'd cooked up something. No, maybe not – not with Hodges.

'You knew where to come,' said Hodges. 'And you yap on about insurance. You bring a couple of randy tramps to my door. And you pitch me a yarn that the nation's in deadly peril because you've seen some tart who looks a bit like a whore you made a fool of yourself with, Christ knows how many years ago.'

He got up. Slowly. I was starting to brace for the next attack but all he did was put his empty glass down, pick mine off the floor and drop it in with the litter. Then he picked up the picture of Sophia and stared at it. Mentally, I counted the seconds. One-two-three-four-five-six-seven. Then he handed it to me. I put it in my pocket.

'I didn't know you still lived here. I came on spec. And the insurance bit . . . well, that's the way it used to be. Nobody in his right mind would chuck away good cover. All I wanted was somebody to run a check.'

He just stood there. Not moving a muscle. What hadn't I covered?

'Those hippies. Look, they drove up after I'd got to the door. They're nothing.' Still no reaction. Nothing. 'Tell you what,' I said. 'If it'll make you feel any better I'll ask you about insurance. Maybe I need some.'

He actually smiled. That thin stretching of the lips that had nothing to do with humour. 'You surely do. But you couldn't afford the premiums, not with all the resources of the Bank of England.'

Yes, I supposed I wasn't much of an insurance risk. Not while I was tangling with Hodges.

'I'd like to give the place a new coat of paint,' he murmured. He seemed to enjoy that. He repeated it to himself; then he actually laughed. I could count on my fingers the number of times I'd heard Hodges laugh.

'Jesus,' he said. 'You're old.'

'Yes,' I said. Then I got really brash. 'Only two years younger than you are.' Quickly, trying to take the sting out of it, I said, 'It was all I could remember.'

He went to the window, moved the drapes a tiny fraction, stared down into the street. A car-horn blared, the sound whining off into distance. 'It's raining again,' Hodges said and turned back into the room. He came close and stared at my face. 'I've got some plasters somewhere.'

My fingers explored the congealed blood above my eye. 'It's nothing,' I said.

But he went out of the room. I could hear him opening cupboards. I sat right where I was. He came back, peeling the pink strip. I reached out for it, but he pushed my hand away. 'Put your head back,' he said. I did as I was told. Hodges was a remarkable man. His touch was as gentle as any woman's as he fixed the plaster over the little wound. 'At least it'll make you look a bit more respectable.'

What next? I waited. The ball, I hoped, was in his court. A lot depended on how he played it.

'You phoned your office this afternoon?'

I nodded.

'Then phone 'em again in the morning. Have flu, or something.' So he was going to do something. But what? 'And stay put.' His voice was getting the edge back. 'I'll know if you don't. Understand?' I nodded again. He went to the desk, brought back a piece of paper and a ballpoint pen. 'Give me your phone number.'

I played along with him. I'll bet he didn't need me to write down any phone number. I gave him the slip back. He didn't even look at it. Just put it in his pocket, went back to his desk and put the pen down. He paused and his hand reached tentatively towards the telephone. But he decided not to do whatever his instinct had prompted he should. I wondered about that, because Hodges rarely changed a decision arrived at in his mind. He had never, to my knowledge, not known exactly what to do next. But here I was watching a man a tiny bit uncertain. He went to the window once more, peeped down at the street.

'You'd better go. And don't do anything stupid.' I told myself I'd do my damnedest not to do anything stupid. 'And you stay put. I mean that.'

His voice told me he meant it all right. I got up, buttoned up my mac and walked out. He held the door open. I didn't look back, but I heard it close behind me.

Bill Nash was sympathetic when I phoned next morning.

'Flu, eh? Just saying to Cedric after you rang yesterday that you'd been looking a bit off colour.'

This was news to me. Up till the moment I'd seen the blonde in the Press Club I'd been feeling fine, fitter than maybe I should have felt at my age. Still, there's not much point in lying if you can't get the other chap to believe you. Anyway, one of the perks of the civil service was pretty liberal sick leave.

'Take it easy, then,' said Nash. 'Good excuse for a couple of hot toddies, eh? Hard luck on the girl friend, though.' The obnoxiously hearty Nash had a habit of judging everybody by the standards of his own virility. 'Panic not. We'll look after your desk. Anything outstanding?'

I'd have liked to be able to say, 'Yes, thirty years of a monumental cock-up,' but he'd have put it down to delirium so I didn't bother. So now it was just a matter of sitting tight and waiting. For what? Hodges hadn't given away even a hint of what he was going to do. But whatever it was it seemed I had to be on tap.

The overnight rain had brought in its train a day of unseasonably warm sunshine. My room was stuffy even in the cold weather and as the morning dragged on it became clogged with bad air. I couldn't settle. The grim headlines in the paper were sufficient to deter me from reading the closely-printed text. The thriller I'd started seemed tame after the memories revived by my meeting with Hodges. I chain-smoked. I opened and drank the first can of beer at half-past nine. By the time I'd downed my second I felt it might be a good idea to switch to coffee. I tried to space the cigarettes by time periods, but the tinny alarm clock must have been running bloody slow. So I had a go at the crossword in the newspaper. That was too difficult, or maybe I wasn't able to concentrate. So I had another crack at the thriller while I supped my third beer. By eleven o'clock I was pacing the room. So I tried something else. I peeled the dressing off my eye. The wound started to bleed again. I cursed but didn't really mean it. It.gave me something to do. Then I found I didn't have any fresh plasters. It took me a good two minutes to straighten out the old one and pat it back on. But the edges wouldn't stay down.

The barmy thing about all this was remembering all the days I'd have given my right arm to have off. Now I had one I didn't know what the hell to do with it. That wasn't true, of course. What was biting at my guts was Hodges. Well, not Hodges so much as what Hodges might be up to. There wasn't any dividend in speculating about that, however. So I reckoned eating might pass some time. But because this wasn't a scheduled be-at-home day all I could find in the microscopic kitchen was some cheese that any mouse with a palate would have despised and the fag-end of a loaf that would be all right after I'd scraped the green mould off it.

Hodges had said, 'Stay put.' So going out to the corner dairy wasn't on. I'd settled to clean up the bread when the phone rang.

'Yes?' I said into it, hoping that whatever Hodges had laid on included lunch.

'How are you, my dear fellow? I've just heard you aren't well.' This was one for the book. Maurice Harding had never called me before. Not at the flat. 'Hope it's not too bad.'

Trying to inject a sniff or two, I told him it wasn't too bad, that I'd live, I thought.

'I certainly hope so, my dear fellow. Place wouldn't be the same without you.' Then, as though the thought had only just occurred to him, 'I say, haven't dragged you out of bed, have I?'

'No. I've just been to the loo.' I could imagine the frown that

41

would pucker Harding's face when I said that. He was the sort of man to whom basic biology was anathema. His marriage must have been a wonderfully spiritual experience.

'Oh,' he said. 'I'd be most unhappy if I'd disturbed you.'

'No. Honest. It's quite all right.' I gave what I thought wasn't a bad imitation of a sneeze while I wondered some more why Harding was going to this trouble of ringing me.

'Well, old chap, as I said, I heard them saying that you weren't any too good. So just thought I'd call. You know, the word of cheer in adversity and all that.' I heard his high-pitched, rather self-conscious laugh. 'Must have a drink when you're back on your feet. Do look after yourself. 'Bye.'

He hung up, just like that. Now what the hell was all that about? A check that I was in fact at home? Couldn't be. Smithson, the principal officer, might do it, but only might. Maurice Harding? It worried me. This Harding, just who was he? He had an office upstairs at the Ministry. I'd never been to it. Come to think of it, I didn't know anybody who had, or if I did, they hadn't mentioned it. Not even for a bet could I have named his job. It was just a name that appeared in lists on files for circulation – you know, the 'Please initial and forward' things. And yet I seemed to have known him for a bloody long time. I tried to track back, remember how I'd first met him. It wasn't on; the memory banks had been wiped clean. There can't have been anything outstanding about the introduction. That made me wonder something else. Who had introduced us? No name came to mind. I just couldn't re-create a picture of ever having met Maurice Harding. But, damn it, I *knew* him. Well, hardly *knew* him. We'd had the odd drink together, sometimes just the two of us, at other times with some of the PR crowd. And I think I'd bumped into him in a coffee-house we used, and three or four times in the tube – or was it on a bus? It must have been a bus: I didn't use the tube that often.

Now why should an acquaintance as casual as that go to the trouble of interrupting what he was doing to phone about my health? Because he must have rung from his office. I had a very firm impression that he was a strict time-keeper, a dedicated bloke, loyal to the department and to the service. I forced myself to picture him. He dressed neatly: dark suits, always dark suits; shirts always fresh, ties immaculate, shoes polished. But it was damn near impossible to fill in the details of his face, or of his figure. This was daft. I mean, if the coppers wanted me to describe Maurice Harding I'd be stuck.

That'd make the fuzz really suspicious, wouldn't it? Imagine them. 'But you *know* him. You've drunk with him. Met him scores of times. You must know what he *looks* like.' Easy for them. But not for me. He was . . . well, he was just a senior civil servant. I supposed he was senior. He did have an air of authority about him. Did he, though? Yes. I was quite sure about that. I don't know why I'd assumed he was married. I couldn't recall him ever discussing his private life, or even where he lived, or whether he grew roses. Then what the hell did we talk about on those occasions when we shared a pint?

For a desperate moment I wondered if I'd even recognise the man if I saw him again. This was crazy. My nerves were starting to twitch I was concentrating so hard. Hodges last night: Harding this morning. I ripped open the last car of beer in the fridge and drank it fast. I almost choked when the phone jangled. I was still coughing when I jerked up the handset. Holding it to my ear, I was still trying to unblock the air passages.

'All right, so you're sick. You don't have to convince me.' It was Hodges. His voice harsh, metallic.

'Just . . . just some beer. Down the wrong way,' I managed to stutter.

'You lay off the booze. Hear me? Lay off it.'

Who the hell did Hodges think he was? I'd tell that bastard . . .

'Now listen,' he said. 'And listen good. Tonight. Eight o'clock. Be at Questro's in Frith Street. Wear your best gear. Go in and tell 'em you're Mr Freeman. There'll be a table for you. Sit down and order a drink. Campari-soda. Take a copy of Bacon's *Guide to London* with you. Put it down on the table where it can be seen.' He paused. 'Got that?'

'I . . . I think so.'

'You'd better bloody know so,' Hodges snarled. 'Questro's. Freeman's the booking. Campari-soda. Bacon's. Eight o'clock.'

'And then what?' Damn it, a bloke just couldn't walk blind into a thing like this.

'Play it as it comes,' said Hodges. 'And get this: don't cock this one up. Just don't cock it up.'

He rang off.

I just made it. Soho was a mad mass of people pushing, poncing, pirating among the street-stalls in the neon glare outside the strip clubs. I shuffled along as fast as I could through the garbage and the litter, the smells a strange mixture of titillation and nausea.

Questro's wasn't a big place, and inside it was a quiet oasis of calm. Only a few of the white-covered tables were occupied. There was a man by himself; a couple; a party of four that looked as if they were going to get noisy later; two more singles, both blokes.

The waiter, his smile looking as if it had been painted on, took his time coming to me.

'Good evening, signore. You 'ave a reservation?'

'Yes. Freeman.'

'Ah, of course. Please, this way.'

He led me to a corner table laid for four. I sat with my back in the angle of the wall. Old habits die hard.

'You 'ave how many guests, signore?'

It was a question. This codger hadn't been told how many there'd be. Nor had I. 'I'm not sure yet,' I told him. 'Just bring me a Campari-soda. I'll let you know later.'

A bit puzzled, he nodded and walked away. I watched him at the bar making some chat with one of his fellow-countrymen, both of them stealing a look at a customer who didn't know how many bloody people he was entertaining.

I laid down the guidebook, front cover up. The waiter put the drink beside me, smiled, and left me to wonder what the hell I was doing here. I sipped the Campari. Five past eight. I sipped some more and the glass was empty. Ten past eight. I flagged the waiter, ordered a refill. 'Lay off the booze,' Hodges had said. Hodges could get stuffed.

I was halfway through the second drink at almost twenty past eight when it happened. Two or three people had come into the restaurant, taking notice neither of me nor of Bacon's *Guide to London*. Then she pushed open the swing doors, her blonde hair piled high, a cuddly anorak over a mini-dress that did barely more than cover the essentials. Long slim legs hesitated, stopped. The waiter almost galloped to her side. She was a good head taller. It was almost funny, watching the little man poise on his toes to impress her. The lovely creature I'd seen in the bar of the Press Club smiled her thanks, fingers on the dimple at the side of her mouth. The waiter fussed his way to a table three away from where I was sitting. I felt a fool. I was half-standing, expecting her to be brought to me. There was much ado about getting her settled comfortably. I sat back in my chair. Then the waiter hurried to the bar. The woman leaned back, put her handbag on the table, opened it. She brought out a copy of Bacon's *Guide to London* and laid it down, front cover up. Lazily, she took stock of the restaurant. Her eyes were sweeping past me without any recognition at all. Then they concentrated. Not on me. But on the scarlet cover of the book, vivid against the white napery.

Her eyes bored into mine. To hell with all the James Bond! I lifted my drink and drained the glass. That's how I missed his arrival.

When, all uninterested like, I allowed my glance to wander in her direction, she was hidden from me by a man leaning across her table. His back was to me, his snugly-fitting dinner jacket blocking any view of her. Then he turned. It was Maurice Harding. His white teeth flashed a smile. Excusing himself to his companion he crossed to my table.

'Good evening Mr Freeman,' he said. 'My name is Godfrey Harmsworth. I believe you may be able to assist a friend of mine. Have we your permission to join you?'

I made a bit of a fuss standing up, to collect my bedevilled wits. 'Why of course. By all means. Certainly.' I wasn't at my best.

'Thank you,' said Maurice Harding alias Godfrey Harmsworth. Back he went. It took a moment or two for her to collect her bits and pieces, long enough I hoped for my features to settle into some sort of normality. Then she was standing facing me, Harding at her side. He was saying, 'This is most fortunate. Sara, may I present Mr Freeman? Freeman, this is Sara Kenyon.' Then came the slightly self-conscious laugh. 'You should have met sooner. It would have saved the price of one guide book, wouldn't it?'

She smiled, and as she inclined her head the fingers caressed her cheek. I tried my best continental bow, a bit inhibited because I was crowded in the corner between chair and table.

Harding reminded me of my lack of manners. 'May we sit down?' he asked.

'Of course. I'm sorry.'

The waiter was there in a flash to help with Sara's chair. The little Italian obviously felt Harding was old enough and big enough to look after himself.

Harding ordered a round of drinks. When I protested, he smiled. 'My dear fellow, it's the least I can do after inflicting us on your table.'

Off went the waiter. 'Very fortunate indeed,' Harding said.

I didn't ask any questions. 'Don't cock this one up,' Hodges had warned.

'It is really very kind of you, Mr Freeman,' Sara said.

'Not at all,' said I, wishing to God somebody would say something that meant something.

'But Mr Harmsworth was telling me only this afternoon that he believed you were in London. And to meet you like this' – she giggled, a trick Sophia would have had if she'd ever been embarrassed – 'two visitors finding their way about London . . . why, it's quite fantastic.' That, I thought, was the under-statement of the century. 'Especially because it's you.' I was getting out of my depth so fast that I hid my confusion behind a smile. Enigmatic: that's me when I don't know what the hell's going on.

So especially because it was me she was pleased. God save us all! Why me?

Harding – no, I'd better get in the habit of thinking of him as Harmsworth – took the next service. And he smashed an ace. Bang. 'Sara was telling me this afternoon that she'd dearly like to meet someone who had known her mother. You did, didn't you? You knew Sophia Kukralovic during the war, in Cairo. I'm sure Sara and you must have a lot you want to talk about.'

SIX

CAIRO: THE REPORT

A headful of questions didn't get asked for a long time after we arrived back at Sophia's flat in the Dopolavoro building. That invitation to 'Come-and-talk-to-me-while-I-have-a-bath' took precedence over a lot of other things. She took her time about getting undressed. I sat in a small chair in the bedroom, watching her take off her street coat, kick off her shoes, fuss with things out of her handbag.

'You could help me,' she complained. I asked how. 'Run the bath,' she said.

Reluctantly, I went into the bathroom, turned on the taps. I found some bath salts, highly perfumed, sprinkled them extravagantly. While the water spouted from the faucets I had time to wonder what the visit to Ida's hideaway had been about. All the build-up of secret police was just so much boloney. Ida hadn't seemed under any stress. Yanni thought it was all a joke. All that had happened was I'd seen Ida without any clothes on, watched the beginnings of a row between the two women, learned that maybe Sophia wasn't the dominant partner and discovered that Yanni had a quite remarkable capacity for hard liquor and surprising strength in his slight body.

Why had Sophia interrupted a lunch just for that? And why wasn't Ida living in the hostel accommodation provided for refugees? Surely it couldn't have been worse than the hovel in which she was hiding. But was she hiding? And if so, why?

Then there was this place of Sophia's, all style and elegance and luxury. Either she had a lot of money or was mighty friendly with people who had.

Another worry intruded. What had I learned that would make any sense to the boss? He'd want a report. And it would have to be good enough to justify unusually liberal expenses for a military security section whose job didn't aspire to this sort of living. For a moment I was tempted to curse Grayling. He'd started this wild-goose chase with his bloody mysteries about a woman who hobnobbed with Nazis in Budapest. But why curse a bloke who'd led you to running a bath for a blonde who, I reckoned, was going to be good value for whatever I could persuade the boss to drag out of public funds? What I would spend couldn't even start to be significant against what was being spent by the British and Allied taxpayers on the war effort — probably less than what Churchill paid out on cigars each day.

Then I dived at the taps. The water was foaming up against the level of the side of the bath. I turned them off in a big hurry. There was going to be one hell of a mess if anyone stepped into that tub. I peeled off my jacket. Then my shirt. Stripped to the waist I plunged an arm into the hot water and ripped out the plug.

'Do you like sharing a bath?'

She stood in the doorway, as naked as the day she was born. But, thanks be to the gods, that was a good thirty years ago. She'd had time to ripen. She was smiling, rubbing a soft finger on the dimple. And she was standing where the light softened her body, the sun's diffused rays pouring through the frosted glass of a window falling across her from the side. Oh yes, she knew what she was about. Her breasts jutted firmly from under rather wide shoulders, the nipples erect. Her belly was flat and the tanned skin wasn't broken by the white strips of bra or briefs: wherever she'd basked it had been in the altogether. Her flood of blonde hair fell loosely on her shoulders and matched perfectly the profusion between her thighs. Her free hand gently stroked the flesh over a hip bone.

The water rushed out of the bath with a sighing gurgle. And there I was, wet arm still poised over the bath, leaning sideways, in a pose that must have looked utterly ridiculous. But I just couldn't move. There she was, all loveliness and lust and loneliness. My tongue licked my lips. I couldn't stop it.

'I asked you to run a bath. Not empty it.'

'It . . . it got too full,' I stammered. 'I had to . . . you know, empty some out.'

She pushed me to one side impatiently. 'Do get out of my way,' she said, kicking my coat and shirt from under her feet. She leaned over to replace the plug, turned on the taps. 'I will do it myself. Go and put your clothes on. You look silly like that.'

I picked up my things, the schoolboy reprimanded by his teacher. What the hell had happened? In one minute flat I was dismissed.

'You said to come and talk to you . . .'

She was watching the water rush into the bath. Her

arms were folded across her breasts. Her back was to me. 'Oh, do go away and put your clothes on. I think perhaps Ida was right. You are quite useless.'

The tightness in my loins was relaxing. So it wasn't going to be any pushover, then. There didn't seem any point in arguing, so I went out into the bedroom. I didn't look behind me but I heard the door close firmly. So that was that. I pulled on the shirt slowly, wondering what the next move would be. In front of the mirror I knotted my tie. I was turning away to pick up the jacket when my eye caught a glimpse of colour in the partly-open drawer of the dressing table.

I walked softly to the bathroom door. The gush of water had stopped, but I could hear splashing sounds. Quickly, then, back to the dressing table! I eased back some fripperies and there it was. A passport: Czech. Holding my breath, I slid a finger under the linen cover, eased it back. The bearer was Sophia Kukralovic. The document had moved slightly. There was the glint of dark metal. Gingerly, using only the tips of my fingers, I picked up the passport: it had been lying on top of a Browning ·32 automatic pistol. Hardly breathing, I laid the passport back where it had been, eased the fripperies back where they had rested, stepped back and put on my jacket.

Now bloody well what?

I sat on the edge of the silk-draped bed. It was firm but soft, designed for making love to a woman like Sophia. But at that moment the thought occurred to me in a wholly clinical context. I had other things on my mind. Had I been dismissed from the bathroom in order to find the passport and the pistol in a drawer left conveniently open? Or had it been a careless oversight on Sophia's part? And what significance did they have – individually and collectively? Owning a gun in a war zone wasn't a sensible act for a civilian, even though Egypt was still technically neutral, and a second passport, in any country at any time, wasn't the way to win friends and influence people in officialdom. But, it seemed, I had at last something positive to report to the boss. It was something for our people to work on. Though I found it hard to accept that Sophia and Ida were much more than stupidly honest refugees, in spite of Grayling's alarmist speculation. What enemy agent would be bothering with a bloke like me? Come to that, what woman with Sophia's material background would want to play along?

I was still trying to nut it out when the bathroom door opened and Sophia came in. She had a huge towel draped around her. 'You are very good at putting the water out of a bath,' she said. 'Will you please do it for me?'

She was all charm and beguiling witchery. I stood up, shrugged out of my jacket, took off my tie and pulled off my shirt. 'That is not necessary,' she said.

'I don't want to get my shirt wet,' I said.

'There is a chain down to the plug. You pull on it . . . so!' She demonstrated with a jerking movement of her hand. The towel slid off one shoulder.

There are times when a man just wants to go away and hide somewhere. I chose to hide in the bathroom, jerking on that bloody chain. I sat on the edge of the tub watching the scented water glug-glug its way down the hole. I went back to the bedroom. Sophia still had the towel more or less draped round her, but with one hand she was holding up what could only be described as a creation. It was so much more than a dress.

'I think this, eh?'

'Depends where you're going,' I said.

Her eyes widened. 'But with you, of course. You will take me to dinner?' She came very close, holding the dress away at arm's length. 'And then we shall come here again. You will like that, I think.'

The towel fell to the floor. She threw the dress on to the bed. Her naked breasts were firm against the bare flesh of my chest. My arms went around her, my mouth searching hungrily for hers. But she twisted away.

'Tonight. Not now. Tonight.' She picked up the towel quickly, held it in front of her. 'There is wine in the ice-box. You will open a bottle. Then I shall drink with you. Take your clothes. And open the wine.'

A hand persuaded me towards the little hall. I went. Other than raping her there didn't seem to be any alternative.

The boss wasn't the happiest man in Cairo when I reported in next morning.

'Where the hell have you been? I've had everybody scouring the bloody streets for you.'

'Look, sir. You knew who I was with . . .'

'And that's why the damn section was out looking for you. You could've had a bullet in your skull. You were absent without leave, sergeant. You're going on a charge.'

'Now just a minute. I wasn't out on any leave pass. I was working. Damn it, you drew expense money for me. You ordered me to get the check on those women completed.' Then I went over the edge. 'Don't talk daft.'

Honest, that man should've stayed with his brass band. He just didn't understand the business he was in. His face purpled. His voice rose to a shiek. 'Corporal! Come in here. At once. You hear me, corporal?'

Little Sanderson stuck his head round the door.

'Arrest this man,' the boss yelled. I had to laugh. I couldn't help it in spite of how I felt after the previous night's frustrations and hangups. I told Sandy not to bother, to go away. Everything would be all right. The poor bloke didn't know what to do. So I pulled a sheet of paper out of my pocket and pushed it into the boss's hand.

'Read that, for pete's sake. Read it. Now.'

The urgency in my voice must have got through. Some of the tension went out of him. He looked at the quick memo I'd scribbled.

I jerked my thumb at Sanderson. He took his head away and shut the door. I punched home the headlines. 'There it is, sir. Two passports; a gun; a lot of money – or access to it: adds up to the same thing. And there's a Gyppo politician in the background somewhere. She wants me around. At least she wants what she thinks I am. A journalist. Somebody with freedom of movement. Like a neutral.' I drew breath. 'I didn't waste last night.'

And I hadn't. I'd taken her to dinner – not to Groppi's but to the bewitching half-lit intimacy of the Café aux Pigeons. Under the sweet-smelling trees and the huge silver platter of a moon, the recorded voice of Maria Marie singing sad songs, I planned to enjoy my work. I was going to make this a night I'd remember, and to hell with the war.

But Robbie Burns must have had somebody like Sophia in mind when he wrote the bit about the best-laid plans of mice and men. It didn't seem I was going to get to first base. Oh, she was full of chat all right. But there was only the promise of sex: in her eyes, her hands, even the little movements of her shoulders. Just out of reach. She was nobody's fool. She went about whatever it was she was doing pretty scientifically. And she didn't overdo the flattery. Just how exciting it must be to be a foreign correspondent: how young I was to have such a responsible job: how lucky I was to be a neutral, and not have to report only propaganda. Not too many questions, just occasional interest. Did I have to travel much? Was I able to? Oh, yes, she realised how difficult it must be in war time. A tiny laugh. She'd been through it. Getting out of Hungary hadn't been easy. Without Ida it would have been quite impossible. How did I get along with the military? Did I know many high-ranking officers? All of it candy-wrapped.

I wasn't in her class, but I did a bit of probing on my own account. The way I saw it, she'd have maybe wondered if I didn't want to know more about her. I told her how lucky she was, having a flat like she had. She laughed at that, rubbing the dimple quite hard.

'Oh, but it isn't mine,' she gurgled. 'How could I afford that?'

I didn't say I'd been wondering the same thing.

'It belongs to a friend of mine. He is away. So he told me to use it, until he comes back.'

'He must be well-heeled,' I suggested. I had to explain the colloquialism. I could see her storing the definition away for future use.

'He is Egyptian. He has a position in the government, I think. And all politicians are . . . are well-heeled, I think, no?' she had something there. 'Like men who work for newspapers, eh?'

This was tricky. No sense in admitting that I worked in an expense atmosphere of maybe a fiver a time, and that it was bloody hard work getting even that. So I shrugged and let her believe what she wanted, while I did some mental arithmetic on how much the dinner was going to cost.

We'd covered a bit of ground by the time the waiter brought the coffee.

'Look,' I said. 'You dragged me all the way out to Bab al-Sharia this afternoon with a cock-and-bull story about Ida and some secret police.' She was apparently familiar with cock-and-bull. 'What the hell was all that about?'

Back came the sadness she'd performed so well at Sans Souci earlier in the day. Either she believed the story or she was a damn good actress.

'Ida swears it is true,' she murmured. 'You know about that attack on Yanni?'

The little red light flashed in my brain. 'Yanni showed me his mouth,' I said. 'Beaten up, was he?'

She nodded. 'They made a mistake when they came to visit me. They went to the wrong apartment. There were some soldiers and one of them attacked Yanni.'

'So?' I prompted.

'They reported it. To the military policeman at the club. And Ida says she has been watched. Yanni, too.'

'Yanni says he hasn't. And he doesn't believe Ida, either.' I let that sink in. 'And even if it were true, what the hell could I do?'

'You know many officers. You could tell them Ida has done nothing wrong. She has suffered very much, but she does nothing wrong.'

'She didn't ask me to do anything.'

'No. She was angry with me. She says I was not honest with you. Did not tell you . . .'

What was she supposed to have told me remained locked in her mind. 'Well,' I said, 'you can start now.'

She stared into the distance. Then suddenly she smiled. 'Later. I will tell you later. But let us talk about tomorrow.'

'What's special about tomorrow?'

'I must do some shopping. You will come with me?'

Jesus, she was turning on the heat. I had to cool this off somehow.

'I'm a working man,' I told her. 'I have to file stories every day, go to press briefings, talk to people.'

'Like today?' she teased.

'I worked this morning.'

'Then work tomorrow morning. We will go shopping at five o'clock, eh?'

'I'll think about it. But shopping with a woman isn't my idea of fun.'

'Oh, but with me it will be different. I buy exciting things . . .'

Her hands were stroking mine across the table. Under it a leg rubbed suggestively against mine. I said I'd probably go with her, then suggested we go back to her flat. That's when things started to come unstuck. She was pretty quiet in the car and as we got near Malika Farida she asked me to stop.

'You will not be angry?'

'At what?'

'If I ask you not to come upstairs.'

'But this afternoon you said . . .'

'I know. I promised. That is why I am so sad. But now I am very tired. I cannot please you if I am tired.' She put on her little-girl-lost face, long fingers stroking the back of my hand where it rested on the wheel.

Sophia, I told myself, had the makings of a first-class bitch. I didn't bother to conceal my anger and frustration. She leaned over, turned my face to hers slowly and deliberately and went to work. It was only when I saw the gleam of white teeth grinning lecherously through the window of the car that I pushed her away. I made as though to climb out and the policeman took to his heels. The Egyptian men in blue aren't noted for personal bravery.

Sophia was smiling, head coquettishly sideways, hand caressing the dimple. 'Soon,' she breathed. 'It will be soon.'

Without warning she opened the door and slid out of the car in one long gliding movement. She swung the door shut and her heels clicked away along the deserted pavement. I decided not to follow her. To hell with it. She was as tired as I was . . . and I was raring to go. It was only then I realised she hadn't mentioned where we should meet next day for the shopping expedition. Still, I knew where she could be found . . . all that remained to be done was to persuade the boss I should be among those present in the big shops on Kasr-al-Nil and Sharia Fouad-al-Awal.

I wanted time to think about that so I headed for a little bar I knew that the soldiers didn't. Out of what was left of my piastres I got lovely. I slept it off in the car and took my hangover back to the boss in daylight . . .

The boss was worried by the time I'd finished. I could almost see him sighing for the uncomplicated command of a brass band.

'You'd better get it down on paper,' he said. 'I'll pass it on and then you'll be able to get some of *our* work done.'

'All right. I'll start the report now. But don't you think we should deliver it? Both of us? Those blokes in the backrooms might have a lot of questions and if we have to do it by courier neither of us'll get anything done.'

This shocked him. 'I know my job, sergeant. This must be handled through channels.'

'Oh, for God's sake, sir! Look, if this woman is up to something we can't afford to bugger about nailing her. We've got to start learning. Fast!' I decided bullying wouldn't get me anywhere. He loved swinging rank, did my boss. 'You see, sir, I've been in the section quite some time now, and one of the things we've learned is to bend the rules when we have to. All right. I accept this thing's blown up. It's too big for us to mess about with. But the least we can do is make sure the other chaps get all the background we've got.' He was listening. 'I think I can

54

help, sir. You see, I know who we could talk to. There's a chap at SIME who can put us in touch with the right people . . .'

But this he wouldn't wear. What, he demanded, short-circuit channels? No. I was to write the report, but he'd handle it from then on.

'Then handle it fast, sir. You see, I'm to see her again this afternoon . . .'

I thought he was going to faint.

By two o'clock I was biting my fingernails. He'd left at eleven. Tempus was fugit-ing and there was a lot to do. I'd written that report very carefully, very, very carefully. I'd emphasised the 'in' I had. I'd stressed that Sophia obviously thought I was going to be useful. And even if a security section wasn't exactly 21 Queen Anne's Gate, I'd at least done one or two jobs of some value to the machine. The masters seemed to think so, anyway. I'd been released from the routine military work. I'd been financed into civvies and had the backing of some cover for my excursions. The boss hadn't liked this when he took over, but he'd had to lump it. He wanted me back on the security-patrol section. My only hope was that he'd be told I was temporarily needed elsewhere.

When he got back at three o'clock he was in quite a state, but not unhappy: vaguely proud. Apparently one of *his* men had contributed something that could be of value. In short, I was to report urgently to a Mr Collins. The address was on a piece of paper. I knew the building – a big insurance company near the Misr Bank, not far from the Continental-Savoy Hotel. And, praise be, I was to take the Chevvy.

'And you'd better pack a small bag. You might not be back tonight.'

Keeping my fingers crossed I did as I was told and headed for town.

SEVEN

LONDON: THE HYPHEN

My appetite for dinner vanished. The huge and ornate menu cards the Questro's waiter pushed into our hands were useful for only one thing: for me to duck down behind while I tried to sort things out. Suddenly I'm somebody called Freeman, without, it seemed, a given name. Maurice Harding had become Godfrey Harmsworth. And Sara Kenyon is sitting there all agog because I'm exhibited as a character who once knew her mother. Christ, the world had gone mad. Why the hell hadn't Hodges warned me? Or Harding for that matter? After all, the bastard had phoned me at the flat. To drop a bloke into this lot wasn't bloody well on.

I was grateful to the waiter that he'd arrived when he did. How I'd have responded to Harding's – no, Harmsworth's – 'I'm sure Sara and you must have a lot you want to talk about' was anybody's guess. And there was all this B-grade movie rubbish of the London guides left on tables. If this was the modern Shop at work they should write a new procedures manual.

Harding – damn it, Harmsworth – was prattling away to Sara, recommending this dish and that. I hoped he was going to pay for it. He wasn't being exactly coy about what he was pushing. He seemed a bit put out when he turned to me and I said all I wanted was an omelette, plain and ungarnished.

'Are you sure?' he persisted. Yes, I said, I was sure. No, nothing on the side. For some reason this put him out of countenance.

'You can't just have an omelette,' he said. 'My dear fellow, we're having *dinner*.'

'I can and I shall,' I told him. 'Though I'm quite prepared to eat elsewhere.'

'Oh, do please stay,' said Sara. To Harding she said, 'If Mr Freeman isn't hungry, why must you force him to eat more than he wants?'

Harding shrugged, but he didn't like my attitude. The waiter went off with the orders. This was a moment I was dreading: the three of us alone.

Sara leaned forward eagerly. 'So you knew my mother, Mr Freeman?' I nodded. She waited. I had to say something. But how much? That was the sixty-four-dollar question.

'I met her shortly after she arrived in Cairo when she escaped from Hungary.' That was near enough to be factual and wouldn't hurt anybody. I wondered if she remembered Sophia at all? I was doing mental sums and it seemed unlikely.

The waiter came back, but it wasn't with the starters for the others. 'You are Mr Harmsworth, signore?' Harding nodded, and took the folded note.

'Excuse me,' he said. He glanced at the slip as casually as if he knew what was written on it. He stood up. 'You must excuse me. I'm sorry. I have to make a telephone call.' He didn't wait for our acknowledgement. Just went. I'd stood up. I sat down again. And I made a decision.

'Known Mr Harmsworth long?' I asked.

She was surprised. 'No. I've only been back in England three weeks.' She hesitated. I felt she was wondering whether to amplify that. I'm fairly patient. So I just sat there. I'd rather have her talk about Harding—Harmsworth than have to dig back into the past.

She gave a little laugh, a finger rubbing her cheek. 'It's awful, but I can't remember how I met him.'

'That makes two of us.'

'I beg your pardon?'

'Nothing,' I said. 'Only this afternoon I was trying to remember how I'd met him.'

Sara gave me a funny look. 'Is that some sort of a joke?'

I shook my head. 'On my life, it's true.' Then I noticed Harding talking earnestly to the waiter. He was indicating our table.

'But tell me about my mother, Mr Freeman. What was she like? Was she beautiful?'

'Your mirror should tell you that. You're very like her.' I almost added the strangeness of the mannerism but didn't. That might be useful at some other time.

'You think I'm a judge of what is beautiful, then?'

Harding saved me having to answer that. He spread his hands apologetically. 'What can I say? I'll have to leave you. I must go home right away.'

Sara said, 'I do hope it's nothing serious?'

'Oh, no. Just one of the youngsters, fallen down the stairs. And you know the state mothers get in.' He laughed. 'But I still insist on playing host. I've arranged that you will be my guests. And you, my dear chap, can really brief Sara on her mother.' He turned to her. 'I *am* sorry. But you'll find Freeman interesting.'

I stood up. 'I'll probably see you later, then?'

'Of course, my dear fellow. Must have a drink soon. And Sara, do watch him. He's a very experienced man.' He thought this was very funny. Sara smiled frostily. She wasn't amused.

'Ah well, must rush. Goodnight. Eat well.'

I sat down. We watched him go, waving to a couple at a table near the door. The man returned his greeting. Without being too obvious, I had a good look at him. Fifty-ish, heavily built, well dressed. What I could see of his face didn't tell me much other than that he was probably foreign. Central European? Slav? I couldn't be sure.

'He must be very devoted to his family,' said Sara.

'I don't know. Didn't realise he had one.'

'I thought he was a friend of yours.'

'Why?'

'Why? Well, this afternoon . . . the way he spoke. That a . . . a chap he knew very well had been a friend of my mother. For him to say that I just assumed he must have known you very well.'

The waiter brought Sara a shrimp cocktail. He asked if I wanted my omelette right away. I said no, later would do, but would he fetch another round of drinks?

Sara didn't seem very interested in food either. She picked and fiddled with the fat little crustaceans.

'What is it you want to know about your mother?'

'Everything, I suppose.' She laid down her fork. 'Everything.'

'I don't know everything about her. Not by a long shot.' I studied her eager, lovely face. 'Why don't you tell me what you know? Then I'll try to fill in the gaps . . . if I can.'

She fiddled with the fork, staring down at the shrimps in their bed of limp lettuce. The cooking at Questro's wasn't so good, if that was a sample.

Not looking up, she said, 'I'm ashamed. I don't know anything really. You see, I can't remember her at all.'

The drinks arrived. Another breathing-space.

After the waiter had gone again, Sara looked up. 'Mr Freeman, I don't even know what she looked like. I haven't even seen a picture of her.'

Should I tell her I had a photograph? Not yet, I decided. Not yet.

'And yet you were talking about her to Hard . . . Harmsworth this afternoon? What brought that up?' These were fair questions, I thought.

She puckered her brows. 'I don't know. I really don't know. It just sort of came into the conversation. It seemed quite natural.' She paused. 'Yes, quite natural.'

What I wanted to know was how the hell she'd met Harding; why she'd been with him during the afternoon; and why, in particular, he'd raised this particular hare. Did it have any connection with the session I'd had with Hodges the night before?

'Eat your shrimps,' I suggested.

'I'm not very hungry.'

'You've got a big steak coming up. Why the sudden loss of appetite?' I smiled at her. Suddenly, she smiled back, a finger tracing the line of the dimple. For no particular reason I had a lump in my throat, watching her. 'Look, I'll make a deal with you. We'll eat our dinner. We'll chat. Then I'll take you home. You live in London?'

'I'm sharing a flat in Kensington with a friend of mine.'

'Right. That's the programme, then. And I'll make you a promise. We'll get together soon because I've got a picture of your mother. I'll get it and I'll tell you all I know about her. How about that?'

'Oh, thank you. Thank you very much, Mr Freeman. You're very, very kind.'

She attacked her shrimps. I sipped my drink. Before I told her anything about anybody, I wanted a few more words with George Victor Hodges.

I leaned on the buzzer. There was the usual crackling static and Hodges asked who it was. I didn't stand on ceremony.

'You should bloody well know who it is. Open up.'

The lock clicked and I pushed open the street door. Up the stairs, along the corridor, into the cul-de-sac to 27. The door was ajar. I went right in, slammed it shut behind me. Hodges was standing in the middle of the room, his hands in his pockets. He wasn't wearing the karate dressing-gown, just shirt and slacks.

'What're you trying to do? Bust my cover?' he said in a mild, matter-of-fact voice. 'Bit late for social calls, isn't it?'

'This isn't social,' I told him, and if he wanted to push my face in he'd be busy for as long as I was on my feet. The sort of anger I had inside me made a nonsense of fear.

'It isn't, eh? Still, you may as well sit down.'

'Not tonight, my friend. I stay on my two plates of meat.'

He shrugged. 'Drink?'

'No. But help yourself.' With a glass in his hand it would take a split second for him to get rid of it if a rough house started, and split seconds with a bloke like Hodges were valuable.

He went to the cupboard, poured himself some lemonade.

'Okay. What's on your mind?'

He was a cool bastard, all right. I fought back an impulse to smash his face in, swallowed hard on the rage that threatened to choke me. 'Just what the hell do you think you're playing at?' He waited, sipping his drink. 'Sending me to that bloody restaurant. Handing out all the James Bond jazz with the guidebooks. Putting me on the hook with that Kenyon woman and Harding . . .'

There was a flicker of something in his eyes.

'Who's Harding?' he wanted to know.

'All right,' I said. 'Make it Harmsworth.'

A tiny silence. 'You mean the newspaper chap?'

I swear to God he convinced me. Hodges on the defensive was a rare sight, but I was looking at it.

But I could be wrong. I barged on. 'Don't cock it up, you said. If it's cocked up you can blame your own varsity arty-farties who run the Shop. They don't even have to work up a sweat in lining up disasters. And I'm out of it. I'm bloody out. As of now. You, Hodges, can get stuffed.'

'Now just a minute.' The crackle was back in his voice, and the first butterfly fluttered in my guts. 'And sit down. This is going to take a bit of time.' I hesitated. 'Oh, for Christ's sake, take the weight off your feet.' I sat down, but I didn't relax. I was relieved when he stretched out in a chair, too. 'Now,' he said. 'How about telling me what happened? Simply, in words of preferably not more than a couple of syllables.'

I had a choice of where to start: with Harding's call or with when Hodges rang me. A little warning voice suggested I start with Hodges. So I did.

He listened without interruption. I reached the point when I'd promised Sara Kenyon I'd meet her again and show her the photograph.

'You say this chap Harmsworth is a bloke you know called Harding?' he said when I'd finished.

'Yes.'

'Who is he?'

'How about you telling me?' I countered.

'Can't,' he said. 'Never heard of him. Who is he?'

Oh, Lord, here we go again. 'Look, Hodges! He has to be one of your lot,' I said.

'He isn't,' Hodges said.

All right, I'd had enough experience to know that left hands rarely knew what right hands were doing in this trade, but this situation was moving quickly from the ridiculous to the idiotic.

'Tell me about Harding,' Hodges commanded.

'He works at the Ministry,' I said.

'What does he do there?'

'I don't know. He's upstairs, on one of the upper decks.'

'Important?'

'I think so.'

'How did you meet him?'

There it was again. Hodges would never believe I couldn't remember. I'd skipped the bit about Sara Kenyon not being able to remember how she'd met him. No, Hodges wouldn't believe it. But I said it just the same. Strangely, he didn't comment. So I don't know whether he believed me or not.

'So? You told Kenyon you'd see her again. Show her the photograph?'

'Yes.'

'When?'

'I said I'd ring her. At the flat.'

'I was coming to that. You told me the two of you just chatted during the rest of the meal after this man Harding had gone?'

I nodded. Retailed back again, it sounded almighty thin.

'Find out anything?'

'Only the personal stuff. Nothing exciting.'

'I'll be the judge of that. Tell me.'

Oddly enough, re-telling what I'd learned sounded more promising. At least I had a picture of who and what she claimed to be. She was the daughter of Alexander Kenyon, commander, Royal Navy, retired, and now something in the City. His marriage to Sophia had been a whirlwind pre-war association of storm and tempest, of a baby born and abandoned by its mother.

'Her father has never discussed Sophia with her. At least, that's what she says. She hasn't ever seen a picture of her.

She's asked questions, but it upsets the old man so she stopped. She's had a go at the nanny who helped bring her up, but she claims she knows nothing about Sophia.'

'She mention her schooling? Jobs?'

'Only that Kenyon sent her to that swept-up girls' school down near Brighton. They live in Hassocks. After that she stayed at home, acting as a sort of secretary to her father. Seems he was writing his memoirs or something. But she got fed up. Took a job as a courier with a travel agency. She's just back from a waltz around Europe, a sort of warm-up before the season gets under way.'

He chewed on this for a while, then asked me again if I wanted a drink. 'I've got stuff more to your taste than this,' he grinned, holding up the lemonade.

'No,' I said. There wasn't anything social about this call. We were meeting on my terms for the first time. 'Right,' I said. 'I've done my share. I'd like to do some listening.'

Hodges had never liked aggression in other people. I could see he didn't enjoy it now. His face tightened. But we'd reached a point where he had to be careful with me. And he knew it.

'What do you want to know?'

'Come off it, Hodges. There's as many holes as a sieve in this set-up. You ring me, give me the cover name Freeman, tell me to carry a bloody guidebook. I wonder you didn't fit me out with a cloak and dagger while you were at it. I go to Questro's not knowing why or who I'm going to contact. And you have the God-almighty nerve to warn me not to cock it up! And what happens? A bloke you claim you don't know gets in on the act. He knows my cover name. He's obviously up-dated on what I told you last night about the Kenyon woman.' I drew breath. 'And you sit there and ask me what I want to know! Christ, you're cool.' I let that lot sink in. 'And there's something else. You chase me to a Soho restaurant where it costs the earth just to breathe their air. No mention of what I'm supposed to use for money.'

He didn't know Harding had covered the bill in some way. Let Hodges bloody well sweat.

'You're a bachelor. You're reasonably well paid. You don't spend so much. If you didn't have cash you carry a cheque book. And you knew you'd get back what you spent. What's your gripe?'

They know. They always bloody well know. Hodges got up,

went across to his desk. From a drawer he took out an envelope. He tossed it into my lap. 'There's fifty quid in there. You may need it.'

I threw it back at him. His flexes were good. He caught it without a fumble.

'Stick it,' I told him.

I made a mess of holding the envelope when he tossed it right back. I had to pick it up off the floor. Psychologically that was bad. I should have left it where it fell.

Hodges sat down. 'Listen,' he said. I was prepared to do that. He might clear away some of the fog patches. 'The reservation was made in the name Freeman because we didn't want your name involved. Okay?' I nodded. 'Now the guidebook: our information was that Kenyon always carried a Bacon's – has done since she moved up to town. She doesn't know London all that well. That check with what you know?'

'Yes.'

'So we gambled she'd have it tonight. She did. They weren't for your benefit. You knew her. They were to pinpoint the two of you to one of my chaps.'

'You mean . . .' He nodded.

'Yes. We had a bloke there. We wanted a report on what happened when she came in. What you did. How you did it. We figured you wouldn't be able to resist making contact. So we set it up. And we used a man who doesn't know either of you. We wanted a report that was unbiased and uncoloured.'

He was a bastard all right. But I had to take it. 'But just a minute. How did you get *her* there?'

'Like I said last night, you don't learn very fast. That was easy.' The contempt on his face made me want to belt him. His explanation consisted of one word, 'Daddy.'

Remembering them, I could picture it all. The message – which suggested they knew where she worked; my information had been superfluous – suggesting her father would be in town. Would she have dinner with him? At the restaurant she would have received another message apologising for his non-arrival. 'But have dinner, darling. I've arranged to take care of the bill.' All right; when she and daddy had swapped notes the thing would have been over, anyway. A little mystery, no more; never explained, but no harm to anyone: a piece of cake.

I was still holding the envelope. 'We want you to make that date with Kenyon,' said Hodges. 'Show her the picture by all means. Talk your head off about Sophia. Your own self-respect won't let you tell her anything that will embarrass us, will it?' He wore his nasty smile.

'What's the point?' I asked him. 'She's nothing.'

'You came running here last night thinking she might be something.'

'That was last night – the shock of seeing Sophia's ghost, her being with Lawson and Pemberton. But now I've met her she's a nothing.' I held up the envelope. 'In this context anyway.'

'Keep contact. See her again.'

There was the crackle in that bastard's voice again.

'And if I tell you to get stuffed?'

'You already have,' he said. 'But you'll do it. I'll tell you why you'll do it. Because it'll be bloody uncomfortable for you if you don't.' He stood up. 'That's why you'll do it.'

I got out of the chair. 'And Harding? What about him?'

'Forget him.'

'Like hell I can forget him. I'll be feeling better tomorrow. I'll be back at the office. Could bump into him any time.'

'So play it by ear. Just so long as you don't cock anything up.'

He was guiding me to the door.

'If it'll make you feel any better . . .'

He stopped.

'Yes?' I prompted him.

He bit his lip, unusually uncertain. He seemed to regret having offered me the prospect of comfort.

'I'll risk it. For your ear, the Sophia Kukralovic file never was closed. So chat up Sara Kenyon. But, like I said, don't cock it up. You're the only hyphen we've got.'

EIGHT

CAIRO: THE SHOP

The public office of the Anglo-Egyptian Assurance Company was a not unhappy mixture of large tiles, marble pillars and heavy mahogany. Typewriters and adding-machines rattled like so many automatic weapons. The staff I could see seemed a balanced blend of British and Egyptian, and women predominated among the paler skins. At the enquiries desk a tasty Coptic morsel asked me my business.

'I have an appointment with Mr Collins,' I said, and gave her my name. A giant Nubian was summoned, teeth in the jet-black face matching the immaculate galabiah for whiteness, his tarbush worn at a jaunty angle. I followed him along a heavily carpeted corridor of obviously executive offices. He escorted me to a small ante-room, asked me politely if I would mind waiting a moment (the excellence of his English was impressive) and disappeared through a door. As it opened, I heard a typewriter being used expertly. The sound stopped as the door closed.

The room I was in had a couple of uncomfortable straight-backed chairs and a coffee-table with back numbers of *Punch* and the current editions of the *Egyptian Mail* and the *Egyptian Gazette*, Cairo's two English-language newspapers. I waited rather longer than I'd expected, but eventually the Nubian came out, inclined his head and went on into the corridor. He was followed by a raven-haired woman of indeterminate age, severe dress and apparent efficiency. She tapped on a door labelled Private and waited.

Above the door a tiny light I hadn't noticed flashed white. She opened the heavy slab of mahogany and motioned with her head. I went in and the door closed behind me. The office was as opulent as everywhere else. It was large, the furniture big and comfortable, the carpet rich. Obviously Mr Collins was an executive of some consequence in the Anglo-Egyptian Assurance Company. But Mr Collins hardly matched his commercial image. He sat behind the huge desk, dwarfed by the magnificence around him. He might have been in his fifties, balding, his round moon face clean shaven. His eyes sheltered behind pebble spectacles. His body was thin, but his lightweight clothes were beautifully tailored.

Standing to his right behind the desk was another man, much younger and tougher-looking, not very big, but his body looked as if it was well put together.

They stared at me. I stared right back from where I stood inside the door. Collins didn't say anything. He simply indicated a straight-backed chair facing him on my side of the desk. I walked to it and sat down. As I did so I noticed a plain buff-coloured foolscap folder in front of him. That, I thought, is me, all they know of me. Now for the grilling. But the approach was so different from what I'd prepared for that I nearly laughed. In a very mild, almost apologetic, voice Collins said, 'I understand you have an appointment at five o'clock?'

Startled, I didn't say anything. Then I nodded.

'We wish you to keep it.' He paused. 'Does she know where you live?'

I cleared my throat. 'Why no. It's never come up.'

'Good. You will go with her on this . . . er, shopping expedition. Then you will excuse yourself. Perhaps you have a great deal of work to do this evening. Then you will go to Number six Sharia Gheziredbadran. That's the Immeuble Mikhanoff. The flat is on the first floor. It is fully furnished and equipped. A servant named Hamid lives on the premises. He will be available to you. You will stay there tonight. You will not go out. You will be contacted. You understand?'

I nodded optimistically. Immeuble Mikhanoff. Number six Gheziredbadran. I concentrated.

'It's in Shubra,' said Mr Collins.

'Take a taxi when you've left her,' said the other man. He slid a bundle of notes across the desk.

'That will be all,' said Mr Collins. He pressed a button on his desk. I stood up and wondered if I should say something. The other man nodded towards the notes. I picked them up. Should I count them? Why the hell not? So I thumbed through them. Fifty Egyptian one-pounds. I stowed them in my wallet.

The raven-haired secretary had the door open. I walked out, through the ante-room, along the corridor and into the sunshine.

Time was pressing on. I wanted time to sort all this out. Sophia had said five o'clock, but not where. That gave me just half an hour for a much-needed drink before it was necessary to make tracks for the Malika Farida. I was heading towards a bar in Adly Pasha when I paused. What should I do with the car? And to dive straight into a bar after the meeting with Mr Collins could look a bit obvious, if one of his hatchetmen was sitting on my tail. After all, they'd just handed me fifty quid on a platter. There were garage facilities around the corner from the Dopolavoro building; I'd drive there, park, have a cup of coffee and then on to Sophia's. That's what I did, though I badly needed a drink. And while I did it I tried to identify who-ever might be doing what I strongly suspected was being done. I might as well not have bothered. Cairo had been stirring for an hour after the siesta; the shops were open again; pedestrians crowded the pavement. Soldiers were everywhere . . . the majority well in their cups.

I finished my coffee and headed for the Malika Farida.

*   *   *

She was expecting me. She opened the door, a vision in a white two-piece suit that hugged her figure.

'I did hope you'd come,' she said. She didn't invite me in. Just picked up a handbag and we walked to the lift together.

'Where are we going?' I asked.

'Galal's, I think.'

I didn't know much about the stores, but that was one mighty expensive-looking shop if its window-displays meant anything to a mere male.

As we turned into Kasr-al-Nil I asked her if she'd slept well. Surprised, she said: 'Of course. Should I not have?'

'Well, sometimes we don't. Not when we're over-tired.'

She nearly said she hadn't been over-tired, then must have remembered why she'd sent me away. She smiled broadly, stroking the dimple. Then she took my arm, snuggling it into her breast. We walked on, as much like a married couple as any unmarried couple could be.

The taxi dropped me at a little cul-de-sac on Gheziredbadran. The Immeuble Mikhanoff stood inside a high wall which bordered the Cairo–Alexandria railway line. I walked up to the first floor. Hamid sat on a chair outside the door of the flat. He was an elderly Nubian, clean but wrinkled. His right hand respectfully touched chest, lips and forehead. He took some keys from a capricious pocket and unlocked the door. I wondered how he knew who I was. I went through into a tiny hall, the parquet floor spotlessly clean. Through a maze of lattice I could see a comfortable living-room, cosy with divans and cushions and low oriental tables. Hamid opened the shutters to admit cool air and the rumble of traffic in the busy Shubra streets. A train screeched by, its whistle piercing the ear drums. He silently took my overnight bag and I followed him into the bedroom. This, too, was shuttered, but in the dim light the acceptably large bed dominated another well-furnished room.

'Coffee, bey?' asked Hamid. I nodded.

He padded off. That was when I noticed a small hold-all in the bedroom. I didn't recognise it, but that was easily attended to. I opened it. I wasn't really surprised to find in it the rest of my modest civvy wardrobe. You had to hand it to these lads. In an afternoon they'd done a lot.

I wandered into the kitchen, passing a small shower-room and loo, with the inevitable bidet. Hamid was busy with the little brass coffee-pot. There was an icebox, a sink and a bench, some cupboards, a table and two chairs – as efficient a bachelor apartment as I'd seen. Back in the living-room I thumbed through a small bookcase: some thrillers, a street-map, a Bible and – surprising discovery – an international press directory. Why wasn't there a typewriter? There was. Not new, it had the used, rather battered look, with half-worn labels on its case, that one would expect a globe-trotting journalist to have in his possession. There was a thoroughness about the set-up that was just a bit frightening. I sat down. Hamid brought in the coffee on a tray. He put it down, waited. I nodded my thanks. He bowed, saluted again with his right hand and walked out, closing the door quietly behind him. He'd be taking station on the landing.

Don't go out, Collins had said. You'll be contacted. I wanted a drink. Maybe . . . I got up, did a systematic prowl of the place. Sure enough, in one of the kitchen cupboards I found the bottles: scotch, gin, zibib, cognac, and some cordials.

I had a well-watered zibib, the coffee and a comfortable chair. I waited.

Hamid must have known him, because he came straight in at half-past ten. It was the man I'd seen at the insurance office.

I'd been dozing and was just a bit bleary.

'Don't get up,' he said. His voice wasn't particularly friendly. Did he think I'd been boozing?

He sat down facing me.

'Well?' he asked.

'Fine,' I said. My arm waved my appreciation of the flat.

'You won't be here long, then.'

What the hell was up with him?

'I'm here to get a report,' he rasped.

'Oh,' I said. 'About this afternoon?'

'What else?'

'We went shopping, and . . .'

'For Christ's sake. We know that. What happened?'

'Nothing much. Went to Galal's first. She wandered about a bit, bought a couple of pairs of panties and a bra. But I feel that was a blind.'

'Why?'

'I had the feeling she was looking for someone or something. Whatever it was she didn't find him or her or it.'

'How do you know?'

'For the simple bloody reason I was with her. I'd have known, wouldn't I?'

'No.'

He was a prickly bastard, this one. But I suppose he could have been right. I mightn't have seen a signal or something else.

'Go on.' He was impatient, his eyes boring into me. It was embarrassing.

'We went to that place across the street and had coffee and pastries . . .'

'What place?'

'I don't know the name of it. It's the . . .'

He got up. 'You fucking amateurs,' he said. I got up, but he pushed me back into the chair. 'Get on with it. I haven't got all night.'

I choked back the anger in my throat. 'We went to Fouad-al-Awal. To Zimmells.'

'And?'

'She bought an evening coat.'

'Pay cash?'

'Yes. Fifty pounds.'

'Her money, I hope?' He said this sarcastically.

'Of course,' I said. 'She never suggested I pay anything.' I thought I'd better be honest. 'There was a bracelet thing she liked. I offered to buy it for her but she wouldn't let me.'

'Then?'

'She said she had a dinner date. Made it easy for me as I had to be here . . .'

'Who was the date with?'

'I don't bloody know, do I? You've got to know somebody pretty well before you start asking questions like that.'

'God save us!' he said, almost to himself. Then, to me, 'It was a mistake, handing this job to you.'

Bugger the flat, I thought. I didn't have to take this. 'I didn't ask to do it.'

He rubbed his hand on his chin. 'You seeing her again?'

'It seems not.'

His eyebrows shot up. 'You telling me you've let her go?'

'No,' I said. 'You're telling me.'

'It's not my decision, friend, worse bloody luck. When?'

'Lunch. Tomorrow.'

'Where?'

'Sans Souci.'

'She meeting you there?'

'Yes.'

'Why aren't you picking her up at the flat?'

'Because she said she'd meet me at the restaurant.'

'Time?'

'Two o'clock.'

'You be there, then.' He thought for a moment. 'Haven't been to bed with her yet, then?'

'No.'

'Then get there. Don't muck about. We want her talking to you.' Another pause. 'You any good at it?'

'Had no complaints. Yet.'

He grunted. Then he pulled a slip of paper from his pocket. 'Memorise that.' It was a telephone number. I was about to put it in my pocket when he snarled, 'I said memorise it. Now. I want that back.'

I worked on it while he went to the kitchen and I heard him pouring a drink. He strode back in. 'What's the number?' he said. I reeled off the figures, handed him the slip of paper. He sipped the drink. It looked suspiciously like lemonade.

'Anything urgent, you ring that number.'

'Who do I ask for?' I could have bitten my tongue out.

'Jesus, you're wet behind the ears. Just ring. Say it's Julius. And talk. But make sure where you're talking from. And only tell essentials. If there's trouble of any sort, just say, "Send me a taxi to" wherever you are. It shouldn't be necessary. But just in case, that's the drill.'

'Think I'll have a drink.'

'You won't. What was the telephone number?'

I recited it again. He grunted, drained the glass, and put it down.

'You start work tomorrow.'

'Don't rub it in.'

'I'm not talking about eating the taxpayers' dough, friend. I'm talking about work. You're a journalist, aren't you?'

'That's the cover I . . .'

'Oh, Jesus. Get on with it. That's your trade, isn't it?' I nodded. 'Right. In this business you don't pretend. You do it. Ten o'clock tomorrow you'll report to the Arab News Agency. Chap called Mortimer. He'll give you some subbing. And you'd better have this.'

He tossed me the green international Press card. God knows where they'd got my photograph, but there it was. And the name of a Dublin agency. It showed accreditation to ANA.

'Right. That's about it. And don't cock this up, friend. Just don't cock it up.'

'Here, wait a minute. There's a hell of a lot more I want to know about . . .'

'The less you know the better. You might talk in your sleep. Mortimer's always good for a few quid if you get stuck. But take it easy, see?' He moved towards the door. Over his shoulder he said. 'And get yourself some decent clothes. I know journalists're a sloppy lot, but you look terrible.'

I stood up. Recited the phone number at him, just for kicks. Then I said, 'You've been pretty free with the chat except who you are. What's your name?'

'None of your business,' he said, and went out.

I wasn't going to find out till later, but I'd just met George Victor Hodges.

NINE

LONDON: A DAY IN THE COUNTRY

George Victor Hodges said I was the only hyphen they had. Hyphen: a transitive verb meaning to join. Join what?

I was less shocked than I felt I should have been when he told me the Sophia Kukralovic file hadn't been closed after all. I bent my memory back to that terrible day in Cairo when I was told I was being flown to London. Had anybody then actually said, 'The file is closed.'? I couldn't remember the exact wording. In some extraordinary way I felt detached about it. Maybe it was because I'd always known it couldn't have been closed, at least, not in the way they let me assume it had been.

All the way back to my bed-sitter I mulled over the events of a daft sort of day and night. Then I began to worry. History was starting to repeat itself. Now why should that be? In those strange Cairo days we'd been at war. Now, give or take Viet Nam, Northern Ireland and the continuing battle between coppers and crime in half a dozen capital cities we were living in an era of peace – well, a period of non-war.

And Harding? I had to believe Hodges when he said he didn't know him. But I was willing to bet that in twenty-four hours he would: he'd know the colour of his underpants. Harding, alias Harmsworth. And the bastards had had a watcher at Questro's.

I got undressed and decided a slug of scotch might help. I sat on the bed and sipped it. It would be back to the office in the morning . . . Morning? It was that now: after midnight. Maybe I should get some sleep and leave the worrying. There didn't seem to be any point in getting all jagged up over something I couldn't do anything about right now. I drained the whisky and got into the cot.

My return to the office occasioned nothing more than the usual polite but couldn't-care-less enquiries about my health. Bill Nash was a bit sour. He'd had a couple of knotty Press queries to handle on my desk, but he cheered up when I said I'd buy him a drink sometime.

I wondered when I should call Sara Kenyon. Better to leave it till the evening when she'd got home.

The clock ticked its way slowly through the dullness of a routine day until just before noon. My phone rang. I said, 'Hello!'

'My dear fellow! I understand you're back on your feet again, eh? Jolly good. Feeling all right now?'

I told Harding yes, I felt fine.

'When I phoned you yesterday I suggested we should have a drink soon. How about it, eh? How about today? One o'clock suit you all right? The Tavern?'

I bought time by coughing. I hoped it sounded realistic. A bloody cool gentleman was Mr Harding. The Tavern? It was right on our own doorstep; we could expect to see any of the crowd drifting in any time.

'I say, you sure you're all right? Nasty bark you have there, my dear chap.'

I cleared my throat. 'Just a bit of spit down the wrong way. I'm fine. Okay. Why not? The Tavern, one o'clock.'

'Splendid. See you, then. 'Bye.'

The place was crowded. They were up to three deep at the bar. Harding must be off his nut: a bloke couldn't hear himself think in this racket. I stood just at the bottom of the steps and tried to focus through the haze of cigarette smoke. In the far corner a hand was waving vigorously. It was Harding. I pushed and elbowed my way over. He was at a small table, a gin in front of him, and standing sentinel over the vacant chair was a welcome pint of beer. He knew my lunch-time tipple.

I squeezed down into the seat and stared stonily at his beaming smile.

'Cheers,' he said, lifting his glass.

'Cheers, Mr Harmsworth,' I said, raising mine.

He looked funny, his glass almost to his lips. His face had gone quite blank, the mouth hanging open.

He leaned forward. 'You all right, old chap?' he wanted to know.

'Sure,' I said. 'Nice to see you, Mr Harmsworth. And thanks for the drink.'

He sat back, sipped his drink, his eyes boring into me. I stared right back. 'What's the matter, Mr Harmsworth? Aren't we buddies any more? You remember me? Freeman's the name. And thanks for the dinner last night.'

I didn't shout, in spite of the noise. But I projected. I think that's what actors call it: making sure your voice would reach its target.

He put his glass down, reached forward and took my jar out of my hand. He put that down, too. His voice was full of concern. 'I say, old boy, you must be running a fever. Look, I'd better get you home. You're not well, definitely not well. Come on. We'll grab a taxi and I'll get you home. Don't worry about the office. I'll fix that. You dedicated characters!' He laughed. 'Reckon the Ministry can't function without you. Come on.'

He was serious. He stood up. Now it was my move. What in hell was I supposed to do? There wasn't any alternative. I played it his way. His hand on my arm, he did a damn good job of pushing us out of the crowded Dive Bar. Up on the street, his hand still on my arm, he waved vigorously at passing taxis. It seemed an age before a 'For Hire' sign showed its yellow light.

'I'm all right,' I muttered. This was getting past a joke.

'Of course you are, old boy. Get in.'

He held the door open. I climbed in. He muttered something to the taxi-driver, then got in and thumped down in the seat beside me.

Wherever we were going it wasn't to Streatham Hill. But, like I said, I was prepared to play it his way. He was holding my arm again, gently. Christ! I was beginning to wonder if I *was* all right. The taxi trundled along the Embankment towards Blackfriars, every red light jerking us to a stop. Finally I said, 'This isn't the way to my place.'

'I know,' he said.

I stared out at the pedestrians, the drivers of other cars passing us, us passing them. It would be good to be just one of them. They thought they had troubles! We swung up towards Ludgate Circus, Harding's hand still on my arm; up Ludgate Hill, left into Old Bailey, across Newgate Street, into Giltspur Street. Ahead of us was the pile of St Bartholomew's Hospital. I started to panic then. Yet, oddly enough, his pressure on my arm was reassuring. 'Chap I want to see,' he said, beaming his smile at me.

The taxi screeched to a stop. He should have his brakes looked at, I thought. Harding clambered out, signalling both the driver and me to stay put. The driver pulled out a copy of *Sporting Life* and immersed himself in the day's runners, picking his nose as he searched for winners. I just sat there. I dismissed an impulse to get out and go somewhere else. If Harding was mixed up in the Sara Kenyon thing then it was my job to stay with him. Job? How the hell had I got into this, anyway? My job was sitting behind a modest desk in the Ministry. But I'd taken the fifty nicker from Hodges, so I was stuck with it. And what was Harding doing in Barts? Setting up somebody to make a pigeon out of me? It was a good ten minutes before he re-appeared: he still had that idiotic beaming smile on his face.

He pulled out some money, paid the driver, then jerked open the door. 'Come on, old chap,' he said. I sat tight.

'Nothing doing,' I said.

'Oh, do get out.' His impatience wiped out the smile.

The driver took a hand. He turned, opened the slide window and said: 'You want to take the cab on, guv?'

Oh well, the Harding situation had to be sorted out. I joined the Ministry man and a muttering cabbie pulled away in a puff of blue smoke. Again there was the gentle pressure on my arm. I went with Harding into reception. The girl at the desk nodded and smiled. Harding beamed back at her. We went along a narrow corridor, flanked by doors, most of them with little brass plates. Harding paused and tapped. I stared hard at the nameplate; I might want to remember it in the future. 'Dr Luke Stapleton' it read.

I heard a voice invite us in. Harding opened the door into a small office. The man behind the desk was wearing a white coat. He was probably fifty, though the beard and heavy black-rimmed spectacles could have made my judgment wrong.

'Ah, Harding.'

They didn't shake hands. Either they weren't close friends or they'd seen each other recently, perhaps a few minutes ago, while I waited in the taxi. Harding introduced us. I was relieved he didn't use the name 'Freeman'.

'The desk said you wanted to see me?'

Harding nodded. Stapleton waved us to the chairs in front of his desk. We sat down.

I noted, The desk said you wanted to see me; just as though Harding hadn't been in the office minutes before. Still, this could've been part of the set-up. Set-up? I still didn't know why the hell I was there. And I also tucked away the hint of a guttural accent in Stapleton's voice.

'Well, yes,' said Harding. 'Passing this way with my friend

and it occurred to me we didn't fix a date last night. So thought I'd just pop in and do it now.'

'I intended to phone you this afternoon,' the doctor said. He leafed through the diary on his desk.

Harding turned to me. 'You play chess?'

The utter incongruity of it all made me stammer. 'Well, yes. Not very well. Know the moves. That's about all.'

Harding's elbow nudged me in the ribs. 'Bet you're good. Never met any player yet who'll admit just how good he is, eh, Stapleton?'

A smile split the doctor's heavily-thatched face. A finger on an open page, he asked: 'How about Wednesday?'

Out came Harding's pocket diary. He flicked its pages. He frowned. 'Oh dear! 'Fraid that's impossible.' Then he smiled, slapped his knee. 'Why not tonight. You were saying you were free. Now why not, old man?'

The jiggery-pokery was making me nervous. I tried to concentrate on the movement outside the window. An ambulance raced out through the forecourt, its siren screaming. I wondered about where it was going, to what it was going. Then I became aware that Stapleton was thinking aloud that tonight might be a good idea.

'Come to my house,' the doctor was saying. 'Perhaps the Commander could come over. Play the winner.' He chuckled. 'At least it'll be practice for whichever of us it is has to play him.'

'Don't be modest, my dear fellow,' laughed Harding. 'Your Sicilian Defence last night was brilliant. I never had a chance.'

Suddenly my stomach felt uneasy. Last night? Harding playing chess? It could be, I thought. He'd left Questro's at — what? Half-past eight? It might have been a few minutes after that.

'Yes, but you owed me a win after what you did in the first game,' Stapleton protested.

Two games. And unless they were absolute novices two games of chess aren't played like hands of gin rummy.

'Sorry we couldn't play the decider,' said Harding. 'But my wife insisted I have an early night. Suppose she was right.' He held his head in mock despair. 'That party the night before was pretty hearty, wasn't it?'

Stapleton laughed. 'I was never more grateful for being a doctor. I mixed myself a pick-me-up.'

'Alex always amazes me, you know,' Harding said. 'Not a

lock of hair out of place. A mighty man . . .'

'He's got fewer locks to get out of place,' Stapleton joked. He rubbed a hand vigorously in his own thick hair. 'But you're right. He can pour the stuff away. Of course, he has a solid base of pink gin. Wardrooms're good training-grounds for winning more than just naval battles.'

My memory cells were getting a bit agitated.

Harding suddenly stood up, glancing at his watch. 'I say, old man. We're holding you up.'

'Not to worry,' the doctor told him. 'So tonight then? I'll phone Alex.'

'Eightish?'

'Not later. I'll have the board ready.'

I got out of my chair. Harding turned to me. 'I say. How about you, old chap? Care for a game?' He faced Stapleton. 'Let's play two boards?'

'Why not?' the doctor agreed, more than warmly.

'I'll run you down,' Harding offered. 'Could put you up for the night. Bring you in to Whitehall in the morning.'

Here it was again, the nervous stammer. 'Why . . . I don't think so. Not in your class. And . . . anyway, I . . . I'm doing something else tonight.' I swallowed. 'Thank you. Thank you both very much. Some other time maybe . . .'

Harding seemed disappointed. But he didn't press the invitation. 'Very well.' To Stapleton, 'Sorry to have interrupted the toil, old man. Till tonight?'

The doctor walked round his desk, opened the door. He shook hands with me, murmuring some polite pleasantry, but didn't shake hands with Harding. We walked in silence along the corridor, through the reception hall and out into the air.

Harding stopped, turned to me. He was smiling.

'You're looking better. But I think you should take the rest of the day off. I'll tell the office.'

What was left of the day I could spend to damn better purpose than at the Ministry. I nodded.

'Nice chap, Stapleton. We really must get you down for a game.' We walked slowly out into the bustle of West Smithfield.

'Care for a coffee?'

I shook my head. 'I think you're right. I'd better get my feet up.'

'Like me to go with you, old man?' His voice sounded full of solicitude.

77

'No thanks. I'll be all right.'

'I'd get the jolly old quack in to have a look at you,' he said. 'Doesn't pay to take chances. Not at our age, eh?' He was beaming again. 'Let me get you a taxi.'

'No, thanks very much.' My voice was firm. 'I'm well enough to use a bus. Honest.'

'That's silly. I'm taking a cab as far as Fleet Street. We'll go round by the Embankment. Be easier for you to pick up a 109 from there. Come on.'

There was about a third of a bottle of scotch in the flat. I drank half of it, neat, in two of the biggest nips I've ever swallowed. Then I stretched out on the bed.

Hodges was a rough bastard. Harding was a smooth bastard. But both of them, for sure, were bastards. And I seemed to be the meat in a bastard sandwich. I wanted to give 'em both indigestion.

The raw spirit was burning my guts. I twisted on the bed while my mind did handsprings trying to make sense of the impossible. It *had* been Harding at Questro's. I didn't have one single, solitary doubt about *that*. But, cleverly, he'd never said he hadn't been in Soho: just proffered supporting evidence that he'd been somewhere else – not as a defence, just as a fact. Maybe it wasn't impossible for him to have been with Sara Kenyon and me and played chess afterwards. Maybe Stapleton was a collaborator, thoroughly briefed and primed in the part he was to play.

But if Harding was Harmsworth, then commonsense suggested he was tied up with Hodges. But Hodges denied any knowledge of the Ministry official. He did it, too, in such a way that I'd had to believe him. There had been a conviction about Hodge's question, 'Who's Harding?'

Then, out of the mental chaos, two little memories jiggled together. Stapleton had said he'd ask the Commander over tonight. Commander? Then a bit about pink gin, wardrooms, the Navy. Sara Kenyon's father was Commander Alexander Kenyon, RN (Ret'd). Alexander: Alex, the man with a good head for booze.

I swung my legs off the bed and damn near threw up. That scotch wasn't lying any too happily in my belly. Blast! Why the hell hadn't I taken up the offer of chess? Not that I was any bloody good at the game. A Russian in Cairo used to read the newspaper while he was beating the pants off me.

I put my head back on the pillow, swallowing bile. Oh Christ! Why had I poured that muck down my throat? Moving carefully, I struggled to my feet. Alka Seltzer might help. Because I had some phoning to do.

Far too many people can afford overseas holidays. It took me twenty minutes of almost continuous dialling before a connected ringing tone replaced the maddeningly high-pitched engaged signal. Astral Travel Services seemed to be doing lively business.

'Astral, at your service,' lilted a sugar-sweet voice. Probably she was a bitch to her boy friend.

'Sara Kenyon, please,' I said.

'Miss Kenyon? May I say who's calling?'

I nearly made a mess of that. Only caught myself in time. 'Freeman.'

'One moment please, Mr Freeman. I'll check if Miss Kenyon's available.'

Miss Kenyon? Now why was a woman still 'Miss' at her age? She had everything: beauty, brains, a well-lined bottom-drawer, too, if her clothes were any barometer. And retired Navy commanders who live in Hassocks aren't usually on the bread-line . . . And Sara Kenyon had to be thirty: she could well be older. Yes, doing my arithmetic, she *had* to be older than thirty. She was wearing bloody well.

'Hello, Mr Freeman. How nice of you to call.'

She sounded as if she meant it.

'Well, I wasn't sure whether I should call you at the office . . .'

She laughed. I could picture the finger on the dimple. 'Why, that's quite all right. Might sell you a holiday one day.'

'Try me now,' I laughed, though my belly still felt a bit unhappy. 'Anyway, I found the photograph. Wondered when we could meet.'

'Oh, you have. How exciting. Now, let me see . . .' I could see her pencil-line eyebrows puckering as clearly as if I were on a video-phone. 'I'm doing a late shift at the office tonight. So that's out. And tomorrow I'm going down to spend the weekend with daddy. I've earned a long weekend – don't seem to have had one for ages.'

Maybe finding out about her mum didn't rate much priority. I wondered why I felt disappointed. It was crazy at my age just to want to see a woman again.

Hesitantly, she said: 'Do you feel like a day in the country?

On Saturday or Sunday? Won't be very exciting, I'm afraid, but there are some lovely walks . . . that's if you like that sort of thing.'

I loathed that sort of thing, but a trip down to Hassocks might be helpful. Obviously Dr Stapleton didn't live too far away nor, probably, did Harding. Damn, why hadn't I checked the phone directory? As Hodges was always complaining, I just never learned.

'Look, I don't want to put you to any trouble,' I said. 'And anyway I remember you telling me your father wasn't too keen on discussing So . . . your mother.'

'He'll just have to lump it then, won't he?' she chuckled. 'Seriously though, he won't be about so much. When he's not playing chess with his friends he's working out the problems in *The Times* and *Telegraph* in his study. He's a fanatic.' She paused, then suspiciously, 'You don't play, do you?'

'Only know the moves,' I said. I wished to God I knew some of the bloody moves in this nonsense game.

'Oh dear,' she said. 'Please don't mention that to daddy. He'll lock you in with him. We'll never get a chance to talk.'

'But won't he think it odd, me just appearing out of the blue?'

'Why ever should he? I'm quite at liberty to invite my own friends to the house. It's where I belong. The flat in London's only for convenience since I've started working here. Listen, make a note of some trains.'

I scribbled happily and said I'd be at Hassocks just after ten on Saturday morning. She promised to be waiting with a car.

I made a mental note to use the opportunity of trying to find out how Harding . . . no, it had to be Harmsworth when I was talking to her . . . had inveigled her to Questro's.

'Goodbye then, Mr Freeman. I'm dying to hear about my mother and see the photograph.'

I stood there, my hand resting on the handset after I'd cradled it. So I was going to have a day in the country with Sara.

Just like some of those I'd had with Sophia in Egypt all those years ago.

TEN

CAIRO: MORTIMER

That first night I spent in the Immeuble Mikhanoff flat brought its surprises. After my unpleasant visitor had gone I unpacked the few things that had been delivered in the holdall. There was a buttoned pouch in a side pocket at the bottom. The contents were hard, unyielding. I opened it. A shoulder-holster rig, a slim box, and in the holster a well-cared-for Browning ·32 automatic pistol, identical with the weapon I'd seen in Sophia Kukralovic's bedroom. Gingerly I drew out the gun. I knew a bit about automatics; I'd spent some time on them when I'd been at the security course. I'd even passed a sort of proficiency test in the handling and firing of them. I unclipped the magazine. It was empty, but in the box were twenty-four rounds of live ammunition. Odd, that: the box should have held twenty-five. I counted the rounds again: twenty-four. The gun had been carefully wrapped in oiled-silk. It was when I was sliding the gun back into the holster that I noticed some slight resistance. A small white card was crumpled under the snout of the barrel. I straightened out the card. On it was a typewritten message: 'This is to be carried or used only when instructed or in emergency, repeat emergency.' You bet it would be. A journalist with a gun parked under his left armpit would learn a lot about the interior of Egyptian jails. I tore up the card, flushed the pieces down the loo, put the holster rig with the gun in it into the pouch, and just stood there with it in my hand.

Where the hell do you keep guns when you're not using them? Like a Browning ·32 automatic? Then I remembered something I'd read once: that Napoleon had worked on the philosophy that to hide anything secret one must leave it in full view. Hanging the bloody thing on a nail on the wall seemed to be about right. In the end I chucked it into a drawer in the bedroom and dumped some shirts over it.

I distributed the rest of my stuff and realised for the first time that I had a pretty thin wardrobe. I'd do something about it when I got time. One suit and the slacks and sports jacket I was wearing wouldn't take me far in Sophia's world.

I felt like a drink, then decided I'd have a look at the Shubra streets while I had it. It made sense to know the neighbourhood I was living in . . . no matter how temporarily I might be in residence. Because if my recent visitor had anything to do with it, that wouldn't be long.

I went into the little hall and found the front door locked. I jerked and twisted and pulled at the handle. It was locked all right, not just stuck. Then I heard a key rattle in the lock. The door opened and in came Hamid.

'Why is the door locked?' I stormed at him.

'It is better, bey.' He held up a massive chunk of shaped steel: the Gyppos who'd built this place God knows how many years before liked security.

'Too big,' said Hamid, holding the key against a side pocket of my jacket. 'But I am here always. Or Silah. Always Silah or me.'

'Well, I'm going out.'

'It is better not. Tomorrow, yes. Tonight it is better not.' He stood there, respectful but adamant. He'd been given instructions. 'If there is something the Bey wishes, I will call Silah. You wish to eat, perhaps?' His English was stilted but intelligible, and if he was an unemotional cuss at least he wasn't unfriendly.

'No, nothing thanks, Hamid. Nothing. Goodnight.'

He bowed slightly, saluted me with the upward sweep of his hand from heart to mouth to head, and went out. The key rattled in the lock. So the Bey was a prisoner. Oh, well. At least the cell was comfortable. I went to bed.

It was Silah who woke me with coffee, croissants and jam at seven o'clock. He was a much younger edition of Hamid with the same passion for cleanliness and good manners. I found later that the partnership was father and son.

I remembered with a shock that I was to report to Mortimer at ten o'clock. Christ, I'd be chucked in among hardbitten professionals, expected to foot it with them on the daily grind of a news-agency's output. I'd probably bump into Grayling again because Anna, as ANA was generally called, had been established by the correspondents of several European countries who'd hot-footed it to the south as Hitler's hordes occupied the north. I believed that. That's how naïve I was in Cairo in those days.

I took Silah with me to do some shopping, leaving Hamid in

charge of the flat. I bought shirts, ties, underwear, and was measured for a suit that would be delivered within twenty-four hours. I was surprised to find that I still had the thick end of forty pounds left. Silah knew his shops and his shopkeepers. It was an education watching him and listening to him.

I wondered what I should do about the Chevvy, which was still parked in the garage near Malika Farida. Silah had the answer to that. I could bring the car to the Immeuble Mikhanoff. There was a mechanic friend who would care for it when I wasn't using it. The organisation was pretty good. I began to feel that I'd have to stretch a bit to keep pace.

I grabbed a taxi for the hair-raising drive along the crowded Sharia Shubra, through the crazy jostle of traffic around Bab al Hadid, the driver with foot flat on the floor, one hand turning and twisting on the wheel, the other pumping away at the old bulb-horn. The taxi-owners were shrewd men. All of them disconnected the electric tooter: batteries would have been flat in an hour. Noise was the paramount factor in driving in that war-drunk city: make enough of it and at least the potential victims could never say in hospital that they hadn't been warned.

My driver jerked to a halt triumphantly. It seemed he'd established some new kind of record for the trip. In a mixture of French, English and some bastard kitchen Arabic I told him he'd die young, but while he lived he'd have fun. He didn't understand a word, I daresay, but appreciated the tip. After all, it wasn't my money.

The Nubian doorkeeper checked my Press card and pointed the way to Mortimer's office. It was at the end of a long corridor. I had to pass the glass-fronted newsroom, almost deserted at an hour when most of the correspondents would be heading for Garden City and the morning military Press conference. Only a couple of shirt-sleeved duty-men lounged at desks, while the tape machines continued to spill out the day's bad news from all over the world.

A smart young miss materialised from nowhere. I murmured my name and that of Mr Mortimer. She smiled, led me through a small office and tapped on a door marked 'Private'. She went in, closing it behind her. I waited. Then she came out, smiled again, and held the door for me. I passed through. The door shut behind me. I was in a typical editor's office. Files of newspapers, typescript, two dirty coffee-cups, stark furniture and a sheet of copy-paper acting as a light shield over the bulb hanging low above the table-desk were all familiar.

Mortimer was a big man, and at this early hour looked as if he had been working all night. He could have used a shave. His shirt was rumpled, the knot of his tie halfway down his massive chest. His sleeves were rolled up above the elbows of hairy arms. Three ashtrays on the table were full of butts, the lengths of some of them suggesting they had been impatiently smoked, extravagantly stubbed out.

'Hello,' he growled. 'At least you're punctual.'

He held out a ham-like hand. I offered mine. He brushed it aside.

'Let's see your card,' he muttered. I handed it over, feeling a bit of a clot . . . not for the first time in the last few days.

He studied it for a long time. I got the impression he was looking for something on it. I wondered what it could be.

'Sit down,' he growled. He went right on examining the card. I must take a look at that myself, I thought. I got as comfortable as I could in a chair not intended for lounging, and waited. Finally, he handed back the card. I put it in my pocket. He sat down, pursing his lips.

'You're young,' he said. There was no point in denying it. 'Much experience?'

He didn't explain in what. 'I've got by,' I said.

'I asked what experience you'd had.' His voice was like wet gravel in a concrete mixer. 'They're pros out there.' He jerked a thumb in the general direction of the newsroom. 'You've got to fit.'

Put that way, it made sense. The thought occurred to me it was a damn sight easier working for a bloke who'd got all his experience commanding a military brass band.

'I'll put you on subbing, down the table. Can't do much damage there. And you won't be missed when you've got to be in other places.' It added up. I'd been warned the night before that I'd probably be subbing. It was a job I loathed, but like all newspapermen who were learning their trade pre-war on a county weekly, I'd done my share.

'Down the table': that meant doing the war-time equivalent of marking up the rose-shows and the church fêtes. I'd probably get casualty lists and the like.

'You'll do your shift like everybody else.'

This had to be stopped. This bloke Mortimer had to be told the score. 'I've got a lunch date,' I said. 'Important.'

'I know. How long will it take?'

'Haven't any idea.'

'Then you'd better do early morning. Eight o'clock start. Through till two.'

'But what if . . .'

'Then when you *do* get here you'll get a bollocking from Carstairs.'

'Who's he?'

'He's the chief sub. A nasty man, but a bloody genius at his job. He doesn't like slackers. And if he fires you, that's it. You're out.'

'God damn it, I didn't choose to come here.'

'Maybe not. But Carstairs is a pro. Best thing you can do is butter up Chalmers, his deputy. He's a bit soft, but he's a tradesman, and Carstairs leaves a lot of the admin to him.'

I wondered how Collins would react if I got the push from Anna? It was a gloomy prospect. The glamour the thriller writers had wrapped around this espionage lark just didn't exist. Then I thought of Sophia standing in the bathroom doorway without a stitch on and I felt better.

'Come on,' said Mortimer. He stood up. 'You'd better meet Chalmers. Carstairs won't be in till noon.'

By the time Chalmers had finished with me I was fighting the clock. And I was worried. How the hell I was going to master the bloody complexities of that damned efficient agency routine I didn't know. But it had to be done. For a desperate moment I'd almost decided to ring the telephone number I'd memorised and tell whoever answered they could stuff this lot.

For Chalmers, whatever was going on outside that newsroom didn't matter except as events of a world war. These were ciphers on sheets of copy-paper, to be slotted into tight running descriptions of what the headlines were all about. He just wasn't personally involved or moved: his approach was clinically objective. A story was either good or it wasn't, well written or badly composed. Human misery and agony and suffering were lead pars to reports. He was a man of few words. And Mortimer had said Chalmers was soft! God preserve me from Carstairs.

I got the Chevvy and started the haul out to Sans Souci. I was going to be late. There was nothing I could do about it. I could only pray she'd wait. The wheels locked as I banged on the brake-pedal and the car skidded to a stop in the sand. I scrambled out, locked the doors and headed through the garden, through the bar, into the restaurant. There was no sign of her, and it was twenty past two. Now bloody what? I trudged into the bar, plonked myself on a stool and gloomily ordered a zibib.

I'd drunk half of it when a voice behind me said, 'Hello'. So much for how clever I thought I'd been, sitting with my back in a corner. I turned. She was in a new outfit, all white and green and hugging, with excitingly deep cleavage. The blonde hair gleamed where the light from the windows made a halo around her.

'You're late,' I accused her, sliding off the stool and only just resisting the temptation to grab her. Male heads were staring at us, and a couple of their women were obviously telling their escorts in some outlandish language that Sophia didn't have anything they hadn't – except Sophia maybe had it more obviously.

She shook her head. 'No. Today I was early. *You* are late.'

'You weren't here when I came in.'

'No. I was in there.' Her head jerked ever so slightly backwards. Behind a drape there was a door. I could see the last three letters of the discreetly printed 'Dames'.

'Oh,' I said.

'It is permitted, eh?' she smiled, a finger caressing her cheek.

She joined me at the bar. Over our drinks she remarked that I seemed worried. Distraught was the word she used.

'Not worried,' I said. 'Busy. I moved into a new flat last night. And this morning it was hell at the office.'

She was all eager to hear about the flat. I didn't hold anything back. And, almost casually, I dropped in the ANA bit, then made a joke about 'Anna'. I thought I might as well build up her confidence in me.

Could she see the flat, please? Of course, any time. Perhaps after lunch? Why not? That was settled.

Sophia had a gift of being able to sustain the banal in conversation. Throughout that lunch she said nothing at all, but was never silent and quite often amusing. She'd been to visit Ida and Yanni (the reason she gave for refusing to allow me to pick her up) and her account of their gypsy existence had me smiling, but added absolutely nothing to the information I had about them.

I managed to get in a question about her dinner on the

previous evening. She'd shrugged. 'My friend the Egyptian has returned. He invited me.'

She made no mention of moving, so I had to assume she was now living with him. I don't know why I should have accepted this as a fact of life. The Gyppo may have used the place only as a *pied-d'amour*: he could be married, live with a fat wife and a brood of kids in a big house at Maadi or Gezira. I decided to have him checked.

Hamid sat guard at the Immeuble Mikhanoff, but he didn't seem even a mite surprised when Sophia and I arrived. He simply unlocked the door and saluted, passed us through, then closed the door behind us. Some instinct made me listen. He didn't turn the key in the lock.

There was something matronly about Sophia exploring the flat. Her hand ran appraisingly over the drapes, the cushions. An exploring finger checked for dust. She wandered through the rooms, nodded absently when I offered her a drink. While I poured the drinks I wondered about her interest in the place. I saw with something of a shock that she was behaving as I imagined a fiancée might on the eve of her wedding. She was in the bedroom when I wandered back with the tray. She was lying full length on the bed, bouncing gently up and down. 'It is very good,' she said. 'Very comfortable. For sleeping too, I think.' The smile on her face was that of a mischievous child, fingers gently, erotically stroking the deep dimple.

I put down the tray but as I stepped towards the bed she slid teasingly away and stood up, facing me across its inviting expanse. She waggled an admonishing finger. 'The servant,' she warned in a whisper.

'He won't come in until I call him,' I said. The pressures around my loins were building up. But she still shook her head. 'Soon,' she promised.

To hell with this. 'It might upset your Egyptian friend. That it?' I asked, not bothering to keep the frustration out of my voice.

Her eyes widened. 'But I do not sleep with him,' she said. Damn it, I bloody near believed her. 'Shall we have the drinks?' she said, and led me out into the living-room.

She teased me because, she said, I was sulking. I was certainly fed up. How long was Collins going to tolerate this stalemate? It was while she was considering whether we'd have dinner together – she had a most irritating indecisiveness sometimes – that I heard the murmur of voices outside the flat. So did Sophia. Her head jerked up. 'You have a visitor?' she asked. There was a peculiar sharpness about the question.

'Not that I know of,' I said. I went to the door, jerked it open. Mortimer was standing there. He was speaking to Hamid, in Arabic.

'Ah,' he said. 'Glad you're here. Mind if I come in?'

He walked past me, not waiting for an invitation. He stopped short in the little hall when he saw Sophia, lounging in a chair, glass in hand.

'Oh,' he said. 'I'm sorry.' But he stood his ground.

I went past him. 'Sophia, this is Mr Mortimer, the slave-boss at the agency.' To him: 'Miss Kukralovic.'

Mortimer walked towards her, his face betraying nothing at all. He bent low over her outstretched hand. He brushed it with his lips. I noticed he'd shaved since our meeting that morning. He was presentable but, like all huge men, his clothes didn't sit easily on his bulk.

'Forgive me,' he said. His eyes were fixed on Sophia. She looked right back at him, her features composed and cool. Maybe she knew the effect she had on men.

Mortimer turned to me. 'Something's come up. I was passing, and thought it might save time if I dropped in. Just in case you were here.'

'I'm here,' I said, not too pleasantly.

'There's a little job in Port Said. Tomorrow. Mean spending the night there. We'll book you at the Eastern Exchange Hotel.' He pulled an envelope from his pocket. 'The details're in here.'

I took it. This situation was becoming farcical. My job was to stick with Sophia. But if my cover was going to get in the bloody way all the time, what the hell did they expect me to do?

'This isn't very convenient,' I told him. And, on the spur of the moment, I added, 'I had an appointment with Miss Kukralovic tomorrow afternoon.'

I kept my fingers crossed that she wouldn't prove me a liar.

She smiled, a finger rubbing thoughtfully against her cheek. 'It is sad, darling. But your work is important.'

I liked the sound of that 'darling'. She switched her attention to Mortimer. 'I suppose this happens many times? He must always be going away?'

Mortimer shrugged. 'We have to use the people we've got. The work must be done.' Then, to my amazement, he said, 'Why don't you take Miss Kukralovic with you? If she's free, that is. And wants to, of course.' He smiled at Sophia.

She got up, put her hands together, her eyes shining. 'Is it possible? I would love this so much. To see Port Said and the Canal. Please, please take me.'

She moved in close, her arms around me. Over her shoulder I looked at Mortimer. His face was expressionless. Had he gone stark staring bloody mad? He knew the restrictions on civilians moving through military zones. We'd be driving through ack-ack sites, the defence boxes they were building in case Rommel broke into the Delta.

Sophia's sharp teeth were nibbling gently at my ear. I almost missed the suspicion of a wink from Mortimer. 'I'll see she gets a pass as your secretary,' he said. 'Get an early start. About eight, I'd suggest. I'll have the pass sent round.'

Sophia didn't see him go. She was still working on my ear. My body rebelling, I eased away from her, followed Mortimer to the door. But it closed behind him. He hadn't looked at me again. In the living-room, Sophia was excitedly finishing her drink.

'You must take me to my flat. To get clothes. Then we shall have dinner. And tonight I shall be here with you. It must be, eh? So that we can leave early as M'sieu Mortimer wants. Oh, darling!'

She threw away the glass. It splintered against the wall. Then her arms were around me again.

'My' flat, she'd said. Take her with you, Mortimer had said. It was getting a bit much for me.

Once again, I disentangled myself, said 'Excuse me', and ripped open the envelope. Whatever was in it would have to be harmless, surely.

I stared down at the typewritten characters. 'Paul Danescu will contact you at the hotel at one o'clock. He will update you on the situation.' It wasn't signed. I frowned at it. Now who in hell was Paul Danescu? Sophia was suddenly standing at my elbow. 'There is something the matter?' she asked.

It wasn't inspiration, just frustration, but I handed her the slip of paper. I wasn't prepared for what happened then.

'Paul? Oh, we are going to see Paul!' Her mouth was open, moist and inviting. Her arms went round me again, her body pressing against mine. 'Oh, darling. How nice. How very, very nice . . .'

My face was nuzzling into her scented neck.

It was she who broke away. She waved the paper excitedly.

'It is a long time. A long, long time.'

I tried to assemble my scrambled wits. 'You know this chap?'

'But of course, darling. Many years ago, in Paris. He is a darling man. You will like him. Please, take me to my flat. I must get my nicest clothes. Paul deserves me to look pretty. Please, darling, hurry. This is so exciting I want to cry.' Far from crying she was laughing her head off, the dimple getting pretty rough treatment from the impulsive fingers.

The visit to Port Said promised to be as confusing as anything that had happened since I'd listened to that idiot Grayling, and Yanni had had his face punched in by a drunken soldier.

ELEVEN

LONDON: CHECK TO YOUR KING

Maintenance gangs on the London to Brighton railway track made the train run late. I didn't mind the delay because I certainly had plenty to think about before I saw Sara Kenyon again.

I'd spent a busy day after her invitation to the house in Hassocks. First of all, I tried to find out just exactly what Maurice Harding's job at the Ministry was. I'd never had to bother before: I'd accepted our casual acquaintance as just one of those things. Now it had become a matter of some priority. It didn't help much to learn that he was attached to the secretariat of the Defence Planning Committee. So he was close to the military people, but just at what level I couldn't quickly find out. Security classifications at individual grading weren't easily come by. But Hodges, I was willing to bet, would break through that barrier.

Harding's name wasn't listed in his local county telephone directory, and a phoned enquiry to the exchange informed me his number was unlisted. That, too, could safely be left to Hodges. At least I now knew that Harding lived in the Hassocks area. This tied up with the exchange of chess visits between him and Stapleton. Dr Luke Stapleton was listed in the directory. His surgery was at Hurstpierpoint, but his home was in the same lane as that of Commander Alexander Kenyon, RN (R'td). But in the Sussex countryside the houses could be a mile or more apart.

And now came the nitty-gritty bit. Harding was known to Stapleton as Harding. I had to assume that that was the name by which he was also known to Kenyon. It had to be his real name, because that's what he was known by at the Ministry. So why in hell complicate things by allowing Sara to believe he was a bloke named Harmsworth? How could he always time his meetings with Kenyon when Sara wasn't there? It seemed incredible that, if he'd known Kenyon for any length of time, at a period when Sara was acting as her father's secretary, they hadn't bumped into each other.

She was standing on the platform when the train finally

trundled into the little station. She was only a few yards away from my window seat and I was able to get another good look at her as her eyes swept along the coaches looking for me. My belly muscles tightened. She was something of a genetic miracle, as much like her mother as if they'd been identical twins. Sara had the same flair for wearing clothes, a body as shapely and as firm. In appearance, she had a look about her that seemed only a step away from innocence. Sophia had had it, too. Sophia and innocence? That had been a laugh. But Sara? There had to be something screwy. Why else was Hodges so bloody interested? I didn't feel happy that I'd got the thing off the ground on the flimsiest of hunches.

Sara had moved away a pace or two, eyes still searching. I took a deep breath, opened the door and stepped down on to the platform. She must have sensed the movement, because she turned, saw me, smiled, a hand caressing her cheek. God help me, I wanted to cry . . .

The house was very old, standing back from the lane in tree-shaded grounds of lawns and flower beds and a tiny pond. She drove the Mini up to the front with easy expertise, bringing it to a stop on the gravel without hint of slide or skid or shudder.

During the two-mile drive from the station she hadn't mentioned the purpose of my visit. Instead, she'd prattled on about the countryside, pointing out places of historical or scenic note. And when we'd passed a half-timbered place that looked ersatz to me she'd casually said: 'One of daddy's chess buddies lives there. He's our doctor, too.' She'd laughed, one hand leaving the wheel to touch the dimple. 'Daddy's one of the healthiest retired commanders the Navy's ever known. Dr Stapleton really keeps him fit.'

So that was Stapleton's house. I wondered idly which of the other places we'd seen belonged to Harding.

Whoever had been responsible for the furnishing and decorating of the Kenyon home had to be congratulated on taste. It had everything, including an atmosphere of lived-in cosiness.

Sara left me in the comfortable lounge while she went to get some coffee. I tried to visualise Sophia in these surroundings and couldn't. The image of her just didn't fit. Yet Sara was obviously at home. Damn it, it *was* her home. But had it been Sophia's? This troubled me. I don't know why. Sara here, yes;

Sophia, no. Now why? Here were two women of such startlingly similar physical characteristics and mannerisms, yet so wildly different against a given background.

Sara put the tray on a coffee-table and sat behind it, facing me. Some tension was building up inside her. Her hands trembled slightly as she manipulated pot and cups and cream-jug and sugar-bowl. I stirred my coffee, took a proffered biscuit and waited. Let her make the first move. I was happy just sitting there, drinking in remembered beauty. She sipped the liquid, winced. I should have warned her. The coffee was hot. She put the cup and saucer on the table, leaned forward.

'Please, can't I see it now?'

I took my time putting down the coffee and the biscuit. I reached for my wallet, fingered the fading picture. Then I pulled it out, handed it across the table. Her hand was rock-steady as she took it from me. I put the wallet back in my pocket, my eyes not leaving her. She stared down at Sophia. I saw and heard the little spontaneous suck of breath. Suddenly she held the photograph in both hands. I could see the pressure of her fingers gripping the edges. She sat very still for what seemed like a long time, then she sighed, a slow exhalation of breath, got up and walked slowly to one of the mullioned huge windows, still concentrating on Sophia's likeness.

She stood in profile to the light. I was able to admire her again, and wish I were a few years younger. Then she looked at me, holding out the photograph, its back facing me.

'May I?' she asked. I nodded.

She read the inscription in the spidery handwriting. It took only a moment, and she raised her eyes. 'You must have known her very well.'

I shrugged. 'Yes, I suppose so.' It can't have been the message that suggested the thought to her.

'It was taken specially for you, wasn't it?'

I thought back to the circumstances in which Sophia had given me the photograph. In a screwball sort of way Sara was right. So I nodded again.

'Were you in love, the two of you?'

What the hell could I say to that? Tell her Sophia was just a nice bit of tail? Or that it was all just a job of war-time work? Or the truth, which was that I didn't bloody well know whether I'd loved her mother or not. I compromised. 'I liked her very much,' I said. She noticed the hesitation, but didn't pursue that gambit, thank God.

She walked slowly back to the table. The coffee was forming an ugly skin as it cooled. She noticed this and clicked her tongue.

'I'll get some fresh,' she offered. I was glad of the break. It would give me time to decide how I was going to handle this Sophia business. She went out with the tray, leaving the photograph on her side of the table.

I was sitting there thinking about it when the door from the hall opened. The man who came in was tall, distinguished-looking, about sixty – perhaps a year or two more than that. There wasn't much flesh on his frame. His hair and trim goatee beard were white, his skin the colour of tanned leather. Only his voice betrayed any surprise he felt at seeing a guest in the house. 'Oh, I beg your pardon!'

I stood up. I had to remember Sara knew me as Freeman. Be daft if I introduced myself by another name, wouldn't it?

'My name is Kenyon,' he said. 'I saw Sara's car outside.' He waited, a question unspoken.

'She met me at the station. I'm a friend of hers. The name's Freeman.'

Kenyon pursed his lips, didn't offer to shake hands. He came further into the room, as Sara backed through a swing-door holding the tray. She turned and saw her father. Quite deliberately she put the tray on the table. 'If you want coffee I'll get another cup,' she said. Her tone was coldly formal – not as I'd have expected a daughter to speak to her father.

'Don't bother,' he said. 'I wouldn't want to break up a tête-à-tête.' There was an edge to his voice that made me uncomfortable.

'As you wish,' Sara said. She stood by the table. I stood there, too, feeling like something a dog had dragged in.

Kenyon shrugged, turned and walked out into the hall. After he'd closed the door, I asked Sara: 'Am I in the way?'

She shook her head. 'Let me pour you some hot coffee,' she suggested and sat down. I sank back into the chair. Sara poured the coffee, gave me the cup and picked up the photograph again. She studied it for a long time. I helped myself to sugar, stirred the coffee, sipped it. This was going to be tougher than I'd thought. Maybe Kenyon was all sweetness and light as far as Harding and Stapleton were concerned, but he didn't like me.

As I sat there, sipping the coffee, watching Sara try to

capture something of her unknown mother through the likeness on a fading piece of card, the thought suddenly struck me that Kenyon might have seen the photograph. Sara had left it on the table when she went out to the kitchen. If it was true what she'd told me — that her father refused to discuss Sophia — then he'd associate my visit with his former wife. I twisted my head. No, it was unlikely he could have seen it: I'd been standing between him and the table in the few moments he'd been in the room.

'You were right,' Sara said. 'She was very beautiful.'

The inanity just popped out. 'Like mother, like daughter.' She smiled politely.

I cleared my throat. 'Look,' I said. 'Your father: he didn't seem deliriously happy when he found me here.'

'It doesn't matter,' she said. Her eyes dropped again to the picture. Without looking up she said, 'Tell me about her.'

I rubbed my hand over my eyes. Where the hell was I to start? Then I became conscious of something. I took my hand away. She was staring at me. Her eyes were fixed on me. Her face was very still.

'You don't want to, do you?'

She was bloody right I didn't.

'You promised, you know.' There was an accusing edge to her voice. True! I had. That didn't make it any easier now.

She stood up, slowly. She still clutched the photograph. I had a feeling I wasn't going to get it back. To gain time, I drained my cup, put it back on its saucer.

'Why?' she asked.

'It . . . well, it's complicated.'

I stood up, facing her. I was half a head taller than she was. It made me feel better.

'Was there something you were ashamed of?'

Was there something I was ashamed of? God, what a question that was. I must have been out of my tiny mind coming down here.

'Or were you ashamed of her? Was that it? Are you trying to . . . to tell me that my . . . my mother was . . . was . . .'

The question dribbled away. Her lower lip trembled. She took it quickly between her sharp white teeth. It sounds daft, but I did what seemed a very natural thing to do. I stepped round that table quickly, put my arm round her shoulders and hugged her, not too tightly, just enough to . . . well, comfort her. I was feeling lousy. She snuggled her head into my

95

shoulder. My free hand gently massaged the side of her neck. Maybe I imagined it, but I thought I felt her body press more closely against mine.

'She was a very remarkable woman,' I murmured into the ordered jungle of her blonde hair. 'There wasn't anything to be ashamed of.' At least that was true enough, as far as it went. 'On either side.' I decided to shut up. This was getting into the realms of fantasy. I was fighting the temptation to put my hand under her chin, raise her face, kiss those full red lips. That's when she raised her face, eased her body up on her toes and kissed the corner of my mouth – not passionately, but not casually either. Then she gently eased away from me. She took my hand, led me to a huge settee and sank down on it. She pulled me down beside her.

'Tell me,' she whispered. 'Tell me. I want to know everything . . .'

I refused her invitation to lunch. It was half-past twelve. I felt drained. And I badly needed to talk to Hodges. For more than an hour I'd told Sara a story that nicely blended fact and fiction – or I devoutly hoped it had. She hadn't queried it, anyway. She'd asked questions, but none that weren't easily parried. But I'd had enough for one session, though on a more personal basis I'd have stayed cheerfully enough. I kept telling myself I wasn't all that much older than she was. After all, Sophia had been quite a bit older than me in Cairo. But there was a lot I wanted straightened out, and only Hodges could do that for me.

She tried once more to persuade me to stay. But, looking past her, through the windows I could see her father. He was pacing slowly across the lawn. At his side was Dr Luke Stapleton. I knew a moment of panic. The doctor didn't know me as Freeman. So what was going to happen when Sara and I went out to her car parked in the drive?

'What's the matter?' Sara wanted to know. She swung round, following my rather fixed stare. Then she laughed. 'Gracious, you don't have to worry about him. He's one of the chess gang. You know, the doctor who lives down the lane.'

I watched the two men turn towards the house. 'Is there any other way out of here?' I asked Sara, my voice sharper than it need to have been.

She frowned. 'Of course. But why . . .'

'Look, don't ask questions. Just take me out some other

way. I'll find my own way to the station.'

'But it's two miles. You can't . . .'

'I don't want to meet that chap with your father. That's all.'
She was puzzled. 'Oh, very well,' she snapped. 'Come on.'

I followed her out through a back hall, the kitchen and into
a vegetable garden. 'Go out through that gate and wait on the
track. I'll bring the car round.'

I wanted to tell her not to bother, but she pushed me towards the gate and went back into the house.

She was right. It wasn't much more than a track, but it
would take a car if the driver knew what he was about. Blast
Hodges. But especially blast Harding. Bugger the two of them.
I was getting out of my depth.

It seemed an age before the Mini nosed its way from
around the old stone wall and drew up beside me. Sara's face
was tight. She flung open the passenger door. I got in beside
her. She jerked away, dangerously I thought on such a rutted
surface. She drove savagely. I didn't have much chance of asking why: I was busy just holding my balance in the little
bucket seat. Her driving didn't improve, even on the main road
into Hassocks. There was anger bubbling out of every pore of
her lovely skin. What the hell now? I wondered. 'Hadn't you
better take it easy?' I suggested. She ignored me, just concentrated on the road. I felt grateful for that. We skidded to a
stop outside the station. She didn't switch off the engine. Just
leaned across me and jerked the door open. I swung my legs
out, turned my head towards her.

'What's the matter?'

'I don't like liars, Mr *Freeman*.' The way she emphasised
the name made my belly roll over. 'And I have a message for
you. I don't know what it means but Dr Stapleton obviously
does, and I can only assume you will. He told me to tell you,
Check to your king. That's all. And now, if you'll get out,
I'll . . .'

'Just a minute.' The rage inside me burst its dams. 'What
the hell is he talking about? I don't know what he's talking
about. Doesn't mean anything to me. Look, is there anywhere
we can go? How about the pub over . . .'

'Go back to London, Mr *Freeman*. I don't know what you're
up to. I don't want to know. Just get out of my car and go
away.'

'If you'd listen for just a . . .'

'Listen? I've been listening to you for far too long. You and your fairy tales.' She was trembling. 'You and your beautiful friendship with my mother. You come down here pretending you're somebody else, spin a tissue of lies about knowing my mother . . .' She swallowed hard. 'Oh, get out. Get out!' She took her hands off the wheel and beat her fists against my chest.

I got out, slammed the door, watched her skid the Mini in a tight circle and roar off, gears grating.

All that Hodges had said on the phone was: 'I'll be in the Horse and Groom at seven.' And then he'd hung up.

I was in my local at half-past six and sank two large whiskies to feed my anger. There wasn't anything Hodges could do in a place as crowded as a pub on a Saturday night. So he'd have to listen. I was minus too much: like a photograph I'd had a peculiar attachment to; like the promise of friendship with Sara Kenyon; like the craziest cover any man had ever been given. It'd been blown right out of the window. And I wanted to know why.

Right on the dot Hodges edged through the swing doors. He didn't make the mistake of just standing there looking for me; he went straight up to the bar, ordered something – it had to be lemonade – and looked around casually while he waited for his order. I was crouched over a table in the corner, my third scotch in front of me. He saw me. We ignored each other. That was all part of this schoolboy business. I watched Hodges go to a table, indicate a chair. The man with the two women shook his head, held out a protective hand, nodded towards the bar. Hodges went through the apology bit, drifted to another vacant chair. The comedy was repeated. Eventually he reached me.

'Anyone using this?'

I shook my head. He sat down. He stared at the dying bubbles in his glass of lemonade.

'Full tonight,' he said.

'Not nearly as full as I bloody am,' I whispered, wearing my brightest and most impersonal smile.

'Glad you don't mind me sitting here,' he said. Not too loudly but loud enough.

Still smiling, I muttered that I hoped he'd still think so when I'd finished.

I drained my scotch. 'Have another?' he invited me. I shook my head. 'Want an early night.' I stood up. To hell with all this nonsense. I yawned prodigiously – might as well make it look good. 'Been a long day,' I said, and threaded my way out through the packed tables.

Let the bastard come to me, on my ground.

He still played it his way. I waited in the bed-sitter for more than an hour before I heard the tap at the door. He wasn't pleased with me, and said so, in that flat, clipped voice.

'And what the hell do you lot think you're doing to me?' I asked. I was good and mad. And I didn't stop talking for a good twenty minutes. I started with meeting Harding at the Tavern bar, the call on Stapleton, Sara Kenyon's invitation. I told him that Stapleton must have blown the gaff on me to Sara. And where the hell was I supposed to go from here? His face didn't change much during the telling. He sat hunched in my easy chair while I either perched on a straight-backed wreck, stalked the room, or thumped myself down on the bed.

'Oh, and there's something else. Stapleton gave Sara a message for me. "Tell your friend," he said, "check to your king." ' I drew breath, sat down again on the bed. 'All right. Over to you.'

The hooded eyes flickered open. They stared at me – hard, unblinking.

'The message. It was "Check to your king" you say?'

I nodded. 'Now look here, Hodges. You can count me out of this bloody nonsense. That girl Kenyon's only interested in her mother. What the hell Stapleton's up to, I don't know. And I don't bloody care. As for Harding, he can get stuffed. Like you can get stuffed. I must've been off my nut seeing you in the first place.'

'Check to your king,' Hodges said. He got up out of the chair. I got up, too. I wasn't going to be caught sitting on my chuff if he was going to start some of his pushing.

'I've had some of our people do some checking. Now we'll have to do some more. Just because you weren't bright.'

There was a crackle in his voice. I backed off, an arm out-stretched.

He took no notice. Just stood there. 'Why didn't you contact me after you'd met Stapleton?'

'Because my brief was Sara Kenyon. That's why. Just Sara Kenyon. You always reckoned I buggered up the Sophia thing because I nosed around too much. Okay. This time I'm not nosing. I'm not bloody doing anything. Just count me out. As of now.'

'You're still the hyphen,' he said. 'You're in. You stay in.' He sat down again. I stayed on my feet. I didn't trust Hodges.

'Sit down,' he said. I hesitated. 'Sit!' he barked. I sat, like a bloody obedient Labrador. Right then I'd have liked to be a dog. I'd have bitten the bastard.

'You're going to listen. And listen good. All right, you buggered up the Sophia thing. This time you're going to do it right.'

TWELVE

CAIRO: APPOINTMENT IN PORT SAID

The Chevvy droned north-east along the Ismailia road. Our destination was Port Said, to make contact with Paul Danescu, a man Sophia already knew. But Port Said was a long way ahead of us. I stole a glance at her, relaxed in the passenger seat, looking out at the northern outskirts of Shubra. I was glad our eyes didn't meet. It hadn't been a good night. God knows what sort of a mug she thought I was.

'It will be so nice,' said Sophia. I grunted. 'Paul is so strong. A very strong man.'

Go on, I thought. Rub it in.

'Look,' I said. 'It won't be a party up there. It's a job. This bloke Danescu and me . . . we'll have things to do.'

'Not all night, darling,' she said, and leaned across and nibbled gently at the lobe of my ear. I jerked away, keeping my eyes on a camel-train that was wobbling along ahead of the car.

There was a tinkle of laughter. She leaned up against the window. So she thought I was a joke. All right, maybe I wasn't in her class. I'd always been used to women who let me make the pace in bed. And I'd never had much time for all the razzamatazz of variety in the cot. It had always been just a matter of getting her down there, get on with it and snore off till you were ready for the next one. But my night with Sophia hadn't been like that at all. We'd picked up her things at the Dopolavoro building. Back at my place Hamid had brought in some food and we'd picnicked. Then it all started to happen . . .

She wanted a shower. And Sophia taking off her clothes was something not to be forgotten. The pros in the strip clubs would've paid a lot to learn just a bit of her presentation. Twice I sort of got carried away but she was spry on her feet. Then she stood for a moment caressing those lovely limbs before she drifted out to the shower-room. Above the hiss of the water I heard her singing. She wasn't any opera star, but the husky voice was throatily tuneful. It was a sad song in a language I'd never heard before. While I listened I stripped off my own clothes, wrapped a thin dressing-gown round me, and waited. My loins were starting to ache from the pressures. Christ, would she never bloody well finish in that shower box . . .

The flow of water stopped. 'Bring my dressing-case, darling.'

There it was, beside the small suitcase. I grabbed it and damn near ran out through the hall. She stood, wrapped coyly in the huge bath towel. About all I could see were the smiling eyes and pink, well-manicured toes. I put the case down.

'And my robe, please. It's in the other case.'

There was a momentary stirring of rebellion. I wasn't going to be ordered round like a bloody servant. I looked at her again. I went and got the robe. I kidded myself it would give me a chance to see what she'd packed for the Port Said trip. The silk robe was on the top. I took it out. Then, trying not to disturb the other fripperies, my hand explored through the contents. Nothing: neither passport nor pistol. I stood up and turned. She was standing in the doorway, still swathed in the towel. She was cradling the dressing-case. She didn't say anything. It seemed as if it was my move. The delicate eyebrows puckered a question.

'You have some lovely things,' I said. It was the best I could do on the spur of a bloody embarrassing moment.

'Yes,' she said. Then, 'You are very inquisitive.'

'Have to be in my trade,' I laughed. That didn't get me far. 'Oh, come on! You asked me to get your robe. All right: here it is.' I'd been standing there like a dummy, holding the flimsy silk.

She put the dressing-case down on the bed very deliberately, and accepted the dressing-gown. She just stood there, holding it, waiting to hear something better than I'd come up with so far.

'Honest, it was just that . . . well, you know. Something about women's things that sort of get at a man. I saw them there and . . .'

The towel dropped from her body; she slid away from my suddenly clutching hands and shrugged into the lightweight robe. The sombre suspicion was still stamping her features into a mask of denial. She knotted the sash.

To hell with her. I walked out of the bedroom, remembering to slam the door behind me. Angry with her and myself, I poured myself a big zibib, splashed in an ounce of water and got stuck into it. I was glad Collins and that tough side-kick of his weren't seeing the balls-up I was making. The tough lad had made no bones about what they wanted. Right here in this room he'd asked me how good I was. I'd told him I'd never had any complaints. Well, I was sure getting them now. And I hadn't even got into bed with her yet. It was all pretty bleak.

The war seemed a long way away. None of us could even be sure that Sophia and Ida and Yanni were part of it, other than as victims. For the first conscious moment in my life I felt a sense of guilt. Conscience jabbed. Why should I, young and healthy, be sitting in a comfortable Cairo flat, getting all het up because I wasn't cuddled up in bed with a desirable female? It didn't seem much of a price to pay for safety and good living. But if, on the other hand, Sophia was one of the small army of cleverly trained people the Nazis were infiltrating with the refugees, maybe my job had some importance. So a bloody big raspberry to conscience. And what the hell was my next move to be? Perhaps another zibib would help. I got it, and sipped it faster than good sense suggested, which left me without any firm decision but at least eased my frustration. Halfway through the third drink I'd decided to play it her way. Let her make the running. And to hell with Collins and his hard boys.

It was late when I didn't want any more zibib. All I wanted was sleep. I wasn't walking too steadily and my head was aching. In a confused sort of way I thought I'd stretch out on the settee. Then I changed my fuddled mind. This was my flat, wasn't it? Well, I was living in the bloody thing. And in the next room was a bed. All right, she was in it. If she didn't like me sleeping there let her have the settee.

I kidded myself I opened the bedroom door silently. She'd opened the shutters and a shaft of moonlight bathed the bed in whiteness. The clicking and the creak had disturbed her. She stirred, then rolled from her side on to her back. She was covered only by a thin sheet. Covered? Her blonde hair spilled over the pillow. One arm was doubled back, resting beside it; the other fell at right angles to her body. Her breasts jutted upwards. The sheet clung closely to what else it covered.

Her eyelids flickered. Her lips moved. I had to strain to catch the murmured words. 'You were so long. I waited. I am sorry. I fell asleep.'

I stood there. Like an ape. I felt saliva dribble out of the corner of my mouth. Silently, I cursed the bloody Arabs for inventing zibib and me for drinking so much of it. I swallowed back the vomit that kept choking up into my throat.

Maybe, once I was in that bed, beside her, it would be all right ...

My dressing-gown fell where I stood. I stumbled to the bed, flopped on to it, my neck resting on the outstretched arm. She completed the roll of her body, the other arm sliding around my shoulders. Her eyes, still full of sleep, were closed, but the lips parted, slowly and sensually. I banged my mouth against them, pushed her on to her back and struggled on to her.

My hands groped and tugged and pushed. She gasped in shock and pain. It was an all-time disaster.

Free of Cairo, we made better time along the Ismailia road. We overtook several military convoys to the accompaniment of wolf whistles from women-hungry troops impressed by Sophia's smile and waving hand. She seemed only mildly curious in a touristy sort of way about the insignia on lorries and uniforms. But when, in the distance, she saw the sky-pointing snouts of an ack-ack battery she asked me to slow down. My foot eased back from the accelerator.

'Want to spend a penny?' I asked.

For all her command of English there were some idioms and colloquialisms which baffled her. This was one of them. I tried to explain, but she wasn't paying much attention. Her eyes were fastened on those distant guns. I waited for the questions. None came. Slowly, I increased speed. She didn't object.

At least she hadn't yet referred back to the shambles of the previous night. I was grateful for that. First there had been anger, then ridicule. The two or three minutes of wild thresh-ing that had followed my forcing my unwilling body on to hers had been a ghastly experience. It had churned up my already queasy stomach. I'd had to lurch to the bathroom to be dis-gustingly sick and then face the humiliation of going back into the bedroom. As I'd slunk on to the bed she'd slipped out on the other side, angrily pulled on her robe and told me her opinion of young boys who got drunk and confused rape with love-making.

We weren't far from the Canal when she transferred her attention from the dreary desert outside to something on the dashboard. I got a bit nervous.

'What's wrong?'

'I am watching the speedometer,' she said.

I glanced down. It looked normal enough. The needle was registering just over eighty kilometres.

'Am I driving too fast?'

She shook her head. 'When I tap your arm, stop the car,' she ordered.

So. Stop the car, she said. I looked around the landscape. Sand and rock; in the far distance a camel-train, threading its ungainly way to the south. It couldn't be a rendezvous with anyone. The road was empty ahead of us, behind us. I looked again at the speedometer: normal.

'It will be soon,' she said.

This didn't make any sense. A gentle tap on my arm. My reaction was slow.

'Now,' she said, urgently. 'Stop now!'

I slammed on the brakes. The car slithered in some sand wind-blown across the bitumen.

'See, she said, and pointed at the speedometer. 'The numbers.'

Three. Three. Three. Three. Three. And on the trip meter another Three.

'Please,' she said. Her hands were reaching for my face. I switched off the ignition, twisted in the seat. Then her hands were behind my neck and her mouth was moving softly against mine. The tip of a tongue caressed inside my lips. I fought the temptation to grab and maul. I responded as carefully as my impatience would permit: this time I would try not to make mistakes.

The hangover was cured in those moments of tongue-probing bliss. She guided my hand on to the silk blouse where it stretched taut over a full breast. I could feel the nipple erect. My fingers explored it. Her hand stroked my thigh. I writhed a little in the seat. Then she drew back and her fingers caressed the dimple formed by her smile.

'That is all,' she said. And meant it. 'We drive now.'

'But . . .' I wanted to ask why, and why here, in this barren place.

'It was always like that. When the numbers were the same. Wherever it happened, we always stopped. And kissed.'

Whoever the other half of the 'we' was had been short-changed. He'd had to wait a bloody long time between kisses.

'Who's we?' I demanded. A hint of jealousy mightn't do any harm.

'My husband,' she said. As simply as that.

I started the engine, engaged the gears and pushed on.

I heard a giggle. 'Once it happened in Piccadilly Circus. That was very funny. The traffic became confused.'

That seemed the understatement of the century. Funny? It must have been a yell. Husband? Piccadilly Circus? Gently, I warned myself, for God's sake tread softly.

'Wonder to me you weren't arrested,' I offered.

'A policeman was very stern with us.' That I could have bet on. She giggled again. 'But he was very sweet. We were very young. And I was *enceinte*: very big.'

So she was pregnant. Out of the corner of my eye I watched her expressive hands shaping the full roundness of how she had been when she stopped the traffic in the heart of London. 'It was very funny. But my husband, he wore a uniform better than the policeman's, so he did nothing to us.'

I drove on in silence, willing Sophia to keep on chatting. Go on, go on, go on, I wanted to yell at her, but her attention was starting to drift again, to the scene outside the windows of the speeding car.

'What uniform is better than a policeman's?' I prompted.

'Oh, many of them,' she laughed. 'Any uniform, I think, is better than a policeman's.'

So I wasn't very subtle.

'You wish to know what uniform my husband wore, I think,' Sophia said.

The only alternative was to lie. I shrugged. 'So your husband was a bus conductor. It doesn't matter.' I hoped that might pique her. She looked about as much like a bus conductor's wife as I looked like the Queen of Sheba. Then I wondered why I'd used the past tense. I'd said, 'Your husband *was* a bus conductor'. Maybe her husband was still around somewhere, and because the traffic had been 'in confusion' in Piccadilly Circus didn't necessarily mean he was English. There was nothing I could do but hope she'd carry on.

'What is that?' she asked, pointing.

Far away, close to the bank of the Canal, was a village of military tents. I didn't know. And said so.

'I thought people who worked on newspapers knew everything,' she taunted.

'We know exactly what we are told. That's why I know so little about you.' That, I thought, might keep the boat sailing.

She laughed, deep in her throat, a delicious gurgling that

made me want to grab her and tear her clothes off. 'But you know everything,' she protested. 'I am the wife of a bus conductor. You have seen me without clothes. You have been in my bed.'

In *her* bed! I was beginning to have a hearty respect for Sophia Kukralovic.

'What more is there to know?'

I took my time about answering. 'Only what you want to tell me.' It was a compromise, but direct interrogation wasn't going to get me anywhere.

She suddenly seemed to lose interest in the conversation. She watched the distant tents until we lost them behind sand dunes, and then concentrated on the black dullness of the bitumen strip ahead of us, shimmering in the morning sunshine.

We made good time to Port Said. It was barely noon when I parked outside the old pile of the Eastern Exchange Hotel, a brown blot with verandahs surrounding each of its floors. At the desk I identified myself and Sophia to the Egyptian clerk. Yes, reservations had been arranged. We signed the guest cards, showed our passes, and a lively young lad grabbed our baggage and led us, helped by a spate of Arabic, to the lift. It was a glass-sided affair, operated by a steel rope. Sophia stared at it doubtfully. 'It is safe?'

I murmured assurances I didn't feel. The old man who operated it wheezed and puffed on the rope, our youthful porter making what must have been hilarious jokes about his performance. For his pains the lad got a cuff on the head, and we were put out on the second floor to the accompaniment of curses from the old man and wails from the boy. I scattered some piastres and a measure of peace was restored.

Sophia's room was next to mine. It was only when I got inside my room that I realised a door connected the two, through what the brochure would have described, I suppose, as a bathroom. I was staring at the archaic tub, the hole-in-the-floor loo, and the ubiquitous bidet, when Sophia's head appeared through the door from her room. The bath didn't impress her very much, either. She turned on a faucet. The water was hot but it spurted a bit spasmodically.

'I will have a bath,' she said. I was to become resigned to her mania for bodily cleanliness. 'Wait for me in the bar.'

I unpacked. It took about three minutes flat. Then I went

downstairs. With luck I might meet Paul Danescu before she came down.

One o'clock came. Fifteen minutes later I was still at the corner table which gave me a field of view of the front lobby and the staircase, but not of the lift. No one had asked for me at the desk. The clerk knew where I was: he could see me. And Sophia hadn't shown up. For the third time in a quarter of an hour I strolled out to the clerk. No, m'sieu, no one had called for me. The mam'selle? Ah, but she had gone out, he thought. When? Oh, perhaps ten, fifteen minutes earlier. Why hadn't he told me? Resentfully, he reminded me that I hadn't asked. How could she have gone out? I persisted. I could see the lobby from where I sat. The mam'selle came out of the lift and went out through the side door. Rubbing it in, the clerk said I had told him I was waiting for a M'sieu Danescu. I had said nothing about waiting for the mam'selle. Leaving him to his injured dignity I tried not to run to the side door, which was down a little passage on the other side of the lift. Cursing myself, I went out into the street. In the bustle of traffic and pedestrians I couldn't see Sophia: with fifteen minutes' start she could be anywhere in the town.

And what the hell had happened to Danescu? He was supposed to contact me at one o'clock. It was now almost twenty-past. Maybe he was waiting at the front entrance to the hotel. I walked briskly around the corner and hurried to the main doors. I went inside. The clerk saw me come in, rather coldly and rudely indicated the bar I had just left. I went across to it. At a table just inside the door was Sophia. Fingers rubbing the dimple, she was laughing at something the man with her had said. He had his back to me. As Sophia threw back her head, she saw me. She quickly got to her feet.

'Darling, we have looked everywhere for you,' she said. A stranger would have believed her.

She ran forward, took my hand in hers and led me to the table. The man had got to his feet. 'This is Paul,' Sophia said. 'You are supposed to meet him.' She'd really taken command. I could have throttled her, cheerfully.

Paul Danescu smiled, all white teeth and pencil-thin black moustache. He bowed, from the waist, with a suggestion of clicking heels, just as the Germans always did in the movies. He was handsome in a perfumed sort of way. His clothes were good, rather better than one would have expected a journalist could afford.

'How do you do?'

He held out a slim hand. I shook it perfunctorily and sat down. Sophia looked at me quizzically, shrugged and drew herself up another chair. Danescu, too, seemed a little put out at my deliberate boorishness. He sat down, but only after fussing with Sophia's chair.

'Sophia won't be staying,' I said. Turning to her, 'I want to talk to Mr Danescu,' I said. 'Go and have a look at the shops.'

'But that is not necessary,' she pouted. 'Paul is my friend.'

'This is newspaper business,' I reminded her.

'But it is not important,' she insisted. 'He has already told me what it is about. Let us have some drinks together. He just wishes to tell you some dull story about ships coming to Suez to take away soldiers. So let us drink and be happy.'

THIRTEEN

LONDON: SACRIFICE A PAWN

By the time Hodges had left my flat I knew I was stuck with a lot of jigsaw pieces without even the clue of what the finished picture should look like. I'd listened to him: I didn't have any choice. A persuasive bastard: that was Hodges. When he'd first mentioned that the Sophia Kukralovic file hadn't been closed when they hurried me out of Cairo all those years ago, I hadn't been really surprised. But what did shatter me was the news that the file was still active. I was still struggling with this an hour after he'd gone. After all, it had been Eppler who was the big fish. But my brief had been Sophia. And, God help me, I'd done my best. If only they'd told me; but they never had, not even now. They were handing out just enough gen to get me into big trouble if I cocked any part of it up – big trouble with them as well as with God knows who else.

I'd been daft to go haring round to see Hodges after I'd seen Sara in the club. But that's how reflexes work when you've had anything to do with the Shop. And the bastards trade on it. They don't give a damn for people like me. Just so long as the machine keeps on grinding, churning out its own brand of destruction, somebody somewhere is happy. About the one good thing I'd enjoyed while Hodges was with me was watching him trying to figure out how much he had to tell me. He was in a jam, and he bloody well knew it. That's why I wouldn't help him. I made him spell it all out. Christ, how I enjoyed watching him wriggle. It made the bastard seem human. He'd hummed and hawed while I sat there, as thick as two short planks. If he'd had half an excuse he'd have pushed my face in. So I was careful not to be silly.

He'd said, 'All right, you buggered up the Sophia thing. This time you're going to do it right . . .'

I memorised that bit. 'Cause if anything went screwy he was going to carry the can. As far as I was concerned it was going to be his briefing that crapped it. That's why I wanted to know it all in words of two syllables. Not that it added up to so much. It seemed that while the politicians were re-drawing the map of Europe after the war one factor had remained constant.

The 'other side' always seemed to know a bit more about British and American intentions than what they were told in diplomatic exchanges. Even the 'other side' changed its identity. Once it had been the Axis Powers; then, suddenly, it was the Soviet Union; later, and more oddly, it had been France. And it wasn't only military stuff that was seeping out. In peacetime, economic planning had its own important role. This, too, was disappearing through holes in the Iron Curtain, surviving the currents of the English Channel. According to Hodges, the latest teaser was that there had had to be a bit of trans-Atlantic explaining. The United States were getting a bit uptight about leaks which their intelligence people swore were originating in London. And, finally, Big Business was complaining. The boys in the boardrooms were buttonholing their favourite cabinet ministers and filling their ears with dire warnings of what would happen to the balance of payments, the employment situation, and the economy in general if somebody wasn't stopped from shooting his mouth off.

By the time Hodges had finished handing me this as if he was distributing Koh-i-noor diamonds from his own personal vault, I was wanting to laugh. Christ, in Cairo it had all been so simple: just them and us, just a matter of nabbing the traffickers across the political no-man's-land. But chuck me the world and economics and big business and the brand new technological miracle hardware of the military and it had to stop being my scene. I told Hodges that. I told him that all he needed was a couple of James Bonds and everything would be just fine and dandy. But me? I was a bloody clerk in a Ministry. And maybe lucky to be that.

He didn't get mad at me. Just sat there, gloomy as hell, muttering about me being a hyphen. They had to use me. He said it as if he hated having to say it. That far, he stayed right in character. Then he said, 'Pawns can win chess games.'

Jesus, I wondered: did everybody play the bloody game?

It seemed a lot of people did. That's why Hodges had jumped on the message from Stapleton: 'Check to your king.' Okay, when Sara had chucked the words at me they didn't make any sense. Maybe Hodges knew something I didn't which meant he didn't have to know much. He stumbled a bit over his explanation of why the phrase seemed to have some significance. One of his men had been in a pub. He'd been watching two customers playing chess. One of them had murmured, 'Check to your king'. The strange thing was, according to Hodges' man, the opponent's king wasn't in check. Maybe the spectator didn't know much about the game? Hodges dismissed that. 'He could give me a rook and still beat me.' He said it in the tone of voice which implied 'I'm good, but he's better.' For Hodges to admit a thing like that, it had to be true.

I had to prompt Hodges. 'And then? Your man says the king wasn't in check . . .'

'That was about it,' said Hodges. 'My man stuck around. But the two players just carried on with the game, normally. Seems they didn't talk much – certainly not about anything other than chess.'

'So?'

Hodges ground his teeth. I'd forgotten that habit of his when he was puzzled. 'I don't know. It just worries us.' Suddenly he stood up, stared down at me, stabbing a finger viciously. 'Maybe you know.'

I couldn't help it. I pressed back against the chair. The butterflies started fluttering in my belly. 'Why the hell should I? If your bloke didn't make sense of it how can I?' I blustered a bit. 'Christ, I'm not one of your tame James Bonds.'

He held the pose which would have been ridiculous on television but bloody terrifying when it was there right in front of you. Then he relaxed. He moved about restlessly. At last he sat down, and I let the breath I'd been holding escape in a long sigh.

'Look,' I said. 'How about we start again? Where does Harding figure in all this? What was all the hanky-panky of *you* calling me Freeman? And how the hell did Harding get in on it? And why call himself Harmsworth? And deny it next day? Why the visit to Stapleton? Why bloody well why all this crazy circus?'

I always felt better when I could push Hodges on to the defensive. But all he said was, 'We're working on Harding.'

'That's not good enough, Hodges. Christ, man, none of it makes any sort of sense. Here's Harding . . . known to Kenyon as Harding . . . yet he's known to Sara as Harmsworth. God damn it, he plays chess with Kenyon. He visits the place. He couldn't control when he'd bump into her. It's . . . well, it's daft. A bloody school-kid could do better than that . . .'

For some reason he remained quite placid. 'There was good reason why we wanted you known as Freeman to the girl.'

'Well, she knows different now. Thanks to Mr bloody Stapleton. So where does that put me?'

He smiled bleakly and without humour. 'We'll have to work on that, too.'

'You don't need to. She's scrubbed me, like a dirty shirt. She can drop dead so far as I'm concerned,' I lied.

'You'll see her again. It's necessary. You, God help us, are all we've got.'

'Crap.'

'It's true.' He still spoke quietly, but the crackle was creeping into the voice. 'Why haven't you asked me who the men were in the pub playing chess?'

'Should I have?'

'Yes,' said Hodges.

After a pause, I said, 'All right. Who were the men playing chess in the pub?'

'My man only recognised one of them.'

Okay, I thought. Bloody well tell me. He picked his nose, then pulled out a handkerchief and blew it. Christ, he was dragging out all the presentation stops. What was he trying to do, impress me?

'Who was it?' I hadn't wanted to ask, but it just popped out.

'Pemberton.'

That shook me. 'You mean the columnist bloke?' He nodded. 'That shit!' He nodded again. 'Well, it makes sense he'd be with a man.'

'His morals don't interest us,' Hodges said.

'Like hell they don't. The day a bent queer doesn't interest you lot won't dawn till the millennium.' Then I remembered something else I had to ask. 'Who was it said this check to your king bit?'

'Pemberton.'

'Look,' I said. 'This isn't my scene, Hodges. I'm way out of my depth. And I can't swim, not in these waters.'

'You stuck with Sophia,' he answered. 'Apart from fucking it all up you did a good job. So now you tick with Sara.'

'You're out of your mind. I'm scrubbed. You and your bloody cover names. Well, mine was blown. I'm on the outside looking in at Sara.'

'Got any lemonade?' he wanted to know.

It gave me a lot of pleasure to tell him I had more respect for my guts than to give the stuff houseroom. He didn't seem to mind.

'Let's understand each other,' I pleaded. 'Oh, I know I came to you about Sara and Pemberton and Lawson. Maybe that wasn't bright, but it seemed right when I did it. You set up a meeting with Sara. That's when you lot had to get all clever. That's always been the trouble, hasn't it? Never do anything the easy way if you can dope out something complicated.'

There was a little pause. 'Wish we didn't have to use you,' he said, mildly enough. ' 'Cause you won't learn. Trouble is, you never understood our business. You still don't. You're a risk.' He permitted himself the fleeting apology of a smile that was no more than a stretching of his thin lips. 'Crazy, isn't it? We can use your kind of stupidity. You're too dumb to be dangerous. So you'll do what we want.'

Rebellion wouldn't get me anywhere. They had ways of handling that, some of them not pleasant. So I tried reasoning with the bastard.

'Let me spell it out, Hodges. I can't go back to Sara. And this time, it's your lot that's buggered up the exercise. She knows my name isn't Freeman . . .'

'She's been told your name isn't Freeman.'

'Christ, it's the same thing, isn't it?'

He didn't say anything, but let me figure it out for myself. So, if Sara could be convinced I was a character called Freeman she'd probably wonder why the family quack had tried to sell her the idea I was somebody else. But where the hell would that get us? Make Sara suspicious of Stapleton, a bloke who was one of daddy's chess buddies? So bloody well what?

'After all, you had enough sense to use your real first name, didn't you?'

'Come off it, chum. It's on the photograph. I'd have looked good telling her I was called Montmorency, wouldn't I?'

'Yet you blew your top at me not giving you anything other than Freeman. Even you couldn't be dumb enough not to think that through.' He got up again, went across to the sink and got himself a glass of water. He didn't like the stuff, but he poured it down, his face twisting. When he came back he stood in front of me. 'She didn't give you any chance for explanations when she drove you to the station?' I shook my head. He chewed his top lip. 'Leave it to me. It'll be all right. I'll come and see you tomorrow. Be here.'

'What time?'

'Don't know. Sundays're a bit tricky. Still, could be the afternoon, latish. If you must go to church, do it in the morning.'

He just walked out. No goodbye, or kiss-my-foot. Hodges wasn't a social animal. Just an animal.

I'd about given him up when he walked in. There was no knock – just the door opening, and there he was.

'Who the hell do you think you are, barging in like this?' I demanded.

'Sit down,' he said.

I sat down. He dragged a chair close to me, but only balanced on the edge of it. He reached into an inside pocket and pulled out a tattered piece of paper.

'Be careful how you handle it,' he warned.

I took it. It was . . . no, it *appeared* to be a copy of a birth certificate, a very official form, with all the proper stamps, even if they were a bit smudged. The dates and places were spot on, except that my family name had suddenly become Freeman. My mother, born Hannah Rachel Robinson, had given birth to a son, fathered by Alfred Freeman. Only that one name made the grubby document a joke: the rest was true bill.

'Treat it gently,' Hodges said. 'It could fall to pieces. The lads had to work on it very hard.'

I held it gingerly. 'They didn't have to work as hard as they did.'

'You shouldn't be as old as you are,' he said, and stretched his lips. 'Phone her. Call at her office. Do what you like. Be puzzled.'

'I am,' I said.

He ignored that. 'Be a bit sore about the way she's treated you – calling you a liar, and that sort of thing. But show her that.'

I folded the certificate carefully, offered it to him. 'It's not on, Hodges.'

'The way I see it,' he said, waving away the paper. 'Way I see it you'll have her over a barrel.'

I was getting desperate. 'Get somebody else. This won't work. God, man, I show her this and one day she has to know the truth: where the hell will that leave me? Eh?'

'She'll be suspicious of Stapleton, and, through him, maybe even of her old man. Nothing like the old divide and conquer bit.' He said this with a grimly smug satisfaction.

'Get stuffed,' I said. I got up and found a dribble of brandy in a bottle. There was no sense dirtying a glass so I put the neck in my mouth and tipped. Of course a dribble had to go down the wrong pipe. When I'd finished getting it out of my lungs or wherever and wiped my streaming eyes, Hodges said, 'You should lay off that stuff if you can't cope.'

He stood up. 'When'll she be back in town?' he asked.

Clearing the last blockage out of my throat I told him she'd probably be due at the travel-office next morning, so maybe tonight.

'Know the number of her flat?'

'Not the phone. Just where it is. Took her there in a taxi from Questro's.'

'I'll give you a lift. Try now.'

'Like hell.'

'Come on.'

'Look, I'm not going. Can't I get that through your skull? I'm out, finished. Stuff you. Stuff Sara.'

'No chance of you doing that if you don't chat her up,' he said. 'Come on.'

That was when the telephone rang. I hesitated.

'Answer it,' Hodges said.

I picked up the handset, wondering who the hell . . .

'Oh, hello,' she said. 'Is that Mr Freeman?'

I hoped Hodges wouldn't have noticed the tensing of my body. But he would. He saw everything.

'Hello,' I said. I tried to keep my voice flat, but even I could hear the quiver of excitement in it.

Mr Freeman, she'd said. Only yesterday she'd been . . .

'I . . . I came back early. I had to. When I found out. I feel so . . . so ashamed. I . . . I don't know what to say . . .'

'That's all right,' I said. For sheer bloody inanity I reckoned that scored bingo. I stole a peep at Hodges. He was watching, listening. Like I said, he didn't know what the phrase 'social graces' meant.

'I can only apologise. And when Mr Harmsworth told me I felt . . . well, awful.'

I pressed the handset hard against my ear. I didn't want the jumble of words to leak across the few feet separating me from Hodges. Harmsworth – Harding – he was back in the act. Oh, Christ.

'Hello? Are you there?'

Her voice carried a hint of panic.

'It's quite all right,' I said, without any emphasis. Playing it cool for the benefit of Hodges wasn't carrying much conviction through the wires to where she was. Her voice had become a

116

noticeable few degrees cooler when she said, 'I can understand you being annoyed. I'm sorry. There was so much I wanted to talk about. I was incredibly rude. I'm sorry.'

I had the feeling she was going to hang up. 'There's absolutely no reason why we shouldn't,' I said.

There was a pause, then. 'Isn't it convenient for you to talk?' she asked.

'Not really,' I said. It was bloody difficult trying to hold a conversation without Hodges picking up the thread of what this was about.

'Oh,' she said. And said, 'I'm sorry,' again.

'Don't be.' What was she thinking? That I was in the cot with some woman? Damn it, I didn't want her to think that. Silly, maybe, but I didn't. 'It's just that I'm dripping water everywhere,' I joked. 'You caught me in the bath.' This was inane, all right. I'd answered that call far too fast for a bloke who had to crawl out of a tub and get to where the phone was.

'Oh,' she said. 'I *am* sorry.' I heard a little tinkle of laughter, could picture her caressing the dimple. Suddenly I knew I wanted to smooth that cheek with my own fingers. 'Then I'd better let you get back to it. I'd hate to be responsible for ruining your carpet as well as . . . as well as everything else.'

'May I call you back?'

'Will you?' She sounded pleased. And somehow relieved. 'I'm at the flat, in town. I'll expect you to call, then.'

She hung up. And I still didn't know her telephone number.

I put the handset back in its cradle slowly. Was it worth the effort to try to bluff Hodges?

'So,' he said. 'She phoned you, eh? Perhaps you'll fill in the blanks.'

Bluff Hodges? 'You're a lousy actor,' he said. 'And we know there's no woman in your life right now. It had to be Sara, hadn't it? You should keep a mirror in this room. Just so you can look at yourself being all cagey and clever. Well?'

'She's a bit upset. Somebody's convinced her I'm Freeman. Just rang to apologise.'

'Somebody? Who's somebody?'

'Harding. Except she knows him as Harmsworth.'

A pause. 'Go on.'

'There isn't anything else. I don't know the details. She simply said that when Harmsworth told her she felt awful. So she came back to town and rang me.'

'Then you'd better finish your bath and call her back, hadn't you?'

'I can't.'

'Why not?' There was a nasty edge to his voice.

'Because I don't know the bloody number, do I?' I exploded. 'I told you I didn't. Only where she lives.'

'Then she must've given you the number.'

'She didn't. She obviously supposed I knew it. And I bloody don't.'

'Right,' said Hodges. 'So I give you a ride to the flat. Come on. Tidy yourself up, like you've had a bath.'

I did as I was told. While I rubbed some after-shave into the ridges and hollows of a face that was starting to show its age Hodges said, 'What does she know about you?'

'Not much.'

'How much?'

'That I'm in PR, I didn't specify where. A bachelor. I've been in newspapers.'

'And Cairo?'

Running a comb through my hair I went out to where he waited.

'What else but the cover your lot gave me?'

'She doesn't query the Irish bit?'

'It's on that bloody piece of paper, isn't it?' I picked up the tattered certificate, put it in my wallet.

He ran his eyes down from my head to my shoes. 'You'll pass. No Beau Brummel, but then you don't shop in Carnaby Street, do you? Let's get on our way.'

He stood aside, forcing me to go out of the flat ahead of him. Then he waited while I locked the door.

'Just remember when you see her that pawns can win chess games. And they're the most expendable pieces on the board. Just keep that right in front of your skull.'

FOURTEEN

CAIRO: PARTY ON A HOUSEBOAT

There didn't seem anything I could do other than order a round of drinks. Danescu seemed in no hurry to talk about whatever it was that had persuaded Mortimer to send me to Port Said. Who and what he was was going to have to wait. Sophia was settled in, and wasn't going to be shifted. They prattled on, the two of them, about the days and the nights in Paris. They'd obviously had a ball together.

'Remember that night after the Opera . . . but the party at the Crillon . . . and the Americans at the King George the Fifth . . . Longchamps . . . Bois de Bologne . . . and when the lift stuck in the Eiffel Tower . . .'

That really must have been a yell. The two of them, suspended between decks, alarm bells ringing, attendants getting excited, a lot of rushing around in bureaucratic circles.

Sophia and Danescu had forgotten me. I sat there, sipping zibib and listening to how the waiting in that trapped cage had first amused them and then bored them. How they'd started to cuddle and kiss to pass the time. One thing, it seemed, had led to another. They hadn't quite finished when the cage was lowered and the gates were thrown open with a flourish. Neither Sophia nor the man sprawled on her heard a thing. They were nearing a point of concentration that had a joint centre of gravity. Sophia, remembering it, was almost weeping with laughter, and Danescu seized my wrist.

'It was formidable, my friend,' he assured me. 'All those people, so concerned for our safety. It was truly formidable.'

He permitted himself a slow smile. Sophia was dabbing at her eyes with a wisp of lace.

'The gendarme was sweet,' she gasped. 'So very sweet. He waved his truncheon, ordered everybody away. He was very stern with them. He closed the gates and stood, like a sentry. I saw him when I looked over Paul's shoulder.'

'He was very young. He showed us a picture of his fiancée when we thanked him. He was very understanding,' Danescu said. He nodded approval of his regard for the gendarmerie.

Unbidden, pictures of the previous night's disasters flickered in my memory. I swallowed. I wasn't in their league. Then other questions niggled at my consciousness. No dates for this orgiastic Cook's Tour of Paris had been mentioned as the two of them swapped reminiscences. There was nothing either of them had said which associated with the Wehrmacht breaking through at Sedan, the blitzkrieg that had swept to the Channel coast, the occupation that had followed. Why had they been in Paris? How had they met? Just who the hell was Paul Danescu, anyway? I had to get rid of Sophia . . .

'Sophia, now you must forgive us.' Danescu's tone was firm. 'I must talk with our friend.'

Without a word of protest Sophia stood up. 'I shall take a bath,' she said. And off she went. I had a lot to learn about the technique of dealing with women. Maybe I should cultivate this Rumanian. He seemed to know what it was all about.

'It is better without her,' he said when we'd sat down again.

'Except when you're trapped in a lift,' I suggested.

'She is for fun, that Sophia,' he said. 'You are from Mr Mortimer?' I nodded. 'You have a card, perhaps?'

He was playing this a bit canny. I produced my Press pass. He studied it carefully, handed it back.

'Thank you,' he said.

'It might help if I knew who you were.'

'Did not Mr Mortimer say?'

'I'd like you to tell me.'

'I am the Anna stringer here in Port Said.'

'And every story you file, somebody comes up to collect copy?' I let that sink through. 'Or maybe you just spill the stuff to women like Sophia? You know, the dull copy, like ships coming to the canal to pick up soldiers.'

His face was very still. Then it puckered. Finally, he threw back his head and shouted, yes, shouted with laughter. When he'd finished enjoying himself he snapped his fingers. A waiter shuffled in. He ordered more drinks. Then sat back in his chair, smiling at me.

'Julius, you are very funny,' he said.

He didn't say it loudly. His voice just reached me across the small table. Julius: the cover name if and when I ever phoned the number I'd been given in Cairo.

'I know,' I said. 'Everybody laughs when I sit down to talk.'

The waiter came back, put the glasses and some fresh iced water on the table and left.

'You are satisfied now, Julius?' he asked.

'No,' I said. 'And who the hell is Julius?'

He slowly raised his glass in brief salute, sipped, then put it down. He leaned forward on his elbows, staring at me. 'You are very young,' he said.

'So?'

He shrugged. 'That is why you are suspicious, perhaps.'

I sipped my zibib, added a little more water. For all sorts of reasons I intended to stay sober. I tried to ignore him watching me, he was going to make all the moves as far as I was concerned.

'Sophia: you are a little jealous?'

I'd been wondering about that. While they'd been enjoying an exchange of intimate memories, I'd tried to analyse my own reactions. Maybe it would be a good idea to let Danescu think it if it made sense to him. So I didn't answer. Silence was perhaps a better admission than words.

'I have told you. She is for fun, that one.'

'Her husband might not agree with you.'

It was a shot in the dark, but it didn't cause any explosion.

'She has told you, then?'

I waited. Maybe he'd say something more. But he took another swallow from his glass and pursed his lips. He gave the impression of being just a bit puzzled.

My patience cracked first. 'Look,' I said. 'I've come a long way to contact a Paul Danescu. Are you Paul Danescu?'

He flashed white teeth in a smile. Maybe it was that pencil line of moustache, but it looked pretty phoney to me. 'Of course,' he said. 'And I accept you are Julius. That is enough for us, I think.'

Was it? Not for me it wasn't. Danescu wasn't behaving like any journalist I'd ever known. But then, I hadn't known so many. The war had come too quickly for me to have got around much. And if journalism for him was the same as it was for me – just common-sense cover for other things – then I didn't know too much about that, either.

'When you return to Cairo you must call on my sister,' Danescu said. 'She is very pretty. Very pretty. And she is jolly.'

God knows where the Rumanian had learned his English. What the hell did 'jolly' mean in this sort of context?

'I'm pretty busy in Cairo,' I said. 'You know, the military briefings every morning, the prodding and poking about trying to pick up the extra bits, getting the stuff filed . . .'

He was smiling broadly. 'You English are very funny.'

I reminded him I wasn't English. He shrugged. 'But you are funny. All of you. You say prodding and poking is work. That is very funny. For me, that is pleasure.'

You didn't have to have second-sight to get the drift of what he was talking about. I wondered again where he'd learned his English. 'With Sophia it is very great pleasure,' he went on. 'But this you must know.'

He liked rubbing it in, our joint possession of the woman upstairs taking a bath. But Sophia's bedworthiness wasn't what I had travelled to Port Said to talk about, or so I, in my innocence, believed.

'Look,' I said. 'How about we finish whatever it is we have to do? Sophia'll be back soon. What is it you have to tell me?'

He looked puzzled. 'But it is finished. Now you can return to Cairo.'

I felt as if my feet were nailed to the floor.

'Mr Mortimer did not tell you?' he asked.

'He said I was to contact you.'

He nodded. 'You have done this. Now I shall tell you where to contact Renée.'

'Renée?'

'My sister,' he explained.

'For Christ's sake, I didn't drive all this way to get your sister's phone number . . .'

'It is important that you meet her,' he said. There was a hint of authority in his voice.

'All right. If you say so.' But I told myself I'd be talking to Mortimer when I got back.

'I do not say so. It is the others who insist.'

The others? Collins? Mortimer? Maybe I should have stayed in the infantry where I'd been posted originally. I suddenly felt a longing for the simple philosophy of kill or be killed.

'Renée lives on a houseboat. At Zamalek. It is very nice. She has many friends. Perhaps she will invite you to a party, with Sophia. That will be very jolly.'

He should have been christened Jolly. 'Tell me,' I persisted. 'Why did I have to come up here?' There didn't seem any point in beating about the bush. I was no match for these double-talk experts: best to have it spelt out in words of two syllables.

'It is best you ask Mr Mortimer,' he said.

You bet I would. That was high on my list of songs.

'There's something else,' I said. 'What was it Sophia said

122

about a convoy coming here to pick up some troops? You out of your mind?'

He laughed again, just as he had when I'd first mentioned it. 'Not here,' he said. 'To Port Tewfik, Suez.'

I waited. 'Well?'

He spread his hands. 'It will be interesting to see what happens. Sophia has been told. Now we shall see.'

'You mean, ships're coming in to take troops *out*? With Rommel advancing on . . .'

I stopped. Christ, I should plaster one of those careless-talk posters over my big mouth. More cautiously, I said, 'We don't know who she is, do we? Where she's from.'

'I know some things. Not many. Just some things.'

He called a waiter. He bloody well knew a lot more than I did, then. Mortimer, I swore, was going to have to do some fast talking.

He ordered more drinks, urged me to finish my glass, still half full of well-watered zibib.

'Tonight,' he said, 'we shall have dinner. I know a good place. Then a night club where there are not many soldiers. Just a few officers.'

'Jolly, is it?'

'Yes,' he said, po-faced. 'It is very jolly.'

Sophia was in splendid form, driving back to Cairo. She sang a lot in that husky, throaty voice that did something to me. Though the songs all had misery for a theme, she sang cheerfully enough. The words were in that strange language I couldn't recognise and which I'd first heard in the Mikhanoff flat.

'What language is that?'

'It is my language.'

'Polish?'

She laughed: those slender fingers caressed her cheek. I swallowed when I remembered how they'd stroked me the previous night.

'I am not Polish,' she said.

That was when I made a bloody fool of myself. 'But you were born in Cracow.' I could've bitten out my tongue. I had to cover up. 'Weren't you? I seem to remember Ida saying something about it . . .' It wasn't very good, but it was the best I could think of. The adrenalin was pumping about inside me. Christ, trust me to arse things up!

'It is Georgian,' she said. Nothing in her voice revealed any disturbance. 'It is a beautiful language. Very sad, but beautiful.'

So she was a fellow-countryman of our good ally Comrade Stalin. 'So you're Russian, then?'

She shook her head vigorously, turning towards me. 'I am not Russian. I am Georgian,' she said.

The vehemence with which she said it surprised me. It showed how little I knew of internal Soviet politics, and it didn't add a lot to what I knew of her. Two passports said birthplace Cracow. She said Georgia. Maybe I should use that Cairo telephone number I'd been given, get some of this straightened out.

But, in a moment, her anger was forgotten. She had her eyes fastened on the distant view of the canal and the encampments along its banks. This gave me time to review the night we'd spent in Port Said. I think I aged a few years in those hours. But not unpleasantly.

When she'd rejoined Danescu and me she'd changed her clothes. She was a vision in cool white with some sort of green motif picked out here and there. The jacket of the lightweight suit was swinging open over a silk blouse unbuttoned far enough down to interest any male with normal appetites.

She flirted outrageously with Danescu and with me, in about equal proportions. Danescu handled it all with an aplomb I envied. And then, at the night club, we'd had Egyptian businessmen and Allied officers making all sorts of excuses to swarm around our table. She'd danced with several of them. And Danescu had had the wit to tap my thigh warningly when I started to get a bit fed-up and wanted to send them packing.

She disappeared for half an hour with a dashing lieutenant-colonel — young, handsome and, I hoped, as intelligent as he looked. What they did and where I didn't know. The officer observed his code as a gentleman. His face betrayed neither pride of conquest nor frustration when he returned her to our table. And Sophia didn't offer a word of explanation, though I remembered a little half-smile straightening out Danescu's moustache. All I wanted to do was fill the officer's mouth with broken teeth. But I didn't.

Danescu had said goodnight in the lobby of the hotel. I told him we'd be leaving early next morning. He said, 'Give my love to Renée.' I promised I would do this, fingering the slip of paper in my pocket on which was only a number. He kissed

Sophia almost perfunctorily. She submitted without any noticeable warmth to the brief embrace, then took my hand and led me away from the lift towards the stairs. It took us a long time to walk up the two floors. She started the love play before Danescu had vanished from the lobby. By the time we'd reached our adjoining rooms I was in quite a sweat. In my room she kicked the door shut and started to take my clothes off.

'Tonight,' she breathed into my ear as she jerked at the tie, 'we shall try again. Not your way. My way.'

I was glad I had drunk sparingly. The triple vodka Sophia had been stowing away during the long evening seemed to have had absolutely no effect. She was rock-steady on those shapely legs and her hands knew how to co-ordinate in undressing a man. Then I was lying on the bed, starkers, and just a mite embarrassed at how I must have looked to the woman now taking all the time in the world about removing her own clothes. The routine was tantalisingly slow, provocative, wholly sensual. Layer by layer the coverings were removed. It seemed a muscle-stretching age before the bra dropped to her feet, another millennium before the brief pants had been wriggled down around her ankles and she had stepped free of them.

Even then she took her time. She stood in front of a mirror, her back to me. I watched her stroke her thighs, her hips, her belly, cup her full breasts in slim hands. I wanted to spring from the bed and grab her, but her posture warned me to stay where I was. I waited, my body stiff with desire for her.

Then she turned, her face still, but her body a writhing movement of enticement. Her fingers plucked gently at the large nipples, bringing them to erection that mocked my own. Slowly, agonisingly slowly, she approached the bed. I reached for her, but she shook her head, moving away.

'Be still,' she murmured. Who did she think she was? Canute? Jesus Christ?

She eased down on to the mattress, gently put aside my urgent, questing hand. Then she leaned forward, her nipples barely brushing my chest and a hand reached down to a part of me that was bursting with frustrated impatience. Unhurried, she stroked and smoothed, sometimes allowing her pointed nails to drag along the flesh, drawn tight around an aching muscle. And then she grasped, savagely, viciously. The orgasm was a pain-filled, ecstatic explosion that threw me back on to the pillows.

I heard a voice, as far away as from another planet: 'Now we can begin . . .'

Remembering, I was grateful that her attention was still riveted on the dun-coloured landscape of sand and rock sliding past the hurrying Chevvy.

I felt the pressure against my pants, tried to control my breathing to quieten a too fast-beating heart. Whoever she was, whatever she was doing, I mustn't lose her, this woman with a lifetime of Arabian nights in her hands, her legs, her thrusting, demanding body.

She had stopped singing her sad songs, sat quietly, watching the dun sand give way to the exotic green of the Delta lands. I pressed hard on the accelerator. I wanted her. In my bed.

But as we cruised at last into the bedlam of the Shubra streets she said: 'Take me to my flat.'

I argued, pleaded, cajoled. But she was adamant. There were things she must do, she said. She must talk to Ida and Yanni. She would come again, she promised, perhaps tomorrow. But this night she could not be with me.

'It will be better to wait,' she said. The slow smile promised new delights. 'Tomorrow I will come.'

I drove on, stopped in a throng of soldiers milling around on the Malika Farida outside the Dopolavoro building. She wouldn't let me go with her, just took her bag, waved, and pushed through the throng of khaki-clad figures who reached for her but were not able to restrain her smiling passage.

I called at the agency but Mortimer wasn't in. No one seemed to know where he was. I went and got the car and drove back again into Shubra. All I really wanted was Sophia. Mortimer could bloody well wait. My anger with him would stay white-hot long enough, but my ache for Sophia's body wouldn't wait. That needed feeding, now.

It was after I'd parked the Chevvy in Shubra that I realised I should update whoever was on the end of the telephone number I'd been given by Collins's man. I'd try it, and see what happened. I went into a sleazy little bar with sawdust and huge brass spittoons on the floor, and few customers. I indicated the telephone. The wallah behind the bar shrugged. I dialled the carefully memorised number. A man's voice answered, heavily accented. I said, 'This is Julius.'

A brief pause, then, 'Attendez, s'il vous plait.'

I waited. Then it was a British voice. I repeated, 'This is Julius. Who is that?'

'Where are you?'

'In a bar. In Shubra.'

'I'll come and see you. In an hour.'

The line went dead. It sounded like the thug I'd first seen in the insurance office who'd come to see me at the flat: the tough lad.

I was groping in my pocket for a piastre to give to the barman when my fingers encountered the slip of paper. Danescu's sister: might as well contact her now as later. I dialled the digits carefully. The phone at the other end rang so long that I thought no one was there to answer it. I was about to hang up when a voice filled with sleep huskily said, "Ello.'

I murmured my name, quickly added that I was a friend of her brother's. It never occurred to me until later I had no right to assume that Renée would automatically answer the phone.

The voice brightened. 'How is Paul?'

'Very well,' I said. 'He sends his love to you. He suggested I should call you. I'm sorry if I've disturbed you.'

'I was asleep,' she laughed. 'It does not matter. It is better that I wake up. You are now in Cairo?'

Yes, I said, I was in Cairo. Perhaps then I could call and tell her about Paul. She hadn't seen him for some time. Perhaps a drink? About seven o'clock? I thanked her, received detailed instructions about which boat she lived in, and rang off.

It was while I was taking a shower that I winced. My hands spreading the soap across my chest had shot pins of pain through my body. I splashed my way to a mirror. Teeth marks showed livid on the flesh, and in two places the skin had been broken. I grinned at my reflection: Sophia's brand. For some daft reason I felt proud of the scars.

He'd said 'in an hour'. Exactly at the sixtieth minute Hamid ushered him in. He obviously wasn't paying a social call. He stood in the little hall, waited until Hamid had gone out, then asked, 'Well?'

He was an unpleasant bastard all right. It was time I dug my toes in. 'Look,' I said. 'I'm a human being. I like to know who I'm talking to. And courtesy won't cost you a damned penny. So, first of all, "Hello". And next, who are you?'

I thought for a second he was going to bash me. He sort of

came up on his toes and I saw a hand clench into a useful-looking fist. Then he sank back on his heels. 'Call me Hodges if you have to. Now, what happened? Why did you phone?'

'Well,' I said, 'it strictly isn't an emergency.'

That made him angry. 'Then why bloody well ring?'

'Because I don't understand a bloody thing about what I'm supposed to be doing. I tried to get hold of Mortimer. He's out. So how about answering a couple of questions?'

'I don't answer questions. I ask 'em,' he said. 'What's happened?'

I told him about Mortimer inviting Sophia to go with me to Port Said; about Danescu having known Sophia in Paris at some date unspecified; about Danescu telling Sophia a convoy was expected at Port Tewfik to pick up troops; and that Danescu had had nothing to tell me. For some inexplicable reason I decided to keep the information about Renée Danescu to myself. It had nothing to do with keeping an eye on Sophia, so to hell with it.

He waited after I'd finished. 'Well?' he said.

'It's bloody serious, isn't it? I mean taking Sophia into a prohibited zone was bad enough, but to chuck her at the head of a bloke she knows, and for him to pass on information about troop movements . . .'

His voice crackled when he said: 'What about the woman? Did she get into any trouble? Give you the slip? Contact anybody else?'

'No,' I said. He picked in a crack that I was lying. He grabbed the front of my shirt. 'Talk,' he said.

'She got to Danescu before I did. Said it was an accident; she'd just bumped into him.'

'Forget bloody Danescu. Anybody else?'

'Only at the night club. She disappeared for half-an-hour or so. But that was all right. It was with one of our officers. A half-colonel.' I tried to make light of it. 'Probably had a woo in the garden.'

He thrust me away, violently. I sat on my bottom.

'Christ, you're useless,' he said. He didn't bother to hide the disgust he felt. I got to my feet, wondered if I should bop him one, decided not to try.

'Where is she? Now?'

'At her flat. Wouldn't come back here with me.'

'What's she doing?'

'Damned if I know. Said she'd see me tomorrow. Good

God, man, I can't go to the loo with the bloody woman.'

'No,' he said. 'But you can watch her go in and come out. That's your job. Where's she going to be tonight?'

I shrugged, then took a quick step backwards. I swear that balled fist of his had started on its way before he checked it. Hodges sure didn't like me, not one little bit. I wasn't much in love with him, come to that.

'Now listen to me,' he said. 'Get round to her flat. Use any bloody excuse you like. But stick with her. That's your fucking job, your only fucking job: to stick with her, night and day.' He paused. 'Or aren't you any good? She kicked you out?'

On impulse I pulled open my shirt, let him see the bites. He grunted. 'Put your own brand on her, then,' he suggested. 'We want to know who she meets, where she goes, what she does. That's why, God help us, you're on the payroll.'

I wanted to ask him about Danescu, the ships and the troops, but I didn't get a chance. He just slammed out, banging the door behind him.

Sophia wasn't at the Dopolavoro flat. At least no one answered when I rang the bell. So I couldn't search Cairo on my own. I piled into the Chevvy and headed for Zamalek.

The houseboat was one of several moored along the south bank just opposite the Bulak shore. I identified the blood-red curtains at the little windows. As I walked across the gangplank I heard music. On board I could hear voices, laughter. A vast Sudanese barred my way. I asked for M'selle Danescu. The Sudanese stood by me, clicked his fingers for a scrawny Arab lad, growled some gutturals. The boy nodded and disappeared behind a bulkhead. It was a long time before a door opened on to the deck. A woman, possibly a year or two younger than Sophia and as dark as the Georgian was fair, stepped out. She ran forward a few paces, her hands outstretched. Her skin was swarthy, her body slim as a boy's. She resembled her brother about as much as I did Farouk.

'I am sorry you have been kept waiting,' she said. She took both my hands in hers. I felt a tingle of pleasure. This woman had something, even if it wasn't quickly apparent. 'Do come in. There are some friends. So Paul is well?'

'Fit as a flea,' I said, and saw her eyebrows pucker. 'He's very fit.'

We were stepping over the high sill into a magnificently appointed lounge, a riot of colourful carpets and drapes, and huge, exotic cushions. I held her back for just a moment. 'He sent you this.' I leaned forward and kissed her cheek. I just couldn't resist the impulse. There was a strange animal magnetism about her that I hadn't experienced before. She turned her head, smiled.

'Thank you,' she said.

Just inside the door was a group of people. One was a woman, blonde hair piled high. She was smiling coldly over the rim of a glass she was rubbing against her chin. I stared back at her with mixed feelings. At least I would be able to report to that bastard Hodges that I'd found Sophia Kukralovic.

FIFTEEN

LONDON: PAWN THREATENS QUEEN

It wasn't easy to locate the house. Damn it, I'd been there only once, in the dark, in a taxi, and she'd got out, run up a path and disappeared through a door. But I knew it wasn't far down Walnut Tree Walk from Kennington Road. I could feel Hodges' eyes probing after me from where he sat in his car at the end of the street where he'd dropped me. I bet he thought I was having him on. I was glad I wasn't. Hodges had a nasty habit of reacting violently to people who tried to outsmart him. So I paused and took stock. The taxi had swung into the street. Sara hadn't mentioned any house-number; she'd just rapped on the glass partition and the cabbie had pulled into the kerb.

This, I thought, might be it. I went up the short path and peered at the name-cards beside the upright row of buttons. One of the cards was new. 'Sara Kenyon.' I went back to the gate and waved a thumbs-up at Hodges. I waited but his car didn't budge. Okay, bastard: bloody sit there all night. I went back to the porch and pressed the button.

'Yes?' she queried in the tone of voice people use when they're not expecting callers.

'It's Freeman,' I said, my mouth close to the grille.

'Oh,' she said. There was a pause. Then the familiar click of a door unlocking. 'It's on the first floor, at the back. Number eight.'

I pushed the door open. Standing on my toes I could just see Hodges over the top of the hedge separating the house from the property next door. The car wasn't moving. To hell with him. I ran up the stairs, got my bearings, walked through a passage towards the rear of the house. Number eight was at the end. I tapped on the door. It opened. I literally caught my breath. The blonde hair was piled high, caught up with pins. She was wearing a loose wrap, caught at the waist with a sash, but loose as it was, the material stretched tight over the breasts. Sophia Kukralovic would never die while Sara Kenyon lived.

'Come in,' she said.

I walked past her into the tiny flat. There was steam escaping from the bathroom through a door left ajar. I heard the door close.

She came into the room. She seemed withdrawn. 'I'm sorry to receive you like this,' she said, and plucked at the thin material. 'But I was expecting you to phone and when you didn't I . . . I decided to have a bath.'

I almost smiled. Mother and daughter shared one thing at least in common – a mania for cleanliness. Sophia was in and out of tubs far more often than she was in and out of bed. And that was no mean record. But if it was a matter of like mother, like daughter, what else was she involved in?

'I didn't know your telephone number,' I said. 'But I remembered where you lived. So I came over.' I smiled at her. 'You sounded upset when you rang. I felt it might be a good idea to let you know I'm not worried.' I tried to joke. 'After all, there was always my birth certificate to fall back on, wasn't there?'

'You didn't know my tele . . .' she started, then laughed, fingers leaping to her cheek. 'But of course you didn't. You rang me at the office.'

I shrugged. 'It doesn't matter. And about the other thing. Don't worry about it. Your doctor friend must have confused me with somebody else.'

She frowned. 'Perhaps. But I don't think so. He was very deliberate about your . . . your name. And he looked at you very hard before he said anything. And there was . . . was the message. No, I don't think he made a mistake.' Then she relaxed. 'But Mr Harmsworth was very angry when he heard about it. He took Dr Stapleton out of the room and I think he told him off.'

'I'm glad it's all straightened out.' There was still a question I had to ask. 'What puzzles me is how the subject of my identity came up at all. You know, with Har . . . Harmsworth.'

'Oh, that was the doctor. He made a point of telling Mr Harmsworth I'd been taken in by an impostor.'

'Did he now?' I laughed. And she smiled. She went to a small bureau and took something from a drawer. She held it out. It was Sophia's photograph. 'I'm sorry. I forgot to return it.'

'Keep it. Please. I hope it gives you pleasure.'

She looked down at it, then at me. 'Thank you,' she said. No protestation that I must have it. She returned it to the bureau – gently, as one handles treasured possessions.

'Well, I'd better get along.' I nodded towards the bathroom, 'Your bath will be cold.'

'Must you go?' she asked. 'It's early. I'd like to make you some coffee. Come and talk to me while I have my bath.'

I'd half-turned towards the door. I swung round to face her. She burst into laughter, the fingers busy on the dimple.

'Oh, dear,' she gurgled. 'Have I shocked you?'

I suppose that was the right word. With Sophia it had somehow been different. She'd been the hare in the chase. But Sara Kenyon wasn't being . . . My thinking stopped right there. Yes. She was as much a hare as her mother had been. Why else should I have raced off to Hodges when I'd seen her in the club with Pemberton and Lawson? She was the quarry, all right. I didn't know why or how, just as I hadn't known how or why in the hunt after Sophia.

'I'm sorry. I didn't realise. It was stupid of me.' Her voice was contrite, but also vaguely puzzled. 'It was just that . . . oh, I'm sorry.'

She ran into the bathroom, slammed the door behind her. I heard the taps rush water, and cursed myself for a fool. I chewed my lip. So I was getting on a bit. But she was no young girl just out of school. She had to be more than thirty. Thirty? Why hadn't she married? Or was she married? She wore no ring but that didn't mean anything. Separated perhaps? Or divorced?

The taps had stopped. I walked slowly and quietly to the bathroom door, listened. There was no splashing of water, just quiet stillness. Was she in there waiting?

I turned away from the door, stared at my reflection in a wall mirror. Battered a bit, with flecks of grey at the temples. But when I held in my belly the shape wasn't bad. Well, it wasn't sphere-shaped. Still no splashing from behind the door . . . I wrestled a bit with . . . what? Conscience? Moral scruples?

I opened the door. She was sitting on the edge of the bath, still wearing the wrap. We stared at each other then, with a foot, she pulled forward a stool. I closed the door, sat on the stool.

She untied the sash, seemed to hesitate for a moment. White teeth pressed into lower lip for a second, then she slid the wrap off her shoulders . . .

I allowed my eyes to range down from her face to neck to shoulders to jutting breasts to gently curving belly to milky

133

thighs tight around the profusion of golden hair that apexed long smooth legs. She stood there until my eyes were on her slender feet tipped by well-trimmed nails. Only then did she slide over into the faintly scented water and the opaqueness of bubbles riding on blue foam.

With a little sigh she slid down until her shoulders disappeared and her knees emerged.

'I am glad you came,' she said. For a single terrible moment I was listening to Sophia Kukralovic, watching her body in the bath.

Hodges was a man of quite remarkable stamina. It was five o'clock in the morning when I quietly let myself out of the flat and turned towards Kennington Road in search of a taxi. His car was still parked where he'd dropped me the previous evening. As I approached he leaned over and opened the passenger door. I got in. I didn't close the door behind me. It would be easy to roll out on to the pavement if things got rough.

Hodges wasn't looking his best. There was an overnight stubble of beard on his chin. Sara had lent me a razor. His eyes were bloodshot, the lids puffy. At least I'd got in a couple of hours' sleep.

'Shut the door,' he said. I had the feeling he wanted to yawn. I pulled the door shut: no sense in forcing an issue before I had to. 'You took long enough.'

'That's the way you wanted it,' I told him.

'You take her to bed?'

'I'm not sure who took who. But yes, we've been to bed.'

'She's young enough to be your daughter,' he said.

'Perhaps. But she isn't. My daughter, I mean. You said to go back to her. Hell, man! You drove me here.'

'You're a fool. You never bloody well learn.'

There wasn't any point arguing that with him. He'd made up his mind years ago.

'What're you trying to do?' he demanded, the crackle replacing the weariness.

'Only what I'm told. Cultivate Sara Kenyon. It's what you want.'

He drummed his fingers on the rim of the steering wheel. 'It was when you started screwing Sophia things came unstuck.'

'It wasn't.' The ugliness was flooding his face. So I tried another track. 'Not the way you think. Anyway, it's what you

134

lot wanted. Get her into bed. This time . . . well, it just happened.'

'You showed her the certificate?'

'Didn't have to. She accepts I'm Freeman.'

That jerked him upright. 'How?' he snapped.

'Harding. The bloke she knows as Harmsworth. Seems this Stapleton character told him I was an impostor. According to her Harmsworth took him apart, and convinced her my name was Freeman.'

As I've said, Hodges on the defensive was something I liked watching. But I didn't enjoy this so much. The man was worried. He'd heard something he obviously didn't have an explanation for. Tension pushed the tiredness out of his body.

'Look,' I said. 'Can't we push off from here? She might take an early morning constitutional.'

Almost mechanically he went through all the proper motions of getting the car under way; he even poked his head out of the side window to check the empty carriageway, switched on his flickers, took a look in the driving-mirror. He was a good driver. I wondered where he'd head for. He turned left into Kennington Road. So he wasn't driving me home. We drove on up towards the Elephant in silence. This suited me fine, and gave me a chance to savour again the pleasures of the hours I'd spent with Sara. It wasn't just the sex bit, though she was good at it. Not like a whore, all motion, no emotion. No. She enjoyed it, for its own sake, I think. But not, I was sure, an easy lay. And yet I wasn't conscious of having taken an initiative, nor could I recall any moment in time when she had – not in a physical sense, anyway. As I'd told Hodges, it just happened.

She'd lain in the bath, very still, for what seemed a long time. She didn't say anything. Nor did I. I just enjoyed sitting there, looking down at bits of her lovely body where it stuck up out of the water. Then, slowly, she'd started to sponge herself, lazily. Things were happening to me. I stirred on the stool.

She turned her head, smiled. She used the big sponge to rub the dimple.

'Daddy would like you to come down to Hassocks and play chess with him,' she said.

I nearly laughed. Here I was, pants getting too small for me in the groin, watching a goddess bathe, and she makes social small talk. 'He didn't give the impression he wanted me as a 'guest,' I managed to say, but my voice had an odd wobble in it.

She leaned forward, jerked the plug free, watched the water start to swirl and eddy. She rested her elbows on her knees. Still concentrating on the plumbing she said: 'He's potty about the game.'

'How did he find out I played?'

'Mr Harmsworth told him.'

This bloody man Harding was going to have a bill to settle one of these days. The last of the water rushed out with a gurgle. She squeezed the sponge over the plug-hole. I reached across and lifted the towel off the heated rail, handed it to her. She nodded a thank-you, got up without any effort from the squatting position and stood there, the towel looped over her wrist.

I stood up, too. She proffered the towel. I took it and for the first time in my life towelled dry a woman's body. And, I swear, it was about the most unsexy thing I'd done in my life. But it was then, I'm sure, we both knew I wouldn't be leaving the flat for quite some time.

She didn't bother about her wrap, just stepped over the side of the bath and walked into the bedroom. I followed her. She got quietly into bed, put her hands behind her head and stared up at the ceiling. I undressed, quite deliberately. Then I got into bed beside her. I lay there, on my back, waiting.

'I could drive you down on Friday evening,' she said.

My body was starting to burn, but I stayed quite still. Her mother had been a good teacher.

'If you're sure . . .'

'Oh, he definitely wants you to come down.'

'But I'm not a good player. Hardly a player at all. I just know the moves; I can just about see a fool's mate coming up.'

'All right. I'm no judge. But he likes winning.'

'Then he'll like me.'

Then she rolled over to face me. She ignored the bedside lamp casting its soft pink light on to the pillows. I turned as well. Our faces were inches apart. Her lips parted. So did mine. We kissed, not urgently or desperately, just slowly and with quiet passion that would dictate its own timetable. Hands gently laid themselves on bodies. An easy rhythmic caressing . . .

'All right,' said Hodges. 'I don't give a stuff what she did. I want to know what she said.'

Hodges was a bastard all right. 'Her old man wants me down to play chess,' I said.

For maybe a second I thought Hodges was going to mount the pavement. But he straightened up quickly.

'Thought you said he didn't like you?'

'That was before he knew I played chess.'

'Who told him?'

'Harding.'

I saw his hands clench on the wheel, the knuckles whiten. I hoped Harding alias Harmsworth was starting to get in his hair as much as he was already in mine.

Suddenly he braked. I was jerked forward. 'Go home,' he said. 'Get a taxi. Get what you bloody well like. But get out of the car.'

'But . . .'

'Get out,' he snarled.

I got out. Holding the door open, I asked: 'What do I do? Go down?'

He hesitated. I hugged the moment. Hodges discomfited was rare enough to enjoy while it lasted.

'I'll contact you,' he said, reached over, slammed the door shut, and over-revved the engine to skid away, tyres protesting. That, too, was out of character. Hodges was in a tizz. I wished I knew why.

By the Wednesday Hodges hadn't been in touch. To hell with him – I'd made up my mind I was going to Hassocks on the Friday evening. I wondered if I should ring Sara. Maybe I should have done so sooner. But the idea of saying something like, 'Thanks for your hospitality!' just wasn't on. So I'd put off calling. Perhaps I could invite her to dinner?

That wasn't easy, either. Hodges had said he'd contact me. That meant he'd expect me to be at the Ministry during the day, and in that bloody bed-sitter of mine at night.

Lunch! That would be a nice compromise. Ring Sara; meet her at the Press Club; tell the office where I could be found. It was impulse that suggested the Press Club. Maybe Pemberton or Lawson would be around. I'd like them to see me with Sara.

I pushed aside the stack of inanities I was supposed to initial and pass on for somebody else to initial, pulled the phone forward and dialled for an outside line. Her office answered, told me sorry, but Miss Kenyon was out of town: Paris.

'When,' I asked, 'do you expect her back?'

'Possibly not until Monday.'

'Monday?' The word jerked out.

'Yes. That's when we expect her to return to the office.'

'Oh,' I said. 'But she may come back to London before then?'

'I'm afraid I don't know.' The girl was getting fed up with the inquisition. 'Sorry I can't help you.' She rang off.

I initialled the file without protest and chucked it into the 'out' tray. To hell with everybody: I'd still go to the Press Club and have a pint . . .

There was some kind of a do up in the Wakefield Room and the bar was almost empty. I nodded to a couple of faces vaguely recognised, sat myself on a stool and ordered a pint of bitter. I chatted with Tommy; ordered a second pint.

That was when Howard Benson came in, all smiling teeth and tiring enthusiasm. 'Just the man I want to see,' he said, and plonked himself on the stool next to mine. There wasn't much I could do other than wave Tommy across, but Benson waved away my proffered money. He would buy the drinks. I indicated I already had one in front of me.

'Then have another. One more pint, Tommy. And a big scotch. What's the buzz on the brouhaha with the States, eh?' he asked, voice carrying loud and clear.

I thought maybe he was talking to someone behind me. But he wasn't.

'What buzz about what brouhaha?' I countered.

An elbow dug me in the ribs. It hurt, and I told him it hurt and for Christ's sake to grow up. He thought this was funny and laughed his fool head off.

'Come off it, squire,' he said, still grinning like a bloody ape. But at least he did drop his voice. 'The warheads: that brouhaha.' Another dig with his sharp elbow.

Tommy put down the drinks in front of us. 'Have one yourself,' Benson invited him. Tommy said, 'I have one, thank you.' Then he added, 'Sir' almost as an afterthought.

'Suit yourself,' said Benson. To me, 'Come on, old cock. Down the hatch. Got to grease that larynx of yours. Oil the pipes.' He winked. 'You know. The brouhaha.'

'Don't know what you're talking about.' And I didn't, so help me. 'Better ring the Ministry.'

'You are the bloody Ministry. So stuff that. It's your job to help the Press. What the hell d'you think we stuff you with booze for, eh? So how about a bit of quid pro quo, eh?' He hitched his stool closer till our thighs were touching. 'Look here, I've got the gen dead to rights.' His voice was down low now. And he wasn't just having fun. He was on to something. You could always tell with Benson. 'All I want is . . . Well, like have the contractors short-changed somebody on that timing unit? Two blokes're dead, blown to bloody smithereens fitting one of 'em. And the Yanks are hot about it. Three more checked and found defective. So . . . who's carrying the can at our end? Could be three million quid down the spout if they scrub the contract. Right? So there has to be a flap in your little corridors of bloody power, eh? And so you have to know something. And I want to know. 'Cause let me warn you, squire: if you don't tell me, I write what I've been told. And tomorrow the MPs'll be off their backsides yelling blue murder. So give, Mr Ministry!'

He guzzled the scotch, ordered another, plus still another pint for me to line up beside the two not yet touched.

Who the hell did he think I was? A PPS?

'You're barmy,' I told him. So he must have been, or pissed out of his mind, though he didn't look it. I slid off the stool and left him with three pints of beer. I didn't go far. The phone booths were empty. I dialled the Ministry. Maybe it was my turn to do Harding a good turn. It took a while but I caught him on his way out. He wanted to be his usual effusive self but I cut him short.

Cupping the mouthpiece I whispered, 'Benson. D notice. Warheads.' Then I rang off. If anyone would know about whatever it was it would be Harding, and he'd do something about the leak.

Only Sam, giving change to a member playing the fruit machines, saw me slip out from the phones and into the washroom next door. I'd scrub up, stroll upstairs, get myself a decent meal and head for Whitehall. But Pemberton was washing his hands. There was the usual buttonhole, the stem of the flower carefully wrapped in foil. Hell! This wasn't my day.

'Hello,' said Pemberton. The columnist was all fruity charm. God, I loathed that man. Not just because he was a homosexual . . . well, maybe that was part of it. But his bloody oiliness put me off: all mincing goodwill to all men. But the stuff that came out of his typewriter was something else. The characters on that machine were fish-hooks.

I nodded. Pemberton rinsed his hands again and again. I could hear him at it while I emptied out the pint of ale I'd drunk. He was still at it when I stuck my hands under a tap, shook them and dried them on a towel.

'How about a drink, dear boy?'

Sorry I told him. Just about to eat. 'Oh, how splendid,' he said. 'I'll join you.'

Sometimes you just can't win.

I headed up the stairs, Pemberton prattling on about the beastly weather and how his flower-beds were suffering so terribly. Hearts and bloody flowers, I thought, and barbed fish-hooks.

There was a table for two. I'd rathed hoped there wouldn't be. I was grateful, though, that his sharp ears hadn't picked up any leads on defective warheads. He asked the usual questions about the Ministry — what was new, sort of thing. Just as though any civil servant would admit anything was.

Then bang: out of the blue. 'Hear you're a chess player.'

Some of the soup dribbled out of my spoon on to my tie. Christ, not another . . .

I dabbed with my napkin at the brown gravy, squinting down below my chin. Pemberton jumped up quickly, hurried to my side of the table, grabbed the napkin and said, 'Allow me, my dear fellow.' His fingers were ridiculously smooth and unpleasant stroking my jaw up out of the way. Then he stood back, after fussing rather more than was necessary, and nodded.

I thanked him, a bit coldly. He sat down. 'You must be pretty good, old chap. I mean, to play a fellow like Kenyon. He's rather hot stuff.' He giggled. Yes, he did – giggled. Noted for giggling was Alistair Pemberton. God, he was an obnoxious character. But he knew I'd been invited back to the Kenyons' to play chess. Now who the hell could have told him that? Damn it, I'd only know about the invitation three days ago. And now, it seemed, it was common gossip. Why should it be? Why the hell should anyone be interested in my playing chess with Kenyon? Sara? He knew Sara, of course. He'd been with her when I'd first spotted her in the club. But she was in Paris. Pemberton was looking at me in an odd sort of way.

'Trouble is I'm no good at it,' I said at last. 'Beats me where he got the idea I'd be able to give him a game.'

He still had that odd expression on his face as though he'd expected me to say something else. He pursed his lips. 'Then let me give you some advice, dear boy. Threaten his queen. That's it. Threaten his queen. With a pawn. A pawn must always threaten a queen.'

I stared across the table at him. Suddenly he smiled.

'I say, my dear chap, your soup's getting cold.'

SIXTEEN

CAIRO: ENTER AN AMERICAN

Renée said: 'Sophia darling. This is a friend of Paul.'

Sophia inclined her head. 'I know him,' she said. That, I thought, was an understatement. But if that was the way she wanted to play it, then it would be okay with me. I wondered if she was annoyed that I'd arrived when she'd obviously wanted an evening to herself and to her own devices, what-ever they were.

'Do meet some people,' Renée suggested. I followed her into a little crush of people. She murmured names, I nodded, shook hands when they were offered. A servant offered me a drink. I took the glass, smiled an acknowledgement when Renée excused herself to greet some newcomers. It suddenly occurred to me that she hadn't seemed curious about what I was. In intrigue-ridden war-time Cairo everybody was always curious about what other people did, or said they did. Had she been tipped off by Paul? I didn't know. Then I remembered some-thing else. Paul had said Renée might invite me to one of her parties, with Sophia, he had said. Well, Sophia was here. So was I. But this was a meeting of pure coincidence. Or was it?

'Say, you're a Limey, aren't you?'

He was a tiny, cadaverous man in a lightweight near-white suit that could have looked better with a press. He was per-spiring freely and his grey hair hung lank and untidy around his weatherbeaten, lined face. He looked old: about sixty, I thought. He was clutching what looked like a scotch.

'No,' I said.

'Oh,' he said, and seemed disappointed.

I watched Sophia. She was talking to a slim swarthy man, well dressed, wearing a tarbush: an Egyptian, probably. The two of them were apart from the little mill of people chattering like sparrows, mainly in French and Arabic. Renée was back and forwards between her guests and the door to the deck as the trickle of arrivals showed no sign of stopping.

'My name's Davers, Harry Davers.'

I nodded. To hell with him. My job was to stick with Sophia.

I was trying to figure out how I could bust in on her and the Egyptian.

'I'm an American.' He must have met a lot of people with insensitive hearing to have to tell me that. 'But I'm not from Texas. No, sir.' He thought this was funny. He laughed, bending over and slapping his thigh.

'No,' I said. 'You're from Boston.'

As God is my judge, I didn't know where the hell he was from, and couldn't have cared less. Why I picked on what people say is a nice city I couldn't begin to guess. But I nearly went into the laughing bit myself as I watched his face collapse.

'Say,' he said. 'You're pretty smart.'

I wondered why Sophia was listening so earnestly to what her companion was saying. She had her head inclined forward as though the man was talking very softly.

Renée walked by. 'You have met Mr Davers, then,' she said. She smiled. 'He must be very rich. He is an oil man.'

'Yes, ma'am. I'm in oil. But rich? Not so sure about that . . .'

But Renée had moved on. Davers got all disappointed again. He plucked at my sleeve. 'You in business here?'

I nodded. Sophia and the man in the tarbush had moved into a corner. She was still listening.

Davers was getting irritated. 'You say you ain't a Limey but, by God, you act like one. You think I got the plague or something?'

I'd just about resigned myself to a conversation I didn't want when the door from the deck opened again. But this time the giant Sudanese major-domo was bowing the new guest in. He was damn near genuflecting. And Renée was almost running across the room. The chatter and the laughter died.

Even I recognised her, even with her clothes on. Hers was a face that stared saucily back at you from a dozen hoardings in the city streets. This was Harida, probably the greatest exponent of the *danse-du-ventre* the Middle East had ever known. It was also rumoured in the cafés that she was a favourite of the king. Certainly politicians and generals courted her. She was wealthy enough in her own right to be able to pick and choose her own escorts, and it was gossiped that only one type of man wasn't welcomed: a poor one. She was breathtakingly beautiful, with huge, slightly almond-shaped eyes, heavily made up. She was tall, with a voluptuous figure. Her thick black hair fell heavily down to her shoulders. She and Renée exchanged kisses. So Renée had to be a person of consequence in this socially conscious city.

Harida accepted the spontaneous applause as a normality. She was soon the centre of an adoring group. Even women clustered close. And for the first time since I'd arrived I noticed something was missing. There were no military uniforms. There was only one other place in Cairo which shared this distinction: the Kit Kat Club, long since out of bounds to all ranks of Allied personnel because of the security risk. Not that the officers who could afford it were deterred too much. It was said they begged, borrowed and sometimes bought civilian clothes to gain entry to one of the most expensive night spots in town. Harida sometimes guested in the floor show. But anyway there was always Maria Marie, the Hungarian songbird who could rival Harida as any man's target for tonight.

'Say, now she's something, ain't she?' Harry Davers was nothing if not persistent. He was plucking at my sleeve, but he wasn't looking up at me. His eyes were trying to penetrate the wall of bodies hiding Harida from his rather prominent eyeballs.

To say anything was to talk about the obvious, so I concentrated on where Sophia and her friend were still talking. They'd glanced up when Harida had swept in. The man had raised a casual hand in salute. He must have known her. Sophia had simply stared stonily, without visible signs of recognition.

'You got an impediment or something?' Davers asked, plucking again at my sleeve. I looked down into his supplicating, pale blue eyes. He had the wistfulness of a dog that has been kicked.

'I'm sorry,' I said. 'I . . . I was thinking about something.'

And I was. Sophia and her companion had disappeared.

'Let me get you a drink,' Davers said.

He hustled away to find a waiter. Renée came up to me.

'You would like to meet Harida, perhaps?'

Would I like to meet Harida? It sounded a daft sort of question. 'Please,' I said.

She took my hand, snaked her way through the tight circle of hangers-on, anxious for a smile that would enable them to dine out in the reflection of it.

In three languages Renée edged her way to the hub of the group. 'Harida,' she said. 'May I present a friend of mine? And of Paul.'

144

So Paul knew her, too. I bowed over the hand she extended and, feeling a bit silly, I kissed it. She used very nice bath salts, quite heady.

I straightened. The huge black eyes were staring into mine.

'You are English?'

'Irish.'

'Ah,' she said, and smiled. 'They, too, fight for freedom, I think.'

Her English was good, accented, but clear and well rounded.

'For centuries,' I said.

'You must come and see me dance.'

'That would be an honour.' For a beginner I thought I wasn't doing too badly. And, hell, I'd like to see her doing the belly dance. I tried to visualise the sinuous body under the clothes. I quickly switched my mind to memories of a cold shower.

'Renée will arrange this,' she said. She gave me a slight bow and turned away to speak to a man standing behind her.

There was a pluck at my sleeve. 'I'd like to meet her,' whispered the hoarse voice of Harry Davers. He'd pushed through the throng, precariously holding two glasses of scotch in one hand. He thrust one of them at me. I swear the man was drooling at the mouth.

I bent my head. 'For God's sake, I've only just met her myself,' I hissed into his ear.

'I've got to,' he said, plucking my sleeve again.

I had the feeling he would perform a bit if I didn't. Renée had slipped away again, so I reached forward, touched Harida's arm.

'Forgive me,' I said.

She turned, her whole attitude one of anger. 'I'm sorry,' I went on. Hell, what did I have to lose? 'But Mr Davers here, he's an American. An oil man. He'd like very much to meet you. May I present him?'

I thought she was going to turn away. But she hesitated for just a moment, then smiled. God, I knew what it did to me, and I'd just had a night with Sophia. What it did to the acidulated Harry Davers I couldn't begin to guess.

'I love America,' Harida said. I could see Davers shaking as she took his hand. Whisky sloshed over the rim of his glass. 'One day I hope I may visit your country.'

Davers thrust his drink at me. Still allowing a hand to rest in Harida's, he thrust the other one into a pocket, pulled out a card, held it out. The hand was shaking as if the bloke had palsy. She seemed to be startled, but she took the slip of pasteboard, glanced down at it.

'Any time,' croaked Davers. 'Any time at all.'

Harida, a good half-head taller than the little American, held the card between finger and thumb. Then she stepped forward and imperiously waved for passage through the huddle of people. My eyes popped when I saw she was still holding Davers' hand and drawing him along behind her. She led him to a low divan. They sat down. She started to talk to him, waving away those who had tried to follow her.

For Christ's sake, I thought.

'You did not say you were coming here.' It was Sophia just behind my left elbow. I turned. I was surprised to find her still beautiful. Not even Harida could extinguish whatever it was that Sophia had.

'I didn't know,' I paused. 'Nor did you, come to that. You said you had to see Ida and Yanni.'

'I must see them. Later. Perhaps you sleep with Renée when I am not available, eh?'

I waited for her to smile, but she didn't. I thought again with nostalgia, but not for too long, about the uncomplicated life of an infantry officer.

'I met her for the first time tonight.' Then I decided to be a bit aggressive on my side. 'You don't do so badly yourself.'

She puckered her brow, then her face relaxed. 'Oh, Hussein? He is nothing.'

'You spent long enough with him.'

'We talk sometimes about how dull life is here in the war. It is not very pleasant.'

'This is a very good party,' I countered.

She shrugged. 'I do not like parties.'

'Then shall we go? I'll drive you to Ida and Yanni. And then we can go to my flat.'

She thought about that for a moment. Then she shook her head. 'That is not possible.'

Renée came over. 'May I speak with you a small moment?' Just where the hell did these Rumanians learn English?

I turned to excuse myself to Sophia but she had gone. She was heading in the general direction of Hussein, now one of a small group animatedly talking.

'Of course,' I said.

'You have other things to do this evening?'

'No. Nothing at all.'

'That is very good. Then you will stay after these tiresome people have gone? You will tell me about Paul.'

I nodded, though I'd obviously have to invent any chat about Paul. What I didn't know about that lad would fill a library.

On a sudden impulse, I blurted: 'Who is the man Sophia has been talking to? I think I know him.'

She looked round. 'The one with the tarbush? He is Hussein Bey. I do not like Muslim men. They wear those silly hats all the time. I do not like this in my house.'

Two others of her guests were wearing the fez; presumably she didn't go much for them either.

'Sophia is very stupid. This Hussein is not good. He is a strange man. Not good for Sophia.'

I tried to sound casual. 'Why's that?'

She shrugged, seemed about to say something, then changed her mind. 'We will talk later,' she said, and left me.

It was two o'clock in the morning before the last of the guests had left. I'd filled in the time well enough. The word had got around that I was a journalist, and a neutral to boot. I was never short of people wanting to know how the war was going. Odd, isn't it, how newspapermen are always assumed to know more than politicians and generals? I did the best I could, cheerfully damning both sides in the conflict, a role I felt suited a neutral.

I didn't see Sophia again, nor Hussein Bey, but Harry Davers turned up at one point. He was still sweating, and very excited. He started the sleeve-plucking bit when I was trying to extricate myself from the boring conversational clutch of a junior French diplomat anxious to justify his army's shortcomings.

When Davers had got me away he found it hard to articulate. His words tumbled one over the other, but I got the drift. Harida had invited him to see her show, as a Guest. I could hear the capital G clearly in the jungle of his Bostonian accent. For a performer who didn't need to, Harida was certainly drumming up business. First me, then Davers. He calmed down eventually, remembered he hadn't had a drink for some time and grabbed at a passing waiter. Renée was busy farewelling the last dribble of stayers out on the deck.

'Well,' said the American. 'Guess I'd better get me some shut-eye. Coming?'

I shook my head, and explained I had some business to discuss with our hostess. His eyes became as round as saucers. He licked his lips.

'Jeez, you young guys,' he muttered.

I told him it wasn't like that. Renée was the sister of a friend of mine. Then he nudged me with a sharp elbow, winked with an exaggeration that amounted to obscenity and drained his glass. He smacked his lips loudly. He looked around the lounge. It was deserted. He walked, I thought a bit unsteadily, to the bar to put down his glass. Because his hand was clutching my sleeve I hadn't much choice but to follow him.

Startled, I realised he was saying something. Not looking at me. His lips barely moving.

'Hussein's only half-wog: his mother. Check out his old man.' He belched, loudly and repeatedly. 'Always the same when I booze,' he complained. His voice must have carried right across Gezira Island.

Renée was in front of us, smiling. 'Why, Mr Davers. You are not leaving us?'

'Dear lady,' said Harry Davers, 'if I were ten years younger I'd be matching straws with this young man.'

He made a great to-do of kissing her hand, was on his way to the door, then stopped.

'Hey,' he said, thrusting a hand into his pocket and pulling out a wallet. 'Better have one of these.' He took out a card, handed it to me. 'Call me. Could be a good story for you. You know, oil and the war effort. That sort of crap.'

He was gone, waving aside Renée's offer to escort him to the deck.

'What a very strange man,' she said as the door slammed shut behind him.

'You should know. You invited him.'

She looked at me sharply. 'What does that mean?'

'Why, nothing. You just sounded surprised. And I thought that him being here that . . . well, you must have known him before.'

She took my hand, led me to a divan. We sat down. 'You would like another drink?' I shook my head.

'Very well. Tell me about Paul.'

'He's very fit.' I paused, then decided it would be more sensible to tell the truth. 'Matter of fact I met him yesterday, for the first time.'

Suddenly she was laughing. She threw back her head and enjoyed herself. I sat there like a dummy. 'You poor sweet boy,' she said, still chuckling. She leaned over, turned my face to hers and kissed me on the lips.

It was over before I'd had the wit to contribute my six-pennyworth. She relaxed against some cushions, her hands behind her head. The thin dress, pulled tight against her body, hardly bulged where it would have done with Sophia. Renée was boyish slim. I suspected that lean body was also tough. There was a litheness about it that suggested strength beyond what a woman could normally be expected to possess.

'You knew, then?' It was all I could think of to say.

She nodded, almost laughing again. 'Of course. But of course I knew.' She twisted her head to the cushion near her. I stretched out beside her, put my hands behind my head, stared up at the low ceiling. The water lapped gently against the hull.

Renée? Who the hell was she? And Paul. And now Harry Davers. Hussein who was 'only half-wog'. Had Sophia gone off with him? I felt a stirring of what could only have been jealousy. Maybe she was in his bed already ...

'You may make love to me if you wish,' Renée said.

Her still face had turned to face mine. How could she know the little misery I was suffering? But how the hell could a man just do it? Like that? There wasn't a hint of passion in her.

'I think it will be better if we make love. Then we shall be friends. We shall be able to talk better.'

She sat up, her back facing me. I saw the long zip. I leaned up, gently eased it down. She stood up, wriggled out of the dress. She was wearing nothing under it. Her body was the colour of tanned leather. Her sunbathing had been done in the nude, and there were no white breaks. Her breasts were barely noticeable, but the nipples were large.

She waited, just standing by the divan. Before I could voice my doubts, she told me the servants had been dismissed. I didn't really want her, but I could hardly not try. When my clothes were in an untidy heap, she signalled me to lie down again. Efficiently, she straddled my quiet body.

There'd been no great excitement, little wild threshing of limbs seeking climax. It was almost cold-blooded. But when we were again lying side by side, and I had a peculiar feeling of fulfil-ment and contentment, I had the sensation of having known Renée for years.

Though I didn't expect an answer, I asked the question: 'Who are you, Renée?'

She smiled. 'Like you, I am a journalist.'

'And like your brother?'

'Yes. Like my brother.'

'But you're Rumanian, like your brother. Yet both of you work in a British military area.'

'We have lived here for a long time.'

'But your country is fighting with the Nazis.'

'Yes.'

'Shouldn't you be interned or something?'

'There are many Rumanians who do not agree with what our country has done.'

'Do you work at Anna's?'

She didn't answer that. Instead, she asked a question of her own: 'Be very careful if you see this man Davers again. You will see him, perhaps?'

'I'm not excited about it.'

'But you must. It is necessary. Be careful, that is all.'

'Why?'

'This Cairo is a strange place,' she said.

She wasn't telling me anything I didn't know.

'And Harida. She is very dangerous. She is a very good friend of Hussein Bey.'

'I don't know Hussein.'

'He was here. Tonight.'

'I know. But I didn't meet him.' I thought about it, then added, 'Sophia knows him well.'

'I think so.' A pause, then. 'He has been away a long time. He has returned . . . perhaps two, three weeks ago.'

The 'half-wog': should I press along on that? No, I twisted, my elbow in the cushion propping up my head. 'You seem to invite some odd people to your boat.'

'It is necessary.'

She rolled off the divan, unselfconsciously walked into another room, and came back wearing a silk robe.

'I think you should go now,' she said.

I put on my clothes. I had to force myself to remember I'd made love to this woman – or rather, she'd made love to me. She'd been right: I felt we were friends, hardly lovers. This wasn't at all like the Sophia thing.

'Shall I see you again?'

She thought about that for a moment. 'It is possible,' she said. 'It may be necessary.'

'Would you like to know where you can contact me?'

'I think Mr Mortimer will know. Or Mr Hodges.'

Now we were getting somewhere. We went out on to the deck together. Across the lightening murk of the river there was the faint tinkle of camel-bells. The air was heavy with the scent of frangipani. The huge Sudanese materialised from nowhere. He was waved away. We stood, Renée and me, staring out at the ghostly silhouettes of mosque and Citadel and the distant blackness of the Mokattam Hills.

'Au 'voir, Julius,' she whispered. 'Walk safely.'

I was alone on the deck except for the Sudanese, who walked ahead of me to the gangway.

Julius. She'd said Julius . . .

SEVENTEEN

LONDON: SUSSEX RE-VISITED

After Hodges had phoned me at the Ministry shortly after I'd got back to the office, I knew the meeting arranged for my flat that night was going to be rough. As a sort of insurance I bought two bottles of lemonade on my way home, large ones. Perhaps his favourite tipple might soothe his temper, though I wasn't optimistic that it would. I reckoned he wasn't going to be pleased with me. I was right. For starters, he said he didn't have time to sit around drinking lemonade.

'Update me,' he said. 'You go to the Kenyons' tomorrow?'

It was useless trying to temporise. 'I don't know,' I said. I tried to explain that Sara wasn't in London, that she was in Paris. All I could do was wait till she contacted me. But his barrage of questions kept getting in the way. At last I had to do some yelling of my own to get sense into a conversation that wasn't getting either of us anywhere.

'Look,' I shouted. '*She* said her old man wanted me down there. *She* said she'd drive me down. *She* laid it all on. What the hell can I do if her bloody firm shoot her off to France? For Christ's sake, Hodges, act your age!'

That, I figured, was going to earn me a push in the face. Instead, his face tightened. The rage went out of him. I sometimes wondered how much of him was actor. His hard eyes bored into me.

'You know the firm sent her?'

I had to admit I was assuming this. He clicked his teeth, tapped his fingers on the arm of the comfortable chair. I was perched on the straight-back.

'She'll be back on Monday, you say?'

'I don't say anything. The office said it. That they were expecting her back at the office on Monday.'

'So she may come back sooner? In time to take you down to Sussex?'

'I've been trying to tell you that. But you kept banging questions at . . .'

'All right, all right. Don't get your knickers in a knot.' He chewed a finger nail. 'This man Harding: he'll be there?'

'I don't know.' Now came the tricky bit. 'He never mentioned it.'

The ferret face jutted forward, a bit like a snake striking. 'Never mentioned it? When didn't he mention it?'

'Today.'

Hodges came out of his chair fast. But not quite as fast as I got out of mine. I put the table between us. His hands gripped the edge. I kept mine free, just in case.

'Tell me.' His voice was very quiet.

'I phoned him.' The knuckles were white where he was gripping the table. 'Christ, I had to. Benson's on to something. I had to tip Harding off. He had to know.' I could have drunk some of that lemonade lying in the fridge. My mouth was like sandpaper.

'Why Harding? Why not me?'

'Benson had to be stopped, fast. Not our . . . not your way.'

He let go of the table, walked away from it.

'Tell me about Benson.'

'You know his style.' Hodges thrust out an impatient hand. It was a karate chop of irritation with word-play.

'Tell me.'

'Something to do with defective warheads we've supplied to the States.' Hodges jerked up his head like somebody had belted him on the chin.

'Say that again . . .'

'Defective warheads we've supplied to the States.' Quickly I added, 'I didn't know what the hell he was talking about. But it had to be bad. So I phoned Harding. After all, he's on the . . .'

'I bloody well know who Harding is.' I'd always known it wouldn't take Hodges long to check on what deodorant the Ministry man used. He wandered about the room, plucking at his lips. He muttered something about being thirsty. I went into the little kitchen and got the lemonade out of the fridge, poured two glasses. He took his, not bothering to thank me. He sipped as he paced the threadbare carpet, occasionally kicking the furniture. Suddenly he stopped, spun on his heel, stared at me.

'You know anything about this warhead thing?'

'I've told you. No.'

'But some creep mentions warheads and you're on the blower double quick?'

'There'd been no statement come through. And Benson was

going to publish. I couldn't take any chances.'

'What's Harding done about it?'

'Christ, I don't know.' Maybe this might be a good time to fill Hodges in about Pemberton as well.

'You screwed up Cairo because you tried to be clever. Now you're trying to box clever again. Don't do it. Don't . . . do . . . it!' He paused. 'Understand?'

'Look,' I said, 'I've wanted out. I still want out . . .'

His face was a mask. 'Do you? Do you really want out?'

Sunday night: the bathroom; Sara's warm, passionate bed.

He laughed then. That bitter snarl that could still bring out goose-pimples on my flesh. 'Don't try to kid me. Don't get clever, and don't try to kid me. You do what you're told to do. Keep on top of the Kenyon woman.'

This amused him. He said he'd be in touch, went out and slammed the door with a jerk that shook the wall.

Hodges, I told myself, was a prize shit.

I chucked the rest of the lemonade muck down the plug-hole and poured myself a large scotch. What I was going to try to sort out needed a strong stimulant. I sat myself down in the best chair, gulped a mouthful and started at my own personal think-in on how I'd got myself involved in this bloody mess. I'd just got to the bit where I was wondering why that bastard Hodges was playing everything tight against his chest when the phone rang. I lurched up, stuck the thing to my ear and said a nasty, impatient 'Hello'. But the operator wasn't going to be intimidated. Maybe she had a boy friend waiting when she came off shift. She was full of happiness.

I grumpily confirmed my identity. Then she said, 'Miss Sara Kenyon is calling you person-to-person from Paris. I'm connecting you now . . .'

I still hadn't recovered when Sara said a hesitant 'Hello'. My lips were framing words, but there was no sound. I was miming an idiot.

'Are you there?' She sounded puzzled.

'You're connected, London,' the operator said.

My voice came back with a rush. 'I know we are,' I snapped.

'Oh,' said Sara.

'Not you,' I said. My voice was still acting daft.

'Have I disturbed you? I'm sorry . . .'

I took a sharp but deep breath. 'Hello there,' I said. This was insane. And the madness was costing her money.

I thought I heard a chuckle. That could only be the operator, because Sara still sounded a bit upset.

'If it isn't convenient I can call ag . . .'

I jumped in fast on that. 'Sara love, *I'm* sorry. Lovely of you to ring.'

'You're sure?' Doubt lingered.

'Sure? I'm delighted.' And so I was. 'I tried to reach you this morning.'

'That's why I'm calling. I felt awful.' I made noises suggesting she didn't have to. 'No, really. I found I just had to come across on Monday morning. Early. And . . . well, I'm dreadfully sorry. I forgot to let you know. That's awful, isn't it? I mean, you must've been wondering about Friday. Going down to Sussex . . .'

'Damn it, Sara. You don't have to let me know what you're doing.' I'm glad Hodges wasn't hearing that.

'It was rude of me. But you're sweet, pretending it wasn't.' Honest, I felt about seventeen. 'Anyway, I just wanted you to know I'll be back in town on Friday morning. My car's at the airport. Where shall I collect you?'

'How about I meet you at Heathrow? What time's your flight due in?' This was potty, but I was enjoying it.

I heard her laugh, could see in my mind the fingers of her free hand caressing the cheek.

'Why should you? You have work to do.' A pause, then, 'I'll go to my flat. Can you come there? About four? Or is that too early?'

'Four o'clock it is. Earlier if you like.'

'No. Four o'clock. I . . . there's something I have to do when I get back. And you will pack a bag, won't you. Make a weekend of it.'

'Weekend? But your father . . . perhaps he . . .'

'He'll have you for chess. Mornings only: the rest's for me.' Pips were pipping insistently. 'Friday, then. Four o'clock.'

'Yes,' she said.

Then something occurred to me. 'Any other people going to be there?'

'Only Mr Harmsworth. On Saturday. But you know him, don't you?' A giggle. 'And once they start playing they'll probably forget about us.'

I liked the implications of that. But Harding?

'I really must fly. I'm late already. 'Bye. See you Friday.'

The line went dead, even as my lips were shaping my own

155

hope that she'd take care of herself.

I cradled the phone slowly. She was late. I wondered for what?

Harding, alias Harmsworth: it worried me. This would be the first time we would be meeting, face to face in our ridiculous James Bond identities, in the company of other people. Because obviously Sara's father also knew Harding as Harmsworth. Should I get in touch with Hodges? Easy for him to tell me to concentrate on Sara, not to get involved with anybody else.

The way things turned out this time of worry could have been used to better purpose. Like going out and jumping under a bus.

I got to her flat on time. I'd left the Ministry at noon, had a couple of pints and a sour pasty at a Whitehall pub. I was still trying to make up my mind whether to contact Harding or not. Finally I decided not. I went home and packed a small bag. I could feel excitement building up, and it had nothing to do with whatever it was I was supposed to be doing for Hodges. I didn't know what the hell I *was* supposed to be doing for him, anyway. So why not enjoy doing it?

Half-past two. I tried to read. Memories of last Sunday, mind-pictures of her body, got between my eyes and the printed text. I drank some whisky, sipping it slowly.

Three o'clock. That was when the phone rang. It was Hodges. 'Well?'

I knew what he meant. 'Yes. I'm going.'

'She's been in touch, then?'

'Yes.'

He was waiting for more. Let the bastard wait.

'I want to know why she went to Paris. What she did there.' I didn't say anything. His voice started to rasp. 'You there? You hear me?'

'I can hear you.'

'Then bloody well answer. Why and what? I want to know. Tickle her up a bit tonight, then start the quiz. Got it?'

I kept my mouth shut. I had to. I might've told him to get stuffed, loud and clear.

'Listen, you,' he snarled. 'I'm talking to you.'

'Now you listen, Hodges. *I'm* talking to *you*. Get cancer.'

I banged the phone down. I felt better. I drained off the

whisky in the glass, picked up my bag, locked the door and headed for the bus-stop.

When I turned into Walnut Tree Walk she was putting a bag into her car. She didn't see me. I watched her run back into the house.

It was spot on four o'clock. I walked up the path, stood on the porch by the open door. I couldn't see her but I heard her voice. She was saying '. . . and it won't be possible, not this weekend. I'm going down to Hassocks. I have to go down.' I heard her laugh. The sound came from the first-floor landing. 'So don't let us have any nonsense. Everything went well in Paris. We can't afford to spoil it now.'

A man's voice, tantalisingly familiar, muttered something about he supposed so, but he didn't like it. Nor did I bloody well like it, but there was no profit in being found there listening. So I walked back down to the car, and waited. She came out within a minute. But that had been long enough for me to ask myself a hell of a lot of questions that didn't seem to have any sensible answers. Paris. 'Can't afford to spoil it. Not now.' She had to go to Hassocks. 'No nonsense.' And all said to a man with a voice I'd heard before. But bloody well where?

She was halfway down the path before she spotted me. Her smile, when she did, was as sincere as any I'd seen. She came out through the gate, offered her face. I held up my bag.

'Saw yours in the car. Thought I might as well wait here.'

She looked a little puzzled, opened the back door of the car. 'Put it in there. Save unlocking the boot.' I chucked my luggage in beside hers. 'Sorry I'm late,' she apologised. It was just two minutes past four.

She got in, started the engine. I settled in beside her.

'A neighbour held me up. Thought I'd never shake him off.'

So the voice I knew lived in the same house. Worth remembering. The car moved away. She set course for the A23.

'Friendly bunch?'

'I'm new there,' she said, eyes on the road. 'But they seem all right. No noisy parties.'

I continued to fish. 'Just pop in and out for sugar and tea?' I tried to make it sound like a joke.

She smiled, rubbing her cheek. 'Silly, isn't it? I found myself without sugar my first night.' She took skilful evasive action to avoid a bus using weight and bulk to intimidate. 'But I was lucky. I knew my next-door neighbour.'

Was this the man she'd been talking to? It was while I was framing my next question that she said, 'Whatever are you wearing a suit for?'

I'd already been conscious for some time of her close-fitting slacks and the sweater thing stretched tight over bra-less breasts, the firm nipples shaping hard little mounds under the soft material. 'A suit's always safe. You know, meals. Guests. Got some casual gear in my bag.'

She concentrated as we ran into thickening traffic. She drove well. She assessed road room, made decisions, acted on them, fondled her way through the gears with precision. I congratulated her. I had to recover some of the ground I'd lost when we'd met at the gate. I must have seemed bloody churlish not kissing the mouth offered. Churlish? After our Sunday night she must be asking herself a lot of questions too, I thought. This job wasn't my scene.

'Treat a car properly and it's predictable,' she said. I felt I should wipe the spit out of my eye.

'Unlike people?' I tried to make another joke.

'Unlike people,' she agreed, her voice as flat as I felt.

I left her to the driving and huddled myself down in the bucket seat. It seemed a good time to just shut up.

It was all so different from what I'd looked forward to. That drive to Hassocks might as well have been in a stranger's car. Oh, we got around to chatting in a spasmodic sort of way about nothing in particular. I had to keep telling myself I'd slept with this woman, that she'd gone to all the trouble of phoning me from Paris. What the hell had gone wrong? I knew what had gone wrong. It hadn't only been concern at the overheard references to Paris and no nonsense and the rest of it. It had been the . . . the *intimate* nature of their conversation. Jealousy? Perhaps. There's no fool like an old fool, they say. Well, I was old enough to have handled things better.

Maybe Hodges was right. Maybe I never learnt any lessons. Damn it, why was Sara any different from her mother? She'd made the play on the Sunday, just as her mother had done in Cairo. Sara was no virgin who'd given me her all in the name of love. She'd been around, had Sara. And that made me feel lousy. I wished I was able to rationalise sex, put it in the same category as good meals I'd enjoyed. Once I tried to be tough about it, then of course I had to bloody ask myself why she'd done it at all: why she'd taken me into her bed, damn near sight-unseen.

We were nearing the Hassocks turn-off when she said, eyes on the road, 'How well do you know Mr Harmsworth?'

How well did I know Harding? Now, that was quite a question.. It didn't help that I'd forgotten the Ministry's mystery man would be among those present at the Kenyons'. Hell! A little memory-bank hammered away, warning caution. Sara still didn't know where I worked: just that I was in PR. She'd never asked. But what did she know about Harmsworth alias Harding? She'd seen him several times on her own. What had he told her? Then I remembered something important. The first time we'd met I'd volunteered the intelligence that Harmsworth was one of those people you know and can't ever remember how or when or why you met, and she, surprised, had said something along the same lines. But did that still apply?

'How well?' I countered, still playing for time.

'Yes,' she said. There was a hint of impatience.

'Not very well.' I wondered then how this would square with Harmsworth's assurances to her that I was Freeman, after Stapleton had tried to blow the cover. Then I had an idea. 'Why?' I asked her. 'Is it important?'

She shook her head, switched on the flicker to warn the road she was turning left into Hassocks.

'Do you like him?' she asked after she had swung the car expertly into the narrower road.

I shrugged. No sense in saying I wished he was dead. 'Do you?'

The bitterness in her voice surprised me. 'I loathe him,' she said.

Something was wrong. As we crunched up the gravel drive we saw three cars outside the house. Two of them were police cars, one of them a panda, and a uniformed constable was standing by the open front door.

I looked quickly at Sara. Her face had paled. Her hands were suddenly gripping the wheel hard, the knuckles white. She put her foot down, drove the last few yards recklessly, skidded to a gravel-spraying stop. She flicked off the motor and hurled herself out of the car. I followed her. The constable barred our passage. She wrenched at his restraining arm, broke past him. More diplomatically, I waited. Through the doorway I saw a uniformed inspector, a sergeant and a couple of constables; an elderly woman who could be the housekeeper, a man in earth-stained clothes, perhaps a gardener; and, his back to me, the chunky figure of Harding alias Harmsworth.

This was going to be a crunch crisis. Whatever had happened, the police were going to want his identity, and mine; our true identities. Not even in the business I'd been press-ganged into did you play silly buggers with the men in blue.

Hodges, I told myself savagely, was going to have a lot to answer for. And I wished to God I'd never had a drink with Grayling in Cairo thirty years ago.

EIGHTEEN

CAIRO: NO MAN IS AN ISLAND

When I got back to the Shubra flat I tossed my clothes in a heap and caught up on some sleep. The drill was that I had to report in at the news agency when not physically on anything to do with Sophia, but I reckoned what I'd been doing came under that heading so I snored off.

It was just after one o'clock when Hodges arrived. He was good and mad. Hamid let him in and he caught me in the cot.

'What the hell d'you think you're doing?' he wanted to know. I mentioned it had to be obvious, didn't it? That didn't help. He grabbed me by a wrist, twisted, and I was on my back on the floor. My arm hurt; so did the base of my spine. The pain prompted me to scramble to my feet and heave a punch in his general direction. He swung away from it and pointed a finger.

'Try that and I'll tear an arm off you,' he said. I glared at him. But he had the confidence of a bloke who could do just what he said. So I rubbed my wrist and tried to forget about my back.

'Christ,' Hodges said. That was when I realised I didn't have any clothes on. 'Not surprising that bitch prefers other men.'

It was while I was trying to get into some clothes with what dignity I had left that I got the drift of what he meant. Mortimer had spotted Sophia in a taxi with Hussein Bey. He'd followed them in his car and seen them making for the Giza road. He'd phoned into the agency and of course bright boy wasn't there. So he'd contacted Hodges. And here was Hodges, like I said, good and mad.

'She's your job. Why aren't you bloody well with her?'

I muttered something about as long as some bastard was keeping an eye on her what was the harm? I had to get some sleep.

The freshly laundered shirt I'd just buttoned got badly crumpled when Hodges grabbed it. I sagged when the oxygen down to my lungs was cut off. Then I landed on the bed. Still, that was better than the floor.

'Get out there. Now. Pick 'em up. And stay on their tails.

She's with a gyppo at the Auberge. Mortimer says it looks like they'll be eating there: He had to get to the office. Get moving.'

Gyppo? All right, you smart bastard.

'That'll be Hussein,' I said. 'He was hanging round her like a bad smell all last night.' Then I reckoned Hodges should know I hadn't been wasting my time. 'But he's only half wog. Mother's side. His old man's worth checking out.'

Hodges' face had gone all puckered. It looked like a prune. I knotted my tie in front of the mirror, saw I was a wreck, unshaven, with not even a chance of a wash. And my mouth was like the bottom of a parrot's cage. Then I saw the reflected image of a suddenly alert Hodges.

'Where did you find that out?'

'Chap called Davers, Harry Davers. American. Says he's in oil. Tipped me off at Renée's party. She's Paul's sister. Has a house . . .'

My hand flew away from my tie. Then it was up near the back of my neck. Flames of pain like lightning-bolts wrenched at my elbow and shoulder. I yelped like a hurt dog.

His grating voice was so close to my ear I could feel the hot breath. 'You won't bloody learn, will you? Do the whole damn job on your own.' He gave my captured arm another jerk. I wanted to pass out, anything to escape the burning, twisting, horrible pain. 'Sophia. She's your mark. Just bloody Sophia, nobody else. Sophia. Understand?'

I nodded feverishly. My free arm scrabbled at his body but it was tucked well behind me. He knew the tricks. I sagged down on to the bed when he released me. Straightening the arm was rough, but it had to be done. For a few moments I was sure something was broken, but he was far too expert for that. I think I was sobbing with the relief from the agony.

When I finally got him back in focus he was standing there unruffled, calm, calculating. I rubbed the still aching arm, tried to speak normally. 'You bastard. What d'you think I'm doing? Bloody enjoying myself?'

He pursed his lips. 'Forget Hussein. And Davers. Forget this Renée woman.' Then, as an afterthought, 'And forget about Harida, too. You're not in her league.'

Now how the hell did he know about Harida? I'd never mentioned her, though I'd nearly blurted out about meeting the belly-dancer. But his instructions just weren't on. 'But how can I avoid 'em if Sophia's mixed up with them?'

'You'd better wash up. You're a mess,' he said. 'Then get out to Giza. Stay with that bitch of yours.'

He went out. I heard the door slam.

I got out to the Auberge des Pyramids in a hurry. Cairene lunches being what they were, if Sophia and her companion were eating there'd still be time to catch up with them. But what I was supposed to do if they were there I didn't have a clue. Hodges was strong on orders, light on method. I found several vantage points both inside and out at the restaurant. No sign of Sophia. Could they have gone to the Café aux Pigeons? Mortimer had told Hodges they were heading towards Giza. Could be. I got in the car and sped back on my tracks.

I wandered about under the trees until the waiters got suspicious. An under-manager looked as if he was heading in my direction. I left.

Sitting in the Chevvy I wondered what to do next. I didn't want Hodges having another go at tearing an arm off. I decided to find a bar and have a long, cool zibib while I thought about it.

Three zibibs didn't solve my problems, but they did help me to live with them. I headed for the Shubra flat. I went up the stairs. Hamid was waiting, po-faced. 'The mam'selle is here, bey.'

There'd been only one mam'selle during my brief tenancy. Sophia was a bright girl. She always knew where and when to show up to get me out of jams with Hodges. She was stretched out on a divan, minus shoes and jacket. The silk blouse was unbuttoned way down and she was lazily fanning herself with a magazine.

'Hello,' I said.

'Why did you follow me last night?'

'Follow you? What's that supposed to mean?'

'To the houseboat. I do not like that.'

'I didn't. Renée invited me.'

She plainly didn't believe it. 'I told you I could not see you again yesterday; not until today. So you followed me I think.'

'Well, you think wrong. But as you've brought it up, I wasn't wild about that bloke you were with. The Hussein fellow. You like wogs?'

She sat up. Not fast. Deliberately. 'What is a wog?'

'Oh, an Egyptian.' Honesty compelled me to add, 'Or an Italian, a Spaniard, you know, anybody on the Mediterranean, I suppose.'

She looked hard at me. 'He is none of those things.'

'Oh yes, he is. Know that for a fact.' Was it only three zibibs I'd had? My speech sounded a bit funny.

She got up. 'I think you are drunk.' She picked up her jacket, shrugged into it. Found her shoes, wrestled her toes into them. 'You can drive the car?' I nodded. 'Please take me somewhere.'

That eased my mind a bit. At least she wasn't walking out. My elbow and shoulder still ached.

'Where do you want to go?'

She glanced at the door of the flat. It was shut tight. 'To Ida and Yanni. It is important.'

'Okay,' I said. 'Then we'll come back here?'

'Perhaps,' she said. 'But come quickly.'

Ida and Yanni were still living in squalor in the squalid, noisy Bulak room. They didn't greet us with any marked joy, but Sophia quickly indicated we wouldn't be there long. She took Ida into the small kitchen. As Yanni, obviously put out by something, reluctantly offered me some cheap brandy I could watch the two women in earnest conversation. Sophia handed Ida what looked like an envelope. Ida took it eagerly enough but didn't open it.

Yanni was grumbling about a job he'd got at Abbasia barracks with the British army. He didn't think the pay was much but, brightening, there were compensations.

'Like what?' I asked him, watching Ida and Sophia. Yanni opened a small cupboard: packets of biscuits, cans of bully beef, packets of tea and coffee.

'We eat better now,' he explained. Then, slyly, he opened a drawer. He jerked his head, inviting me to look inside.

There was a Luger pistol, two boxes of 9 mm ammunition. Lowering his voice he said, 'You can have it, cheap. Ten pounds, eh?'

I told him I might be Irish but I wasn't with the IRA. Then I jerked my head towards the kitchen. 'What're those two up to?'

He glanced across, shrugged. 'This is a very good pistol.'

'I don't need a gun,' I said. 'What sort of a job have you got at Abbasia?'

164

'I am a clerk.'

Food; a gun! I wondered if that was all the Greek was bringing out of the Cairo barracks. Yanni poured himself another glass of brandy. In the brief silence I heard Sophia say, 'Hussein is prepared to pay more.' Pay for what? And had the envelope she had handed over contained money?

Then Ida's voice, louder and angry, 'You forget what I am.'

My eyes flickered in her direction. Sophia was looking at me, and had hold of Ida's wrist. I turned away, picked up the gun. It was a well-cared-for weapon. But it had been used.

'All right,' said Yanni. 'Nine hundred piastres.'

I shook my head.

'You are right,' said Sophia at my elbow. 'It is too big. It is for the military, that.'

You, I told myself, should know. I wondered again why she had that slim Browning in her baggage.

'We must go now,' Sophia said. I laid the gun back in the drawer, refused Yanni's offer of a second brandy, nodded to Ida and walked with Sophia to the door. I held it open. Sophia insisted I go out ahead of her and when I was in the passage she muttered something, went back to Ida. She whispered for a moment, then joined me. Ida slammed the door shut.

'She is not very clever, that one,' Sophia said. She took my arm and we walked to the stairs.

She came back to the flat. I desperately wanted to contact Hodges. I went into the kitchen and poured her the vodka she liked so much, then quickly and quietly poured nearly all of what was left in the bottle down the sink.

I took the glass and the bottle back in to her. 'I'll have to pop down and get some more,' I said.

'Hamid will do that,' she said.

'He takes too long. He gossips. Won't be a minute.'

I hurried into the little bar nearby.

Julius was told that Hodges wasn't available. But there was a question about an insurance policy. Perhaps Julius could find it convenient to call to discuss it?

I was sorry. I was entertaining a friend.

Then perhaps a message could be delivered by Hamid? 'Very well,' I said, and rang off.

I ordered a zibib and sat at a table to scribble my note. It was brief, but they would know what it was all about.

I remembered I hadn't bought the vodka. I got two bottles,

hurried back upstairs. I thrust the folded paper into Hamid's hand, told him to deliver it urgently. He knew where. He nodded, padded down the stairs, his sandals making a flapping noise.

Just a mite out of breath, I went into the flat. Sophia was standing in the hall, a Browning pistol aimed steadily at my chest. I came close to dropping the bottles. Instinctively I braced my muscles for the shock of the ·32 slug hitting me. Then she started to laugh, the fingers of her free hand working overtime on the dimple.

'Your face,' she croaked. 'It was so funny.'

Funny wasn't how I'd felt. I gulped, walked into the lounge, dumped the bottles down.

'What the hell sort of a game was that?' I demanded. I didn't need to pretend anger. Still laughing her fool head off, she sank down on the divan. I got the cap off one of the bottles and for the first time in my life took a swig of neat vodka. It bloody near tore the lining off my throat. God knows how she coped with the stuff.

'You looked so funny,' she gurgled.

I took the gun off her. 'Where did you get this bloody thing anyway?'

Still smiling, she pointed to the bedroom. 'It is yours. It was in the drawer. I needed a handkerchief.' She held up the square of cotton looped in the waistband of her skirt. 'And there was the gun.'

I unclipped the magazine. I knew that unless she'd loaded it it would be empty. It was empty.

'Why do you keep a gun?' she wanted to know.

'For the same reason you do,' I said. To hell with what she made of that. I watched the laughter drain from her. I didn't bother to tell her that the handkerchiefs were in a different drawer from the one in which I kept the pistol. So she'd had a snoop around. I'd done the same with her gear. Honours were even. I went back into the bedroom, opened a drawer, slid the gun back in its holster, and there was a little pile of handkerchiefs. Either I was getting forgetful or she'd made sure her story would stand up if it came to the crunch.

She was behind me. 'Let us go to bed,' she said.

Both of us were pretty exhausted after a tempestuous hour of acrobatics. Sophia liked experimentation: she regarded the impossible as just another challenge to ingenuity. 'You are much better now,' she complimented me. Coming from a woman without any inhibitions at all, I felt rather good about that.

I was lying there, hands behind my head, staring up at the ceiling and allowing the strength to flow back into me.

'Would you take me to Istanbul?' she asked, just like suggesting a sight-seeing trip in a felucca on the Nile.

I screwed my head round. She was facing me, her face very still.

Istanbul? All right. Turkey was still neutral. But both sides in the raging conflict were wooing a nation strategically vital to their different aims.

'I wish to visit my uncle.'

'It won't be easy,' I said. I tried to sound casual.

'You are neutral. It should not be difficult.'

'My job's here.'

'There is much to write about in Istanbul,' she countered. 'It will be very simple. We go to Haifa. There is the Taurus Express which will take us to Istanbul.'

'Why can't your uncle come here?'

'It is not possible.'

'You don't like Cairo?'

'Very much. But I must visit my uncle. It is very important.'

'Why?'

Her long fingernails started to trace intricate patterns on my chest, on my belly. I began to feel restless. I fought the temptation to put my hands on her, thrust myself into her. One bloody thing at a time.

'Why didn't you go to your uncle from Budapest, then? You must've come through Istanbul.'

'Because he was not there at that time. Now he is there.'

'So he's in touch with you?'

'No. With a friend. My friend says I must go.'

The fingers were still busy. Down the inside of my thighs, up again, exploring, exciting . . .

'Hussein?'

Her eyes widened a little. She moved her face closer, her mouth opening. The fingers tightened, the nails biting suddenly in stretched flesh. For half an hour I forgot about Istanbul.

She insisted that I drive her back to her flat shortly after midnight. This was also 'very important'. But when I got back to

Shubra I wasn't too disappointed. She'd talked. She'd had to. If I were to be persuaded to get her to Instanbul she had to tell me something. But how much of it was true? Hodges would have to sort that out.

I grabbed some sleep and phoned the contact at eight o'clock. Hodges would see me at the insurance office at ten.

It was Silah's shift on door duty. He brought me coffee and croissants and a newspaper. The headlines hit me. The Luftwaffe had bombed Port Tewfik. Shipping had escaped major damage, the report said. Some shore installations had been hit. Three of the raiders had been shot down.

Suez. The convoy. Paul Danescu. Sophia. Maybe Hodges would have to listen to me now.

Hodges was with Collins when I reported in at ten o'clock. The two of them sat behind the desk, stonily staring at me. I sat in a straightback chair facing them. I held out the newspaper. It would make a good starting point.

Collins waved it away. 'Well?' he asked.

'She wants to go to Istanbul,' I said. There didn't seem any point in beating about the bush.

They didn't even blink. Just waited for whatever else I had to tell them, which, to me, seemed plenty. I started in with our visit to Ida and Yanni: Yanni's job, the food in the cupboard; the envelope given to Ida; the proposition that Hussein could be persuaded to pay more. Then the bits Sophia had told me in bed at the Shubra flat: how her uncle had saved her life as a child when the Bolsheviks had butchered her parents during the stormy days of the Revolution; how he'd smuggled her to Estonia where she'd been educated; how she'd drifted to Cracow, to Paris, to London. She'd married in London, had a daughter. But this had broken up. She'd gone back to Paris, to Berlin, to Rome. Her brother, I told them, was fighting in Russia. And, off my own bat, I reminded them that White Russian troops were fighting with the Wehrmacht. That was really carrying coals to Newcastle. I started to launch into some theories taking shape in my mind when Collins held up a restraining hand.

'Please wait outside,' he said.

Pompous bastards, I thought. But I went out into the little anteroom and cooled my heels for a good half-hour. Who the hell did those blokes think they were? I'd got them a bucket of information. I'd done a good job. And I was being treated like a bloody office boy. When I got back in there maybe I should tell them a few home-truths.

Hodges came out. He shut the door behind him. 'Go back to the flat. Wait there till I can get around to you,' he said.

'Can't. I'm meeting Sophia for lunch.'

This irritated him. 'Do you have to?'

'Come off it. You said it was my job to stay with her. I'm doing my best. Anyway, she wants an answer on this Istanbul thing.'

'Oh,' he said. 'Wait here.' He went back into Collins's office. He was in there for another ten minutes.

'All right,' he said. 'Meet her for lunch. Where're you taking her?'

'Sans Souci.'

'That bloody place?'

'She likes it.'

'Very well, if you must.' He wasn't at all happy. 'About Istanbul. Tell her it'll take some time to fix, but you're working on it. Don't press. Just find out anything you can. Then get rid of her. Go to the flat. I'll be in touch.'

'But, look, there's . . .'

'Do as you are told,' he snarled. He stood there, watched me fumble with the door and storm off down the corridor.

He arrived at seven o'clock. I'd been varying my diet of zibib with a few slugs of vodka. It hadn't been a good day. The lunch had been a damp squib of a thing. Sophia had been impatient that I didn't seem able to fix a journey for two to Istanbul more quickly. The wine hadn't been to her taste. And when I said she couldn't come back to the flat because I had work to do she got downright huffy. Then, when I'd put up some questions about uncle, she said he was very old now, wanted to see her; then she'd shut up.

So when Hodges got there I was prepared to risk having an arm torn off.

'What the hell's going on?' I demanded. 'You bastards push a bloke round and don't tell him a damned thing. What cooks?'

'You're going to England. That's what cooks,' he said. He seemed pleased about it.

England? As far as it went, that was fine. But why? Then I cheered up a bit. Maybe it was to do a bit of probing into Sophia's marriage. I was going to miss her in bed, but that would have had to come to an end anyway. So it was now. Not good, but far from fatal. I thought of all the women short of men in London . . .

'We feel you could be a liability if you stayed on here. Even back in the army.'

I stared at the man. He stared back. But he was trying to smile, just so I'd know how he felt about it.

'Liability? What's that supposed to mean?'

'Like it says in the dictionary: the opposite of an asset.'

'You mean I'm sacked?'

'In a word, yes.'

He went out to the ice-box, got himself a lemonade. He came back, sipping the gut-rot, sat down.

'There's an aircraft going back. You'll be on it, in uniform. And you can wear your sergeant's stripes. We'll let you keep those.'

Questions hammered around in my brain. But I didn't know where to start asking them. He drank some more, smacked his lips appreciatively. 'That's the way it is,' he said.

'But Christ, man, we haven't even started on her yet . . .'

'Look, sonny,' he said. 'Maybe we haven't. But this is for the professionals. You've done your best to screw us up. So you're out. As from now.'

That 'sonny' rankled. He was two, at most three, years older than I was. I wanted to belt him. God, how I wanted to smash his mouth. But that was an area where he'd win. There had to be another way.

Then he said, 'Forget it. The file's closed. We know what we're doing . . .'

'Then how about telling *me*? I'm the mug who's been pushed around from pillar to post. Told to do this, do that. I gave you a basinful of stuff this morning. What the hell d'you want? Blood?'

'That's the name of the war-game, isn't it?' He got up, drained his glass. 'By the way, I wouldn't try to go out if I were you.'

'And why bloody not?'

'Because Hamid or Silah or both of them will stop you. And even if you get past them, there'll be others. Not gentle; no, not gentle.'

I choked back my rage and frustration. 'Okay. You kick me out. Why? You can bloody well tell me that.'

'I've told you. You screw things up. Well, got to be going.

Things to untangle. Stay put. Food'll be brought in. And I'll be in touch.'

He left.

And I sat there, not knowing one goddam thing about what was happening to me.

NINETEEN

LONDON: NOT QUITE CHECKMATE

Alexander Kenyon, Commander RN (Ret'd), was dead. The top of his head had been blown off by a shotgun blast.

The inspector, an unusually kindly man for a policeman, was very gentle with Sara, and though the elderly housekeeper, Mrs Cummings, had actually discovered the body, she was a level-headed soul not much given to hysterics. She helped too.

Inspector Solomons was apologetic. The CID were on their way, but they would create as little disturbance as possible.

I badly wanted to have a word with Harding but there was no way I could. Beyond the briefest of nods he ignored my existence.

The gardener, Harding and I were ushered into a small library and a stolidly uncommunicative constable stayed with us. Mrs Cummings was with Sara, who seemed to have taken the tragedy calmly enough. Information about just what had happened was scarcer than teeth in a hen.

Through the mullioned windows we watched the CID cars arrive. With them was a woman detective, and all the paraphernalia of investigation, including what I suspected was the murder bag. Was this murder? And if so, why? And by whom? Fortunately the when of it wasn't any of my business, nor of Sara's.

There was a lot of coming and going. Then an ambulance, siren wailing, chugged to a stop in front of the house. The library door opened and a man in civvies whispered something to the constable. The policeman crossed to where Harding was standing by the window. More whispering. Harding nodded, followed the policeman to the door, went out. The constable remained.

'Sorry business, this,' I said to the man who looked like a gardener.

'Ay,' he said and seemed inclined to say more but the policeman coughed and said, 'It would be better if you didn't talk, gentlemen, until after you've spoken to the officers.'

He was polite, but firm. I lit a cigarette and strolled along the shelves of books. Kenyon had obviously been a man of catholic taste in literature, and equally obviously with the means to indulge it. Some of the tomes were old: first editions I suspected. Then I came to a section devoted wholly to his passion: chess. Manuals and text-books and volumes of problems, in French, English, German. I selected one of the books at random, then put it back quickly when the policeman coughed again and said, 'If you don't mind, sir.'

There were three chess-tables in the room, two of them with arrays of pieces as though the games had been adjourned. Or perhaps they were problems. I stared down at the boards. Both games were showing the black king in check, but that was the end of any similarity between them.

'Check to your king,' had been Stapleton's message to me brought by Sara. 'Check to your king' had been Pemberton's statement to his opponent in the pub. But the king hadn't been in check, according to Hodges' man. Well, I thought, Kenyon had been well and truly checked – checkmated, in fact.

The gardener produced an evil-looking pipe, began slowly and methodically to fill it. Like all men who work in the dirt of the earth he was unhurried, patient. He was used to waiting for things to happen, knew they couldn't be hurried. For some strange reason I envied him. Here were Hodges and his crew scurrying around like frightened rabbits to achieve . . . what? A slight change in political balance that probably wouldn't matter a damn if it stayed the way it was.

I wandered back to the two chess games, stared hard at the pieces. Whoever had been playing black in one of them knew even less about the game than I did. That made him a tyro. His king had been left so exposed that his opponent had been able to put him in check at long range with a bishop and, with supporting forces of knight, rook and queen, was going to create all sorts of havoc without black being able to do much about it. On the other board the game was being played by exponents of some sophistication. The situation was complex with, it seemed to my not-very-expert eye, black only temporarily embarrassed and poised to mount an attack of his own.

I sniffed. The gardener had lit his pipe. The room was starting to stink: even the stolid constable's nose was twitching. I concentrated on the chessboards, hoping to be able to ignore the stench. The only hope for black in the novice game was for him to sacrifice his queen. But it was always difficult to convince a novice that the loss of a queen wasn't the end of the game. I was prepared to bet he'd sacrifice a knight and that would be very much that.

The policeman coughed at my elbow. 'If you'll come this way, sir.' I followed him to the door, a shade irritated at being interrupted. I was interviewed in the kitchen, but the detective sergeant and detective constable at the table were very polite. They stood up, invited me to sit down, told me I could smoke if I wished.

They understood I knew the late Commander Kenyon. Slightly, I said; I'd met him once. They hoped they wouldn't have to bother me for long, but perhaps I understood it was necessary? Yes I understood.

The constable poised pencil over notebook.

'May we start with your name, sir? Address? Occupation?'

I gave them my name, address and occupation. What was going to be their reaction when Sara gave them a quite different name for me?

I cleared my throat. 'Look, sergeant, there's something I'd better explain.' Explain? How the hell do you explain something you don't understand yourself? 'It's a bit difficult.'

'Ah, yes,' said the sergeant, as though he knew something I didn't. 'The chief superintendent informed me, sir. It's a matter of identity, isn't it? Miss Kenyon is under the impression you are somebody else.'

'Well, yes,' I said.

'Not to worry, sir. We co-operate as fully as possible with you chaps.' He dropped his voice, and got just a little bit roguish. 'Even though we can't always approve of the methods you use sometimes, eh?' If we'd have been on the same side of the table I'm sure he'd have nudged me in the ribs with his elbow. He turned to the constable. 'Don't record that,' he ordered, his voice all official again. The constable obediently scored over the spidery shorthand outlines and waited.

'How did you know?' I asked him. He winked, laid a finger on the side of his nose. The man obviously read too many spy thrillers. Then he got businesslike again. There wasn't much I could tell him, though he wanted to know why a man I'd met only once and with whom, on my own admission, I hadn't got along too well, should invite me to visit his house socially. I told him I was as much in the dark about that as he was. He looked disappointed. Maybe he thought we James Bond people might have given him something to retail to his wife and the locals in his pub. He didn't press me very hard on my relationship with Sara, but was keen to know what I thought about the relationship between father and daughter. I told him what I'd seen and heard on the one occasion I'd seen them together.

Did I know any friends or acquaintances of the late Commander Kenyon?

Maurice Harding, slightly. Dr Stapleton, one brief meeting. It all went down in the constable's notebook.

I decided to risk a question of my own. 'Was Kenyon murdered?'

The sergeant had his chance. He took it. 'Our job is rather like yours, sir.' He winked again. 'We don't like giving too much away. Not before we're sure.'

So they were treating it as 'suspicious death'. Fair enough. Then the sergeant said, 'That will be all, sir. But I wonder if you would mind waiting in the library?'

'Why?' I didn't need to ask. The surprise must have been writ large on my face.

'It's possible the chief super might want a word with you.'

The sergeant escorted me to the door, showed me into the hall. There were still detectives coming and going. I went into the library, back into a fug that now stank to high heaven. The gardener must have been smoking compost.

The pipe-smoker was called next, but he left behind strong evidence of his presence. Without any prompting, the constable crossed to the windows, ran a professional eye over them, located the catches and threw them wide. Wind gusted in. I smiled my thanks. The policeman tried not to smile, but a grin lurked at the corners of his mouth. He was a man very conscious of his duty.

I went back to my contemplation of the two chess games. Were these the keys which would unlock . . . what? I still didn't know what I was doing, being mixed up in all this nonsense, any more than I'd known what was happening in Cairo all those years ago. To hell with it: I'd study the boards as problems. But I'd already found one of them too easy, and the other was far too complex for my simple knowledge of how to move the pieces. Still, it would pass the time if I worked on the difficult one. I sat down at the black side. Me to move. What should I do?

The door opened. Harding came in. With him was a huge, florid man. Flesh hung over his collar. He wheezed as he walked.

Harding saw my fingers poised to touch the king. 'Don't,'

he shouted. Startled, I knocked over the chair, stooped down, and stood it on its legs.

'Sorry, my dear chap,' he said. 'I don't think you've met Chief Superintendent S. Holmes?'

Harding grinned. The detective didn't look at all pleased. The policeman briskly rubbed his mouth in the background.

'Honestly,' said Harding. 'S. Holmes.'

'The S stands for Stephen,' the detective said wearily. He held out a hand the size of a leg of mutton. 'Hello,' he said.

It was a relief that Harding introduced me by my own name. What we were going to do about Sara would have to be sorted out later.

The chief superintendent told the constable inside the door to wait outside. The uniformed man saluted and went.

'How is Miss Kenyon?' I asked.

Harding looked at Holmes. The detective said she was upset, naturally, but composed. 'Very sensible woman, that,' he added. 'Got her feet on the ground. Blimey, the hysteria we have to battle through sometimes.'

His eyes, immersed in their layers of puffy flesh, screwed heavenwards. He waddled to a chair, sank into it with a puff of exhaled breath. Harding sat on the edge of a desk, leg swinging. I sat down again at the chess-table.

'My sergeant's had a chat?'

It was phrased as a question but it wasn't. I nodded. 'Just for the record, that,' Holmes said. 'Maybe we can help each other.'

He squinted up at Harding but got no help. Impatiently, the detective asked, 'Well, can we or can't we?'

'Don't know, old chap. I just don't know,' Harding said.

'Now see here, Maurice,' Holmes said. So they knew each other, I noted. 'We've had to come in on something your lot's interested in. I say we might be able to help: us, you; you, us.'

'You're satisfied, then, old boy?'

'I'm never satisfied,' the big man wheezed.

I wanted to talk to Sara. 'Excuse me, Mr Holmes,' I said. 'The sergeant said you might want a word with me. Do you?'

Holmes thought about that for a moment. 'Not sure,' he said. 'Depends on Maurice, doesn't it?'

I turned to Harding. 'I'd like to see how Sara is. I'll be in the house if you want me.'

'Sorry, dear old boy. Doubt if our friends of the constabulary would like it.'

'Wouldn't like what? Me talking to Sara?'

'Yes. And wandering about the place, you know. Might trample valuable clues into the carpets. Never do at all, old boy.'

He slid off the table, wandered slowly past the chessboards. 'Keen, wasn't he?'

'Sara said so. That's why I'm here. Supposed to play him.'

'Ah,' said Harding. 'Know the game, then, old man?'

'The moves, yes.' This was bloody nonsense.

Harding was standing over the empty board. 'Care for a game?' he asked. I looked at him. He looked serious enough.

'Hardly the occasion, is it?' I said. And meant it.

Holmes wheezed on, but I saw his piggy eyes weren't missing the little duel developing between Harding and me.

'Oh, I don't know, dear boy,' said Harding. 'Nothing we can do at the moment. And I don't think the dear old chief super here would like us to leave just yet?' He turned to Fatty. 'That so, Steve, old man?'

The detective didn't say anything. Harding wandered about, located a box, slid open the lid, tipped thirty-two chessmen on to the empty board. He picked up one white pawn, one black, put his hands behind his back, then presented two clenched fists. This was crazy, real nutty. I tapped the back of his right hand. He turned it over, opened it. In the palm lay a white pawn. He shrugged, started to set up the board. I didn't move, just watched him. Patiently, he laid out his black pieces, then the white, for me. Then he sat down, waving me to the opposite chair.

'Your move,' he said.

Holmes puffed on to his feet, waddled across to our table. His heavy, laboured breathing worried me.

There didn't seem anything else to do but play. I moved the pawn to king four. Harding countered with the same move. And because all this was a nonsense I moved my queen to king's bishop three. He moved a pawn to queen three. To hell with it! I put my king's bishop on queen's bishop four. He looked at the board, then turned a searching stare on me. What with the wheezing and the staring I began to feel uncomfortable. Then, deliberately, he moved his queen's knight to queen's rook three. It was my turn to stare at him. This wasn't

177

chess. It wasn't even beginner's dominoes. He couldn't be serious. But there he sat, contemplating the board with a concentration that suggested there would be more moves. I swept my eyes across the board. No. It was on, all right. I picked up my queen and lifted it carefully to his king's bishop two, removing the pawn. I couldn't help sounding apologetic. 'Mate,' I said.

His face betrayed nothing. He simply said: 'The fool's mate.' He stood up, offered his hand. I shook it briefly. Then I got out of my chair, started to put the pieces back in the box. He watched me.

'You play well,' he said.

'No,' I told him. 'You play badly.'

'Perhaps,' he said. He wandered away. I could hear him murmuring, 'Yes, perhaps, my dear chap.'

Holmes wheezed an 'Excuse me' and lumbered out of the room, closing the door behind him.

I was learning to take my chances as I found them. 'By what name do I address you?' I asked. God, it sounded stuffy.

He turned, smiled. 'A good question, dear boy. A very good question indeed.'

He strolled back to the two boards with the unfinished games, studied them for a long time. I waited, got fed up, decided I'd explore elsewhere, police permitting, perhaps try to find Sara. My hand had closed round the knob when Harding said, 'Would you mind staying with me, old chap? I don't much like being alone.' I swear he shivered; delicately, but certainly a shiver.

'I'd got the impression you weren't in the mood for conversation,' I said, turning back.

'You're sometimes very perceptive, old man. No, I'm not in the mood for conversation. This is a time for thinking, and I sometimes think aloud. You could make a good enough sounding-board.'

That put me in my place, I suppose, but he said it gently enough. I was beginning to wonder how gentle and meek that dapper man really was.

Still staring at the boards, he said, 'Now, you play very good chess . . .'

'I don't. And you know it.'

'You play well enough to give me an opinion, my dear chap.' He pursed his lips, ruffled his hair. 'Would you say that these er . . . contestants were good players?'

Pointing to one board I said, '*They* are, very good. Would lose me in five minutes. The other . . .' I shrugged. 'They're not even beginners.'

'I see,' he said. I didn't bother to mention that *I* didn't. I wondered instead how Sara was bearing up. Somewhere in this rambling house she was maybe still answering questions, trying to explain why her father should have died.

'Look, Mr Harding. I'm worried about Sara. Think I'll just pop out and see what's happening.' He didn't answer and I turned to leave him. Then a thought occurred to me. 'The housekeeper found the body, didn't she? Then when did you . . .'

Not even bothering to look up he said, 'She thinks she did.' The significance of what he was saying didn't penetrate for maybe two seconds. I stared at his back.

I had to ask. 'When *did* you get here?'

'Just before it happened.'

That really shook me. Bloody Harding! Here when a man died violently, and couldn't care less.

Suddenly he was looking at me. He must've seen the suspicions and the accusations and the wondering in my face.

'They know,' he said. His voice had changed. All the affectation had drained out of it. So the fuzz knew. And Harding was still a free man. So he hadn't done it . . . Done what? Had Kenyon put the gun to his own head? I was still trying to sort it out, to find the right words to shape the questions I wanted to ask, when he'd turned away again and was staring at those bloody chessboards.

'What I can't understand, my dear fellow, is why two dunderheads should be playing chess in the house of an acknowledged master.' The words were mincing out of him again. Harding was a screwball. He had to be.

'He could've been teaching somebody how to play.' It just popped out. It wasn't a reasoned statement. But it had a remarkable effect on Harding. He whirled round, snapping his fingers. He reached the door, it seemed, in about two bounds, wrenched it open. 'Excuse me,' he said. And disappeared.

I wandered out into the hall. The constable who'd been in the room was the only policeman in sight.

'The chief superintendent about? Or Inspector Solomons?' I asked him.

'I suppose so, sir,' he said. A real helpful bastard.

'Then I'd better find one of them.'

'Very good, sir.' He made no attempt to stop me. Nor to

help. I envied a bloke who knew just what he was supposed to be doing and did it. I went into the lounge. Holmes, still wheezing, was listening to Solomons. The inspector was being emphatic in a big way – careful, though, to punctuate whatever he was saying with a scattering of 'Sirs'. I could catch the sibilants, but not much else.

They ignored me, if they saw me at all. I turned to leave when the detective sergeant pushed past me.

'He's on his way, sir. Yard's sending a man down with him.'

Holmes wheezed. 'So they found him, then?'

'No trouble at all. Should be here within an hour.'

I followed the sergeant and caught him by the arm.

'Look, sergeant. What's the score? Do I have to stay on here?'

'That's a matter for the chief super, sir.'

'Then perhaps you'll tell me if I can see Miss Kenyon. I'm rather concerned about . . .'

'She's there, sir. And now if you'll excuse me . . .'

Off he went and I swung round to face the stairs. Sara was walking down them slowly, but steadily. She was pale, but her face betrayed no evidence of grief at all. She looked no worse than if a favourite household pet had been run over. I hurried across to her, took her hands in mine.

'I'm desperately sorry,' I said, and meant it. It was no way for anybody's father to die. She nodded, a smile flickered for a moment and was gone.

'Is there anything I can do?'

She stood very still, her eyes fixed on the stolid constable inside the front door.

'Will you stay here with me?'

That didn't need any thinking about. 'Of course.'

'They are trying to find my brother. Bring him here.'

Brother? This was new. But it wasn't the time to ask questions. So I said, 'The sergeant said something about somebody arriving here in about an hour.'

She nodded. 'I don't know why they're bothering. They hardly knew each other. I only found out about him a week or two ago.'

A dozen questions hammered in my brain.

'Shall we have some coffee?' She led the way to the kitchen. We passed no one. The kitchen was empty. There seemed fewer policemen about. 'I think you know him.'

'Know who?'

'My brother – half-brother, really.'

'Do I?'

'Howard. Howard Benson.'

Benson! The Ministry's journalistic pain in the neck, and – God I was dumb – the voice I'd heard on the landing when I'd been waiting for Sara. Sara was watching me carefully, but it would have taken a better actor than I ever could be to hide the shock of what she'd told me. Then her arms were around my waist. She was snuggling close.

'You have to stay. You *have* to!'

'I've said I will.' My arms went around her. Then I saw there were tears in her eyes. Her body was trembling.

'I'm frightened. My God, how frightened I am.'

Frightened? That made two of us. I was scared stiff. What the hell had I started? What I didn't know about what was going on around me would have filled a bloody library.

TWENTY

CAIRO: ESCAPE TO BULAK

Why? I kept asking myself that. Why? So I screwed things up, Hodges had said. That was balls.

Christ, I'd done everything they'd said. I'd really stuck with that woman. Okay, there'd been perks. She'd been good in bed. I'd learnt a bit in the cot with her, but I'd done my share of picking up the gen between the grummit. And she could have had the pick of a lot of blokes in Cairo. There was that politician who owned the flat she lived in. And that character Hussein Bey – probably loaded. All right, maybe she was having them, too. I wasn't going to kid myself too much.

She was no refugee, that was for sure: not the sort of refugee the security people were dealing with, anyway. She had too much money, too many brains to get herself on the run. She was a phoney all right. Look at the places she'd been to – Berlin, Rome, London – and always when things had been hotting up politically.

That reminded me of something. Something she'd said, not long since. We were filling in the time, getting some breath back. And I'd made a crack about Churchill, just to jolly things along, as any fed-up Irishman might. And she'd said something. What the hell was it? About Hitler. Something about the lot of them being painted with the same brush. I was remembering it because she'd got the expression all wrong. I'd told her it was *tarred* with the same brush, not painted. She made mistakes like that sometimes. But it wasn't what she'd said. It was how she said it, as if she was talking about someone she knew. It was daft. How could she know Hitler? I thought about that for a while. Well, why not? Grayling had said Ida Clapham was always hanging round the Nazis in Budapest. And . . .

It hit me. Hard. Ida and the Nazis. Ida was Sophia's stepmother, according to the Lebanese in the refugee control place. And Davers had said check Hussein's father. My bet was Mr bloody Hussein senior – but that wouldn't be his name – would be German.

So the bastards were going to heave me out, eh? They bloody

well weren't. I wanted another session with Hodges, with Collins as well.

The door was locked. I rattled it. Hamid opened it a crack.

'Look,' I said. 'You've got to get Hodges bey here. Quick.'

The one eye I could see was white in the coal-black face. It didn't blink.

'Igri. You understand? Bloody fast.'

He shut the door. There was a pause. And then I heard his sandals flap-flap on the stairs.

Somehow I had to convince Hodges that it was all bloody rot for them to kick me out now. Sophia had talked once. She'd talk again, especially if I did a bit of horse-trading on this Istanbul trip. Her uncle, she'd said: maybe if I could get a lead on who he was . . .

Ida could know. Come to think of it, Ida could know a hell of a lot. And there was a bit of needle between the two women. Maybe I could use that. I hadn't bothered much about Ida. I'd written her off as a scrubber, which wasn't very bright. Right. I'd see Ida. Now.

Then I remembered what Hodges had said. 'I wouldn't try to go out if I were you.' That Hamid or Silah would see to it I didn't if I tried and if not them somebody else. Then I remembered something else. When Hamid had shut the door, I hadn't heard the key turn in the lock. Holding my breath for some daft reason, I turned the handle gently. The door swung open. I braced for the shock of crashing past anybody who'd try to stop me. The landing was empty. Hamid must have forgotten. They hadn't moved the Chevvy and it was only when I'd started the motor that the thought struck me: Was this a try-on? Were they letting me out deliberately to see where I'd go, and to give them an excuse for roughing me up good and proper? The hell with it! I let in the clutch and headed for Bulak. Just a glutton for punishment . . .

She was alone, wearing the same sloppy wrap in the same haphazard way. She looked disappointed when she opened the door.

'Oh, it's you.'

There didn't seem any point in confirming it. So I said, 'May I come in?'

'Where's Sophie? She not with you?'

I shook my head. 'I'd like to talk to you,' I said.

'What about?'

Some kids came racing down the stairs screaming Arabic abuse at some adult unseen, but not unheard, higher in the rickety building.

I had to shout almost. 'Can't I come in?'

Ida held the door back unwillingly. I went past her. She shut the door, stood with her back to it.

'Yanni won't like it if he catches you here.'

If you'd cover that left tit it'd look better, I thought – not the tit: that was quite handsome – if Yanni came in.

'We shan't be in bed,' I said.

'You bet we won't. I don't go for skinny kids.'

Yanni wasn't any giant. But I remembered his handshake. He was strong. Maybe that made the difference. This wasn't getting me very far. I'd have to break down the hostility. 'How's Yanni settling into the job?'

She peered at me suspiciously. It occurred to me that what I didn't know about Yanni's background would fill a library.

'You didn't come here about Yanni,' she said. 'What d'you want?' She must have seen my eyes pulling back all the time to the exposed left breast. She pulled the wrap over. That gave me a fair view of the right one. I concentrated on her unmade-up face, tousled hair, unlovely skin, the not very good teeth.

'Well, it's about Sophia,' I said. 'I'm worried about her.'

Ida shrugged. 'What's she up to now?'

That was where I decided to gamble. 'Look, she once told me you were a bit upset because the secret police were keeping an eye on you . . .'

'She was a fool.'

'All right. But I'm damn sure some odd people're getting interested in her.'

I wasn't prepared for what Ida said then. 'Serve her bloody well right, then.'

'Oh,' I said. What the hell was the relationship between the two of them? 'Well, I don't like it. And if they nail her for something, I don't want to get caught up in it.' I tried to look like I felt guilty about something. 'And maybe it wouldn't help Yanni in his new job. And there's you. You and Sophia came in together.'

Not very subtle, but it was spelling out a message. The wrap was slipping. The right breast was there to be admired in all its fullness. Pity she didn't have a face to match the body.

Ida chewed at her bottom lip. God, she had awful teeth. 'You want a brandy?' she asked.

I didn't, but I said yes. It might keep her talking. She produced a couple of doubtful-looking glasses and half a bottle of some cheap Greek stuff. She poured generous measures.

'You're a bit keen on Sophie.' It wasn't a question. I nodded. At least I could be truthful about that.

'Don't be,' she said. 'She'll gobble you up.'

'I give people indigestion.'

She started to laugh. I got the discoloured teeth and coated tongue full frontal. Then she stopped, suddenly.

'You one of *them*?' she wanted to know. There was something in her voice I didn't like. And who in hell were *them*? I gulped some brandy, then asked the question.

'Who're *them*?'

'If you were you wouldn't say. Forget it.' She drained her glass in one long swallow, splashed in another shot, then offered me the bottle. I took it. The bloody stuff was playing hell with my taste buds but I hadn't been chucked out yet.

'She's your step-daughter, isn't she?'

It was something to say while I splashed a tot of brandy into the glass. But it really broke her up. She stared at me, her mouth a bit open. Then her body started to shake. It was the sort of laughter that was too big a belly-laugh for just the mouth and throat to handle: the gusts of it must have started in her pelvic cage before working their way up. She doubled up, slammed the glass down on the table, wobbled to the unmade bed, threw herself on it. The wrap became only a token covering. It twisted from her body as she rolled about. Only the belt held firm. I concentrated on the brandy. wondering what the hell I'd sparked off. She struggled to a sitting position. There were tears in her eyes. 'Oh, Christ. You come to ask mum's permission to ... to ...'

She gave up and flopped back again to enjoy what must have been the best laugh she'd had in years.

'No,' I said. 'I haven't. We won't be getting married.' I didn't smile. Just spoke the words flat. That sobered her a bit. She sat up again, used the corner of the murky sheet to dab at her eyes.

'Gimme the glass,' she said. I passed it over. She propped herself against the pillows, ignoring her nakedness. 'Come and sit here.' She patted the bed. 'And put the bottle on the chair.'

I got the bottle, put it on the chair beside the bed. Then I sat down beside her. She got rid of a few more chuckles, then said, 'You feel like a bit?' She twisted and thrust her breasts and belly at me.

'I'd like to,' I lied. 'Later. You know, when Yanni's not likely to pop in.'

'Oh, him.' She nearly spat the words. But she didn't seem to be offended.

'What was so funny?' I asked.

She checked another gust of laughter. Then, the glass of brandy in one hand, the fingers of the other plucking persistently at a nipple, she filled in the background. I listened carefully. I had to make sure everything registered. There was going to be a big job of persuading to do. Hodges was going to be good and mad when he caught up with me. My story would have to be spot on. Ida didn't spare me any of the sordid bits. How she'd drifted around Europe after being junked by a dance-troupe boss who'd skipped with what there'd been in the kitty. She'd been getting old for the strip job in Soho, so she'd teamed up with the girls headed for Hamburg. Then came Berlin, Paris, Marseilles, Rome, living as best she could with whoever would have her. The war and trying to get away from it. Budapest.

'He was a silly old coot. Nearly eighty. But he liked my tits. Had money, too. So why not, when he said he'd marry me? Suppose I'm a countess, really. Said he was a count.' She gurgled with laughter. 'Reckon he didn't know how to spell.' She'd married the Hungarian. He'd showed her off a bit. And what Ida hadn't got in his bed she'd had in plenty among the young bloods of a town getting ready to die.

'Know something? A real do-gooder, that old boy was.'

She giggled when she talked about his prison visiting. And that's how he found Sophia, in jail as a political prisoner. Nervous authorities had slammed the door on the blonde. So old Stephan, attracted by the glamorous prisoner, had chatted up his friends in high places. Finally he'd adopted Sophia. It was the only way the politicos would wear her release . . . by making the old man responsible for her.

'So I suppose I'm her foster-mother or something,' Ida gurgled. 'Foster-mother to a full-blown bitch.'

'Why a bitch?'

'You joking, sonny? What else could she be?'

'Why? Lot of people get chucked in the can.'

'Okay. And how many frame the bloke who gets 'em out to the coppers so she can beat it, eh?'

186

Sophia had wanted out of Budapest. The old man said no. But Ida was getting frightened of the place. There were too many Germans now, and the Wehrmacht was poised just beyond the frontiers.

'That's me. Guns and things scare the hell out of me. Sophie said she could fix everything with an army bloke she knew, an officer. Stephan got mad with both of us. Said he had influence. Well, he hadn't, not enough. God knows what Sophie told the police blokes. But in one day flat the old boy was in the same clink he'd got her out of.' She laughed. It was a nasty sound. 'Full-blown bitch.'

'You came out with her, though.'

'Who wouldn't? Me, a bloody Englisher in the middle of a Hun army? You gotta be joking, sonny. Sure I came out. No money, no nothing.'

'Why was she so keen to get out? Can't imagine the Nazis frightening her very much.'

She stopped plucking at the nipple, stared at me. 'Frighten her? Christ, you say some bloody funny things.'

'What's funny about that?'

'This frightened stuff.' She laughed again. 'Sophie? Frightened?'

'That's what I said.'

'Yeh, I heard you.' She laughed again. 'You want to start asking yourself how you're able to get between her legs, sonny.'

'I have. I'm useful. That's all.'

She nodded. 'Long as you know.' She went back to teasing the erect nipple. ' 'Cos she's been with the best. Like that Turkish feller she picked up. Guard on the train from Ankara. Got us a compartment. Even taught me a bit, watching 'em.'

'We can all learn,' I said. 'Can I pour you another drink?'

She nodded. This suited me fine. But I wished she'd cover up those tits; they were getting in my line of vision. I slopped brandy into the glass she held out.

'She certainly knows how to grab them,' I said.

Ida gulped at the brandy. It was taking a long time to get into her bloodstream. 'You don't know a thing,' she muttered. 'How about the big Nazi bloke in Berlin, eh? How about him?'

'All right. What about him?'

The liquor was getting to her, after all. Her speech was blurring.

'Knows Hitler, that's what about him. You know Sophie's met that bloke? That Hitler bastard?'

I shook my head. I didn't believe it, but if I could keep Ida yakking she might say something I could use with Hodges. But it was going to have to be good.

'Why stick with her, then?'

'How else do I live? You think Yanni can keep me?'

'He's working. Should be able to. Anyway, why should Sophie have to?'

The sudden splurt of anger surprised me. 'Why the hell shouldn't she?' She drained the brandy, imperiously held out the glass. I filled it. Right up. Waited till she'd gulped a good half of the stuff, then topped it up again. Her drinking suddenly became an act of defiance. She drained every drop of brandy from the small tumbler, then hurled it across the room. The violence shocked me. Then she threw herself on her back on the rumpled bed. She spread her legs wide.

'Come on, sonny. I want a bit. You'll have to do.' Her speech was slurred, heavy.

God, I thought. I tried to be crafty. 'But Yanni might come back. I don't want a knife in my ribs.'

'Oh, Jesus,' she said, and struggled up on her elbows. 'Whassa time?'

'Half-past eight.'

I had to help her off the bed. She pulled her robe clumsily around her body. She was starting to sweat. She didn't smell so good. Staggering, she pushed me towards the door.

There had to be time for one more question. 'Look, Ida. What's Sophia up to? I'm a bloody journalist. I don't want to get mixed up in . . .'

She was wrestling with the door handle. I grabbed it, eased her away so she could lean against the wall.

'She's up to something, isn't she? I don't want any part of it.'

There was hate in the drink-sodden face.

'She's a bitch.' Her tongue wasn't framing the words clearly, but I got the message. 'Ask her, son . . . sonny. And her bloody fancy co . . . colo . . . colonel. And the bloody corporal. But the sergeant's the bloody best. Try that little bastard. Give 'em lang . . . lan . . . oh, Christ. You know. Them foreign words.' She croaked with horrible laughter. 'And money ain't all they give her. You fucking bet it ain't.'

There was a gutter background pouring out of the twisting, slobbering mouth.

'And that bastard Huss . . . the bugger with the red hat.

Like a bloody monkey. Him . . . bloody German . . . thinks he's fucking Hitler, he does.'

I had to be quick. 'What's his name, Ida? Hussein. What's his real name?'

She slid down the wall, landed on the floor with a bump. She didn't give any indication she felt any pain or that she was anything but perpendicular.

'Why shouldn't I, eh? Bloody German money, ain't it? More I take, less those stinking Nasties'll have, eh?' She started to giggle uncontrollably, her body swaying from side to side like a gross pendulum. She must have had a skinful of booze before I'd arrived. She was paralytic.

'So I take it, see? Every bloody piastre John bloody Eppler shells out . . .'

I slid through the door fast. Slammed it hard-shut behind me. I could still hear her drooling on as I damn near ran towards the stairs and the street.

And right into Hodges.

Three hours later, at the Shubra flat, I was sick, physically as well as mentally. He hadn't hurt me much, just roughed me up a bit. It had been the hard driving of stiffened fingers into my guts that had made me puke.

He'd nearly fooled me out there in Bulak. I should've known better. But as he was always telling me, I never learn. He grinned, just like an old mate from the local; he seemed all surprised that he should bump into me in Bulak. Now this was crazy. I'd sent Hamid to phone him, to tell him to go to the flat, while I'd done a quick bunk to Ida. Of course, I kept telling myself while I drove him back into town, maybe Hamid hadn't been able to reach him. He'd made contact all right. Because when Hodges had said he'd just come up to the flat for a few minutes, the out-of-character matiness disappeared down the drain like my vomit did a while later.

He'd shut the door and, still grinning, had brought his open palm across my face. Without a break in the rhythm the hand had swept back again, the flattened knuckles of the fingers banging against the other cheek-bone. Then he'd pushed me in the chest with his flat hand. I collapsed on the divan, more with shock than pain. I'd have to talk fast.

'Listen, Hodges. Ida talked. Talked her drunken head off. She . . .'

'I told you to stay put. Here. Till I came.'

'I know. But it suddenly struck me. To talk to Ida.' I got up grabbed his arm. 'Look, we've never bothered with her. But she had to know, didn't she? Christ, she *had* to. So I . . .'

I landed back on the divan with a bounce. Hodges knew his stuff. He moved like a snake strikes.

'So you screwed things up. It's all you've ever bloody done. Screw things up. Fucking amateurs.' The venom in his voice scared me a bit. But when Hodges was around I scared easy.

'Look, for God's sake. She talked, I tell you. The whole bit. Sophia in Berlin. How she got out of Budapest. Even the Hussein bit . . .'

I jerked to my feet. Christ, he was strong! His grip on the front of my shirt was choking me. I clawed at his hand, but a knee in my testicles doubled me up. All that kept me upright was that vice against my throat.

'What about Hussein?' His voice was a whisper, almost gentle, it was so quiet.

This was when he'd have to listen. 'His name's Eppler. John Eppler. A German.'

He'd released his grip on my shirt so I could croak out the headline. I stood there, rubbing my throat, waiting for the break in the hostility. Hodges stared at me for a long moment. Then he chopped with the edge of his right hand. Not on my neck. He'd have broken it. But down on the hollow where neck meets shoulder. I lost the use of my legs, sprawled on the floor.

'Don't get up,' he said.

I got the message. He was telling me that he didn't intend to use his feet. So I stayed where I was, wondering why he wasn't impressed, and why I was aching so much.

'Your job was that bitch, not Ida; not Yanni; not Hussein: just Sophia,' he said.

'You took me off her,' I managed to get out through my sore throat.

'That biting at your balls, then? Missing it? That it?'

I shook my head, but not for long. It hurt my neck. That was when I felt the first surge of nausea erupting up through my guts. I swallowed it back. It didn't taste good. And it hurt my throat.

'I . . . I'm going to be sick,' I muttered. I crawled away from him. I scrambled to my feet. He just stood there, watching me. Inside, I'll bet he was enjoying it. I staggered out and threw up. That hurt the sore places, too.

He was still standing there when I walked back in. I was

feeling a bit better. Maybe if I tried again, tried to get him to see how good the stuff was that I'd got.

'Look, Hodges. You beating me up isn't getting us anywhere. Maybe you don't understand. I was trying to tell you . . .'

'Sit down,' he ordered. I sat down. Easier to do that than have him put me down. 'You're staying here. Understand?' I nodded. 'No funny stuff or, God help me, I'll tear your arms off. You stay put, till they're ready to fly you out. Ask Hamid or Silah for what you want. But stick a nose out of that door and it'll be chopped off.'

I nodded again. 'Won't you listen, Hodges?' I said it, though I knew he wouldn't. It didn't make any sense, but they just didn't want to know. Perhaps if I could get to Collins or even Mortimer, it would . . .

'And forget about trying to contact Collins or Mortimer,' Hodges said. 'Got any more lemonade?'

I started to get up, but he pushed me back, not roughly; just firmly. 'I'll get it,' he said. He came back, sipping the stuff. 'You bloody amateurs make me sick,' he said. His voice was almost gentle, like a mother chiding a small boy. 'They shouldn't use them. Always screw things up. Makes it rough for blokes like me. But do they listen? Christ, no. Never do.'

He sat down in a chair, staring at the lemonade left in the glass. 'You've done all right for yourself, though.' That wasn't my view of it, but there wasn't any point arguing. 'Be back in London soon.' He sighed. Maybe he was human after all; maybe he didn't like the business he was in. 'Hell of a lot of blokes out there'd like to be in your boots.'

I nearly told him they could have my bloody boots, any time.

'You got a girl back home?' I shook my head. 'You'll do all right, then. Must be hundreds of 'em dying for it. And you've had a bit of practice. Should do all right for yourself.'

He drained the glass, got up. I got up, too. I kept an eye on him but he didn't make any move towards me.

'I mightn't see you again,' he said. And paused. What was I supposed to say? That I'd be sorry if we didn't meet? 'They'll come for you when they're ready.'

He went out, shutting the door behind him. I heard the key turn in the lock, a murmur of voices, then his shoes on the stairs.

It was going to be quite some time before I saw Hodges again.

TWENTY-ONE

LONDON: A THREAT OF STALEMATE

Sara recovered quickly. She made two large mugs of instant coffee and we sipped it in the kitchen. We didn't talk much. I was still chary about how to approach her father's death. For her part, she seemed satisfied to be doing something, even if it was only brewing coffee.

I was trying to think of a conversational gambit when she said, 'Do you know Howard?' I nodded. If I didn't open my mouth I wouldn't put my foot in it.

'Strange, isn't it?' she said. 'I mean having a brother for all these years and not knowing.'

Maybe, I thought. But from what I'd overheard at her flat they seemed to have made some ground in the few weeks since they'd discovered each other.

'How well do you know him?'

I'd wanted to dodge that. To her I was still Freeman, a vague sort of PR man. Blast Hodges! Blast Harding! Christ, would I have to guard my bloody tongue about him? Was he still Harmsworth to Sara? Bugger, bugger, bugger.

'Not very well. You know: PR and journalism trip over each other sometimes.'

Trip was the right word. I could fall flat on my middle-aged face any tick of the clock. Middle-aged? God, when I was a kid people my age were old. But Sara hadn't seemed to notice it, and in bed with her I felt about thirty.

I swallowed some coffee and figured I might do better if I led the talking.

'Tell me about Howard,' I suggested.

She shrugged. 'I don't know much about it. Daddy never mentioned it at all.'

I couldn't resist it. 'Who did, then?'

'It was the doctor.'

I didn't press it but she could only have been talking of Stapleton, the bastard who tried to put my weights up by blowing the damn fool cover Hodges had given me.

'Seems an odd thing for him to do. A friend of your father's, I mean.'

'I've wondered why he did.'

I'll bet you have, I thought. 'Do you want to see him? Benson.'

'I haven't any choice. He'll be here.'

So he would be. And how long would I remain Alfred Freeman once he arrived? I'd have to talk to Harding. I gulped down the rest of the coffee.

'Look,' I said. 'Will you excuse me? For just a few minutes?'

She looked surprised. 'You're not leaving? You did say you'd stay . . .'

'I'll be staying. It's just that . . . well, I . . . I've got to . . .'

She laughed. 'If you want to go to the loo why not say so? There's one just along the hall to the right of the kitchen door.'

I put down the mug, grinned like the fool I felt, and sort of just crabbed my way out. I made for the hall. The constable was still stoically doing his duty.

'Where'll I find Mr Harding?' I asked him.

'He went upstairs with the chief superintendent just a few minutes ago, sir.'

I thanked him and took the stairs two at a time. When I reached the next floor I nearly knocked Harding down.

'Sorry,' I muttered.

'My dear chap, my fault entirely.' He jerked a thumb. 'It's down there. Second on the left.'

I was beginning to wonder if my bladder was showing.

'I don't want a loo. I want you.' Maybe I should have been a lyric writer.

He looked a bit taken aback. 'But of course, old man.'

He waited. I looked along the passage, then down the stairs behind me. 'Can't we find somewhere less public?'

Harding blinked. ''Fraid I can't discuss the case, old chap. Have to chat up the constabulary.'

Impatiently, I told him it wasn't the death of Commander Kenyon I was worried about.

'Oh,' he said. He didn't look happy. 'Well, if you must, my dear chap.' He led the way into what I suppose would have been a small morning-room in more gracious days. I shut the door behind us. This was no time for protocol. 'Who are you?' I asked him.

He spread his arms, smiled. 'My dear fellow. Thought you knew. Harding. Maurice. Defence Secretariat. Principal officer grading. Married. House in Sussex. Two kids. Hobbies are . . .'

'All right,' I snapped. 'That's the funny bit out of the way.

I'll try again. *What* the hell are you, then?'

I watched the affability drain out of him like bathwater down a plug-hole. There wasn't any of the pansy la-di-da in his voice when he said, 'I've told you. I'm a principal officer in the Defence Secretariat. And you're a nothing clerk in PR-ten. Remember that.'

So the bastard was going to pull rank, was he? So I didn't have anything to lose, not now. They'd pushed me around once: they wouldn't again.

'Look,' I said, stabbing a finger at him. 'This is the second time in my life the cloak-and-dagger lads have given me the run-round. I don't like it. No, Mr Harding, or Harmsworth, or whatever your bloody name is, I don't like it, not one little bit.'

He just stood there. I could see him shaping his face to get back into the silly-ass role he seemed to like playing.

'There's a woman downstairs you lot've got me in dutch with,' I went on. 'She thinks I'm a bloke called Freeman. Now, I like her. I think she likes me a bit. Sooner or later I'm going to have to tell her I'm not Freeman. That I'm who I am. And when I do she's going to ask why. That's something I've got to sweat out, 'cause for sure you bastards won't help. So right now you're going to answer a few questions.'

I sucked in a long breath. Maybe Harding was too long in the tooth to fall for bluff, but I had to try. If he didn't talk there wasn't anything I could do, except maybe smash his teeth. I reckoned Harding was more my weight than Hodges. So I watched him.

He smiled. 'My dear fellow,' he said. So it was going to be the Burlington Bertie act. All right.

'You can cut that ponce stuff,' I snarled. 'I've got an itchy fist.' I held it out. Let him have a good look at it. So I wasn't Muhammad Ali, but a fist is a fist is a fist.

It didn't seem to worry him. He kept right on grinning. But his eyes were watchful now, and he dropped the nancy voice. 'We're both a bit old for the schoolboy rubbish, aren't we?'

I really could have hit him then. But he was right. Hodges seemed to be good at it, but pushing people's faces in didn't get anybody else very far. So I said, 'Okay. Let's forget the kid's stuff, and all the cloak-and-dagger. Suppose you start being adult, then? What the hell's all this about?'

He thought for a moment. The he shrugged. 'Nothing I can tell you, really.'

My blood pressure started to get out of control again. He saw it, shook his head. 'Honestly, old man.' The music-hall pansy boy was creeping back into his voice. 'You see, my dear fellow, this isn't my show.'

'Then how about telling me whose show it is?'

'Bit difficult that, old man.' He bit his lip. 'Wish I knew myself.'

That was when I really blew my top. 'For Christ's sake,' I yelled at him. 'Has Whitehall gone stark staring bloody mad?'

The door slammed open. The chief superintendent wheezed his way in. The stairs must have been a strain on his bulk. 'Huh,' he grunted. 'Took a lot of finding.'

Holmes was talking to Harding, not to me. 'Want to see you,' he rumbled. Harding nodded. They went out together. I fumed alone for a second or two, then decided I'd better get back to Sara.

She was still in the kitchen. 'More coffee?' she asked. I shook my head. 'He's arrived.'

'Who's arrived?'

'Howard.'

So that would be why Holmes wanted Harding. 'You've seen him?'

'No.' She drained her mug.

I wondered again why the death of her father hadn't upset her. she was behaving unnaturally normally. It was weird, watching her standing by the table, drinking coffee, not a hair out of place, in a house where her old man had been found only an hour or two earlier with the top of his head blown off. She wasn't cold-blooded, that I knew: her performance in bed made a non-starter of that idea. Her blood was rich and red and hot.

The policeman on hall-duty appeared in the doorway. 'Someone to see you,' he said.

'Me?' I asked. He nodded. 'Who?'

'Didn't say, sir.'

The 'sir' sounded like an afterthought. I reached out a hand towards Sara. 'Come on.'

The constable blocked the doorway. 'Only you, sir.'

'You'd better go,' Sara said.

I went, the man in blue leading. He led me to the room I'd just left. Hodges was there. The policeman shut the door behind me.

'You really screw things up, don't you?'

195

'I suppose I do,' I said. 'But there he was. And there was the gun. It just seemed a good idea to blow his head off.'

He looked for a moment like he was going to blow a gasket. But he didn't. 'Sit down,' he said.

'Why?'

That caught him on one foot. He was surprised. Then he shrugged. 'Suit yourself. Just thought it might be more comfortable.' He sank into a chair by the chess-tables, reached out and picked up one of the pieces.

'Harding doesn't want those touched,' I said.

He didn't take any notice. He stared down at the rook, twisting it in his fingers. 'How's she taking it?' he asked. There was something up. Hodges was being far too mild.

'Like you'd expect,' I said. Some ambiguity wouldn't do any harm.

'And how would I expect her to be taking it?'

'I don't know. I don't know how you'd expect anything or anyone to be,' I told him.

'So what you said wasn't an answer.'

He put the rook back on the board, on the same square he'd taken it from. 'Why don't you sit down?' he wanted to know. His voice was strangely petulant.

I eased myself into a chair. There was no sense in antagonising him and I decided to keep my mouth shut.

'Well?' His voice was impatient rather than abrasive.

'She's all right.'

'Not upset?'

'Doesn't seem to be.'

He chewed his lip. 'Why?'

'I don't know. Why not ask her?'

His eyes narrowed. 'Don't be smart. She's your contract. So talk. And I might forget you're here.'

'I had to be here. It's where she is. You know: my contract.'

For a fleeting second I thought he was coming out of the chair at me. Or maybe he was just getting more comfortable. It was always hard to tell with Hodges.

There wasn't any choice. 'She doesn't seem to give a damn.'

He waited. 'Go on.'

'That's it. She doesn't seem to give a damn.'

'She's a woman.'

'I know.'

'I know you know. And a bloody waste of time it's been while you've been finding out.'

'Okay. Why use me? I screw things up.'

This time he got to his feet, fast. I'd been watching him but still he caught me sitting. My shirt collar started to throttle me, his knuckles pressed into my windpipe; I could feel my eyes popping. My fingers scrabbled at his hand. But I might as well have saved my energy and what oxygen still remained in my lungs. He jerked his hand away, the edge of it cutting up under my chin. It damn near broke my neck.

He stepped back, his face expressionless. 'Why won't you learn?' he said, his voice barely above a whisper.

Maybe I was just stubborn. I gulped in mouthfuls of air, jerking the knot of my tie loose.

'You're a masochist,' he told me. Idiot was a better word, I thought. He sat down again, crossed his legs, started to swing one foot. I coughed, my shoulders hunching forward, but the pain was passing.

'Now,' he said. 'Where were we?' As though he didn't know. 'She doesn't give a damn about her father getting killed, or killing himself, or whatever. Now why should that be?'

I got some spit into my mouth, swallowed it. 'She didn't like him.'

'She tell you that?'

I shook my head. 'Saw it. Last time I came here. He didn't seem to take any shine to me, come to that.'

'So he asks you down for a game of chess, eh?' I nodded. 'Why didn't she like her father?'

'I don't know. Maybe it was . . . was not telling her about Benson.' Maybe Hodges didn't know the relationship. 'He's her half-brother.'

'Really?' said Hodges. He wasn't good at sarcasm. 'I brought him down.'

'Then you know as much about the family set-up as I do.'

'Yes,' said Hodges. 'Benson and your girl-friend don't know each other very well.'

Not much they don't, I told myself. But right now what Hodges didn't know wouldn't hurt him.

We sat looking at each other for a while. I got the impression that Hodges wasn't quite sure what to do or say next. I thought I'd help him. 'I had quite a long chat with Harding,' I said.

His foot stopped swinging. I'm sure his body tensed. 'That's the bloke in your department, isn't it?' His voice was level enough.

'No.'

'Oh yes, he is. We've checked . . .'

He stopped. Maybe I should make a habit of being helpful to Hodges. 'I'm in PR. He's top echelon. Secretariat. Principal officer.'

'All right. He's another of the Ministry wallahs. I know he's here. Pal of Kenyon's, wasn't he?' It wasn't a question. Just a statement.

'Played chess with him,' I said.

'Quite a cosy little club' said Hodges.

Cosy? 'Stapleton came here, too.'

'The doctor? Yes. I know.'

'He tried to bust that fool cover-name you gave me.'

'So you said.'

Had I? I tried to remember. Hodges seemed to have settled down again. His foot was swinging idly.

'What was all that about, anyway? I mean, the Freeman nonsense?'

He shrugged. 'They didn't want you associated with the Ministry.'

'Bit daft, wasn't it?' He didn't say anything. So I plunged on. 'Harding calling himself Harmsworth. What am I going to tell her?' I pointed at the floor. 'She's going to have to be told, sooner or later.'

'Why?'

That had a sinister ring about it somehow. Was I going to be hauled out? Not be allowed to see Sara again? I didn't like the thought of that. Not see her again? Christ, I wanted to see her. That's the worst of getting older: your reflexes slow down. I *had* to see her, all the time. I wanted her not just casually, in bed. I suddenly knew it had been good watching her make coffee in the kitchen. Christ, was I in love with the woman?

Hodges had stretched his thin lips into his mockery of a smile.

'Fallen for her, eh?' I heard the harsh crackle of laughter. The bastard was enjoying himself. 'Forget it,' he said.

I got up, slowly. I didn't want him to get any wrong ideas. Even so, he uncrossed his legs, brought his feet close together close in against the chair. But he stayed put. I walked past him, stared out of the window. There were still two or three cars on the gravel below me. Without turning, I said, 'What's it all about, Hodges?'

'The security of the State.'

I turned. His face was very still. I'd been going to give him the 'ho, ho' treatment but the man was deadly serious.

'All right,' I said. 'Maybe I wouldn't screw things if you put me in the picture.'

He thought about that for a while, then got up out of the chair. I backed up against the window, but he didn't move in my direction. Just stood plucking at his lower lip.

'What do you want to know?'

That surprised me. 'Every single bloody thing.'

Impatiently, he said, 'You know that's impossible.'

'Okay. So why have I been dragged into this? You said I screwed up Cairo. You say I've screwed this. I'd like to know what I'm supposed to have screwed up.'

'Trouble with you is you've got no discipline. Always trying to be clever.'

'Look, I picked up a lot of gen in Cairo, not trying to be anything, just listening. Like I've been listening in this nutty set-up. That's why you'd better chat up Benson . . .'

I wanted to bite my tongue out. Hodges was right. I was too clever. Far too bloody clever.

I didn't see him coming. But a hand was knotted into my collar and the breathing was getting hard again. 'What about Benson?' he grated in my ear. Not loud. With the trapped blood pounding in my head his voice sounded like the hissing of a snake. I tried to shake free. Then he threw me away from him. I lurched back against the window. An elbow smacked into one of the panes. I felt it give. Then came the tinkle of breaking glass. Trying to save my arm, I tumbled round. My face was staring down into the drive. Harding was helping Sara into the back of a large car. I saw them jerk round, look up. She saw me because she tried to break away from Harding. But he bundled her inside, climbed in after her, slammed the door. Whoever was driving already had the motor running. He let in the clutch and the car was gone in a shower of gravel.

Hodges was beside me. He saw it all.

'Stay put,' he snarled. Then he was across the room and the door swung shut behind him.

My first impulse had been to chase after him, except that when I ran out into the corridor a constable was coming up the stairs. He asked me, politely but with the arrogant assurance of those who wear the uniform of authority, if I would mind waiting in the room I'd just left. He was bigger than me. Anyway, I generally try to respect the law. I went back in. The policeman stood outside. I stared down from the window. Nothing was happening down on the drive. The car Harding had put Sara in had gone. The other vehicles were still parked.

With the bluebottle parked outside there wasn't anything I could do but sit it out. I found the most comfortable chair and settled in. This might be a good time to try to sort things out – like why Harding had taken Sara away. Where? Oddly enough, I wasn't worried about what was happening to her. I would have been if it had been Hodges. But not Harding.

Now why the hell should I think like that? Harding. I hardly knew him. And what I did I didn't like, and for sure didn't trust. There he was, gallivanting somewhere with a woman I was keen on, and I wasn't minding.

Sara. Now why the hell was someone my age getting gooey over a woman just about young enough to be my daughter? And how the heck had it started? The club – seeing her – remembering Sophia – dashing off to see that bastard Hodges. And next thing I'm in the cot with her: no wrestling, no fighting. Just two willing people into the cot. Which raised the point: why? Why had she given a middle-aged no-hoper like me a tumble? She'd been around. I didn't have to be a Casanova to get that message. She had money. Her old man was somebody . . . correction: had been somebody. 'Cause a corpse wasn't anything. And why had he changed his mind? Like asking me down here when he'd made it plain enough the first time he'd begrudge giving me a cold in the head? Head: his was blown off. Who did that? And why? And those unfinished chess games . . . Stapleton . . . why did he blow my cover?

I leaned my head back. Closed my eyes. Tried to make sense of it all. It was a comfortable chair, deep and soft. That must have been when I fell asleep . . .

'My dear fellow, so sorry to've wakened you.'

I blinked my eyes open, jerked my head round and damn near broke my neck: the muscles had cramped. I rubbed, tried to stand up and bloody near fell down: one of my legs had gone to sleep. Christ, I was in proper shape to cope with Harding!

He stood there, leaning forward from the hips, his face a bubble of concern.

I tried to unscramble my wits. 'What time is it?'

'One o'clock, old boy. Witching hour, eh?'

'One o'clock?' I tried to figure out how long I'd slept, but the sum wouldn't work out. I yawned, rubbed my eyes, shivered. I felt like the wrath of God. 'Where's Sara?'

''Fraid she had to leave, old man. Asked me to apologise.'

The man was a fool. He must've seen me staring out of the window when he pushed her into the car.

'Had to leave's dead right,' I told him. 'I'm asking where she is now, at this minute.'

'Terribly upset she was. Said she'd invited you to stay.' He sighed, an exaggerated exhalation of breath that would have had the audience at a melodrama on its feet applauding. 'But there it is. Plans of mice and men and all that, eh? I'll give you a lift back.'

'I want to talk to Sara.'

'Of course you do, old man; quite natural. Well, shall we get your bag?'

Harding wasn't Hodges. I reckoned I could just about cope if I was pushed. 'I'm not going anywhere.' He looked surprised, then pained. 'I'm not going anywhere till I get some answers to a hell of a lot of questions.'

Harding scratched his ear, rubbed the side of his nose. 'Difficult, that, my dear boy, very difficult.'

'Oh, for God's sake, be yourself. How about dropping the Bertie stuff?'

'Bertie stuff?' He sounded shocked.

'Yes.'

'Bertie stuff?' He was talking to himself. He shook his head. I began to wonder if it was I who was off my nut.

Footsteps were approaching along the corridor. Harding tensed. I could see it. He turned to face the door. It was Hodges. He stood in the doorway, very still. Harding matched the stillness. Hodges said, slowly: 'What're you doing here?'

I moved quietly so that I could see Harding's face. He was wearing his Bertie grin.

'Here? Oh, I see. Well, matter of fact, old man, I was just offering . . . ah, this young man a ride to town.' I made a mental note to thank him some time for that 'young man' bit. 'You know, nothing we can do here. Constabulary's got everything under control, eh? None of us in shackles, what? So may as well toddle off . . .'

'You get in my hair,' Hodges told him. His voice was flat, like a blade of steel. He was concentrating all his attention on Harding. Maybe that's why he didn't hear anything. Mind you, I didn't either. Holmes had come along the passage remarkably silently for so huge a man. I saw him appear behind Hodges. The detective sergeant was there, too. Then Hodges whirled. His hands were reaching up. Suddenly he relaxed, smiled. 'You shouldn't do that, Mr Holmes. Might get yourself hurt.'

Holmes smiled, but without humour. He leaned forward, whispered something in Hodges' ear. I saw Hodges frown. He looked a question at Harding, at me. Holmes whispered again. I noticed Harding was picking his nose, but in this screwy set-up it seemed a perfectly normal thing to do. Then I saw Hodges nod. Holmes and he and the sergeant walked away.

Harding said: 'Well, old man, shall we get your bag? It's in the hall, I fancy.' A hand politely covered a yawn. 'Have you home in no time flat, eh?'

I hesitated, then checked a torrent of questions.

'Okay,' I said at last. 'And thanks for the lift.'

'Not at all, old boy, not at all. My pleasure, really. Like I always say, do your fellow man a good turn whenever you can. You know, cast bread on the waters. Nothing like it, my dear chap.'

I walked ahead of him down the passage and the stairs. The constable in the hall handed me my overnight bag and opened the front door.

The questions would have to wait.

TWENTY-TWO

CAIRO: 'DON'T ASK QUESTIONS'

Maybe the grog I poured down my throat didn't cure my aches and pains, but it helped me to bear them. I was next door to being properly pissed when I threw off my clothes and crawled into bed. Stuff the lot of them! The bed swayed a bit for a while, but I hung on to the sides, lying on my still sore belly. I was giddy when I closed my eyes, so I kept them open, staring at the muddy wallpaper behind the pillow. Stuff 'em! So they didn't want to know. All right: that was okay with me. Christ knew what they were up to. I cursed having bumped into Grayling with his story of bumping into a woman he'd heard about in Budapest. Stuff him, too. Stuff the war. I don't remember stopping the dribbling and the cursing. And I don't know what time it was when a hand shook me awake. I opened my eyes . . . then closed them again fast. The light hanging from the ceiling bored into my head like a searchlight.

'Sorry about this, but it's necessary.'

Well, whoever it was, it wasn't Hodges. The voice sounded sympathetic, but not too sympathetic. But for sure it wasn't Hodges. I forced my eyelids apart just enough for them to give my aching eyeballs some protection. I struggled up, using my hands as levers and tried to focus. My head was pounding, my mouth was like the bottom of a birdcage, and my belly and shoulder still throbbed.

Mortimer was sitting on the bottom of the bed.

'You've had a skinful,' he said.

He wasn't telling me anything I didn't know. I eased myself painfully back up the bed till my head rested against the pillows I propped behind me. It wasn't easy to do, but I managed. I squeezed my eyes shut, then opened them. Mortimer was etched a little more sharply in my vision.

'Already?' I muttered.

He shook his head. 'Just a chat.'

This was going to be new, them wanting to talk. So I waited.

'You know you're going home.' No question. Just making sure I wasn't in any doubt. 'It's important that you realise your responsibilities.'

I pressed my fingers into my eyes. That light was hurting. I manoeuvred my legs over the side of the bed. 'Got to get a drink. I'm parched.' I lurched out into the kitchen, gulped down two glasses of water from the carafe in the icebox and grabbed a piece of ice and rubbed it across my forehead. I shivered and kidded myself I was feeling a bit better. I crawled back on to the bed. Mortimer hadn't moved. He was a patient man. I thanked him silently for that.

'You're familiar with the Official Secrets Act, I take it?'

I nodded. It didn't do my head any good at all. 'I read it before I signed the declaration.'

'You know the penalties tacked on to it?'

'Yes.' Life imprisonment in time of war, or so I'd been told in the security training school.

'Good.' He pursed his lips. 'You'll be travelling back as an infantry sergeant. No harm in saying you were posted to a security section.' Then he added: 'No harm. But you don't have to volunteer it. But that'll be the lot.' He got up, shook his shoulders. 'Let's go where there's a comfortable chair.'

I got out of bed again, followed him into the lounge. I still felt lousy but if I wasn't going to be able to sleep I might as well listen. I could even learn something. That was what Hodges always said I should do: learn something.

Mortimer didn't seem to be in any hurry. He yawned, stretched, then sat down. So did I. We stared at each other.

'You're being boarded home. They're fixing the papers now.'

'I'm as fit as a flea. At least I will be, given time.' Like when my hangover was over.

'You're not. Not according to the certificate. You've got flat feet.'

He didn't look like a bloke with a sense of humour. And I didn't feel much like laughing, not with my pounding head. So I just said, 'You're joking.'

He shook his head. 'That's what it'll say on the paper. Unfit for active duty.'

The poor bastard didn't think it was funny. I wished I didn't feel so grim. I'd have been laughing my head off, instead of wishing, as I did, that it would fall off.

'You're not to blame, you know.'

'Not to blame for what?' I asked him.

He shrugged. 'It takes a lot of training. And you hadn't had it. They shouldn't have dragged you in.' He chewed his lip. 'Bad luck, really.'

'Bad luck, shit,' I told him.

'I can understand your disappointment. But it won't do any good adopting that attitude, you know.'

I suppose the bastard was doing his best. All I wanted to do was belt him, hard. I'd learnt some bad habits from Hodges.

'You'll be still engaged on work of . . . er, national importance,' he added. Then he said, 'I hope.'

'So what I've been doing was important, then?' I rasped at him.

He jerked his head up. 'Why, of course. Of the utmost importance.'

'Then tell me why I'm being turfed out,' I suggested. I watched him flip through the index of his mind for the words he wanted.

'Look,' I said. 'I got some information that your people didn't have. They must've reckoned I could be of some use. They moved me in with you lot. I did the job I was given. And I didn't do so badly, did I? I mean, there was this woman able to pick and choose whatever men she wanted. I got right alongside her, didn't I? And she talked. I was good enough to get her to talk, and to give you lot a whole heap of stuff you couldn't have got without me. Right?'

He regarded me carefully. I think he was an essentially kindly bloke doing a lousy job. But he blew my growing regard for him right out of the window when he said, 'No. Wrong.'

I'd been forgetting my hangover. Now I was feeling it again. He was as big a bastard as Hodges.

'All right,' I shouted. 'Bloody well tell me.'

He sighed. 'It's very difficult. You see, you had the wrong training. Infantry, wasn't it?' He bloody well knew where I'd come from. 'All rush and grab and stick a bayonet or whatever into a chap who wears the wrong coloured uniform. We work a little differently. It's not your fault.' He started to speak more quickly. He didn't want me interrupting. 'Don't misunderstand me, but this wasn't an infantry operation. But they thought you'd be less dangerous with us than wandering around outside. Once you'd got that information about the Clapham woman we had to make a decision.' He pulled a wry face, shrugged. 'I didn't make it. Spoke against it, as a matter of fact.' Suddenly he smiled. 'Nothing personal, mind.'

I'd forgotten all about my hangover again. These blokes, I told myself, should be certified. They shouldn't be allowed out. Christ, if the Germans could only begin to guess . . .

Mortimer said: 'It's very embarrassing. You were so enthusiastic. That was the root of the trouble, of course.' He sighed again. 'We've had to part with a lot of very nice people because of it. A pity. But there it is.'

He stood up. This was one I wasn't going to win. But I didn't want him to leave just yet. There were far too many questions I wanted to ask. All right. He wouldn't answer them, but at least I could try.

'Do you have to go?' I asked him.

He shrugged. 'Is there any point in my staying?'

He fiddled with a button on his jacket.

'Well,' I said. 'At least I'd have someone to talk to. I don't feel so good.'

He nodded gravely. Had a moment of indecision then sat down again.

'Can I get you a drink?' He shook his head. I wondered if another couple of slugs would help me and knew they wouldn't.

Casually, as though making small talk at a party, Mortimer said: 'Oh, by the way, your friend Ida Clapham: she's dead.'

I suppose I must have gaped at the man. A woman I'd been with just hours before was dead, and he trots it out as an afterthought.

'It wasn't your fault. You were quite right not to buy the Luger. But he used it before it could be recovered.'

'You . . . you mean, Yanni . . . used it? He killed her?' I stuttered.

He nodded. 'Some domestic quarrel, we think.' Mortimer picked at a fingernail. 'All very sordid.'

I wondered if I wanted to be sick and decided not just yet. The anger was building up inside me. She wasn't my friend, and maybe he knew that bloody well, but, hell, she was a human being. And 'all very sordid' was her epitaph, written by a bunch of manic depressives who didn't seem to know what time of day it was.

'That's bad luck, then, isn't it?' I snapped.

He raised his eyebrows. 'It doesn't matter,' he said.

'It matters all right. You've lost the best witness you ever had.'

'Witness?' He looked honestly puzzled.

'You bet. Witness against that bitch.'

'Ah, you're talking about your special subject, aren't you?' He smiled. 'I'm afraid Clapham wasn't very much use to us. She . . . er, tended to complicate matters.'

206

The hangover had gone. My head was remarkably clear. I found myself able to think, to reason, to analyse.

'So you had her killed?'

He looked pained. 'My dear chap, whatever gave you that preposterous idea? Why should we kill anyone? We're not savages, you know. Just civil servants doing a somewhat unsavoury but essential job of work.' He laughed. 'Soldiers like you do the killing. We simply provide information to the generals, and try our damnedest to prevent the other side's generals getting any. You mustn't get emotional about it.'

All right, I wouldn't be emotional. So I got control of my voice, decided to match his contempt with cold reality.

'Perhaps your lot hasn't been listening. But I'm stuffed with information up here.' I tapped my skull. 'If I started to talk about what I know you'd be in trouble, big trouble.'

Blandly he said: 'Your medical certificate: there's time to put any reason for your discharge we like on it. So don't be childish.' Sharply, he added: 'Claim to be a Casanova if you must, but not a Sir Galahad. Broadmoor's not a pleasant place.'

Calling my bluff had been easy. So I'd try reasoning with this devious man who seemed to hold all the aces in the pack. 'Look. Sophia's no refugee. You know that. I know it. She's been sent in here. And I'm satisfied she used Ida as a front. Damn it, Ida told me herself, tonight. She yakked her poor bloody head off. Is that why she died? Did Sophia's lot have her gunned? Makes sense to me. 'Cause that Yanni . . . he's a bastard. Do anything for a few quid.'

'You read too many thrillers.'

So reason wasn't going to get us very far. What was there left? Nothing except chuck my hand in. Bow out without any more fuss.

'Why're you worrying about it?' Mortimer asked.

That surprised me. He can't have been bothered about what I was feeling. Or was he scared I might just cause them some embarrassment after all?

'You did the best you could,' he went on. 'You just weren't one of us. They shouldn't have put this on you.'

'All right,' I said. 'Far as I'm concerned you can shove off.'

I waited for him to go. All the questions thumping round my head weren't going to be answered. He was plucking at that fingernail again.

I got up and went into the kitchen. I drank two glasses of ice-cold water, poured a third and emptied it over my head. I mopped my face with a towel. It was good to feel normal again. There was a shadow. He was standing in the doorway.

'I think you deserve to know we've taken some of them.'

Unpredictable: that was Mortimer. I wasn't going to show any surprise, though. I'd play it as he was playing it.

'Eppler?'

Was it a flicker of surprise on his face? I couldn't be sure. Then he nodded.

'Sophia?'

He'd turned away, gone back into the lounge. I followed him slowly, as though I wasn't very much interested.

He'd sat down again. I stayed on my feet.

'The file you were working on is closed,' he said.

So they'd taken her. And Paul and Renée Danescu? Harida? And that chap Davers, the American? What about him?

'There was a man called Davers, Harry Davers. Said he was an oil man. American. Where did he fit?'

Mortimer screwed up his face, maybe to persuade me he was thinking. That was a laugh.

'He could be an oil man. A lot of them over here.'

As Davers would've probably said, that was crap. Mortimer and his gang would know everything worth knowing about who was what and where. I let it go.

'You've got Yanni?'

'Gracious me, no. Nothing to do with us: I told you. Just some domestic thing. Matter for the local police, that. Oh, I suppose the Embassy'll take an interest. She was British, after all.'

He made it sound like she'd been the syphilitic offspring of a Canton fisherman and a Bombay prostitute.

'I'm sorry about her,' I said. 'Damn silly way to finish up for a woman who really got us inside the Sophia operation.' The fingernail was giving him a lot of trouble. He didn't look up.

On impulse I asked: 'What did I do wrong? Can't be any harm in telling me that. Not now.'

Without looking up from that blasted fingernail he said, 'Wasn't that you did anything wrong. Just that you tried to do too much, sort of got carried away. It started to worry us.' That really shook me. I sat down facing him. 'It's understandable, I suppose,' he went on, still worrying the fingernail. 'Must be a temptation for anybody not trained in . . . er, what we do. And not knowing exactly what we want.'

'And whose bloody fault was that?' I blazed at him.

'Ours, I suppose,' he admitted, plucking at a sliver of nail. Then he winced, examined his hand. Finally he put his head back, looked at me. 'But it's difficult sometimes. Occasionally we're not quite sure what we do want.' He permitted himself the ghost of a smile. 'You don't have to feel bad about all this. You aren't the first, and you won't be the last of the . . . er, amateurs who get involved. And it's always dicey knowing what to do with the likes of you afterwards. You'd be surprised the trouble it is to get you fixed up where you . . . you'll be doing something useful.'

I would have bet a thousand piastres right then he'd just avoided saying 'where you can't do any harm'.

'Well, now I'm going to be out of your hair you'll be able to get back to the news agency. Start filing some stories out to the great, wide, waiting world.' I punched into it all the sarcasm I could muster.

He didn't rise to it; he just shrugged. 'I'm lucky. I have a good deputy.' A pause, then, 'You were in the trade before the war, weren't you?'

I nodded. They were great lads for confirming what they already knew.

'Interesting life, isn't it?'

I nodded again. Then I began to wonder why he was still with me, prepared to chat about nothing at all. Suddenly I felt tired. There was the slight hint of a headache. I wanted shot of him. I got up. 'You'll be wanting to get away,' I said.

'Yes,' he agreed, but didn't move.

I walked over to the window. The shutters were locked in the interests of black-out. I badly wanted some fresh air.

'Mind if I put the light out?' I asked him, indicating the window.

He shrugged. I walked to the switch, flicked it, then went back to the window and snapped the wooden slats open. Moonlight flooded the room. There was just a suggestion of cool breeze blowing in from the Nile, but all I could smell was the rotting garbage stacked outside the little bar on the corner. I leaned out.

'Goodnight, then,' said Mortimer. I didn't bother to turn.

'Goodbye,' I said. We didn't shake hands.

'Good luck,' he said and went out into the hall. I heard the door open, close. I also heard the lock snick. Hamid wasn't taking any chances. Or would it be Silah on duty? I didn't care, one way or the other.

I leaned on the sill, dragging in the air, and the stink from the garbage. I yawned, was about to turn back into the room when I saw Mortimer emerge from the deep shadows below me. But he wasn't alone. There was a woman with him. She'd probably been waiting while he talked to me. Odd, that. Why hadn't he been in a bigger hurry to go? If it had been Sophia waiting, I wouldn't have been wasting as much time as he had. I stared down in utter disbelief. The woman with Mortimer *was* Sophia. I'd got to know that walk, the sway of hips, the swing of shoulders. I knew I couldn't be mistaken, not in the white moonlight. It was Sophia all right. And as I gaped down I heard the laughter, watched a hand move up and stroke her cheek...

A man I'd never seen before came for me three days later. It had been a time of torment, cooped up in the flat. In fairness to them, I'd been supplied with everything I wanted. Hamid or Silah would come flapping in each time I rapped on the locked door. Booze, food, books: all I had to do was name it and it appeared. But the torment had been with me all the time. Mortimer walking away with Sophia. 'The file you were working on is closed,' he'd said. 'We've taken Eppler,' he'd told me. Put those two statements together and Sophia should have been out of circulation. But she wasn't. She was walking with Mortimer, laughing with him. I was the bloody prisoner. Three days of brooding on that damn near drove me up the wall. I was ready to be tied. So it was a relief when he came. He didn't introduce himself. Just said he would 'help' me to the aircraft. I didn't argue; I was past that. I started to throw some things into a bag. He stopped me, said it wouldn't be necessary; just leave everything, even a razor. He allowed me a comb in a jacket pocket. Press card, cigarettes, everything I had that associated me with Cairo was dumped on the table.

'I'm allowed to wear a suit?' I asked him.

He nodded, refusing to acknowledge the sarcasm. 'You'll change before you get on the plane,' he said.

He kept looking at his watch. Deliberately, I sauntered through the rooms, drank a long zibib for no reason other than a show of petty independence, then went down the stairs with him. Hamid was on duty. He didn't even bother to look at me. It irked me to find it was the old green Chevvy that was to take us wherever we were going. Another bloke in a sports jacket was behind the wheel. My escort pushed me ahead of him into the back seat. The driver never turned his head, just started the engine and drove out into Sharia Gezired Bahdran. It was siesta time and traffic was light, so that we made good time. But I soon lost all sense of direction as the car threaded its way through a maze of narrow streets. I gave up trying to orientate. What the hell? I wasn't coming back.

It was an RAF base, God knows where: I didn't. But we'd taken a long time to get there. I was hurried through a side door in a Nissen hut into a tiny cubicle. There was a cot with a palliasse, a small table, a chair, a cupboard, and a kit bag, properly stencilled with my number, rank, name and the infantry unit in which I'd originally served. But the unit's name had been crudely blacked out as though it had been done in a hurry. It was still legible. I wondered about that.

My escort carefully locked the door and stood by it while I threw off the lightweight suit.

'Wear the battledress,' he said. 'It'll be cold at the other end.'

Maybe, but it was bloody warm here. I struggled into the clumsy battledress. It was rough, felt scratchy against skin that had forgotten the irritation of it. I put on the boots, gaiters, webbing, the lot.

'It might be a while. Feel like a beer?'

I said yes, I did.

'Something to read?'

I nodded. He opened the door a crack and whispered something to whoever it was outside. After about five minutes a bottle of Stella beer, a tin mug and a paperback were passed through. I'd already found a packet of issue cigarettes and matches in a tunic pocket, and, believe it or not, my paybook. In it were a medical slip and a movement order.

He shook his head when I held up the beer. All right, I thought, be like that. I got stuck into it. I chucked the paperback into a corner. It was a spy thriller, an old one. I'd had too much of that at first hand. They could stuff it.

*   *   *

The Liberator squatted on the dusty tarmac like a fat, tired hen. The setting sun bathed it blood-red. I shivered in the heat, even under the lumpy bag of the kitbag on my shoulder. I wasn't excited about flying. I chucked my bag up through the hatch and an RAF corporal gave me a hand up the ladder. I clambered inside. It wasn't going to be a comfortable flight.

There was a lot of stuff in sacks and boxes and cases lashed down under heavy nets. There were maybe a dozen canvas sling seats, but they were for the high brass, it seemed. The corporal jerked his thumb towards the back. There was a little folding chair.

'That's yours, sarge,' he said and turned away to lend a respectful hand to a puffing half-colonel. I sat myself down, fiddled with a skimpy-looking belt, discovered how it fastened across my belly and waited. The plane filled up. A red-faced, sweating staff major seemed about the most junior of the other passengers. That lot I'd worked with could surely pull strings: no sitting round waiting for a hospital ship for me. That would give me too much time to think, too many of my own kind to talk to.

I was sweating in the stuffy confines of a cabin that was crowding up. To take my mind off it all I tried guessing at what was beyond a heavy curtain up towards the front: maybe the VIP section? I fidgeted in my seat, and wondered what the hold-up was all about. Even a full colonel ahead of me was getting testy. Then there was some commotion at the hatch. The corporal was joined by a flight-sergeant to drag in a couple of suitcases. These were followed by a man who muttered panting thanks in rich American. He staggered to recover his balance after the final jerk from the corporal. It was Harry Davers, the oil man from Boston. Now maybe I'd get some answers. If he was travelling on the plane I'd . . .

I leaned forward, saved him from pitching on his face.

'Hello,' I said.

His face was inches from mine. I saw the flash of recognition in his eyes. But that was all. He jerked away.

'Let me go, jerk,' he snarled, and squeezed his way down the cabin and disappeared behind the curtain.

So *he* was the privileged VIP. And he didn't want to know me, the bastard!

The hatch beside me slammed shut. One by one the engines whined into stuttering, then shattering, life. The aircraft quivered and strained. My muscles tensed. Fear replaced anger. I don't like flying, never did, and probably never will.

In the effort to look normal in that shuddering mass of metal I forgot about the answers Harry Davers could have given me. I'd get them one day. And some of them were going to be even crazier than I would have believed possible.

TWENTY-THREE

ANOTHER CUL-DE-SAC

Sitting beside him, I envied Harding's energy. In spite of the sleep I'd had I was bone weary, but he sat behind the wheel, nearly relaxed. His eyes were alert on the white smudge thrown ahead of the car's headlights. For the first half-dozen miles on the near-empty highway he concentrated on the driving. I'd given up any hope of discovering what all this was about, and I'd resigned myself to waiting. Somebody was going to have to tell me something sooner or later. So I lay back and thought about Sara. Where was she? And why had she been taken away? Some strange instinct told me she wasn't in any physical danger. After all, Harding wasn't Hodges. She might have been taken to a police station to make a formal statement about her father's death. But no: that couldn't be it. Harding wasn't a copper. Or was he? No, damn it, the man worked at the Ministry. So she wasn't at a police station. Staying with friends, perhaps? No: if she'd been persuaded to do that she'd have told me, or sent a message. That was when I remembered I hadn't seen Benson. He'd arrived, according to Sara. But I hadn't seen him come, or go.

'What happened to Howard Benson?' I asked.

Harding didn't take his eyes off the road. 'Who?'

'Benson. B-E-N-S-O-N. Howard Benson. A journalist. Sara Kenyon's half-brother. Hodges brought him down.'

My nose flattened against the windscreen when Harding hit the brakes. He'd warned me to use the seat-belt, but I was fed up with being told what to do, so I hadn't. I collapsed back in the seat, my hand feeling for the wetness of blood. But only tears were gushing down my cheeks. My nose hurt like hell, though.

Harding changed gear; the car purred up.

'Sorry, old man. Damned rabbits: nuisance at night. Hurt?'

'No,' I lied.

'Do use the belt, old boy. That's what it's there for.'

I pulled the strap across my belly, locked it. My fingers gently explored the bridge of my nose. It seemed to be in one piece.

Rabbits, he'd said.

'I didn't see any,' I told him.

He laughed. A throaty gurgle. 'Two, my dear fellow. Two of 'em. Doing what they oughtn't. Right in the middle of the Queen's highway. Seemed a pity to spoil their fun, eh?' He was making good time along the tree-lined road. 'Nice little animals. Cuddly. Farmers don't like 'em, but I do. Pity to kill 'em when it isn't necessary. They've got enough to cope with, dodging their natural enemies without us getting after them. Now, stoats and weasels and ferrets I can't stand: vicious unpleasant things. Only thing I've got against living in the country, really. Can't escape seeing it – the hunting and the killing and the unpleasantness. Every furry creature's chasing other furry creatures.' He sighed. 'I sometimes wonder about nature. Its cruelty, you know. Rather beastly.'

I'll bet you do, I told myself. Got to give your conscience a break somewhere along the line. Living in the country, he'd said. Then why the hell was he driving me up to town? The fuzz could have done that. But no, Harding does it, drives away from where his house is.

His voice was droning on and on. He seemed to be hooked on the Sussex fauna, and I just hoped he wouldn't get on to flora as well. He obviously wasn't going to talk about Benson. Specks of rain flecked the windscreen. He switched on the wipers. Now he was talking about squirrels. His voice, the rhythm of the wipers, my own frustration took their toll. I closed my eyes, allowed my face to fall forward.

I snapped awake to hear him saying, '. . . and it isn't good enough, old man. I mean, they shouldn't have done it. Quite uncalled for.'

Who shouldn't have done what? The farmers? The squirrels? The Government?

'Sorry,' I said. 'Must've dozed off.'

His eyes jerked round to me for an instant, then back to the road ahead. It was raining, but softly. The wipers continued to swish-swish. He clicked his tongue impatiently. 'One of your shortcomings, old chap. You don't concentrate. That's why you get confused.'

'All right,' I snapped. 'So I'm confused.'

'Quite,' he agreed.

The self-righteous bastard, sitting there, all smug!

'Look,' I snarled. 'I didn't choose to get mixed up in all this, any more than I did last time.'

Not quite true, that. Still, maybe he wouldn't know any different.

'Last time?' His head flicked round, then back to the road in front of him. I'd got behind his complacency. But now what? This was going to be tricky. Back in Cairo they'd meant what they said when they warned me about talking.

'Oh, that was back during the war.' I tried to make it sound of no account at all. I stared out through the windscreen. The rain was easing off. I started to whistle between my teeth, then stopped. It made me sound guilty.

'Tell me.'

'It was nothing. Just . . . well, sort of an accident. Something I tripped over. I reported it. And I was asked to lend a hand.'

The car slowed as Harding applied the brakes. He allowed it to roll on to a grass verge. He switched to his parking lights, cut the wipers, but allowed the engine to idle. Then he eased round so he could see me full face.

'Tell me,' he said again. 'It might help.'

Help? Christ, was I in some sort of a jam?

Harding was sharp. He reacted as if he'd heard that unspoken question. 'We don't know much about you, do we?'

The Bertie act had been switched off along with the engine. It seemed he was prepared to make a long session of this. And who were the 'we' who didn't know much about me? Hodges knew plenty. Maybe that was the easy way out.

'You'd better talk to Hodges.'

'I'm talking to you.'

It wasn't said nastily, but there was an edge to his voice. He didn't intend to be buggered about.

'Look,' I said. 'I don't have to look for trouble. It finds me.'

He nodded. As though he believed me. And he waited.

I didn't want to talk to him. I didn't know enough about who or what he was. 'Switch on the engine. I'm getting cold,' I told him.

'Switch yourself on,' he suggested. He was still waiting. Somewhere in the night sky above us a jet screamed its way into touchdown at Heathrow, just as a Liberator had once hammered its homing to an RAF runway 'somewhere in England'.

I still remembered that awful night of long hours of thrumming vibration as the Liberator skirted its way from the unsociable skies over occupied Europe. The flight seemed to go on for ever, and I envied the passengers able to submerge in uneasy sleep. But everything has an ending. The cotton-wool through which we'd cut a path got lighter in texture. My ears did funny things. We were coming down. Below were green downs, clumps of trees, and houses: England. The wheels thumped down on to concrete. The throbbing engines rested. Taut muscles relaxed. Suddenly there was laughter and a babel of talk in what had been a tomb of silence. Everybody behaved as if we'd been on a picnic. Bullshit artists, every one of them.

I watched the curtain up front. There was no movement. Then the hatch near me clanged open. A bowler-hatted head appeared.

'You,' it said. 'Come with me.'

This was VIP stuff. First off. I dumped my kit through the hole and followed it down.

'Not smuggling anything, are you?' bowler-hat demanded. I shook my head. 'Come on, then.'

I followed him across the tarmac. There was going to be no chance of trying to talk to Harry Davers. The kit was weighing heavy when we reached a car. An elderly chap in chauffeur's uniform was behind the wheel. We got in and off we went.

'Where're we going?' I asked.

My companion didn't answer. Stuff you too, I thought. He didn't open his mouth during the long, long ride into London, and with the road-signs down I could only guess where we'd landed. I suspected it might have been in Hampshire, but I couldn't be sure. Then we were at the gates of a barracks. Bowler-hat whispered something to the MP; we drove in and finally stopped outside a Nissen hut standing apart from the more permanent buildings.

I lugged my kit along behind bowler-hat. He turned into a cubicle, nodded to a bespectacled, moon-faced lieutenant wearing RAMC badges. The two of them sat behind a table. I stood at a sort of rebellious attention in front of them. Bowler-hat flipped open a folder, extracted a piece of paper, slapped it down in front of me.

'Recognise it?' he demanded. I nodded. I was getting a bit fed up with the Official Secrets Act.

'Sign here that it's been shown to you and you understand it.' He held out a pen. 'You can read it if you want to.' This was said in a 'and-you-bloody-well-dare-to-waste-my-time' voice. I signed.

'Lieutenant Cramer here'll handle your discharge. You're

unfit for active duty. So you'll be moving into a reserved occupation.'

He stood up. 'You'll be given travel warrants and told where to report.' He tapped the document I'd just signed. 'And remember this. Not that you'll find many people to talk to who'd believe you, anyway.' He nodded to the officer and left us. Cramer gave me a tentative sort of smile. He looked like a man who didn't know quite what the war was about. He was the only person I spoke to in the four days it took to process me out. He did his best to be pleasant, but he'd had orders. This was my first experience of 'solitary', and I didn't like it.

Harding faced me, one arm looped over the wheel.

'Well?'

He sounded tougher than I believed possible. But was he tougher than Hodges? I felt like the ham in a sandwich. What was it Confucius had said? When rape is inevitable relax and enjoy it?

'I was with a security section in Cairo,' I said. 'Working in civvies. You know. I picked up some gen about an English-woman in Budapest, and followed it up: that led to Sophia Kukralovic . . .'

Telling it wouldn't have taken long, except that Harding wanted a hell of a lot of detail. I had to concentrate to remember all the bits. He really dug them all out of me, the bits I'd forgotten without all the prompting. Trying not to name names was a waste of time, and so he heard about Grayling and Collins and Mortimer and Hodges and the Danescus and Harry Davers and Harida and Ida and Yanni. And, of course, about John Eppler, alias Hussein Bey. God knows how long the telling took, but I was shivering with the cold when he finally switched on the engine, and warmth slowly spread from the heater grille.

'Thank you,' said Harding.

'I could wind up in clink,' I reminded him.

'You won't,' he said, prodding the car into gear. He switched on the lights. The sky in the east was paling. I settled back and closed my eyes.

Fuck the lot of them, I thought. And fell asleep.

The train journey to Waterloo seemed to take for ever. Some bomb damage from the previous night's raid hadn't improved the track south of the river. The coaches were chokker with uniforms in khaki, navy blue and sky blue. I got a lot of dirty looks in my ill-fitting civvy hand-out gear.

I'd be met. That's what I'd been told. So I dumped my pressed-paper suitcase without much in it on the platform. There were uniforms everywhere, and I felt like a pariah.

'Come on.' It was bowler-hat, who'd materialised from somewhere. I got my fair share of bumps from unfriendly uniforms as I toiled along behind him. He whistled up a taxi, and in silence we honked our way through bomb-damaged streets to the War Ministry. We walked along endless corridors. Bowler-hat kept flashing some card or other to bored sentries.

'Wait,' he said and left me in an airless cubby-hole of a room. Twenty minutes later he came back. With him was an elderly, stoop-shouldered man with a blank face, a bronchial condition and a dewdrop hanging from the end of his nose.

'Ah,' said this ancient. 'A journalist, eh? Bit young for this job. But we can't be choosey, eh? Not in times like these. Do the best we can with you. Long as you can write cheerful copy. Got to keep the public cheerful. Mustn't let 'em get down-hearted, eh?'

He looked as though he was going to start crying any tick of the clock. Bowler-hat stared at me, hard. I got the message. I was now, it seemed, engaged on work of national importance. My days in the cloak-and-dagger industry were over. I followed Mr Hamilton-Fyfe-Smythe along more musty corridors. I think I'd have been happier in Pentonville.

We were on Purley Way when I woke up. Harding didn't waste any time when I moved to ease my cramped muscles. 'You saw Sara in the Press Club. Why did you go to Hodges?'

I went through it again. And, to be honest, it didn't make much sense in the re-telling. I knew what Harding was thinking: that I'd been in touch with Hodges since the Cairo days.

Hell, what had happened in between couldn't be important. So I stuck to my story.

In the Ministry I wrote my pieces. But I'd been out there and the very old and the very young and the cripples hadn't, and so they wouldn't accept my words. They slashed at the copy or spiked it in furious anger. The sort of war being fought in far-away places with strange-sounding names didn't belong inside the Ministry. And the dreariness and frustration of life inside the grey-black Whitehall building was matched by the dullness of living outside, I'd found a bed-sitter, just off Leigham Court Road in Streatham Hill. It was cheap and ordinary. My social life was almost non-existent. Not many blokes my own age were out of uniform. And the women . . . well, they hardly matched Sophia and Renée. But even if they'd been Renoir models I doubt if I'd have done much about it. I kept seeing bowler-hat rather more often than coincidence suggested I should.

So I became a loner. I'd sip a pint or two, go to the cinema, occasionally treat myself to the Windmill when I was in danger of forgetting what a woman's tits looked like, then back to the bed-sitter to thumb my way through thrillers which made Hodges and his kind look pretty ordinary. This always pleased me.

The car stopped with a jerk. We were at the corner of the little cul-de-sac where I lived.

Harding said: 'Hodges. I want to know how and when and why you contacted Hodges. Before the Sara thing.'

I hadn't contacted Hodges – well, not the way Harding meant.

VE Day had come and gone, then VJ Day. That's how long it was. The Ministry was getting back to a peacetime footing. Suddenly the information section had blossomed into public relations. I was dishing out the puffs to a Press that couldn't have cared less about anything military. So we teased them with skives to here and there, and lots of booze. I didn't like it, but I was stuck with it. I could guess what would happen if I tried switching jobs. So I just soldiered on. Then it was . . . when? 1947? How the hell can anyone remember that far back? Especially when all it added up to was a thick ear and a nasty taste in the mouth?

Bowler-hat hadn't been in evidence for quite a while. Maybe now the war was over they'd forget about me: not that I cared much any more. The war was just a page or two in school history books; the bloke with the little moustache who'd died in a Berlin bunker was just a pub joke now. When you're dead you're nothing. You wondered what the hell you'd got in a tizz about: hating and getting scared and shaking impotent fists at the droning in the sky high above the searchlights. I didn't feel alone any more. Everybody was in civvies. And a weary

219

nation turned away in boredom from the men who remembered stripes on their sleeves and pips on their shoulders and the days of brief authority.

My own memories of Cairo and Sophia were getting furry round the edges. Things were getting back to a sort of normality. I began to date the odd girl, welcomed the occasional wrestle in a bombed-out house. But it was strictly fun-stuff. Then I met Laura. The new face in the typing pool at the Ministry had a pert freshness that was going to wither pretty fast if she stayed in that barn. Her young figure drew its share of wolf-whistles, which seemed to scare her a bit. We got to chatting one day at the tea-trolley when she'd delivered some typing back to me. The cinema was her strong interest, but she wasn't just a blind fan: she seemed to know a bit about it, and when she talked about a show she was going to that night I decided to box clever. I got to that cinema early and hung about on the opposite side of the road. It was all sort of childish. I'd show those jerks at the office how to date a girl who always turned them down. I watched her join the queue. A taxi and a car blared at me as I snaked across the street. I came up behind the queue, tacked myself on to it. Two couples separated me from Laura. We shuffled along. I let her buy her own ticket, but I was right at her side as the line stacked up at the stalls' entrance. That's when, all surprised, I said, 'Hello, Laura.' She didn't suspect a thing. We even got seats together. But my hands didn't fumble in the darkness. It was played straight as a ruler.

She refused a drink afterwards, but agreed to a coffee. She lived in Islington with her parents. Her old man was a bricklayer. He was going to be employed for a long time. At seventeen she was a bit of a romantic and still inclined to starriness about war heroes. I stuck to the infantry gambit, and flowered it up, but not too much. Then I walked her to the tube and said goodnight.

That was the beginning. Once a week, then more often, we'd be at the pictures. She was finally persuaded to go into a pub for a nightcap. Daringly, she sipped at a lemonade shandy. But always we said our goodbyes at the tube, she to travel north, me south. We hadn't even held hands.

Then, subtly, she started to change. While we'd talked about everything under the sun other than ourselves, she'd been surprisingly articulate. Get on to personal ground and her shyness wrecked any chance of progress. But now, and it took a visible effort for her to do it, she was asking questions, about me, my background, my job, my ambitions. And she became demonstrative. This was so out of character I wondered about it. She offered her face for kisses when we met, when we parted. And she graduated from lemonade shandies to gin and tonic. I could see she loathed the stuff but she forced it down. I tried to stop her. It was no good. She claimed it made her feel good. With a shock I realised that her leg was rubbing against mine under the pub table.

Questions. More questions. And then, one night, she'd downed a third gin. 'Got any medals?' she giggled. Out of the blue. Just like that.

'Medals? For what?'

'Oh, go on. You know. The war.' She hiccoughed. 'Oops, pardon. Bet you were brave. Bet you were the bravest of them all.'

This was crazy. I tried to laugh it away. 'Me? Medals? They don't hand 'em out for cowardice. And that was me. Devout coward: head down, bum down, everything down – flat, like a lizard. No medals. Not the sort you're talking about, anyway.'

'Want another drink,' she said. Her mouth was going slack.

I shook my head. 'You're going home.' I stood up. 'And I'm taking you.' Trying to get my own voice right I said, 'Can't have a bundle of charm roaming the streets of Islington all by yourself.'

She stood up, too, wavered just a bit then found her balance. 'Good idea. I . . . wanted you to do that. Folks're out tonight. Won't be home for . . . for ages.' She giggled again, then clumsily snuggled against me. 'Have some fun, eh? The two of us.'

Christ, I thought. The damn fool's drunk. I did a quick sum in my head. I could just about do a taxi, one way, anyway.

'Come on,' I said.

Harding was getting restless. His fingers drummed on the wheel. 'Had quite a love-life, haven't you? But I want to know about Hodges. Why you made contact . . .'

'I'm telling you,' I said.

My standards weren't very high, God knows, but the street where she lived was grubby. A few kids still yelled while they played football with an empty can, even though it was getting late.

I paid off the cab, reckoned I had enough left for tube fares back to my place. She'd gone ahead of me up the short path to the front door of what looked like two-up and two-down. While she fiddled with the key I tried to sort out just what kind of girl she was. Though we hadn't done much wooing in the taxi, her offer in the pub had been clear enough. Why? Why the sudden 'have some fun'? Why the sudden boozing? We'd gone around for weeks. Nothing: she just hadn't seemed the type. And now she was having trouble getting the key in the lock, and giggling. I took over, opened the door. She tripped on the sill but I caught her before she fell. The house was dark.

'Don't put the light on,' she muttered and giggled again. 'Don't want the street to know . . .'

We'd come in a taxi; we'd got out under a street light; come up the path and gone inside the front door together. Christ, she *was* an amateur.

Unsteadily she led up some narrow stairs, into a tiny room. The light from the lamp outside showed me a simply furnished room. Narrow bed, narrow wardrobe, a rather makeshift dressing table, and what looked like a badly-painted chest with a sort of rug askew on it.

Laura collapsed on the bed. She hiccoughed, giggled, and I just stood there, feeling like a bloody executioner. This wasn't on. Then she'd stopped giggling. I waited. She struggled up, her shapely legs dangling over the side of the bed. She licked her lips, looked at me, shivered. To hell with it, I wasn't going to help. So I went on waiting.

Her eyes started to dart around the room. She wrapped her arms around her body. She took a deep breath. Then she was remembering something. Her lips trembled, and then she lifted her face and stared at me.

'You do like me, don't you?'

The bloody simplicity of her shook me. All I could do was nod.

'I . . . I've thought about it. And uncle's right. I . . . think . . . no, I'm sure he is . . .'

It wasn't making any sense so I just stood there in the pale darkness.

'Now mum and dad . . . goodness, they'd kill me. Very strict they are. But uncle . . . he said not to be frightened. I mean, if . . . if . . .'

She stopped. She was stone cold sober now, and shy. I had to step in and help.

'Look, Laura. What you said in the pub – it doesn't count. Forget it.'

'But I don't want to. Forget it, I mean. I . . . I . . .'

She got off the bed, wrapped her arms round my neck and hid her face in my chest. I let her rest there.

'Laura, honey,' I said. 'I'm too old for you. You . . . you're only a kid. I . . . I'm grateful. Honest. But I'll get along and . . .'

She lifted her mouth and kissed me, on the lips. She didn't know much about it, about how to do it, but the intention was there. I kissed her back. Then I kissed her again. There was the slightly sickly taste of gin. I don't remember if she just naturally opened her mouth or whether my tongue forced her lips apart. But in seconds she was panting. And the feel of her rounded softness under the clothes really got me going. I had to push her away. She stood back, not quite sure what to do next.

I said, 'See you tomorrow, Laura.' But I didn't turn towards the door. She never took her eyes off me as she slowly pulled off her coat and let it drop. She struggled, and then unzipped her dress. She was wearing a slip. She shrugged that over her head. The tight breasts filled the small bra. The briefs moulded her slim hips. Still staring at me with wide round eyes, she unclipped the bra. The breasts were pear-shaped, firm and beautiful, jutting out from the deep shadows thrown by the street light. I saw her swallow, then deliberately her hands pulled down the briefs. She stepped out of them. Then her hands peeled away the warm leotard-type stockings, rolling them slowly down the long slim legs. She stood there in the half-light, naked as she was born but with all the budding freshness of untouched womanhood. There was a short pause, and then she sat on the bed, shivered, and reached out her arms to me.

I took her hands. Slowly she fell back, pulling me on to her.

'Hodges,' said Harding. He was cold. And irritable.

'I'm telling you,' I told him again.

The blaze of anger in me as I ran out into the street burnt up caution. All right, so he'd beat me up. But, by Christ, this time he was going to get hurt, too.

It'd been hell on that bed. The pressure in me to take her filled my pants, choked my throat. My hands couldn't stop themselves exploring that young body. And she was sobbing for what I wouldn't give her. God knows why I wouldn't. But I didn't. Because there was something screwy. I remember thinking there was a catch there somewhere.

I tried to calm her, explain. I told her how much I liked her, wanted her, but it wasn't on. For me and her it wouldn't work. I was too old. The passion destroyed her inhibitions. She clawed at me, hurting me, sobbed hysterically that she loved me. That at first she hadn't believed him . . . but he was right . . . a girl had to give to deserve a man's love . . . and she wanted to give and give and give . . . he knew what he was talking about . . .

I dragged myself off the bed and knelt beside it. I took her tear-stained, stretched face in my hands and shook it. 'Who knows what he's talking about? Who?'

It took time, but I pieced it together eventually. And when I did she'd become ashamed of her nakedness. She wrapped herself in the bedspread and wouldn't look at me. It was her uncle. Well, not really her uncle, but the friend of a real uncle. She liked him. And he'd been so kind when she'd told him about me. He'd asked so many questions, given her advice . . . He was in insurance and knew all about people. That was his job. So she listened to him, and to his plea that she should match my worldliness with her own offering of unselfishness. It all sounded daft, but not the way she told it. And not to an innocent like Laura. This 'Uncle' George had done a pretty thorough job of hooking me into the 'family'. Because her 'uncle' was George Victor Hodges. And he lived in a flat in Trebovir Road, Earls Court.

I found the house and the card with his name on it. But I ignored the bell that would force me to identify myself through the little microphone. Instead, I hung around in the shadows, prepared to wait as long as I had to.

It was twenty minutes before a lean tall figure walked up the steps, thrust a key into the door. By the time it swung open I was right behind him.

'Thanks,' I said.

'No trouble, mate,' said the twangy Australian voice.

I walked up the stairs with a confidence I hoped would fool the Aussie. But he'd disappeared.

I found the flat at the end of a little cul-de-sac of a passage. I knocked. I thought I heard a door open somewhere behind me. I was only interested in what was on the other side of the door in front of me. I knocked again. This time a hammer blow with my fist.

The door opened. And there he was: George Victor Hodges.

'What do you want?' he asked. The voice was quiet enough, but bloody unfriendly.

'Just this,' I said. And for the only time in my life I caught that bastard off balance. I felt the skin on my knuckles tear as my fist crashed into his mouth. That's when I made a mistake. As he staggered back I followed him into the room and, like a demented fool, kicked my one line of retreat shut behind me as I went after him.

'You fucking bastard,' I was screaming. 'I should bloody do you. Playing ponce to Laura, you crummy piece of shit. Have a tame watchdog on me, eh? You sod!'

'What happened then?' Harding asked.

'I was off work for a few days. He beat me up, scientifically. He didn't like being hit.'

Even the memory of what he had done to me on that night all those years ago still hurt. He'd left me on the floor of his flat till the small hours. Then he lifted me up as if I was a kid, took me through his bedroom and out of the second door to the place. That was the one I must have heard while I was knocking. Then he'd dumped me in the street, just far enough away from his flat so as not to be noticeable. He'd leaned over me.

'Don't tell the coppers anything,' he'd whispered. 'Nothing. See? Let 'em guess what happened. I'd hate to really rough you up.' He'd sounded like he was real sorry. Then he'd walked away. I heard him whistling softly.

Harding didn't say anything for a while. Then, 'You'd better get some sleep. Don't leave your room. I'll contact you. Understand? Stay at home.'

I nodded, got out of the car, rescued my bag and left him. He was still sitting in the cold, silent car when I shut the front door behind me.

TWENTY-FOUR

THE END OF IT ALL

Harding kept his promise. He arrived at my digs just before twelve o'clock. I was still asleep. That's the advantage of a clear conscience. He wasn't pleased that he'd had to knock seven times, and he thrust the bottle of whisky at me as though he regretted having brought it. I put it on the table, tried to stifle a yawn. I pulled the dressing-gown sash tight and flexed my shoulders, wishing to God the man had been human enough to want some sleep himself.

'You'd better have some of that,' he said. I looked at the bottle, then at him.

'I'll get glasses,' I said. I went into the box of a kitchen, found two tumblers. I decided he'd probably want water, so I emptied souring milk out of a jug, rinsed it under a tap, filled it with cold water. I went back. He was still standing at the table.

'Oh. Sorry. Won't you sit down?'

He grunted, crossed to the one easy chair. He sat down, then stood up again. He fingered his raincoat. 'Mind if I take this off?'

'No. Sorry.' I decided I'd have to stop apologising. That's the trouble when you've been wakened: you're not at your best.

He shrugged out of the coat. I suddenly realised he'd left his Bertie voice somewhere else. Right then I'd have welcomed the affectation: I didn't go much for the no-nonsense grimness.

I uncorked the bottle, tried a joke. 'I suppose it's okay. The sun's over the yard arm.'

'It's raining,' he said. I noticed then that the coat he was still holding was damp.

I took the hint. And the coat. Then I had to find a hanger for it. By the time I had it draped I was starting to tick on all my limited cylinders.

'Sorry,' I said again. And cursed myself. Being apologetic wasn't helping. I was starting to feel bad about Sara.

'Where is she?' I asked.

'Where's who?' he countered.

So it was going to be like that. 'Sara.'

'She's all right.'

'I didn't ask that. I asked where she was.'

He wasn't taking much notice. He was fishing something out of an inside pocket. It was a folded sheet of newspaper. He held it out. I took it. I opened it up. The huge black headlines of a sensational feature dominated the top. And there was a picture. There was no mistaking who it was: Hussein Bey, without the red tarbush with the black tassel.

I looked up at Harding. He was staring out of the window, lips pursed in a soundless whistle.

HOW I CAUGHT HITLER'S TOP SPY, the two-inch-high letters thundered. Christ, I thought. I plumped into a chair, remembered the whisky, got up, sloshed myself a treble. Then I remembered Harding.

'Have one?'

'I'll help myself.'

I tossed back half the drink, spluttered and coughed. Dear God, I prayed, let me behave like a bloody adult. I settled down, trying to take my time about it. Then I got myself behind the screen of newsprint. Somebody called Major Austen Smythe-Emerson was being interviewed about how he'd caught the Nazi spy John Eppler, and, through Eppler, a ring of eighteen others. Smythe-Emerson? The name didn't ring any bells. But as my eyes raced down the columns of six-point type, broken by the catchy crossheads, the facts seemed to fit the little I knew about it all.

Harida was mentioned, and there were vague, guarded references to the Danescus, without any clear statement of who or what they were. I searched for Hodges' name. It wasn't there. But the real rocker was that I couldn't find Sophia Kukralovic either. There were names I didn't recognise, of course. Could she have had another identity? How could I know that?

The adrenalin started to pump just from my reading about those long-ago days. But the story I was scanning so eagerly wasn't how it had been, not as I knew it. Oh, the main facts were there, but overall it was all wrong.

But my pulses were hammering as I realised that my hunches had been right. Out there, right under my nose, the enemy had been operating. And all my reports to Hodges and Mortimer and Collins had been spot on. And then I realised where this story fell apart at the seams. Sophia's part in it was missing. I put the page down. Harding had moved to the chair opposite, was sipping a minute drink. I leaned forward.

'Whoever this reporter Carstairs is, he doesn't know what it was about.'

'Carstairs is dead. He died three months ago.'

'Christ, how long do bloody papers hold stories?'

'Take a look at the date.'

I grabbed at the tear sheet. The month and date weren't important any more. There was the year: 1963.

'I dug it out of the files,' Harding said. 'And don't knock Carstairs. David was a good writer. Honest. He took down what he believed to be true. And published it.' He paused. 'And there wasn't any D-notice.'

So the boys in the backroom hadn't minded the piece. I wondered why.

'This Smythe-Emerson,' I prompted. 'Look, I was there. Never heard of him.'

Harding shrugged. 'Dead, too. But he was in the Army list all right. In charge of Field Security Section No. 432.'

That made me sit up. 'Field security? Who're you trying to kid? Eppler was way above that level. Take me for an idiot?'

He didn't answer that. I shook the sheet at him.

'Just what the hell does this mean? Eh?'

He shrugged again. 'Propaganda. Cold war. That sort of thing. Just to let the Americans and the Russians know the British aren't mugs. Eppler was big, and clever. So why not remind the world that the British caught him?' He sipped, then, 'At least, I suppose that's why they did it. Can't think of any other reason.'

I gulped down what was left in my glass. It went down easier than the first half. I slopped more whisky in the glass. Now I had Harding across a table I'd make a meal of him.

I was shaping up the words when he said, 'They thought it would be better if you knew how important Eppler was.'

All right, I muttered, so when did I doubt it? Davers had tipped me off, hadn't he? And Ida. And I'd passed the word back about John bloody Eppler alias Hussein bloody Bey.

He listened patiently enough. While I got some more whisky down my throat he said, 'You still don't understand, do you?'

You bet I don't, I told him. But I'd contributed my little bit. You bet I had. I'd led 'em to Sophia, hadn't I? Not all the clever Charlies in their precious outfit had tumbled to her till I got in the act. I celebrated my cleverness with another swig of whisky; it was beginning to go down as easily as lemonade.

'You know,' he said, very quietly, 'you're either very dull or very stubborn.'

He put his glass down on the table. He'd drunk very little of the small tot he'd poured. Okay, I thought. That's more for me. I helped myself to another generous splash.

'I accept you've had a rough ride,' Harding said. I took the glass away from my mouth. There was a 'but' coming. 'But they didn't have any choice, did they?'

I felt better. So I couldn't be dull, could I? I'd heard that 'but' a long, long way off. So maybe I was stubborn, stubborn enough to want to know what the hell he was going to say next.

'I'm listening,' I said, and felt mad that my voice sounded a bit blurred round the edges.

He sighed. I got the feeling it was more out of impatience than sympathy. 'Well, you *were* a nuisance. And short of . . . er, getting rid of you they didn't know quite what to do.'

Christ, I must really have got in the hair of those bloody experts. I swallowed some more booze to celebrate that.

Harding said: 'Pity about Hodges. He was a good operator.'

That caught me on the wrong foot. All I could think of to say was, 'Wish they'd hang the bastard.'

'They won't. But I suppose they could. Treason's still a capital offence.'

Treason? Hodges? Then I remembered Holmes, and the whispering, and the departure of Hodges. My head jerked up from my glass. Harding wasn't as clearly in focus as he'd been, but I could see him.

'I'd think he'd prefer it,' Harding said. 'The rope. He won't like rotting in jail. He'll think about you, a lot.'

Jesus, I thought. Hodges. One of the other lot. Maybe I'd done a better job than . . .

'Forget it,' said Harding, just as if he'd read my mind. 'It didn't have anything to do with you.'

But Hodges had been my . . .

'You're duller than I thought,' said Harding. 'But Sara'll be all right.' A pause. 'I think. Maybe just a suspended sentence.'

I swallowed more whisky. Perhaps that would help. It didn't. But at least it gave me something to do.

'Tell me,' said Harding. 'That girl Laura. You still friendly with her?'

It wasn't fair the way he kept jumping about. Even his

image in front of me wasn't keeping still. Laura? But yes, he knew about her. I'd told him last night. I mouthed the words carefully. 'She . . . I don't know where she is. When I got . . . got back to the office she'd . . . she'd gone. After Hodges beat me. Left me in the street. I . . . I dunno where she is. Left home. No . . . no note, no message, just buggered off. Dunno where.' I tried to pull myself together. 'Bitch. That's what. Didn't give it to her. So . . . so she took a powder. Wanted it. Didn't give it to her . . .'

'A pity,' I heard Harding say. I shook my head, trying to clear it. I realised Harding was moving about, heard noises from the little kitchen. I must have dozed off for a minute. Next thing I knew there was steam rising in my face and the smell of strong, black coffee.

'Drink this,' he was saying. My hands clutched at the mug. It was hot. I sipped. It burnt my lips, but he forced me to drink, and drink, and drink. The stuff was bitter, and black, and hot.

'I haven't got unlimited time,' Harding said.

I felt lousy and told him so.

'Drink the coffee,' he ordered. I drained the mug, put it on the table. Harding went back to his chair. I thought I was feeling better, and I thought it might be a good idea if I started leading the conversation. My voice managed to clamber through the cottonwool of my mind.

'Hodges. He was a baddie, then?' Christ, it sounded inane. But Harding nodded.

'Had been. Ever since Cairo. And Sophia.'

Jesus, I thought. They still arresting Nazis? 'Talk sense,' I suggested.

It took quite a while to tell. But Harding kept it simple.

Sophia was a top Soviet agent who'd infiltrated the Nazi machine, and who, during the uneasy Anglo-Soviet alliance during the dark days of 1942, had been 'loaned' to British Intelligence in the Middle East.

It got a bit more complicated when Harding tried to explain how, before the war, Sophia had been assigned to Britain and how she'd cheerfully married a Royal Navy officer in her efforts to help her Kremlin masters. She'd given him not only a daughter, but a cause as well. Communism had become more than just a political ideology to the man who was to become Commander Alexander Kenyon. As events in Europe had marched to their inevitable climax, Sophia had as cheerfully left him, moved into the capitals where her services were more urgently needed.

Ida Clapham had served a purpose in Budapest. And I hadn't in Cairo.

'You do understand, don't you?' Harding said. His voice sounded, for the first time, almost sympathetic. 'You had stumbled on to something that was going to be an embarrassment to people involved in a very . . . er, delicate exercise. Something had to be done about you. And because you were young and callow and quite inexperienced they did what they did. Sophia's solution for you was much more . . . how shall I put it? . . . final. But she was persuaded to do what she did. Though she did find you a nuisance, a time-wasting nuisance.'

To hell with the suffering, I thought. I reached for the bottle and the glass.

'Our own people found you a liability,' Harding went on. 'Or so I'm told. It was a long time ago. But they couldn't leave you running loose to spread the message around the bars that you'd found a spy and nobody was interested. So you had to be taken inside, and put in the hands of professionals who'd see to it that you'd do the minimum amount of damage.' He nearly smiled them. 'But they say you gave them a run for their money. You did strange things. You seemed to want to tackle the entire German Abwehr on your own. Report has it that they got very cross with you. Very cross indeed.'

I drank some more scotch. I'd let the bastard talk. So they tried to write me out of the script, eh? 'Go on,' I said.

'You must have the message by now, for God's sake.' I kept staring at him. 'All right. If you can take it you may as well have it.'

I was beginning to wonder who or what or where he'd been in those days. He was pretty well-informed. If he'd been briefed by somebody else he had to have a colossal memory.

'This woman Sophia. Apparently she kicked up a fuss when she was ordered to take you to . . . er, I think they said Port Said, on one occasion. But somebody had to keep an eye on you and no one else could be spared right then. But she had to be there. So she had to take you along. And not even being introduced to another boy friend put you off.' He paused. 'I've heard you described as being as welcome as a boil on the back of the neck.'

He nearly smiled again. 'Hodges, of course, argued all the time in favour of an accident, a fatal accident, with you as the headline.'

I poured some more scotch. He was getting blurry again, but who wanted to look at a bastard like him, anyway? Maybe my eyes weren't so good right now, but there was nothing wrong with my brain. I was getting the picture, loud and clear. No: pictures: you didn't hear pictures. You *saw* pictures. I started to laugh. That was funny that was. Getting a picture loud and clear . . .

Harding's voice was coming at me in gusts, like wind. Sometimes the words hammered into my head, then they'd just touch me, like a gentle breeze. What was he saying? 'You had to be got away from Cairo; our people were ready to move in. They couldn't risk you messing up the operation. So you had to go. And Hodges had to lean on you; Mortimer, too. They couldn't take any chances.'

Christ, they'd really brainwashed old Harding, and me. The joker who'd sorted out Sophia. And that bastard Eppler. Well, Davers had tipped . . .

Davers. 'And they put Davers on that plane to keep an eye on me, eh?'

Harding's face screwed up a bit. That I could see. He was trying to figure something out.

'Davers?' he said, as if he didn't know who the hell I was talking about. Then he relaxed. 'Oh, the Yankee oil man.' He smiled. 'They had to get him out, too. Been to a couple of parties with some of the Hussein outfit . . . you know, Eppler. They thought he could be useful. He wasn't, it seems. But he was pretty sharp. He'd twigged something was screwy and started playing the sleuth. He was a worry, too. They had to get rid of him.'

Now that was a bloody giggle. Who the hell did Harding think he was fooling?

'Oh, for God's sake, come off it,' I mumbled. I poured another drink.

' 'Fraid they had to put you in a bit of a spot with him, though. Still, you're not likely to meet up again, are you?'

I gagged on the booze. Maybe I should steady it down. Meet Davers again? Who'd bloody want to? That rude shit of a bloke who couldn't even say hello on the . . .

'Hey,' I snarled. 'What if I did see Davers again?'

'Well, I'm told he might be a bit annoyed. You see, they told him he was persona non grata in Cairo, on . . . er, security grounds. And you, they told him, were in security.'

I struggled out of the chair. By Jesus, who the hell did this lot think they were? God the Father, Son and Holy Ghost?

Harding stood up. 'Sit down,' he snapped. The shock of the authority in his voice stopped me from doing whatever it was I was going to do. I wasn't sure what it was. 'Sit down,' he said again. I flopped into the chair, savagely poured myself another scotch.

'You should be grateful,' Harding said. 'At least you made that much contribution.' He lowered himself into the chair, not taking his eyes off me. 'Tell me,' he went on, speaking very slowly and distinctly (I appreciated that. It was getting harder to sort out the words). 'Tell me why you haven't said anything about Hodges.'

'Easy,' I muttered. 'Always knew he was a bastard.'

'But you didn't know he was working for *them*?'

'Germans, Russians – all the bloody same.'

He nodded. 'I suppose so. It's only the name of the enemy that changes. There's always an enemy.' A pause. Then, 'She must have been quite a woman.'

She was, I agreed. But we weren't talking about the same thing. And he knew it. Even my bleary eyes caught the flash of contempt.

'You didn't know Hodges was her . . . er, regular lover?'

No, I didn't. But it explained a lot.

'She had the knack all right: Kenyon, then Lord knows how many Nazis in Europe; then Hodges.' He shook his head. 'Hodges: a professional.'

It was this that was worrying him. He had to be one of them. And he must have been ticking the lengthening list on his mental fingers. Burgess – MacLean – Philby – and Hodges. But Hodges hadn't got away. They had him. But for thirty years he'd cocked a snook at the Establishment and probably played his own part in helping Burgess and MacLean and Philby. For a tiny second I felt sorry for the lot of them. But that was before Harding said, 'You just weren't in the league. Then when you got into the act a second time you can imagine how they felt.'

'Yeah,' I almost shouted. 'Especially that bastard Hodges. I was getting bloody close to him, wasn't I?'

He didn't bother to disguise the contempt. 'You? You'd never have tumbled Hodges in a million light years.'

'That so?' I snarled. My voice was thickening with the booze, but I was getting braver every minute. Braver, but not brighter.

'You ran to Hodges because a girl you saw looked like a woman you'd known. That's not how the professionals work,' Harding said. 'And,' he added, 'you damn nearly skittled the get-Hodges exercise. Oh, yes . . . they were on to him, and Kenyon, and Stapleton. Then you pop up, giving Hodges a nice little diversion to play with. And when he pitched the tale that you'd have to be brought "inside" again they had no choice but to go along with the idea. They didn't want Hodges wondering, which he would have done if his advice had been ignored. They were getting too close by then. So everybody had to put up with you.'

Trying to sound sober, I mumbled something about not doing any harm, only trying to help.

'Harm? God, that shows how dumb you are. Stapleton was getting edgy. So he blew your cover. And we . . . they had to straighten that out. We . . . damn. They didn't want the birds flying the coop.'

Drunk I was getting. But I hadn't missed those two 'we's', hurriedly corrected. They made me feel better.

'All you did was damn near jam the works. You were up everybody's nose, and Hodges was as sore as a boil. He had to turn his woman over to you to keep you busy in the cot while they got on with it. He didn't like that, not a second time. First Sophia – then he'd tried to get you out of his hair with that kid Laura. With her he could have kept an eye on you. But you decide to play Saint George and take a poke at a dragon. Then he had to hand Sara over.' He stopped, looked as though he wanted to spit, and said, 'Hodges doesn't like you.'

Sara! I wanted to cry. Harding saw it. Uncharacteristically, he said: 'You lamentable piece of shit,' and got up to stare through the steamy window.

I poured the last few drips from the bottle and tossed what was left in the glass down my throat.

'What the hell,' I croaked. 'You've got 'em. What're you moaning about?'

His fury was mounting. He wheeled and pointed a fingerful of rage at me. 'I'll tell you what they're moaning about.' So, he'd been careful to say 'they' this time, eh? 'We didn't get all of them. That's what we're moaning about. They didn't get the communications set-up, all because you came barging in, full of patriotic enthusiasm. Patriotism?' He snorted the word. 'It's for the seagulls. This is a business, a profession. It's not cops-and-robbers wrapped up in a fifty-pence paperback with a nude on the cover.' Then he sagged. 'What's the use? I might as well talk to you in Urdu.'

I wiped away a dribble at the corner of my mouth with a sleeve, and sat up straight in the chair. I'd show the bastard. So he thought I was boozed, eh? I sorted out the words in my head, then mouthed them carefully. 'I knew Sara and her brother were up to no good.'

Witheringly he reminded me Sara wasn't pronounced Shara. Then he sat down again. Wearily, he rubbed a hand across his eyes. 'I'm going to tell you the set-up. But only because I've been instructed to.'

He didn't want to do it. But 'they', whoever they were, had said so.

'Maybe it's because, if you know, you won't start spouting fantasies wherever you may be. Anyway, all of Britain'll know in time. They'll read the evidence. Why the hell we have to blow the gaff by holding trials beats me. Still, that's the way it is.'

He gave me the story in a flat monotone, a bit like a teacher talking to a backward child. Kenyon, a serving officer during the war, had been an easy victim of his wife's wiles. Yes, that was the phrase Harding used. He was a bit old-fashioned. Russia and Britain had to find common purpose, and even after Sophia had gone and the Soviet Union had come into the conflict, Kenyon continued to use the contacts in London she'd given him.

Co-operation in wartime had become treachery in peacetime. But Kenyon, either through choice or necessity, had continued his work, and Sara, out of sympathy with him on so many things, had willingly acted as his courier to Europe. And the child of his second marriage, Howard, had taken his mother's maiden name, gone into journalism, won himself a place in Fleet Street because of the information he was fed from better sources than those available to his colleagues. Russia knew what stories they wanted to be printed.

Dr Stapleton, an intellectual Communist: Pemberton and Lawson, 'pink' Leftists: all useful in their own fields. And what more natural than that Hodges, back in Britain, should be told to team up with the one man the Soviets could rely on: Commander Kenyon, RN (Ret'd)?

'I suppose they were a clever lot, working out a code all wrapped up in chess problems. You know, those problems were so good they even had some of them published?' Harding didn't bother to hide his admiration. Hodges had, of course, been the cornerstone of the whole operation.

And it had been me who'd helped to blow the cell sky-high after all. I gloated a bit when Harding told me how Sara (she was just a bitch, too, I told myself) had got fed-up wet-nursing me. The odd row or two blew up. And Hodges was finding it rough trying to maintain harmony in the group when he himself wasn't any too happy.

'Who blew Kenyon's head off?' I stuttered. I didn't bloody care one way or the other, but I thought I might as well know.

'He did. Kenyon. When he realised the jig was up.'

I wanted to sleep. But every time I closed my eyes it felt as if I was riding a dinghy in a rough sea. I wished there was more whisky. I needed a drink. Harding got up, crossed to where his raincoat was hanging, pulled a half out of a pocket. I grabbed it; helped myself. The bastard was smart, a bloody mind-reader, but generous, definitely generous. He was saying something, but I wasn't listening. I'd done my share of that. Stuff the lot of them!

'So where would you prefer?' He'd raised the decibels a notch or two.

'Prefer?' I slurred at him. 'Talk sense.'

'Canada – Australia – New Zealand? Nice places, I'm told.'

Now what the hell was the man talking about?

'The Ministry'll pay you a decent pension, though you hardly deserve it. And . . . er, there'll be an ex gratia payment, a more than reasonable amount. You should be quite . . . er, comfortable.'

I needed another shot of scotch. Were these bastards going to emigrate me? Sounded funny, that. Emigrate me. Maybe I was getting a bit high.

'You're the sort of disaster we'd prefer to happen three or ten or twelve thousand miles away. You'll be expected to sign a covenant, of course: no writing for Sunday newspapers. And there'll always be the Official Secrets Act if we're . . . if they're pushed into using it. Pity you didn't handle that Laura girl better. You need a wife.'

I struggled out of the haze that stank of whisky. 'You . . . you tell me I . . . I've got to bugger off?'

He nodded. 'Got to. That's exactly right.'

'To hell with the lot of you.'

'I see,' said Harding. 'They rather hoped you'd be as reasonable as they're prepared to be. A pity.'

'Whoever they are can't force me out of England.'

'True,' he agreed. 'But my own opinion is that freedom in another country is much to be preferred to incarceration in this one.'

Incar . . . incar . . . why the hell couldn't he use words I could get my thick tongue round? In . . . Jesus. I wanted to laugh. But suddenly it wasn't funny.

'They couldn't bloody do it,' I blurted.

'Nonsense.' His voice was crisp. He was on his own ground, now, not delivering messages. 'Your association with the woman Sara is enough. And you were a friend of Benson's. You knew Lawson and Pemberton. You visited Kenyon's house.'

Out of the blue, Burlington Bertie was back.

'My dear fellow, it's quite ridiculously easy. Amazing what these lawyer chaps can make out of a suggestion. Fantastic fellows, lawyers. And the way you were always running to Hodges. Wouldn't sound awfully good to a jury, old man.'

I struggled out of the chair, knocked the bottle over as I lurched against the table. The spirit squirted on to the wood. Harding was on his feet much faster and I suppose I'd have pitched on to my face if he hadn't caught me. My legs wouldn't straighten. And I wanted to be sick. Harding saw it, helped me to the bathroom, waited patiently while I threw up. My whole body was trembling when I'd finished. Harding held out a sponge. I wiped my face, squeezed water on to my aching head. The blurred blodge of suet-pudding whiteness facing me in the mirror wasn't my face: it couldn't be. I squinted, trying to bring it into focus.

'Better hop into the cot, old man,' said Burlington Bertie. 'Sleep it off. I'll be back tomorrow with the necessary papers. And, my dear chap, stay at home. Not, I take it, that you'll feel like doing much else. But do stay here, my dear fellow. Fewer complications that way, if you follow me.'

I followed him – back into the bed-sitting room, and flopped on to the rumpled bed. Hazily I watched him mop up the mess on the table. He looked at the half-bottle of whisky. Some of the spirit remained. He put it back on the table.

'You'll need that later.'

He took down his coat, shrugged into it.

'Oh, by the way, Sophia's dead.'

He'd got rid of Bertie again. I twisted my head to stare the question. So she'd got in the way, had she?

'Pure accident, in fact. Two years ago, in Vienna. Crossing the street. Hit by a tram. Funny, isn't it? Even the professionals can't organise against downright bad luck.'

He was at the door. His hand on the handle, he turned.

'When the professionals can't win, amateurs should get the message.'

He went out, shutting the door behind him.

Harding had sounded just like Hodges.